He set her as… f
Poppasquah P… l
away from her. Sh… d
never seen it all before, never seen the white birches flashing silver in the sun, or the bay spilling seafoam and seaweed onto the shingled beach. She had never felt a breeze like this, so soft and hushed, or heard a thrush singing quite so sweetly. Nothing in her world, she thought, would ever be the same.

She went into the house and up to her bedroom, and she took off her clothes. She took them all off until she was as naked as she had been with him, and she thought, He touches me there and there and there, in all my woman's secret places. He touches me.

"Extremely satisfying. . . . A valentine to friendship and the love that crosses all boundaries."

—*Kirkus Reviews*

"A great read that makes you believe in love against all odds and shows you many facets of human nature."

—*Affaire de Coeur*

Please turn this page for more praise for THE PASSIONS OF EMMA . . .

"4 1/2 Stars! (Exceptional). This novel truly speaks to the heart as Ms. Williamson delves into the human soul to find the strength to grasp happiness, forgiveness, and the inherent goodness in the world. Few authors have the power to so beautifully impart these feelings. She imbues her stories with a deep compassion and her characters with real emotions and gifts her readers with a story of stunning grace, eloquent prose, and a lasting impact."

—**Kathe Robin, *Romantic Times***

"The best book I've read all year. . . . THE PASSIONS OF EMMA is music to the eyes. The words flow so smoothly off the page, it's like listening to a symphony. . . . Forget the hanky, curl up with an entire box of tissues."

—**Carrie Romero, *CompuServe Romance Reviews***

"What a fabulous book! . . . Makes one's own heart soar with the beauty of the words created by the incomparable Penelope Williamson. Bravo! I know I'm never missing a book by this great author. A must read!"

—***Belles and Beaux of Romance***

The Passions of Emma

ALSO BY PENELOPE WILLIAMSON

The Outsider

Published by
WARNER BOOKS

The Passions of Emma

PENELOPE WILLIAMSON

A Time Warner Company

WARNER BOOKS EDITION

Cover design by Diane Luger
Cover photo illustration by Diane Luger and Franco Accornero
Handlettering by David Gatti

Warner Books, Inc.
1271 Avenue of the Americas
New York, NY 10020

Visit our Web site at
http://warnerbooks.com

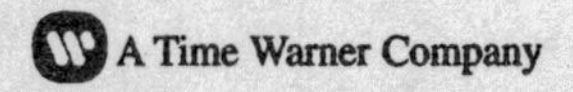

Printed in the United States of America

Originally published in hardcover by Warner Books.
First Printed in Paperback: August, 1998

10 9 8 7 6 5 4 3 2 1

For Candice Proctor

Sister . . . and, at last, the best of friends

Acknowledgments

Thank you, Helene Tessler, of the Bristol Historical Society for your help in bringing the Bristol, Rhode Island, of 1890 to life.

And thank you, Lindsay Casablanca, for all your valuable research, and for being such a dear friend. It's not often a gal can find a kindred spirit who shares a passion for Giants baseball, shopping at Saks, and expensive French restaurants all in one person.

And thank you, Kristin Hannah, Frances Jalet-Miller, and Claire Zion, for your insightful critiques of the manuscript. You not only showed me where I went wrong, but offered brilliant suggestions on how I could make it right. I truly, honestly, no-doubt-about-it couldn't have done it without you.

And thank you, Tracy Grant and Catherine Coulter, for being there through countless lunches and coffees, listening to me whine endlessly about how hard this book was to write, and all the while politely refraining from telling me to shut up and just do it.

And, finally, thank you to Aaron Priest and Larry Kirshbaum for believing.

Acknowledgments

Thank you, Maxine Taskin of the Bristol Historical Society, for your help in bringing the Bristol, Rhode Island, of 1890 to life.

And thank you, Lindsay Casablanca, for all your valuable research, and for being such a dear friend. It's not often a gal can find a kindred spirit who shares a passion for Guinness, shopping at Saks, and expensive French restaurants all in one person!

And thank you, Kristin Hannah, [illegible] Miller, and Chase Zion, for your insightful critiques of the manuscript. You not only showed me where I went wrong, but offered brilliant suggestions on how I could make it right. I truly, honestly, no-doubt-about-it couldn't have done it without you.

And thank you, Terry Dean and Catherine Coulter, for being there through countless late [illegible] and coffees, listening to me whine endlessly about how hard this book was to write—and all the while politely refraining from telling me to shut up and just do it.

And finally, thank you to Anna Pinto and [illegible] Whitehouse for believing.

Chapter One

Bristol, Rhode Island
April 1890

Emma Tremayne felt their stares like slaps on bare skin. She was so shy that simply being looked at was a torment, although she ought to have been used to it. She was a Tremayne, after all, one of the wild and wicked and outrageously rich Tremaynes. And she was beautiful—or so she had been told all of her life.

She had never liked being out in society, but she was a girl who knew her duty and usually tried her best to do it. She had come to this last fox hunt of the season because it was a tradition among the Great Folk of Bristol, and the Tremaynes tended to take special care of Great Folk traditions. "You are our last hope now," her mother had reminded her only that morning.

So she had come, for Mama and the family. That and because she loved the hunt. Well, not actually the hunt—it was the riding she loved. Galloping full tilt across plowed fields, through red deer grass and woods of birch and pine. Over stone walls and brambled hedges, hurling herself headon toward that one instant in time when her horse left the ground and she could be weightless with freedom.

At the moment, though, she was standing firmly on the gallery of her cousin's farmhouse. Her wide-open gaze took in the restless horses and yelping dogs, the master's scarlet coat and all the buff breeches and black habits and black silk top hats. She had known these people all her life, yet she was reluctant to go out into the yard and join them. But when she thought about the wild ride to come, she felt a surge of giddy and shameless pleasure.

She saw the Alcott brothers at the edge of the yard, near the gate, astride a pair of matching bay geldings. She had forgotten how alike in looks the brothers were. Both with those long narrow faces and long narrow noses, topped with shocks of light brown hair.

Geoffrey sat his horse easily but very upright, elegant in his black bowler hat and neatly tied white stock. Stuart slouched in his saddle, looking both dashing and decadent. But that had always been the way of Stu. He hadn't been home in over seven years, and she was so pleased to see him that she imagined herself lifting her skirts and running down into the yard, shouting his name. Seven years ago she might have done such a thing, even with everyone watching, but it would hardly be proper now.

No, she would never have done such a thing, even as a child. The Emma Tremayne of her imaginings had always been a much braver, more daring girl.

Geoffrey lifted his hand to her, and she smiled, although she didn't wave back. Geoffrey Alcott, whom she had seen only last Wednesday, and whom all the world, or at least all of Bristol, thought of as her beau. As the man she would marry, except that he hadn't come around to asking her yet.

They had danced together twice at the Christmas Ball, though, and at midnight he had taken her arm and walked with her out onto the balcony—to see the stars, he'd said. When she'd laid her hand on the railing, he'd covered it with his own, and she'd thought she could feel the heat of his palm even through the silk of their dancing gloves. Their breaths wreathed their faces like veils, and they had looked at each other, not at the stars. She'd thought he would ask her then, but he hadn't. Afterward she couldn't decide if she was disappointed or relieved.

Now Geoffrey was staring at her with his mouth pulled tight, and she wondered what she had already done this morning to make him frown at her so.

She gathered up the heavy, trailing black kersey skirt of her riding habit and walked down into the yard. A man wearing a black pea coat and a slouch hat brought up her horse. The man's hat concealed his face in shadow, but it didn't matter, for she didn't really look at him. Not even when she accepted his boost up onto the back of her skittish roan mare.

She wrapped her leg around the near pommel and adjusted her skirts. The saddle leather felt cold and slippery. The mare bucked and snorted, shaking her head, and that was when the man reached up and grabbed Emma's ankle.

His fingers pressed hard into the soft leather of her boot. A strangeness and something breath-stopping, near to panic, swamped her. She stiffened, making a sound that was half cry, half gasp.

"Your girth is loose," he said. "And splendid little miss though you are, surely, if some kind soul like myself doesn't tighten it, it's arse over teakettle you'll be come meeting the first fence."

His rough words shocked her less than did the roughness of his voice. It had an Irish lilt to it, but it was harsh and raspy, barely above a whisper. Menacing, somehow.

He had already let go of her ankle to lift the saddle flap and hitch up the girth straps. They were large and square, his hands, and battered.

She stared at the top of his slouch hat, at the way his hair hung long and ragged over the collar of his coat. Slowly, he lifted his head. For a moment longer the brim of his hat still shaded his face, and then she was looking into a pair of startling green eyes.

His face matched his hands. A white scar thin as a razor rip slashed from his right eye down across his cheekbone. His nose was crooked, bent slightly to the left. And he bore a scar on his throat as well. A thick purple welt.

I'm sorry, she almost said, and then realized how foolish that would have sounded, since she had nothing to be sorry for. If anyone should be sorry it was he, for touching her without her leave. And for speaking so to her, accusing her of thinking of herself as a "splendid little miss."

But he had already turned his back and was walking away from her.

Or rather, he swaggered, she thought, and she felt wistfully envious of his confidence. He with those tough black-Irish looks. He went right up to her cousin Aloysius, who as Master of the Hunt sat his horse amid his pack of hounds. The dogs were yelping and climbing all over one another in their excitement, but they quieted as soon as that man went among them. As if his mere presence commanded obedience.

She was aware of him after that. The Alcott brothers rode over to her and she was able to smile at Geoffrey and tease him some, and she only blushed a little, for of all the people in her world she'd always been most at ease around Geoffrey. She was even able to tell Stu how pleased she was that he'd come home after being so long away. But always her gaze came back to that man.

Once, he must have felt her eyes on him, for he turned around to stare right back at her. She looked quickly away, her fingers tightening around the whalebone stock of her whip.

Her cousin Aloysius took up the copper horn that hung around his neck and blew a wailing, warbling note up into the morning sky. He was serving as her cousin's whipper-in, the Irishman, for she noticed that he had mounted a chestnut hack and was gathering the hounds. They all rode through the gate, then, hats bobbing, saddle leather creaking, and the road rang hollow under their horses' hooves.

April morning mist rose from the road, pale blue and cold. Frost flaked the long, salt meadow grass. The Irishman struck his boot with a leather thong, and the pack trotted on ahead. And then he was no longer there for her to watch.

The Bristol Hunt Club always gathered for the last hunt of the season in the stableyard of the old Hope Farm.

The farm had once belonged to the Tremaynes, but it had gone to a daughter who had married unwisely, and so it wasn't as grand as it ought to have been. Most of its onion fields lay weed choked and fallow, and the house itself wore a tawdry air. It had been built of an exotic marbled stone, yellow like a cat's eyes, brought out of the heart of Africa as ballast in a slave ship. The house was said to be haunted, although no one had ever actually seen or heard anything more sinister than bats in the attics.

Ghost riddled or not, the hunt took place there every Friday morning from November through the first week in April. Hope Farm and the surrounding countryside were nothing more than a sprawl of old mills, swamp and scrub, stagnant ponds, and poison ivy. But the first hunt had been held at Hope Farm over two hundred years ago, and the event had been repeated every winter Friday morning every year thereafter.

All the old Bristol families who mattered belonged to the club. The Great Folk, they called themselves—those old, moneyed families. The mill owners and boat builders, the bankers and lawyers, and all their sons and daughters and grandchildren, generation upon generation. They might not all ride to the hounds every winter Friday, but everyone who was anyone made it to the last hunt of the season. It was a tradition, and Bristol folk both great and ordinary had never been ones to let go of any tradition without a fight.

Like serving eggnog before the last hunt of the season was a tradition. The gentlemen and ladies of the hunt, in their polished boots would sit astride their polished horses, and mill in the yard, toasting themselves with eggnog served in sterling silver cups engraved with running foxes. When the master blew his horn, the Hunt Club would ride through the gate and all the way to the first bend in the road. Where, with a hearty cheer, they would toss their empty cups over the hawthorn hedge.

It was a gesture meant to show off Great Folk wealth and giddy extravagance. But everyone knew the servants were always given strict instructions to follow along after and gather up every silver cup, to be used again next year.

The gentlemen's cups were always spiked with whiskey. Only on this particular morning Stuart Alcott had passed up the eggnog and was drinking his whiskey straight from a flask that was silver as well, but a battered and tarnished silver.

This was not the way things were done at all—to bring along one's own whiskey flask to the hunt. Everyone was staring and frowning at him because of it, and this was irritating his brother, Geoffrey, no end. Geoffrey Alcott hated the thought of anyone bearing the family name being caught out in an impropriety.

As they rode together through the gate, Stu caught his brother's eye and waved the flask toward Aloysius Carter. The master of the hunt and present-day owner of Hope Farm led the way, wallowing in his saddle like a leaky tugboat. Aloysius was so fat he filled the seat from bow to cantle, and he'd been inebriated for over thirty years.

"Look at him, drunk as a pickled skunk," Stu said. "Yet I'll wager you a short bit the old boy still makes it over every fence, and well ahead of the rest of us."

Geoffrey sighed at the thought and took a swallow from his own cup, consoling himself with its sweet warmth. His cup, like the ladies', was filled only with eggnog. He rarely drank spirits, and *he* certainly wasn't going to go galloping across fields and flying over fences woozy-headed from booze.

He looked up and caught his brother watching him. Stu's eyes were bright with whiskey shine and derisive laughter. "They'll run like the very devil today. It's just nippy enough," Geoffrey said, for lack of anything better, and then felt himself flush. His brother could still, after all these years, make him feel and behave like a fool.

"Shit. It's cold as the proverbial witch's teat." Stu took another long swallow of the booze and pretended to shudder. "Which is why, instead of glowering at me like a pinch-lipped parson every time I take a little nip, you ought to be congratulating me on my good sense. After all, a fellow's blood can hardly freeze when it's ninety proof."

That won't keep a fellow from breaking his damn fool drunken neck, Geoffrey thought, although he kept it to himself. But his brother, who could always read his mind, grinned and lifted his whiskey flask in a mocking toast.

Geoffrey set his jaw and looked away.

But a moment later his gaze had gone back to studying his brother. Stu's was a handsome face, with its shapely patrician nose and high cheekbones, the wide mouth that held a certain wild charm even now when it was slack with drink. Geoffrey looked at that face, as familiar to him as his own, and felt something like fear roil up sour in his belly.

It was the way his brother had looked at Emma.

Not that everyone didn't always look at Emma. She had walked out onto the gallery of the yellow stone farmhouse, and every man present had stopped talking, stopped moving. Even the horses had gone still. Emma had stood alone, framed between the gallery's white wooden pillars, and her presence there had the power of a thunderclap on a clear day.

Geoffrey had heard his brother ease his breath out in a low, slow whistle and had looked around in time to catch the light flare in his brother's pale eyes. "Good God," Stu had said. "If it isn't our dear little Emma, and my, how she has grown."

"She's mine," Geoffrey shot back, surprising even himself with the force of his protest, so that of course he flushed.

Stu turned his head slowly away from the girl on the gallery and cocked one pale eyebrow at his brother. "Ah, but does she know she's yours?"

"Stu, damn you . . . You can't go gadding about the world for all these years only to show up back here and expect—" Geoffrey clamped his jaw shut so hard his teeth ached.

Stu laughed. "I don't *expect* anything, brother mine. That is my one saving grace."

Geoffrey couldn't help laughing a little himself. "God, what a scapegrace you are. And you even have the audacity to admit it."

"All right, so I have two saving graces."

The brothers shared a smile. Then, as if of one accord, their gazes had been pulled back to the girl on the gallery. So young and lush, she was. But her beauty was surely more suggestive than real, something out of a man's dreams. For they were too far away to see that beneath her black silk top hat her dark hair shone like lacquer. That the white linen ascot she wore was wrapped around a neck impossibly white and long. That the violet in the buttonhole at her breast quivered with some strong emotion that might have been fear or perhaps excitement.

They were too far away to see her eyes, which were neither gray nor green nor blue, but the color of seawater lit by a rising sun, bright and luminous and deep. Only Geoffrey, who loved her, knew that all the world's longing was in those eyes. And that once you looked into them it was impossible to look away.

Chapter Two

She smelled him first, pungent and musty.

Then she saw him—crouched on top of a stone wall that was shadowed and webbed with old vines. He held himself still, as if mesmerized by the sight of her waiting for him there in the road.

His russet fur was molting, falling off in patches. The blood of some prey stained his cheek ruffs. His eyes were bright and black and staring right at her, and she had the strangest notion that he was begging her with those eyes not to give him away.

They had spread out along the edge of the woodland, the horses and their riders, waiting for the hounds to draw the covert and flush out the fox. Emma and her mare had wandered off by themselves to where a stone wall separated the birch woods from the fields of an onion farmer who was trying to wrest a poor living out of the briny marshland.

The fox crept slowly now out of the shadows, his belly low and brushing the rough stones of the wall. Then he went still again, and Emma realized that she and the fox weren't so alone, after all. The Irishman and his horse stood among the slender gray trunks of the birches. She thought he had to have seen the fox as well, and she waited for him to do his duty as whipper-in—to stand up in his stirrups and shout the view holloa. But he did nothing, as if he were trying to give the fox a chance to get away.

They stared at each other, and the fox stared at the two of them, and it was as if a skein of something bright and electric, like lightning, had wrapped itself around them, holding them fast.

The fox moved first. He whirled and dashed along the top of the wall, his tail floating long and beautiful behind him. But with every step he took, the glands in the pads of his feet left a trail for the hounds to follow.

Emma and that man stayed caught by each other's eyes long after the fox was gone. An eternity, or perhaps it was only a moment later, the hounds began to bay, crying out that they'd picked up the scent. She heard her cousin Aloysius cheer a shrill, "Holloa!" followed by three quick, pulsating notes from his horn.

The hounds were running.

Emma took the wall head-on, soaring, flying, landing clear. She galloped across a tussocked field, not chasing the fox so much as just riding, riding.

The wind roared past her ears. The mare's strong back bunched and flowed, bunched and flowed, beneath her legs. Sky and earth and trees rushed through time and space to meet her.

She heard a shout and pounding hooves coming up hard behind her. It was he, she was sure of it, and she urged the mare to go faster, faster. She was running from him now, not chasing after, and her excitement sharpened, became tinged with fear.

They soared over a wide hedge with a steep drop into a salt meadow on the other side. She heard a yelp of surprise and saw out the corner of her eye a horse go down. It was a Thoroughbred bay, though, not a chestnut hack. It had been the bay behind her all along.

She looked back over her shoulder and saw Stu Alcott pull up to help the fallen rider. Slowly, she brought her own horse down to a squelchy canter, throwing up little splatters of water, and then to a walk. The mare's belly heaved against Emma's legs like bellows, and white streams of breath shot from her nostrils. The air stopped rushing, and the world grew still.

They were in a clearing filled with cattails and asters surrounding a salt pond. Next to the pond stood an abandoned gristmill. Over the years the windmill's sails had worn a deep rut in the wind-ruffled marsh that smelled of wet peat.

Close to the mill lay an old graveyard. A lone pine tree grew out through the collapsed roof of a crypt. There was no house here. Only tall grasses and swamp and the ghosts of Indians.

The clouds broke open and beams of sunlight shot through the holes in the sky. Emma tilted back her head and felt the warmth of the sun pour over her. The land had seemed locked in winter forever, but now the first breath of spring was here. For Emma spring always brought with it a faint disappointment. As if she expected her life to be changing along with the seasons, and yet it never did.

A branch cracked and she started, jerking around. A horse trotted into the clearing, a bay whose rider was splattered with mud.

She waited for him to ride up to her, feeling shy and yet strangely buoyant. When he was close enough she took a white linen square out of the hanky pocket of her saddle and leaned over to wipe the mud off his face, daring to tease him a little. "I've heard of throwing your heart over a fence," she said, "but not your head."

Geoffrey Alcott laughed and shrugged. "You ride as if there's no tomorrow, Emma. You're going to break your neck one of these days. Or I'll break mine, trying to keep up with you."

She pulled away from him, her gaze falling to the handkerchief she now held crushed in her fist. He might have laughed as he said it, but she hadn't missed that barest hint of censure in his voice, It wasn't proper, she knew. The way she rode.

She could hear from deep in the woods the confused baying of the hounds. The horn sounded, two long blasts, which meant the dogs had for the moment lost the scent, and she was glad, for this time she wanted the fox to get away.

"Emma . . ."

She continued to look down at her hands, but she made her voice be light and what she imagined was flirtatious. Although she'd never been much good at that. "Oh, dear. Now you're going to scold me for larking over unnecessary fences and not following the hounds."

"Marry me, Emma."

She thought her heart might have stopped. And when it started up again, it beat in unsteady lurches. She had been waiting for months for this moment, and now that it was here she didn't know what to do with it.

She risked a look up at him.

His eyes were the clear gray of pond ice, his hair the pale brown of sun-steeped tea. He was considered a handsome man by all who knew him. She had known him all her life, and she had no idea at all whether she loved him or not.

"I didn't mean to go and blurt it out like that," he said.

"You wish to take it back?"

"No!" He flashed a rueful smile. He wasn't as handsome when he smiled, for he had long, slightly protruding teeth. Yet, Emma had always liked his smile best of all. It had a touch of sweet whimsicality about it that made her feel warm inside, as though they shared something precious.

"I'm willing to shout it from the rooftops if I must," he said. "Although I'd just as soon not have the whole world listening for your answer—in case it should be a refusal."

But he didn't really expect her to turn him down; she could

tell by the way he was looking at her, with possessiveness and a bright expectancy, and something else. A raw and powerful thing akin to hunger that both frightened and excited her.

She wondered if he was going to say he loved her. It was probably numbered among the rules that so carefully governed their lives—that moment when he could first say the words. Perhaps on their wedding night he would be allowed to proclaim his devotion. She hoped so, for it often seemed in the world in which she lived that after one or two years of marriage there was little devotion left to proclaim.

"Emma," he said again, impatient now. She couldn't look at him anymore but she felt his gaze hard on her, on her mouth, as if he could will the words into being. He was known for getting what he wanted, was Geoffrey Alcott, and apparently he wanted her.

"I suppose I should have properly requested permission from your father first, but given as how he isn't here . . . and we've known each other all our lives, and you're already twenty-two, and it's 1890, after all, and you're such a modern girl, I thought . . ."

Emma lowered her head to hide her smile. Geoffrey Alcott was actually babbling. Did he really think of her as a modern girl? And she *was* twenty-two, a veritable old maid. How Mama would shudder to hear those sentiments spoken aloud.

"Emma, you have me in torment, waiting for your answer," he said, but then he laughed so she would know he teased. Geoffrey never allowed himself to be in torment over anything.

Yet, when he reached up and stroked her lips once with the pad of his thumb, she felt breathless of a sudden, the way she got when she was soaring over fences. Perhaps she did love him after all.

"Yes," she said, surprised at how her voice sounded, such a breakable thing. "I will marry you, Geoffrey Alcott."

She looked up at him at last and she smiled, feeling happy

and shy. She thought he might kiss her, and she waited for it, still a little breathless, so that she jumped when he took her hand.

Slowly, one by one, he opened the three dainty jet buttons of her riding glove. He brought her hand up to his mouth and pressed his lips to the inside of her wrist, where the blue veins pulsed hard and fast beneath her skin.

The fox had scrambled up the lightning-scarred trunk of a downed cedar tree. He was off the ground, just out of the dogs' reach, but he was trapped now. The hounds surged and leaped at him, their teeth biting at the air. They hadn't been fed that day, and their hunger gave their baying a savage edge.

"Let the dogs have at 'im!" Aloysius Carter bellowed to his whipper-in. "I said, let the dogs have at him, damn your dirty bog-trotting Irish hide!"

But the Irishman, Emma saw, wasn't listening. Cracking his whip above his head, he had ridden into the middle of the pack and was trying to force the hounds back, away from the downed tree. The dogs, excited though they were, hungry though they were, obeyed—until the fox's claws slipped on the mist-wet wood of the rotting log.

For an instant he hung suspended in the air, then he fell into the middle of twenty snarling, snapping jaws.

The fox gave one great cry as the first set of teeth fastened onto his throat. For a moment, all that could be seen of him was the white tip of his tail flailing at the air, then all of him was smothered by the dogs.

The horn blew, one long mournful note, sounding the mort.

Emma had looked away as soon as the fox fell, but she could still hear her cousin Aloysius shouting at the dogs now to, "Tear at 'im, boys! Kill him!"

She and Geoffrey sat side by side on their blowing horses.

He was watching the fox die, but she couldn't tell by his face how he felt about it.

"Geoffrey? Don't you sometimes hope the fox would get away?"

He looked at her as if she'd just been prattling at him in Chinese. "What?"

"The fox. I wanted him to get away."

A tender look lightened his face. He leaned over and patted the leg-of-mutton sleeve of her riding habit. "My poor darling," he said. "Such a soft little heart you have."

Emma's eyes ached, as if she were about to cry. She slipped her arm out from beneath his touch and backed her horse away from his, although she didn't know why. Geoffrey was no more or less responsible for the fox's death than she was.

Geoffrey saw his brother and hailed him over. "Stu! Miss Tremayne has just done me the honor of agreeing to become my wife."

Stu's laugh had a sharp sound to it. "On a fox hunt? Good gad, Geoff—such marvelous spontaneity. I didn't think you had it in you."

She was being careful not to look at him anymore, at that man, but now he was watching her. She could feel it, just the way she could feel the pulse beating hard at the base of her throat.

"Who is that man?" she blurted out.

"Who?" Geoffrey twisted around in his saddle. "Him? The whipper-in?" he said, as if surprised that she had noticed a servant. They were invisible, usually; they didn't even have names.

Geoffrey tried to stare the man down, but he stared back. At her.

"Apparently," Geoffrey said with a curl to his lip, "he's a stableboy who seems to be using the day to get above himself. I'll have a word with him. He has no right to look at you."

It was an absurd thing to say, Emma thought, for the man

had a right to look anywhere he wanted. And what's more, she was the one who had been looking at him. Yet she said nothing, for she hoped Geoffrey would speak to him. She wanted that man . . . she wasn't sure what she wanted. For him not to be there for her to look at, she supposed.

Stuart Alcott rode up to her. From one elegantly gloved fist swung the fox's tail—a wet, matted mess of bloody red fur. It was no longer beautiful at all.

"The belle of the day deserves the brush, wouldn't you say?" he announced loud enough for all to hear, and there was a hint of meanness in his smile.

There was more than a hint of crowing in Geoffrey's answering smile. "She deserves the world."

"And instead she gets you," Stu said.

But Geoffrey only laughed and took the brush from his brother's outstretched hand.

"Geoffrey, I don't want it," she said.

But her betrothed was already draping the bloody fox tail over the pommel of Emma Tremayne's saddle.

A woman waited for them back at the gate to Hope Farm. She had a dead child in her arms.

A whale's giant jawbone had stood sentinel by the gate for over a century, put there by a long-ago Tremayne sea captain. The jawbone had weathered to the pale gray of driftwood, and the woman seemed to hover before it like a burning bush. A mass of long, flaming red hair obscured her face, and she was enveloped in a pumpkin-colored coat that looked plucked out of the dustbin. Shabby and frayed at the hem and much too big for her.

The woman was small and frail and she staggered beneath the weight in her arms. There was no doubt the child was dead, for he was *mangled.* His arm had been torn from its socket so violently the shoulder bone showed white through the bleeding flesh. His head gaped open and bloody where his hair had been.

The woman's dark, haunted gaze went from one Alcott brother to the other. "And which one of you, then, is the fine, fair gentleman who owns the Thames Street mill?"

"Hell's fire, don't look at me," Stu drawled into the raw silence that had followed the woman's words. He cocked a thumb at his brother. "I only spend the money. He's the one who makes it."

A few of the men actually laughed. Although their laughter cut off abruptly when the woman took a single, lurching step toward them.

"Murderers!" she screamed. "All of you are wicked murderers!" Her wild gaze snapped over to Geoffrey Alcott. "But it's you especially I've come here to see."

Geoffrey blanched a little, but then he bowed his head as if acknowledging a parlor introduction. "At your service, madam."

She tried to lift the child's body up to Geoffrey as if presenting it to him as a gift. For a moment it seemed she would fall over backward under the weight of it.

Tears poured in steady streams from her dark eyes, but now her words were gentle and lilting, as if she were crooning a lullaby. "He fell into one of your ring spinners. Slipped and went flying, he did, right into the spinner, while hurrying with his bobbins like the wee good lad that he was. I thought you'd want to see what your great black monster of a machine did to him afore we put him in the ground."

Emma couldn't look at the dead child, but she couldn't look away either. Her gaze fastened onto a thin bare foot that was black with dirt and grease.

"It took his arm, did the spinner. And ripped the pretty yellow curls right off his head. Scalped him, it did, like one of your red Indians."

Geoffrey cleared his throat. "I deeply regret your loss, madam," he said, and Emma noticed that his voice had taken on that gentling tone he often used with her. "But I must remind you that when you sent your boy to work in the mill, you put your mark on a document agreeing to make no claim for any damages or injuries that might result from his own inexperience and carelessness."

A ragged sob burst out of the woman's throat. "*Aaugh*, carelessness, you say. And was it carelessness that made his bare feet slip on the greasy floor that's doubtless never seen broom or mop in all the years you've owned it? Was it careless of him to be carting your bobbins back and forth for hours at a stretch and with nary a rest nor hope of one, 'til his poor legs got so wore out they couldn't hold him up no longer? Maybe it was careless of him to slave all his darlin' life for a pittance and then die so's to make you rich Great Folk all the richer."

To Emma's horror, the woman's gaze suddenly shifted onto her. "*A mhuire*. And would you look at your fine lady sitting up there on her fancy horse. Wearing her fine clothes woven of such a misery as the deaths of poor wee children, and her not caring a jot for it."

The woman's eyes, her whole face, bled pain. Emma's head bowed before her fierce gaze. She looked down . . . and saw blood dripping from the fox tail's gory stump onto the polished black toe of her riding boot.

The rest of the hunt had bunched in a tight group around the gate and the whale's jawbone, unable to ignore the woman's presence and ride through, and yet unsure of how to meet this sort of unpleasantness that had suddenly been thrust into their day. No one spoke or moved. It was as if they were all merely waiting for the woman to go away and take the messy business in her arms with her.

Their silent indifference didn't defeat the woman; she seemed to feed off it. Her head came up proudly. Her eyes glittered brightly with tears and an inner fire.

"His name was Padraic," she said. "Should any of you be wanting to know."

Slowly, she turned and walked away from them. She staggered under the burden she carried, and once she stumbled, though she didn't fall.

"Bad form, that," Aloysius Carter said, when she had disappeared around a bend in the road. His thick bulk teetered slightly in the saddle as he bent over to slide the polished brass horn carefully back into its leather case. "Bringing a dead child to the hunt."

Stuart Alcott emitted a crack of wild laughter. "Indeed. Only one carcass at a time, please."

"For God's sake, Stu," his brother said.

Emma sent her mare cantering through the gate and into the yard. She kicked her foot out of the stirrup and jumped from the saddle without even waiting, as was proper, for a man's arm to assist her. She was so cold. She had to get inside the house by a fire and get warm. She didn't think she would ever be warm again.

Only a lifetime of rigorous training kept her from running across the yard. Still, she was walking so fast she had to lift the skirts of her habit high above her ankles.

"Miss Tremayne."

Her name, spoken in that man's rough, grating voice, startled her so that she nearly stumbled over her own feet as she whirled to face him. She gasped when she saw what he had in his hand. What he was holding out to her as if it were a gift, like the woman had held out the dead child to Geoffrey.

His face, as he looked at her, bore no expression. Only his eyes were that same startling green she'd noticed about him the first time. She was used to admiration in a man's gaze, but what was in this man's eyes she had never seen before.

She was now so cold she was shivering; she had to clench her teeth to keep them from chattering.

"It's forgetting your trophy, you are," he said. The smile on his face was biting, not really a smile at all. "And here after all the trouble you've been at to get it."

She shook her head no, and a small moan escaped her tight lips. She had wanted to make Geoffrey take the horrid thing back or to toss it away, but she hadn't because . . . because in the world in which she lived, to refuse the honor of the brush just wasn't done.

Yet, as cowardly as it had been for her not to refuse it in the first place, it would be even more cowardly of her not to take it now.

She took the brush from his outstretched hand, careful not to let her fingers come close to touching his, and made herself turn and walk slowly across the yard to the farmhouse as if she didn't care.

When she got inside, she set the mangled fox tail with exquisite care on the marble shelf of the hall tree. She took her handkerchief and tried to wipe the blood off her hand-stitched ecru kid riding glove that had come all the way from Maison Worth in Paris. But although she rubbed and rubbed, the bright red stains wouldn't come out.

Later that night, when she would go to put the gloves away in their satin-lined box, she would wonder how she'd gotten the little Irish bobbin boy's blood on her hands, when she hadn't been anywhere near him.

Chapter Three

Bethel Lane Tremayne cinched her lips together until they were as thin as a buttonhole. She hurried along the path that led to the old orangery, and with each tap of her heels on the cobbled stones her anger grew.

What an aggravation her daughter was. What a . . . what a . . . but she couldn't think of a word *forceful* enough to describe the cross she had to bear that was her daughter Emma.

She didn't like coming out to the old orangery. When the new conservatory had been built closer to the house, the old orangery had been allowed to fall into disuse. Emma had taken it over, and Bethel didn't like to think about what her daughter did out here with her chisels and mallets and grit-stones. It wasn't proper, what she did. It was downright disgraceful, and yet there was no stopping her.

Not that Bethel hadn't tried. She'd locked the girl up in the cellar with the rats and spiders; once she'd even had her tied down to the bed so that she could beat her back with a cane. Yet none of those punishments had done any good. In many ways Emma had always been as malleable and obedient a daughter as she ought to be. But in other ways she was every bit a Tremayne. There was a wildness in her, something untamable that frightened Bethel.

She had to stop as her breath caught suddenly, stabbing at her chest. Her corset stays gouged deep into her ribs. Her lungs felt starved for air. It was all Emma's fault—that she had to rush about so, when she ought to be preserving her strength for the trying days and weeks and months that lay ahead.

First there were the betrothal visits to be faced. And then the betrothal ball—an event that would pale before the glory and fury of the wedding itself. Every moment of those days would be fraught with shoals of impropriety and social disaster, which would have to be navigated around with the utmost care and attention.

And it will all fall on my shoulders, Bethel thought. For she alone was now the keeper of the Tremayne name and reputation and traditions.

By the time she got to the orangery's warped wooden door, Bethel had worked herself into such a state that she jerked on the latch hard enough to break a nail down to the quick. She gasped at the sting of pain. Then gasped again as the point of one of her whalebone stays poked her in the belly.

Then she gasped again, as she did every time she saw the inside of the old greenhouse.

It was no longer a repository for orange trees and orchids. Indeed, its main occupant now seemed to be a huge crane with pulleys and winches that Bethel had some vague idea were used to move the heavy blocks of stone and marble that filled one corner of the room.

Instead of the sweet perfume of exotic blossoms, the place smelled of wet clay, stone dust, and soldered metal. Once, the air inside here had been hot and moist. But not so today, for it was gray outside and many of the frosted glass panes were cracked or broken.

And there, bathed in the pale wash of light streaming through the broken windows, stood her daughter Emma.

The girl was bundled up against the chill in an old gray sweater and a stained painter's smock. She stared raptly at a heavy four-legged stand with a turn table top. In the middle of the stand sat a lump of yellow clay, which was held in place by a rusting iron frame.

She couldn't have taken up pastels or watercolors like other girls, Bethel thought. Oh, no. In a world where daughters were supposed to pass unremarked, her Emma fancied herself a sculptress.

"Emma!" Bethel said, her voice loud and sharp.

But she might have been speaking to one of the blocks of stone. All of the girl's attention was focused on the mound of moist clay that was half-formed into a shape that looked, to Bethel, vaguely human. Except that it had no head.

Bethel was trying to imagine just what the thing was supposed to be, when her daughter picked up a spatula from off a table littered with stained rags and stroked the blade down . . . It was a leg, Bethel realized suddenly.

The leg of a naked man.

Bethel shrieked as a sharp pain pierced her chest. Twinkling lights danced like fireflies at the edges of her eyes, and the floor suddenly began to pitch and sway beneath her feet. The light pouring through the windows faded, faded, faded into darkness.

She opened her eyes as Emma was draping a wet cloth over her forehead. Her daughter was kneeling beside her, and she was lying on something . . . a filthy old green-striped chaise that was losing its ticking.

Bethel tried to sit up, but the world spun crazily. "What . . . ?"

"You fainted, Mama. You've had Jewell lace your corset too tightly again."

"I did not." Bethel swatted the girl's hands away—hands, she noticed, that were stained with yellow clay. Her gaze went back to the headless, naked man. Even half-formed and decapitated there was no doubt of what it was, what *he* was. So blatantly . . . *masculine.*

Bethel shut her eyes against the indecent sight of it. She wanted to tell Emma to cover it up, but she would not even acknowledge its existence aloud.

"I'm going to loosen your laces," she heard Emma say. "You're huffing worse than a beached whale."

Bethel pushed her daughter's hands away again. "You are not to do so, for they aren't the least bit too tight. At least they're no tighter than they need to be. And I'm not *huffing.* What a wickedly ungracious thing to say to your mama."

Bethel could hear the Georgia drawl in her own voice thickening like clotted cream. It always got worse when she became agitated. And she had the uncomfortable feeling she was creating a scene. Nothing was more ill-bred than scenes.

She took a deep breath to calm herself, and her stays stabbed into her sides again.

She made her face go all soft and wounded-looking. "You've simply no idea of the torment I go through to appear before the world as I ought. You, who've always been as skinny as a poor man's chicken. Why, without my corset I would look like I'd up and swallowed a watermelon, and your father cannot abide fat women. You don't know how many times I heard him say those very words, and I did try so not to let myself go. But then you children came along and . . ."

Her daughter had sat back on her heels and was staring at her with those changeling eyes. "You're wrong in what you're implying, Mama, and what's more, I think you know it. Papa didn't leave us because you had babies and your belly got a little plump."

Bethel hauled back her hand and slapped her daughter so

hard across the face the girl's head rocked on her long, slender neck. But Bethel was the one who burst into tears.

"What did you go and make me do that for?" she cried, for nothing was worse form than a display of temper. "I declare, there are times when you are pure hateful to me. All my children have always been hateful to me."

Emma brought a trembling hand up to her cheek. "Mama, please, please, don't lie to yourself anymore. Don't lie to *us*. It was what happened to Willie that drove Papa away, what we . . . did."

Bethel clapped her hands over her ears. "You hush up, hush up! I can't bear to speak of that night. You know I can't. Why, even just hearing you say his name is like a knife stabbing into my heart. And we did nothing. Nothing! It was Willie, Willie was the one. He shamed himself and he shamed the family." She seized her daughter by the arms and shook her hard. "And don't you look at me like that, don't you dare. You think I don't mourn him, but I do. I cry myself to sleep every night just thinking of my poor darling boy and what I've lost."

Emma's face was white, except for the livid mark on her cheek. "I think of him, too," she said in a strained whisper. "Of what we did to him that night, of how we betrayed him, and I can't bear it. If it didn't take more courage to die than to go on living, I sometimes think . . ."

The unfinished threat hung, pulsing, in the air between them. Charged with accusation and recrimination, and a dark secret only the two of them shared. It must, Bethel thought, be the strain of the impending marriage that had precipitated the memories of that terrible night being brought out into the open, for they rarely spoke of it, hadn't spoken of it in years.

And this was what came of it. This was what came of broaching aloud things better left to lie shrouded in silence.

"We'll not speak of it anymore," Bethel said.

Emma stared back at her with those impossible, unreadable eyes. "No, Mama."

It was the way things were done in their world, and the knowledge brought Bethel comfort. The way things ought to be done. To ignore the unpleasant, to turn one's face away from the disagreeable. And it was better this way—to carry on as if none of it had ever happened.

"We'll never speak of it again," she said.

"No, Mama."

Bethel made a show of checking the chatelaine's watch pinned to her waist. "Mercy sakes alive, will you just look at the time. We're at home today, and here you are looking as though you've been raised like a hog in the woods. It will not do, Emma. You will return to the house this instant and change your frock. Put on the beige velvet tea gown."

Emma pushed herself to her feet. Bethel could see the girl's chest lift in a hard, hitched breath, although she made no sound. "Yes, Mama," she said, but instead of obeying she went over to a big soapstone sink and began to prime the pump.

"This instant, Emma."

The pump handle squealed, and water splashed into the sink. "Yes, Mama. Only just let me wrap my model up in a wet cloth, or it will dry out."

Against her will, Bethel's gaze slid over to the clay model. A naked man . . . She shuddered. She absolutely would not abide such goings-on. It would not do.

Tonight, after her daughter had gone to bed, she would come out here and take up one of those mallets and smash that disgraceful thing into so many pieces it could never be put back together again.

~

She had grown up with the sweat sour on her skin, in a place so hot the sun bled the sky bone white. A place of red dust and yellow cotton, and a two-room shack with a rotting front porch.

When the war came it first took away all the men, and then it took the mule they'd used to pull the plow. That was when Bethel's mama had held the back of a tin pie plate up to her face and said, "You're prettier'n a July mornin', honey, the prettiest lil' gal in all of Sparta. You can go far, Bethel Lane. As far as the back of the moon, if you but put your mind to it."

Mazie sold the plow, and one of the first things she bought with the money was a *Beadle's Dime Book of Practical Etiquette.* The way Mazie had it figured, the war was going to change things, to bust things wide open. Even for the child of a dirt-poor cotton farmer who lived in a weather-rotted shack at the end of a dust-palled road in the heart of Georgia. Especially if that child was possessed of a face and body that could send a man's thoughts sinking right down to the hunger between his legs.

Mazie set about teaching her daughter every bit of knowledge there was to be found in Beadle's book. Bethel learned to say, "Be quiet, please," instead of, "Shut your golblamed mouth." She learned how to crook her little finger when she drank a cup of tea, although she always complained that it gave her a cramp. She learned to keep her knees pressed together at all times, even when sitting on the privy house hole, and not to belch when she swallowed air.

By the time they'd gotten to the last page of Beadle's book, the war was over and Sparta had long since given up on itself and the glorious cause of Southern independence. And a Yankee by the name of Jonathan Alcott had come to town.

He was said to own a whole fleet of mills up north somewhere and had come down to encourage the planting of cotton on the battle-ravaged land. To introduce himself and his grandiose plans he decided to give a ball, and the whole of Sparta was to be invited.

The Lane women planned for that event as though it were a military campaign. Mazie took the last of the plow money and went to a secondhand shop, where she bought a white brocade wedding dress that she made over into a ball gown. She borrowed some marabou feathers off an old hat and used them to fancy up the gown's scalloped neckline, while Bethel spent the hours practicing her curtsey and waltzing with a broom.

On the night of the ball, Mazie wove two perfect white gardenias into her daughter's hair. "Lord, child, you are so beautiful you make my heart ache," she said, and the tears softened her tired, washed-out eyes, making her for a moment look young and pretty, as well. "You're gonna have every man there at your feet, see if you don't. Only you remember what I told you about keeping your drawers buttoned and your knees together until after a ring is on your finger."

The ball was being held in Sparta's grand old hotel, and Bethel floated there on clouds of pride and joy. It was everything she had dreamed it would be. Chandeliers glowing with the warmth and dazzle of a hundred suns. A string quartet playing lilting tunes as sweet as any meadowlark had ever sung. Lace-covered tables groaning beneath the weight of so much food it made Bethel dizzy just to look at it.

Oh, the ball was indeed everything she had dreamed it would be . . . until she heard the whispers:

"Do you believe the gall of Bethel Lane, bringing herself here in that made-up dress? And those feathers! Why, they look plucked right off the hind end of a swamp duck."

"That's what comes of inviting just any-old-body to your to-do. But then he's a Yankee, so he can't be expected to know better."

"If he lets share-cropper trash like Bethel Lane come waltzin' through the door, then I'm surprised we aren't rubbin' elbows with the coloreds, as well."

"Land, even a Yankee's got more sense than that."

Bethel sat alone on a chair against the wall, smiling, smiling, smiling until the tears she kept swallowing grew like a tumor in her throat, and her eyes shone fever-bright with agony.

And then she saw him. Or rather he saw her.

He was a boyhood friend of Jonathan Alcott's and he'd accompanied the man on his trip to Georgia as a lark, or so he'd said. Later, she understood pity and a soft heart had drawn him across that room to bow over her hand. Then, she thought it was her bluebell eyes and sunshine yellow curls, and the pretty face she'd first seen reflected in the back of a tin pie plate.

She had laughed and charmed him and said, "How you do go on," every time he complimented her. By the end of their first dance, she'd discovered his New England blood was bluer than ink, and he had bank accounts and portfolios stuffed plumb full with good ol' Yankee greenback dollars.

She would have fallen in love with him anyway, even without his society connections and all that beautiful money. For he was tall and slender with golden, sun-tinted skin and a head of raven-black hair. And when he touched her, she felt the way the air got in the dead heat of summer right before it was fixing to thunderstorm. Crackling and heavy, charged with both promise and danger.

But Mazie Lane had taught her daughter well. Bethel was sure enough going to keep her drawers buttoned and her knees together until a ring was on her finger.

He had only intended to be in Sparta for three days. By the end of two weeks she had him so desperate for her he was down on his knees. She didn't give him what he was begging for, though—not until they'd eloped across the county line and woken up a judge to pronounce her officially Mrs. William Tremayne.

And so that was how Bethel Lane, of Sparta, Georgia,

came to live in a fine northern mansion called The Birches on Poppasquash Point, in the state of Rhode Island and her Providence Plantations. How she came to find herself part of a family known as the "wild and wicked" Tremaynes. A family that had made the first of its many fortunes off slave trading, rum, and privateering, and whom all the world believed cursed because of it. Tragedy, so it was said, had claimed a victim of the Tremaynes at least once in every generation.

It amused Bethel's secret Confederate heart to discover that her husband's proud and venerable Yankee family had built the foundation of its great wealth on trading in black flesh. Especially since the Lanes themselves had never owned any slaves, being too poor most years to count even a plow among their meager possessions, let alone the mule to pull it. Nor was she fazed by stories of any ol' curse—where she came from, bad luck was as common as fleas.

And if the family had once been dashing and reckless, and if maybe their blood was tainted still—the way Bethel saw it, the Tremaynes had already put a lot of good time and effort into scrubbing themselves clean as a new pair of drawers. For two hundred years they'd cultivated respectability as diligently and carefully as they tended to the hothouse blooms that filled their house year after year. Bethel promised herself, from the moment she became a Tremayne, that she would never let the cause down. The Lanes might never have amounted to much themselves, but Bethel Lane Tremayne would do her new family proud.

She surely could not have dreamed up a place like The Birches, with its gables and towers and wraparound piazzas, with its iron lace gates and acres of birch stands and green velvet lawns stretching to the bay. She had ridden in William's fancy new landau, with all its gilt and velvet and leather, through those massive wrought-iron gates and down a lane that was as white and smooth as a fresh snowfall. She found out later the lane was paved with the crushed shells of thousands of little clams called quahogs, and she had been awed with the utter wonder of it all. She felt that by coming north, to this place, she had indeed gone as far away as the back of the moon.

To her it was an alien world of sailboats and clam bakes and long-faced people with a way of talking flatly through their long noses. A world where the old, rich families had the audacity to call themselves the Great Folk and then go on and live right up to it. A world defined and ordered by an enormity of rules and traditions not found in Beadle's etiquette book.

Up north here, only William knew she'd come from a two-room shack at the end of a backcountry road. It was a gilded world her husband had brought her to. A world where appearances and rituals were all, and the real thing was never said or done or even thought.

She had to work so hard to fit in, and with a ruthlessness that frazzled her soul and left her in the silent darkness of her bed at night shaking with fear that she would be found out, found out . . . Day by day, year by year, she scrubbed away the outer layers of herself as if she were washing the red dust of Georgia off her skin. Scrubbed and scrubbed until all that was left of Bethel Lane was her cane-syrup drawl and a taste for coffee made with chicory.

Bethel learned how to be one of the Great Folk by observing how they walked through their carefully orchestrated lives. She learned how any deviation from the expected thing, the done thing, was so swiftly punished.

She saw what happened to the banker's daughter who was caught kissing the fishmonger's son beneath one of the Thames Street piers that Fourth of July. She saw what happened to the young wife who appeared at the yacht club's private beach in a bathing costume that revealed too much of her naked calves. She saw what happened to the matron who lost her composure and quarreled openly with her husband's mistress in the middle of High Street one winter's drizzly afternoon.

Bethel saw what happened when you flaunted the conventions and courted scandal, what happened when you were found out, and she carved those lessons into her heart. The gilded world was ruthless to those who defied it. Once you entered that world, once you submitted to it, then you had no choice but to abide by its rules.

Or be ostracized forever.

Sometimes, though, Bethel would wake in the middle of the night with her face wet with tears and a hollow, heavy ache in her chest. In the silence of those dark hours she would remember dazzling sun-scorched days of wading barefoot through a tea-colored creek, the oily smell of cotton boles dripping in the hot air, and a pair of loving hands weaving gardenias in her hair.

"I'll send for you, Mama," she'd scrawled on the note she'd left for Mazie on the night she'd run off with her Yankee gentleman. *I'll send for you, Mama*, she had promised.

But she never did.

Chapter Four

It was strange, Bethel thought, that her heart would be so full up with memories of her mama today. Or perhaps not so strange, what with her head so full of plans for her own daughter's wedding. Getting married was, after all, the biggest thing that would ever happen in a girl's life.

At least Emma, with all her peculiarities and that streak of Tremayne wildness, had had the sense to make a splendid match.

Geoffrey Alcott . . . Bethel breathed a little hum of satisfaction. Geoffrey Alcott of the *New York* Alcotts. The family had lived in Bristol for over a hundred years, but they were called the New York Alcotts because the first Alcotts had been born there, in New York. Folk in Bristol had always had long memories and unforgiving natures, and they were suspicious of newcomers.

Still, Geoffrey Alcott was manly in looks, possessed of good manners, and unfailingly civil to his elders. A true gentleman by blood and birth. And wealth, of course.

Well, perhaps his method of proposing left a bit to be desired—popping the question on a fox hunt, no less. Bethel didn't approve of such shortcuts through the conventions; they made her nervous, for who knew of what other, worse things they could lead to. It would be up to her now to ensure that the wedding overcame the groom's small breach of etiquette and tradition.

"It will be the wedding of the century," Bethel vowed, and her words echoed over and over like a chanted prayer in the vast black and white marble foyer of The Birches.

She had left the old orangery and returned to the house through the front entrance. She often did that, even if she'd only taken a short turn around the garden—she would come back inside through the massive, coffered ebony doors as any guest might do. That way she could get the full impact of the glory that was The Birches. And she would remind herself of how far she had come, and of how vigilant she must always be to keep alive the destiny and the fortunes of the great old family into which she had married.

Only this time a sudden thought brought her to a standstill in the middle of the enormous, echoing, domed and marble-lined hall:

William would be coming home for the wedding.

She touched the back of her hand to her burning cheek. Her heart pounded so hard she feared her ribs would crack. Oh, surely, surely he would come home now. He'd have to come home. He *must* come.

She would write to him—no, no, she would have Emma write him, write him and beg him to come. A girl would want her father at her wedding, to give her away.

And Bethel would have a chance to talk to him then, to explain things to him. She would tell him how wrong he had been to blame her for what had happened that night. She would explain how she'd only been doing what needed to be done, what the world *required* be done, for the family, for them all.

It was wicked and mean and unfair, what he'd said to her that day he'd left—about her not having a kind and loving heart. She'd tried so hard to be the perfect, genteel wife he deserved, and she did so love him and their children, truly she did. It was just that sometimes other duties had to take precedence. The family as a whole had to come first, beyond any one individual. As a Tremayne he should have understood that.

She wasn't the cruel and selfish creature obsessed with fripperies that he had accused her of being. She knew what was important—she'd always known. And she was still as pretty as she'd always been; she was only forty-two, after all. She could bring back that look of wild hunger that had burned so brightly in his eyes the night of the Sparta ball, all she needed was a chance. All she needed was a little time alone with him.

Bethel was smiling now as she smoothed back imaginary loose strands of hair off her forehead. She was smiling as she straightened the stiff Belgian lace collar of her shirtwaist. William would be coming home, and she would have her chance. But she would have to think it through more carefully later, plan her strategy later. Their afternoon callers would be arriving soon, and she couldn't be found out here in the foyer disheveled and with her face all flushed and the drawing room not yet seen to. It simply would not do.

She finished crossing the hall in a more stately fashion, passed through the heavy, green damask portieres, and entered the drawing room.

She had called it the parlor the first week she'd been here, until one of the servants had corrected her—and what a humiliating moment that had been. The room was a magnificent mix of the exotic and the traditional. Two ribbon-backed Chippendale chairs flanked an antique Chinese rosewood chest with dragon-claw feet. A silk carpet woven by Tibetan monks lay spread over a beautiful teakwood floor that was washed down every week with steeped tea leaves.

Two immense gold bowls from India graced either side of

the rare sienna marble mantelpiece. Every day the bowls were filled with freshly cut American Beauty roses grown in the new conservatory. Bethel had set about reassuring herself that the roses were indeed fresh when she noticed a parlor maid bent over the onyx and lapis lazuli piano lamp, trimming the wick.

Bethel didn't shout, but her voice still cut, quick and sharp, through the air. "You!"

The girl whirled, one hand pressed to her breast, her eyes wide.

"What are you doing in this room at this time of day?" Bethel demanded. Servants in properly run households did not show their faces abovestairs when family and guests might be forced to be reminded of their existence.

The girl jerked her knee and head in a curtsey. "The lamp was smoking and I . . ." Her gaze fell to the floor and her hands drifted helplessly down to twist in her starched apron. "Forgive me, madam."

"It will not do."

"No, madam."

The girl started to give Bethel a wide berth on her way to the door, but then she paused and cast a shy glance up at her. "We've been saying, those of us belowstairs, how it's that happy we are to hear of young Miss Emma's betrothal to Mr. Alcott."

For a moment Bethel almost smiled, although it wasn't the done thing, to exhibit emotion of any sort in front of a servant. "Why, thank you, Biddy," she said.

They were all called Biddy, the multitude of Irish girls who scrubbed and dusted and "did for" the Great Folk. Years ago, when she'd first arrived at The Birches, Bethel had made a special point of learning all the servants' names. Until someone had warned her that such familiarity just wasn't done.

"He's right handsome," the girl was saying. "Right handsome is Mr. Alcott, and oh such a gentleman."

"Indeed, he is generally conceded to be the most eligible bachelor in all of New England. For not only has he inherited a fortune of more than three million dollars, but he—"

Bethel cut herself off, so shocked she almost shuddered. To speak of money, and to a servant no less, was a vulgar, vulgar thing. She couldn't have been more horrified at herself than if she'd suddenly taken it into her head to flip up her skirts and show off her bloomers.

Bethel's hand fluttered up to the lace at her throat, and she could feel that she was flushing. This, she thought, is what happens when you allow your vigilance to slip even for a moment; when you lose sight of appearances and remember things, speak of things that you shouldn't.

"That will be quite enough," she said.

"Yes, madam," the girl mumbled to the floor, and scurried from the room.

A movement through the brocade-and-velvet–swathed windows caught Bethel's eye. Her younger daughter, Madeleine, sat in her wheelchair on the veranda, among the potted ferns and a pair of old twig rockers. Emma stood behind her, her hands resting on the chair's handgrips.

Bethel frowned at the sight of them. A servant would have to be fetched now to take Maddie and her chair back into the house for tea. It would create a fuss they certainly didn't need on such an afternoon.

And as for Emma . . . She had obediently changed into the beige velvet tea gown, although she must have positively thrown it on to get back outside so quickly. And now she risked rouging her cheeks and frizzing her hair by standing out in the damp like that.

As Bethel watched, Emma half-turned toward the window. She was laughing, and her face shone opalescent in the watery half-light of the gray afternoon. The wind fluttered soft tendrils of her dark brown hair. The bone of her cheek was like the curve of an angel's wing.

Bethel felt an odd hitch in her chest. It wasn't fair, she thought, that a daughter could stop her own mother's breath with her beauty.

The sky lightened just then, glazing the windowpanes and showing Bethel her own reflection in the glass. She reached up and touched the image as if she could make it go away, like stirring still water in a pond. How old she seemed to be growing of a sudden.

Am I still pretty, Mama?

The sunshine-yellow hair had faded some, and she had to enhance its thickness now with rats. She wore high, lacy collars to hide the sagging skin of her neck and chin. Her eyes were still the color of bluebells, but they were fanned with wrinkles that had stayed long after she had quit smiling. After she'd no longer had a reason to smile.

A hollow emptiness clutched at her belly. Somewhere deep inside her there surely lived still that girl who had gone to a ball with gardenias in her hair and hope blazing in her heart.

A gust of wind slapped against the window, and she closed her eyes. When she opened them again the day had darkened and she couldn't see her reflection anymore, only her daughter Emma, so young and beautiful, and with all of her life stretching before her like a shiny road, straight and sure.

And as her daughter's head tilted back again in laughter that Bethel couldn't hear, she had the strangest feeling of having missed something important.

"You must be so happy, Emma. It's a wonder you're not positively bursting and dripping with it. Like a ripe juicy summer peach."

Smiling, Emma looked down on the seashell roll of her sister's pale hair. "What a sticky thought," she said, her smile growing when Maddie laughed. She laid her lace-gloved hand on her sister's shoulder and gave it a gentle squeeze. "And I'm not so happy at all when I remember that I'll be leaving you and Mama."

Leaving home.

Emma looked out over the winter-worn lawns to the thick grove of white birches that encroached on the back of the house. Low clouds snagged their bellies on the treetops, and a salt-laced wind whipped at the bare branches. Yet spring was a certainty still, for it came every year. Emma could feel the promise of spring knocking at her heart.

Maddie reached up and patted her sister's hand, twisting around in her chair. Her eyes sparkled wetly, but whether from their earlier laughter or held-back tears Emma couldn't tell. It could even have been the bite of the wind.

"Oh, tosh," Maddie said. "Don't be such a ninny. To begin with, the wedding won't happen for another two whole years. And besides, you'll only be going as far away as the house on Hope Street. You could still see us every day if you wanted, although why you would I can't imagine. It's a dream come true. To marry the man you love."

Emma looked out at the birches again so she wouldn't have to meet her sister's eyes. She loved Geoffrey, she did. Only she had a hard time remembering if it was truly her dream or only everyone else's dream for her.

"But then you're so pretty," Maddie was saying. "You could have had any man you set your heart on."

"Now listen to who's being the ninny," Emma said. She tried hard to pretend that her beauty didn't exist, for it held a power she wanted to explore but was afraid to. "It so happens that it's Geoffrey I do want, not just any-old-body."

"And heaven forbid that you would ever become Mrs.

Any-old-body," Maddie said in their mama's Georgia drawl, and Emma laughed.

Maddie turned back around in her chair and her hands fell together in her lap. She sighed, although it was not an especially sad sound. "Remember how we used to fight over which of us would marry Stu?"

"I certainly never did any such thing."

Maddie laughed with delight. "But you did, you did. I remember it so distinctly."

"Oh, the very shame of it." Emma pressed the back of her hand to her forehead and pretended to be on the verge of a swoon. "I suppose I was young then and more impressed with style over substance."

"Stu has plenty of substance," Maddie protested. "It's only that it's always been so hard for him, what with Geoffrey being such the perfect son. Poor Stu. I worry about him sometimes." Her voice softened and a faraway yearning came into her eyes. "Still."

Emma swallowed around a sudden lump in her throat. She hadn't told her sister yet that Stuart Alcott was back home, for it would only bring the girl pain. And a horror of the inevitable moment when he would first see her as she was now. Seven years ago, when Stu had left, Madeleine Tremayne had been a gay child of twelve, with a kiss of freckles across her nose and a wide, laughing mouth, a child who was always running off somewhere, to swim, or play tennis, or skate. Not this pale wraith of a creature with her wasted, crippled legs.

Emma suspected that her sister had been in love with Stu all her young life. For Maddie, marriage to the flamboyant and wickedly handsome Alcott second son had probably always been something more than a wistful, girlhood imagining. Although she'd certainly never spoken of such feelings aloud.

But then, they never spoke about either the horrors or the

dreams that lay so powerful and enormous among them all. And there wouldn't be any marriage for Maddie now anyway. Not to Stu Alcott, not to any man.

A memory stirred at the edges of Emma's thoughts, of a day when they'd all been children and they'd been lounging right here on the south piazza, where she and Maddie were now, among the potted ferns. Next to these old twig rockers with their balsam-stuffed cushions, which had sat in this very place when their father was a boy.

It had been summer then, though. One of those rare sun-baked days when it was so hot the leaves of the birches curled and crackled in the heat.

She remembered she'd been barefoot and how marvelous that had felt—to be able to wriggle her toes on the smooth painted boards of the piazza. They were wearing their bathing costumes that day because they had just been swimming in the bay, and the yards of black wet flannel covered them from wishbone to ankle and clung to their sweating skin, making it itch. They had been so very young—well, she and Maddie had been. The Alcott brothers, at seventeen and fifteen, had already been edging up to being men.

Somehow the subject of weddings came up, and Stu had claimed he was going to marry a hootchy-kootchy girl. Maddie had laughed and laughed as if that was the funniest thing she'd ever heard, although she'd been only seven at the time and couldn't have had the vaguest notion of what a hootchy-kootchy girl was.

Emma, not to be outdone, had said she was going to run away to live in Paris in a garret with a man who wore a beret and smoked cigarettes and practiced free love, although at ten she'd had only the vaguest notion of what *that* meant.

And that was when Geoffrey had said, "What a stupid little snot-nosed brat you are, Emma Tremayne. You are going to marry me."

Emma had tried to punch him on the nose for calling her

a snot-nosed brat. Only he'd ducked, and she'd hit the veranda post instead and cut her hand so badly on a carved wooden pineapple that she had needed three stitches.

And now here she was—engaged to marry Geoffrey Alcott. It had been inevitable, Emma thought, and she felt a strange, slow tearing down her chest, a rip of fear. It had been inevitable and now it was indissoluble. It was too late to change things, even if she wanted to.

But with her brother dead, and her sister as she was, Emma was the only one left to marry, to have children and carry on the family traditions and bloodline. If only Willie . . . But she had no right to think of Willie, to think that if he had lived he might have set her free.

Maddie had been quiet for some time now. Emma leaned over a little, enough to see where a tear had dried, leaving a salty trail on her sister's cheek. She felt ashamed of herself for decrying all of her many blessings when here was poor Maddie mourning those things she would never have.

Suddenly Emma wished desperately that she could speak to her sister of Willie. Of the truth about how he had died and the hole he'd left behind in their lives.

We'll never speak of it again.

Willie, Emma remembered, had also been with them that hot summer's day, sitting so quietly as was his way on one of the old twig rockers. He had laughed at Maddie for laughing over the hootchy-kootchy girl, and he had been the one to wrap his handkerchief around Emma's bleeding hand. But he hadn't said much that day. Of them all, Willie had been best at guarding the secrets of his heart.

The wind lashed through the birches, and the gray sky spat rain. Behind her, Emma heard a boy's gentle laughter and the creak of the old twig rocker.

Yet when she turned around it was empty.

Chapter Five

The Carter sisters were the first to come calling that day.

They entered The Birches through its enormous scrolled wrought-iron gates in an ancient landau, pulled by a pair of matching chestnut horses decked with plumes of red, white, and blue.

They passed through the black and white marble foyer in a sweet cloud of dusting powder and violet sachet, wearing flounces and feathered bonnets that dated from before the war. The Carter sisters were the wealthy, unmarried daughters of a Providence beer baron, and time, for them, had stopped thirty years ago.

Miss Liluth, the younger sister, was what the Great Folk politely called a "little tetched," although it was generally acknowledged that she had not been born that way. But the man she'd been engaged to marry had been killed at Antietam and she'd never gotten over his death. He'd left on the Tuesday afternoon train to Providence, and somehow Miss Liluth had gotten it into her head that the same train that had taken him away from her would bring him home. And so she had spent every Tuesday afternoon since the war's end at the Franklin Street Depot, waiting for him.

"I declare, I must somehow have dreamed you ladies were

coming today," Bethel said, as she saw the sisters settled into a pair of brocaded armchairs, "for I had our chef bake your favorite lace cookies just this morning, Liluth. And for you, Annabelle dear, some of those delicious custard cream cakes I know you so adore. And don't you dare tell me you won't have any. Why, you've gotten skinny as a spindle lately."

Emma winced to herself at her mother's sly cruelty, for the elder Miss Carter was what the Great Folk politely termed a "fleshy woman." She was also wretchedly homely, with small, squinty, pumpkin-seed eyes and a faint birthmark like a water stain on her cheek.

What's more, everyone knew she had fallen into a violent and unrequited love with William Tremayne when she was sixteen, and had stayed in love with him through his marriage to another woman and the birth of his three children.

"As for myself, I surely can't allow a bite to pass my lips," Bethel was saying, "for I confess that I have been on a fast that would wring tears from a Chinese peasant. But whenever I feel my resolve waver, I remind myself that one of the first things my William noticed about me was my slender figure."

She waved a hand at the blue and white Canton china tea service that sat waiting on a silver cart. "Emma, dear, why don't you pour this afternoon?"

The purpose of her pouring, Emma knew, was to show off her betrothal ring. For while a young lady should never brag about her good fortune, a little subtle flaunting was allowed.

The Carter sisters wouldn't be able to miss the ring, for it flashed like blue fire even in the dull light of a gray day. The ring was a huge sapphire encircled by a dozen diamonds, and he had slipped it on her finger only yesterday. Afterward he had turned her hand over and kissed her palm and then the inside of her wrist, and then at last, at last, he had kissed her mouth.

She had been startled by how his mouth had felt on hers, so

strange and sweet and urgent. And afterward, when he'd let her mouth go, her own lips had felt thick and hot. She'd touched them with her tongue and tasted him.

The ring was duly exclaimed over and admired by the two elderly ladies. Emma smiled shyly at Miss Liluth as she handed her a cup of tea with no milk and two sugars. Liluth Carter had been an acknowledged beauty in her day and she was pretty still, with cornsilk hair, pale and fine, and violet eyes.

Emma wondered if Miss Liluth had been kissed by her young man before he had gone off to die in the war. Perhaps they had even made love the night before he left. Emma found the thought of committing such a delicious sin with the man you loved terribly exciting—like sailing before a squall. And dangerous as well, fraught as it was with discovery and scandal. She liked to imagine herself doing it, although she doubted in her heart she would ever find the courage. Certainly she couldn't imagine Geoffrey ever suggesting it.

But in all these years that she had known Miss Liluth, Emma had never spoken with the woman about the man she had loved and so tragically lost. Powerful feelings drove Liluth Carter to that train station every Tuesday to wait for a man who would never return. Yet no one ever acknowledged those feelings aloud, and so they did not exist.

Emma knew she would never learn the secrets that lived inside Miss Liluth's heart. She would spend the next hour in her company, just as they had spent hundreds of hours before this, and the conversation probably wouldn't progress much beyond the weather.

A lady was required at all times to have an ample supply of small talk at her tongue's end, most of it about the weather. Emma had often wondered, though, why they should all care so much about the elements when they so rarely went out in them. The ladies of Bristol fretted more over the weather than did the fishermen.

"The weather," Miss Annabelle Carter said as if on cue, "has been most variable lately."

"It never settles this time of year," Bethel chimed in. She sounded sorely aggrieved, as if it behaved so just to vex her. "At least winter and summer are settled seasons. One knows what to expect."

Emma caught her sister's eye, and they shared a bemused smile. "I find this unsettled weather most unsettling," she said. "Don't you, Maddie?"

Her sister's face lightened with quiet laughter. "Indeed. But then I've discovered that with the weather in particular, one must keep one's opinions flexible."

"It was raining the day my Charles went off to the war," Miss Liluth said. "I always feel so sad on rainy days. Perhaps tomorrow it will be fair."

Bethel leaned over and patted the woman's arm. "I'm sure it will be, my dear."

Emma swallowed around an ache in her throat that felt strangely like tears. There sat Miss Liluth, waiting for a man dead nearly thirty years. And her sister, who came week after week, year after year, to the house of a love who had married another woman. And Emma's own poor mama, abandoned by that same man, starving and strangling herself with whalebone, and behaving as if she would see him that very night across the supper table.

But it was against every rule in their world that they should even hint at what was truly in their thoughts and in their hearts. Emma wondered what would happen if for once someone spoke the unspeakable.

"A bobbin boy was killed in the mill last week," Emma said.

Her words fell into the room like stones down a dry well, clattering and echoing into nothingness.

Then Miss Liluth sighed loudly and rattled her teacup in its saucer. "Oh, dear."

Her sister sniffed so hard her nose quivered. "They say that Irish woman brought him to the last hunt of the season, of all places. It's unsettling to think of."

"Like the weather," Emma said.

Miss Liluth plucked at the lace jabot around her throat. "Oh, dear. Oh, dear."

This time her sister was the one to pat her arm. "Now, now, Liluth, don't upset yourself. I was saying as much just this morning, wasn't I? That the middling and lower orders can no longer be depended upon to know their place."

Bethel clucked her tongue, shaking her head. "Society is disintegrating before our very eyes."

" 'Disintegrating.' What a clever turn of phrase, Mama." Emma could hear the rising hysteria in her voice, but she couldn't seem to stop it. "The child had his scalp and one of his arms torn off. He bled to death."

The face Bethel turned to her daughter was empty, but a frown darkened her deep blue eyes. "To be sure, dear. But one doesn't speak of unpleasant things over tea."

Bethel then turned a smiling face to their guests and said, "Now you all must surely have heard the latest news. Young Stuart Alcott has at last come slinking home, impoverished no doubt, and most certainly in disgrace."

Maddie's gaze jerked over to Emma and then away again, and two bright spots of color blossomed on her cheeks. Her hand shook so hard the cup rattled in its saucer, and tea slopped onto the lap rug that lay across her legs.

Bethel reached for the silver bell on the tea cart just as more callers arrived. A trio of Great Folk matrons, who exclaimed over the beautiful sapphire engagement ring on Emma's finger and pretended not to notice Maddie's white face and trembling hands. They spoke no more of dead bobbin boys and scapegrace young men, but of the weather and a wedding that was two whole years in the future.

Their callers all left promptly at five o'clock, as was the

rule. A heavy silence settled over the drawing room, and Emma thought she could almost see her mother's anger, like a stain on the air. She knew she would pay dearly now for discussing unpleasant things over tea.

But it was Maddie on whom their mother bent her fury.

"You are a disgrace, Madeleine Tremayne," Bethel said, her drawl soft and yet somehow cutting deep. And though she was a small woman, she seemed to tower over the wheelchair, so that with each word Maddie shriveled deeper and deeper into the cane seat. "Here our friends come to see our Emma, and you make a spectacle of yourself—worse than a dime-show freak, you are. Since you can't seem to manage yourself in polite company, I can no longer allow you to be there."

"They are *my* betrothal calls, Mama," Emma said, and although she tried, she couldn't keep the shaking out of her voice. "I want Maddie with me."

"It won't do, Emma. She makes herself conspicuous, sitting there in that . . . that obscene contraption, unable to partake properly of the refreshments, *spilling* her tea. Her very presence makes our guests uncomfortable. It will not do."

"But, Mama—"

Her mother gripped Emma's chin hard with her fingers, turning her head to the light of the window. "And you are not to go out on the veranda again on those afternoons when we're at home. The wind flushes your cheeks most unbecomingly. I'll not have people thinking I allow you to wear rouge like some Thames Street harpy."

Tears burned in Emma's eyes as she watched her mother leave the drawing room, stiff-backed in the armor of her whalebone. But it was the sight of her sister's pale, anguished face that tore at her heart.

"Oh, Maddie, I'm so sorry." She knelt beside Maddie's chair and took up her hands. They were cold and shaking, and she chafed them with her own. "Mama's furious with me, and in her uncanny way she knows just the thing to make me feel utterly wretched about it and that's to take it out on you."

"Why, shame on you, Emmaline Tremayne, you're flushing again," Maddie drawled. "It will not do."

Maddie was smiling, but Emma saw the tightness of her sister's throat as she swallowed. The brightness of tears held back in her eyes.

Maddie's gaze fell to her lap. She pulled her hands free and then plucked at the fringed rug that covered her legs. "Emma, will you be a darling and prevail upon one of the servants to carry me up to my room. I very much wish to be alone for a while."

"Oh, Maddie. Shouldn't we—"

"No, we shouldn't. I don't want to talk about him, because there's nothing to be said. I suppose now that he's home our paths must cross eventually. Whereupon he'll see that I've become a cripple, and then that will be the end of that."

Emma couldn't bear to stay in the house a moment longer than it took to see Maddie comfortably settled in bed with a glass of warm milk and her favorite book of poetry. Emma was determined to go for a walk if only to subject her cheeks to the ravages of the cold and the wind until they were redder than a pair of peeled tomatoes.

Her half boots crunched on the winter-brittle grass. The coming night was already casting its black shadows over the dying day. The low dense clouds promised more rain.

When she got to the edge of the lawn she turned and looked back. Her slave-trader ancestor, the first William Tremayne, had built what he called his "plantation house" in 1685, in the square and stolid style of his day. But his pirate, whaler, and merchant heirs had embellished it with wings and bays, towers and cupolas, coves and cornices. Over two hundred years' worth of hot summer sea breezes, fall hurricanes, and winter snowstorms had weathered its shingled walls to a delicate silver gray, the color of the birches that gave the house its name.

Most days, The Birches looked enchanted, with its steeply gabled roofs, and its piazzas spread all around it like the skirts of a curtseying debutante. But on this day the house appeared to be cowering under the heavy sky. A sullen fortress of rules and duties and reproaches, of must-do's and must-nots.

Gaslight flickered in her sister's window and then went out. She had known that as soon as she left the room, Maddie would take the bottle of chloral hydrate out of the drawer in the bedside table. Their uncle, who was a doctor, had prescribed it for the pain in the girl's back and hips. But Maddie had confessed once that she drank it more for the pain in her heart. "It brings me such sweet and gentle dreams," she'd said.

Oh, Maddie . . .

Emma turned her back on the house and entered the forest of birches, following the old Indian trail that ran along a broken stone wall down to the bay. The bare white branches dripped water onto her uncovered head. The leaf mold on the path gave off a melancholy smell, like forgotten old love letters. The world had been stripped of its color; it was all white and black and gray.

She thought of how this stone wall, these white birches, had borne witness to the whole of her life. They knew the entirety of who she was, and yet to her ownself she was a mystery. She felt as if she'd always been holding a part of herself back, saving it, and she had a terrible fear she would end up saving it forever. That she would die with whole parts of herself unused.

When she stepped out of the trees onto the beach, the wind came whipping up off the bay with a lacing of rain that stung her face. She lowered her head and so didn't see the man standing on the dock until she was almost upon it.

The dock was part of a boathouse that thrust out into the tossing waves. It was where Emma's slender little racing sloop, the *Icarus*, was spending these early days of spring, awaiting the first sail of the season. Emma could hear the muffled creak of the boat's masthead, the slap of water against her hull. Willie's boat had been kept there as well, but his slip was empty now.

And that man, that rough and swaggering Irishman from the hunt, stood at the very end of the dock. Her dock.

He must have seen her coming before she saw him, for he was facing her, his back to the wind and water. In the failing light she couldn't see his face, but his very presence stopped her in midstep on the beach.

A seabird wheeled and cried overhead. The foamy waves made hiccuping sounds as they washed over barnacled rocks and speckled pebbles. The wind tore at her hair, pulling it free of its pins. Her hair swirled around her head, a wet shroud that smothered and blinded her. They both stood unmoving and they might have been the only two people on earth.

She broke the spell by reaching up to capture her hair. She wrapped its thickness around her wrist so that she could see him better. "You were going to steal my sloop," she accused, although she had no proof of it, beyond that he was in a place where he should never have been.

"Ah, *Dhia*," he said in his ruined voice, and the sound of it was like the pull of a dull saw through wet wood. " 'Steal,' you say. Such a harsh word, that."

She suspected he was exaggerating his brogue, flaunting his Irishness. Just as he was flaunting the great size of him. He stood dark and tall against the gray water, with his shoulders thrown back and his legs splayed wide, absorbing easily the roll of the dock's weathered boards on the waves. His black wool pea coat flared darkly in the wind.

He made her think of pirate skiffs slinking over moonless

waters, of cloth-muffled oars and the black, silent shadows of dangerous men.

"This is private property you're on," she said. Her own voice sounded rusty, as if she hadn't used it in a hundred years. "The whole of Poppasquash Point belongs to us Tremaynes, and you've no business setting so much as a foot on it."

He threw his head back dramatically, his eyes beseeching the wet slate sky above. "God save us all. The next thing she'll be telling me is that the Great Folk own the very air I'm breathing."

He startled her by moving suddenly, so fast it seemed he was off the dock and coming at her before she even had time to think about running.

The closer he came, the larger and more frightening he seemed, and yet she still didn't run. He came right up to her until only a hand's space separated them.

Her head fell back as she looked up at him. There was something striking about his face, even with the scars and the bent nose, or perhaps because of them. He had brave but somehow broken eyes, and they were beautiful. The color of bottle glass that has been polished by the sea and glazed by the sun.

He stared down into her upturned face, and she waited with her heart pounding louder than the surf in her ears for him to do God knew what. But instead he simply stepped around her, passing by her so closely she thought the sleeve of his coat might have brushed her cheek.

She didn't watch him go. Indeed, she walked away from him, in the opposite direction. She pretended to be fascinated with the beards of wet green moss that wrapped around the pilings of the dock, while she listened for the scrape of his boots on the white sand. When all she could hear was the roar and the pulse of the sea and the wind, she turned around.

And she saw that he had stopped and was looking back at

her. She felt a rushing well up inside her, then. Of excitement and fear, and of expectations only half-imagined. She whirled, turning her back to him, and drew in a deep breath, tasting the brine.

When she looked around again, he was gone. But she could still see where their tracks in the sand had come together and then walked away from each other.

It grew dark and became quite cold, and yet she waited there on the beach until the tide had come in far enough to wash their footprints all away.

Chapter Six

It was a blue, wind-booming day. The first day of May.

Emma took the *Icarus* out onto the water for the first time that spring. And when the wind caught the mainsail, bellying it out with a great snap, Emma Tremayne threw back her head and laughed.

She felt as wide and free as the sky.

She squinted out into the dazzle where the water met the last fraying tatters of morning fog. The sun was just up and the world glowed rosy, like the hollow of a conch shell.

She trimmed the sails and the sloop heeled deeper, the bow slicing through white lips of waves, foamy wake spilling from the stern. She kept one hand on the tiller, while the other held aloft a parasol. She braced her feet against the coaming and turned her face to the salt spray. And lost herself to the strange rushing silence of a fast boat under sail.

Bristol girls learned how to sail almost as soon as they could walk. The Tremaynes had always met their fates and made their fortunes off the sea and boats; it was in their blood. Mama would never have allowed her to go sailing alone otherwise, if it weren't such a venerated Tremayne tradition. It was the only time Emma felt truly free—in her little racing sloop, running with the wind.

Even so, she had to dress properly, in a yachting costume fashioned by Monsieur Worth. She was required to wear a hat, of course, and carry along a parasol so that her face wouldn't become flushed, or, horror of all horrors, *sunbrowned.*

Today, she stayed on a close tack far out into the bay, sailing around the end of Poppasquash Point and the lighthouse on Hog Island so that when she brought the boat about she would be on a long, steady beat toward the town and the harbor. It would take hours but she didn't care. On the water, time was without limits or horizons. The world was only sun and sea and wind.

She had never ventured out of the bay and into the ocean, although she'd often imagined herself doing so. Once, she'd looked up in an atlas where she would land if she sailed due east from Bristol. It was a seaport in Portugal called Viana do Castelo.

She liked to imagine such a place when she was sailing. To imagine red-tile roofs and crooked cobblestoned streets, a sunwashed harbor and rolling hills of olive trees and grape vines. But although she longed for it, she knew she would never sail there. It wasn't the danger and the loneliness of the wide-open sea that frightened her. It was its infinite possibilities.

When she finally came about, the sun was dancing high in the sky, throwing lacy collars of light on the water. The bones of the town were stark on the horizon, trees and roofs etched against the sky.

She chose Saint Michael's belfry to sight by, as many a homebound Bristol sailor had done before her. Saint Michael's, where every Tremayne born in the last two hundred years had been baptized and buried. Except for those, like her brother, who had been swallowed up by the sea.

The wind filled every corner of her sails. The boat cut and dipped through the waves, drawing closer to the shore. She passed some men in a skiff who were taking up eels with long forks. She could see the mansions on Hope Street now, and the arched roof of the railroad station. And the cotton mill, with its high, narrow windows and its chimneys spewing white steam-smoke.

The mill stood right at the harbor's edge and had its own wharf with piers that stuck out like comb teeth into the water. Emma let the mainsail fall slack and glided up to a barnacle-crusted piling. The rushing silence of the wind spilled into a clash of noise: the jib fluttering, a seagull crying, a man singing as he raked for clams. The loud, vibrating hum that was the constant whir of hundreds of spindles inside the mill.

She tied up her sloop, making the mooring lines fast to the deck cleats with quick, efficient hitches. Yet she didn't climb ashore—not just yet.

For so long, for all of her life, things had always just happened to Emma Tremayne, without her seeking, sometimes without her understanding, and often without her caring. So it had taken some while before she had fully understood what it was she wanted to do. And longer still for her to find the courage to see it through.

Slowly, she lifted her eyes to the red brick, arched gateway of the Thames Street mill. The cotton mill where the Irish bobbin boy had died.

Emma Tremayne had been in all the best houses in Bristol, but never had she set so much as the slender toe of her glazed white kid boot inside the Thames Street cotton mill. She hesitated just past the thick, iron-banded door, next to a time clock and row after row of little yellow cards. Around her the walls and floors trembled to the throbbing cadence of the machines.

A thin man, wearing a shiny black suit and reversible paper cuffs, stepped out of a wooden cubicle that made Emma think of a prison guard tower. She had never seen him before, yet it never occurred to her that he wouldn't know her. The Tremaynes had always been known by everyone in Bristol.

She held out her hand to him, although it shook a little. She always imagined herself being brave, sailing forward to conquer worlds. But the truth was that even an occasion as familiar and simple as a tea party, with people she'd known all her life, could sometimes send her heart to bucking wildly in her chest. She knew her fears were irrational—fears of being stared at and judged so strictly—but she couldn't seem to prevent them.

As this man was staring at her, his eyes wide behind a pair of spectacles that were thick as milk-bottle glass. She told him she wanted to take a tour of the mill, and his Adam's apple bobbed hard in his long slender neck. But in the end he only swallowed and nodded and led her to an office down the hall. There, he turned her over to a Mr. Thaddeus Stipple, a short man with the blubbery roundness of a walrus.

Mr. Stipple tried to tell her that she did not really want to see the mill, for it was dirty and noisy and full of the Irish. Not at all a sight for a gently reared lady such as herself. Emma laced her fingers together in her lap and made herself smile at the man. She reminded him of who she was, as Mama would have done, even though she thought she sounded embarrassingly full of herself.

He gave one more halfhearted protest, then sighed, pushing himself heavily to his feet. He had her follow him back out into the courtyard, up a flight of iron-plated stairs, and through a tin-covered door. They came out onto a latticed catwalk. Overhead, the ceiling was a tangled mess of belts, wires, pipes, beams, and shafting. But Emma looked down, into an enormous room full of clanking, whirling, shuddering machines. This, Mr. Stipple told her, was the spinning room.

He gave the machines names: twisting frame and ring spinner and worsted mule. But all Emma saw was a maze of pulleys and cogs, spinning gears, and whirring bobbins. The din of steel jamming against steel hurt her ears. The rank smell of sweat and oily vapors choked her nose. The air was hot and so full of cotton flint she could barely breathe.

It was a roaring hell, a hell full of children.

She saw wan-faced girls, stoop shouldered and thin chested in their ragged dresses, some so small they had to stand on stools and boxes to do their work. Their pale fingers danced between spinning bobbins, catching and tying the snapped threads before they could tangle.

She watched a boy, with legs as white and thin as birch twigs, crawl beneath one of the great iron monsters to squirt an oil can at a rack of sharp, whirling spindles. Another boy ran by beneath her, rolling a bushel full of spools over a floor slick with grease and tobacco spittle. She could imagine his bare feet slipping on that filthy floor, imagine him thrusting out his arm to catch himself and being caught instead by the cogs of an unguarded machine.

She wondered which had been the one to kill the Irish bobbin boy. Padraic.

Emma never knew how she was able to pick the woman out from among the press of machines and workers on the factory floor. Perhaps it was her red hair, which was like a flaring torch even in the dim light of the cavernous room. Or because she alone was no longer tending to her machine, which was drawing cotton fibers exquisitely long and fine and winding them around dozens of whirling bobbins.

Her dark eyes, fever bright, were staring up at Emma. She had tied her flaming hair back with a piece of twine, but wisps of it clung to her cheeks. Her face had a pale sheen to it, like a lit wax candle. This time she wasn't bundled up in a coat, and Emma saw that the woman's shapeless lye-boiled dress was stained with grease and stretched taut over a belly that was great with child.

She took a step toward Emma and lifted her head, as if she would call out. But then a harsh, racking cough seized her. Her thin shoulders hunched, and she pressed a fist hard to her breastbone, as the coughs tore through her one after another, and her whole body shook.

She fumbled with the sleeve of her worn dress and pulled out a handkerchief and coughed into it hard, almost choking, as if her next breath would be her last.

A man on the floor, who must have been the overseer, saw her then and shouted something Emma couldn't hear. As the woman turned back to her ring spinner, she stuffed the handkerchief back up her sleeve. But Emma had seen that the ragged bit of cotton was stained with strings of blood.

Emma watched her, not moving, barely breathing herself. She wondered how she had come to be what she was, Emma Tremayne, born to such wealth and privilege. And not that woman, coughing her life out on a cotton mill floor.

Chapter Seven

It wasn't often that a young man of only twenty-eight would be so certain in his heart and mind and soul of where he was going and what he was doing in this life, but Geoffrey Alcott was such a man.

Early every morning, except for Sundays, he went down to his office in the old warehouse that was the headquarters of Alcott Textiles, and there he ran his family business with a steady hand on the tiller and a keen eye on the horizon. Besides the Thames Street facility, he owned eight other mills throughout New England, and Geoffrey could have lived well off their income without once ever setting foot inside a spinning room. But such was not his way.

He made it a point of pride that he could himself perform every task he paid others to do. When he was ten, he'd talked his father into allowing him to be a bobbin boy for a week—he still bore the scar on his left hand from where he'd cut it on a buzzing steel spindle. He could disassemble and put together again a carding engine almost as quickly as his best machinist. One day just last year, he'd stood before a ring spinner for a full shift, untangling and tying up broken threads along with the lowliest of the mill rats.

Indeed, Geoffrey's overseers and secretaries often complained that he tried to do too much. If he'd had his way, he would have examined, paid, and received every bill himself. As it was, he did insist on keeping the books for the Thames Street mill, all in his own meticulous handwriting.

At precisely ten minutes before noon every day, Geoffrey Alcott would leave his office in the warehouse and walk home, strolling at a modest pace down Burton Street toward the harbor, before turning uptown on Hope Street. Folk joked that you could set your watch by Geoffrey Alcott.

Most days he enjoyed his walk. Down the cross streets and between the houses and storefronts he could catch blue glimpses of the harbor. When the wind blew steadily, as it did today, he could smell fish and brine, and the spent steam from his cotton mill.

It was on his walks that he did most of his dreaming. Geoffrey Alcott was well favored and rich, but these things he had inherited from his father and grandfather. He had always wanted to make his own mark.

So in the last five years, since his father's death, he had built Alcott Textiles into one of the largest business concerns in the state. To the mills he had added a bleachery and dye works. This year he would extend their operations to include a foundry for the building of the machines that powered his mills.

Just this week, the *Providence Evening Bulletin* had referred to him as "Rhode Island's textile tycoon." He'd clipped the article, and he carried it now in the breast pocket of his fashionable windowpane-checked suit. From time to time as he walked he tapped the pocket, smiling to himself at the crinkling sound the newsprint made.

When he crossed Church Street, he entered a vaulted arch of giant maples and elms and chestnut trees. He left behind the noise of commerce and took up the music of gentrified life. Great Folk life. Here, carriage wheels didn't clatter, they softly crunched over the dirt and gravel street. Coal didn't rumble down chutes into bins; it gently slid. No one shouted or cursed, babies didn't cry, but sometimes from behind wrought-iron gates and privet hedges he could hear a child's laughter.

When he passed the ivy-shawled house of the Carter sisters, he heard the squeak of a porch glider. He stopped and bowed to the two ladies. He smiled when he heard Miss Liluth giggle.

His own house was the biggest and grandest of the mansions on Hope Street. He walked through an iron archway and up an alley of marble flagstones. Linden trees lined the way, and on sunny spring days like this one their scent was sweet and haunting. It always made him feel a little sad, the smell of the lindens in spring, although he could never say why.

He stopped at the bottom of the portico and let his gaze roam slowly up the two-story fluted Corinthian columns and tall Palladian windows. Alcott pride had been built into the house, and he always felt an answering pride well up inside of him at the sight of it.

He put his custom-made kangaroo congress gaiter on the first marble step just as the mill's shrill whistle blasted, the town clock pealed, and Saint Michael's bell tolled the noon hour.

By the time the last chime had been carried away by the wind, he was through the door of the Hope Street mansion. He hung his derby on the hall tree and put his ivory boarhead walking stick in the elephant's-foot umbrella stand. He adjusted the columbine in his buttonhole and slicked back his hair.

He breathed deeply, filling his head with the house's familiar scent that was both sweet and musky. Some folk might say it was the hundred years' worth of beeswax polish rubbed into the olivewood paneling. But Geoffrey Alcott knew it for what it was: the smell of old money.

As he did every afternoon, Geoffrey went first into the morning room, where he found his grandmother sitting in her white wicker rocking chair among her camellias and ferns. Twice a week she had the *Bristol Phoenix* delivered hot off the presses so that she could check the obituaries and gloat over whom she'd managed to outlive for another day.

She had been waiting for him, and her eyes came alive in her fleshless face when he entered the room. She waved the newspaper through the air so hard her cap strings fluttered.

"Amelia Attwater!" she shrieked. She was nearly deaf and she behaved as if everyone else was also. "Right here she is—Amelia Attwater, dead in the paper. It says it was softening of the brain what did her in, but that's a bald-faced lie if ever there was one. Her brain was always soft as stewed tomatoes, so why should that affliction suddenly up and kill her? Huh? I ask you."

He leaned over and kissed the air close to her crepe-papery cheek and got a strong whiff of camphor balls and fresh printer's ink. "Perhaps it was a progressive disease," he said.

"Hogwash. It was her gallstones that did it. Last time I saw her, at Olivia Wentworth's funeral—and what a sorry affair *that* was: brass instead of sterling on the casket and a paucity of white blossoms among the flowers—I remarked how she'd been looking awfully jaundiced lately. Amelia, that is, not Olivia. *Olivia* looked like a pitless prune because the undertaker had forgotten to put her teeth in. As for Amelia, she was as yellow as cow piss. It was gallstones, I tell you, only the Attwaters would never admit to something so pedestrian. Always giving themselves airs, that family." She thumped the newspaper with a gnarled, opal-ringed finger. "They made up this bit about softening of the brain."

The old woman drew in such a belabored sigh her chest rattled. "Poor jaundiced Amelia. Dead in the paper. Nipped in the bud."

Geoffrey leaned over his grandmother's white-lace-caped shoulder for a closer look at the obituary. Her palsied hands caused the paper to tremble, but he was able to catch a glimpse of it. "It says there that she was ninety-three."

"In the bud, poor soul. But then the Attwaters have always been known for dying young. Never has been any grit in that family, beyond the stones in their bladders."

Outside, a gust of wind blew through the blooming lindens. A swirl of pale yellow petals grazed the windowpanes. And it came over him again, that feeling of diffused sadness, like a tender place in the heart.

"Better plan for rain this afternoon," his grandmother said. "There's a strong west wind blowing, and a west wind always brings wet weather."

Geoffrey smiled and patted her shoulder. "I will," he said. But he wouldn't. All his life his grandmother had looked for signs in the wind and the clouds, and she always saw rain.

He left his grandmother to her obituaries and went, as he did every afternoon, to his library to take care of household affairs before luncheon.

The library was a beautiful room, with carved pine pilasters painted to imitate black marble veined with gold. And a round, arched fireplace with a real black marble mantel flanked by Tiffany glass bricks. Geoffrey thought of it as his sanctuary.

Which was why he was aggravated to find someone else sprawled in *his* Morris chair, in front of *his* mahogany and ormolu desk.

Stuart Alcott leaned far back in the chair, tossed the hair out of his eyes, and crossed his boots on the green felt blotter. He had a cut-glass Waterford tumbler cradled in his palm. "Lord, Geoff," he said. "What's happened? You look like hell."

The statement disoriented Geoffrey because he was feeling just fine, thank you kindly. Except for that strange touch of melancholy brought on by the blooming linden trees, all was right with his world. Indeed, all couldn't be better.

His brother, though, was a different story. Or rather the same old story. "You're soused," Geoffrey said, "and it's barely past noon."

Stu tilted the tumbler at him in a mock toast. He tried to smile but it came out sour. "Gin and lime juice. It keeps away the scurvy."

When Stu was nineteen their father had had him committed to the asylum up in Warren to cure his alcohol addiction. When he had walked out of those black iron gates nine months later, he hadn't come home to Bristol. He hadn't come home for seven years, not even for their father's funeral. A stay in the Warren asylum, Geoffrey thought, hadn't stopped his brother's drinking, but it seemed to have cured him of whatever real joy he had once taken in life.

Stu plucked a Havana cigar from out of the cedar humidor on the desk. Geoffrey watched his brother's hands shake as he peeled off the cigar's silk wrapper and clipped the end with the slender silver knife on his watch chain. Stu pushed himself out of the chair, lurched slightly, and bumped into an ivory inlaid chess table. A sterling silver rook rolled to the floor.

In the harsh light coming through the library's French doors, Geoffrey took note of his brother's bleary eyes, the sandy stubble on his chin. His tie hung like a noose around his neck. The collar of his sweat-stained shirt was open, and Geoffrey saw to his utter shock and disgust that its points were frayed.

Growing up, Stu had developed a love for fast yachts and faster horses, and a thirst for champagne and brandy cocktails. The world they lived in really asked very little of its rich young men, except that they exhibit good manners and dress well. But his brother wasn't even managing that anymore.

Yet, still, when he looked into Stu's world-wearied face, Geoffrey saw echoes of the charming, wild-hearted boy he once had been. The younger brother he had admired and envied, and loved.

Stu had made his wavering way over to the fireplace mantel where there was a brass vase of long spills for lighting cigarettes. He took one and then realized that the fire wasn't lit. In their Hope Street mansion, the fires were always left to go out on Easter and weren't rekindled until after Thanksgiving no matter what the weather.

Stu flung the spill into the empty grate. "Christ. Nothing ever changes around here. It's enough to drive one mad."

"There's a match safe over there," Geoffrey said, pointing to a rope-legged mahogany table that supported a brace of heavy old crystal decanters in their silver cradles. "And you may as well pour yourself more lime juice while you're at it. There's been a veritable epidemic of scurvy in Bristol this spring."

Geoffrey recaptured the now empty Morris chair, settling behind his mahogany desk with a small, satisfied sigh. He rubbed at the scuff marks his brother's boots had left on the felt blotter. He pushed the mother-of-pearl letter opener back to its customary place between the telephone and an onyx postage-stamp box.

When he looked up again Stu was smiling at him with flat eyes. His brother gave him another one of those irritating mock toasts, and this time the drink splashed over the lip of the tumbler and onto the cabbage-rose carpet.

"Hail the conquering hero," Stu drawled. "All the yacht club and chophouse banter this past week has been about your wooing and winning the glorious Emma Tremayne."

Geoffrey smiled as he moved the cut glass inkwell back to the center of the desk. He always felt a warm glow deep in his chest, followed by a little hitch of wonder, when he thought of how Emma was truly his now. *His.*

His brother's return had perhaps precipitated his proposal to Emma—he had planned to ask her this summer, the Fourth of July, to be exact. But the way Stu had looked at her that day of the hunt . . . Geoffrey gave himself a mental shake. It was ridiculous, of course, to think his brother had ever had a prayer of taking Emma from him. Of the two of them, Stu had always had the better looks and the greater charm, but Geoffrey was the one with all the money.

He looked up to find his brother staring at him now, the drink in his hand poised in midair. "What?" Geoffrey said.

Stu widened his eyes and slowly shook his head as if moved by utter wonderment. "Good God. If you could have seen your face just then, when I said her name . . . One could almost believe you love her."

Geoffrey wiped the corners of his mouth. "I . . ." He straightened his brown silk four-in-hand tie. "She . . ."

Stu threw back his head and boomed a laugh at the coffered ceiling. "My brother, Geoff. Still counting his words as carefully as he does his penny change."

"I do love her," Geoffrey said, and the words startled him coming out. "I've loved her since . . ." He spread his hands, flushed. "Forever."

A strange look came over Stu's face. Geoffrey could almost believe that whatever thought his brother had just had, it had cut deep.

"You'll never make her happy," Stu said.

"Of course I'll make her happy." He turned the humidor around so that its decorative brass eagle was again facing the door. "Why wouldn't I make her happy?"

"Because our dear little Emma has always had much too much imagination. She might actually get a glimmer, on occasion, that there's a whole other world beyond riding in a gilt and lacquered carriage with velvet cushions, eating oysters and sipping champagne, while wearing a ball gown from Maison Worth. And when that happens, she'll end up doing something that will frighten you to death, and our world will destroy her for it."

"What nonsense." The mantel clock chimed, and was joined by the standing clock in the hall. Geoffrey took out his gold hunter pocket watch and nodded, satisfied that time was safely harnessed and under control.

He slipped his watch into his vest pocket and looked back up. "My Emma could never bring me anything but joy."

"Naturally you would believe that," Stu said, "since you have no imagination whatsoever."

Geoffrey felt a flash of familiar irritation. His brother always made it seem as if being steady and reliable and responsible were character flaws.

"And you," Geoffrey said, "have always exhibited an unfortunate tendency to put your own overwrought thoughts and emotions into the hearts and minds of everyone else. Just because you feel this compulsion to rebel against 'our world,' as you call it, it doesn't follow that the rest of us are secretly harboring similar longings. And I find it rather amusing that you can do all that while getting tight from drinking booze out of a glass worth more than one of my mill workers will earn in a year."

Stu smiled suddenly and tossed back another healthy swallow of gin. "You're right, of course. The rebel's life is only romantic in the abstract, and a luxury I probably can't afford. Which brings us around, again, and rather adroitly if I do say so myself, to the subject of money and my lack of it—"

Geoffrey cut him off with a wave of his hand. "I thought I had made my position quite clear on that. I can't draw another check on your trust fund before the quarter's end. As trustee, I've certain obligations to carry out the letter if not the spirit of our father's last will—"

Stu slammed the flat of his hand down hard on the desk. "Fuck your obligations! Fuck you and him both. God, you're as bad as our dear pater ever was—tighter than a nun's pussy." He caught himself up, drawing in such a harsh breath he shuddered with it. "Don't make me beg, Geoff, for Christ's sake."

Geoffrey reached out to straighten the inkwell, which had been knocked askew again by his brother's fury. There was no need for Stu to be spewing foul words like cow dung at his head. If his brother had exhibited some of those character *flaws* of reliability and steadfastness when he was younger, maybe their old man wouldn't have tied up his inheritance tighter than a nun's . . . whatever.

He looked up to say as much, when the library door opened and suddenly Emma was there.

Standing in the doorway, she seemed but a silhouette of a girl outlined in silver light. Then she crossed the threshold and her head came up. The stiff patent brim of the yachting cap she wore lifted to reveal her face, and his heart gave a leap of surprise, as it had been doing for as long as he could remember.

She was dressed for boating, in a navy skirt trimmed with gold braid and a shirtwaist with a big sailor collar. He thought she looked adorable.

He leaped to his feet and crossed the room to meet her. Her cheeks were flushed with color, and he hoped it was only the wind, and that her innocent ears hadn't been sullied by his brother's vulgarity.

He slid his arm around her waist, drawing her over to a maroon tufted-leather sofa. His palm pressed into her side, just below her ribs, and he could feel the give of her flesh, the gentle motion of her breathing. He was allowed that, he thought. Now that they were engaged he had the right to touch her more often and more intimately. But he had to be careful, for he wanted her desperately.

"My dear," he said, his voice breaking a bit with the force of his feelings. "What a pleasant surprise."

The face she turned up to him was as translucent as a tide-rinsed seashell. "I've just been to your mill, Geoffrey. It was . . . I can't even think of what to say to you. I was in terror the whole time that the machines were going to run amok at any moment and eat the children."

He was shocked that she had gone to the mill, for it was no place for a gentlewoman of tender sensibilities. No wonder she was so trembly; the noise and smells alone must have made her feel faint. This was all the fault of that foolish woman, bringing her dead child to the hunt last month. His dear little Emma had always had such empathy for all of God's creatures, even the Irish.

He settled down beside her and brought his head close to hers. She smelled of lilac water and the sea.

He picked up the hand she had clenched into a fist in her lap, uncurling her fingers one by one. "No children are going to be *eaten* by anything. You're allowing your imagination to run away with you."

Stu made a sound that was halfway between a snort and a laugh. He had gone to lean with Byron-like negligence on the mantelpiece, but Geoffrey was determined to ignore him. Rather, his gaze had fastened onto Emma's face, onto her eyes, which had changed to the color of the sea reflecting a cloud-whipped sky. He was sure he knew her, but sometimes he thought he saw, deep inside of her, a thin white flame that was consuming her from the inside out.

She pulled her hand out of his grasp. "And afterward I had a very enlightening conversation with Mr. Stipple. He told me you pay those poor children a dollar-fifty a week. They can't live on such a paltry sum. It's ridiculous and cruel of anyone to think they can."

"It's hardly a paltry sum to them. They were born to get by on potato scraps."

She had such a fierce grip on her parasol that her wrist bone shone white above the edge of her glove. She looked around the room, wide-eyed, as if she'd suddenly found herself in the wrong place.

Her gaze came back to him, and the flame in her eyes burned brighter, hotter. "I think I despise this side of you, Geoffrey Alcott."

Stu snorted again. "Not only imagination, but insight as well. Deadly combination, Geoff. Deadly."

Geoffrey tried to take up her hand again, but she pulled it away. "Don't you think you're judging me unfairly, Emma? Those people come here from their wretched country penniless and ignorant, and I give them work. A place to learn solid Christian virtues and the benefits of honest labor."

"And what of the law?"

Geoffrey's gaze had become fascinated with the way her lower lip trembled and her bosom rose and fell with her agitated breathing. He'd lost track of both his thoughts and her words. "Law?"

She stood up and strode away from him. Then turned and came back and sat down again. "The law that forbids children under the age of twelve to work in the mills. Geoffrey, if there was a child there *over* the age of twelve, I would be surprised."

"Their parents stipulate to their ages. They don't exactly arrive here from Ireland with their certificates of birth pinned to their chests. And besides, most are probably older than they look."

"A diet of potato scraps," Stu said, "does tend to stunt one's growth a bit."

Geoffrey thought about telling his brother to shut up. Instead he reached for Emma's hand again, and this time she allowed him to have it.

Her hand trembled like a broken-winged bird in his. Her feelings were flashing over her face almost quicker than he could read them—blame, sorrow, pain. He had a sudden and somewhat frightening realization that perhaps he had never understood her as well as he'd thought he did. To him, she always seemed as if she were only waiting for something, and up until this very moment he had always assumed that something was he.

"Don't treat me as if I'm a fool," she said. "That little bobbin boy who was killed couldn't have been over six."

He covered her hand with his other one, stilling it. "It so happens that I've commissioned a report to be done on ways to improve conditions at the mills," he said, and it was the truth, although the report was to focus on areas of productivity and efficiency. Still, he wasn't averse to broadening its scope, if that would please his Emma.

He rubbed his thumb along the seam of her glove. "When it's finished, perhaps you would be so kind as to read it over and offer your suggestions. From a woman's perspective." Smiling, he reached up with his free hand to trace the delicate shell of her ear. "Gentle feminine eyes and ears often see and hear things we callous men do miss."

"If I'd eaten any breakfast," Stu said, "I would be losing it long about now."

"Are you being truthful with me, Geoffrey?" She was studying his face, and something shifted behind her eyes again, turning them grayer, flintier. "Because I've already thought about it some, about things that can be done. Something as simple, for instance, as bringing in more light, for the place is as dark and dingy as a prison with only those grimy, narrow little windows."

"Darling . . . Will you believe me when I tell you that I'm not a heartless monster, that the lives of my workers are already better by far than most? What happened to that boy was an accident—unfortunate, terrible even, but an accident."

She let a long, trembling breath go. "I want to believe you, Geoffrey." Her gaze fell to their entwined hands, her mouth softening, deepening at the corners. "I *can* be useful to you in this way, Geoffrey, after we are married."

"Of course you can," he said, giving her another tender smile. He was confident that once they were married she would be too busy being his wife to concern herself with the plight of the working Irish. "Now, will you stay and take luncheon with us?"

She came gracefully to her feet with a rustle of taffeta petticoats. "Thank you for asking, but I must start for home. I came here in my sloop and you know how Mama always frets when I do that."

He looked out through the French doors. The lime-green leaves of the lindens shuddered and flapped in the wind. "Surely it's become too blustery of a day for you to manage the boat on your own. Let me drive you back to The Birches in the landau."

But she was already walking away from him. "Now, don't you, too, be fretting over me, Geoffrey. If I sailed myself here, I can surely sail myself home."

He went with her to the door and watched her walk down the marble flagstones, between the trees, passing through sunlight and shadow, sunlight and shadow, and with sweet yellow petals drifting through the air to kiss her cheeks and hair.

Tears started in Geoffrey's eyes. He didn't think it was possible to love her more than he did in that one perfect moment of a blossom-filled spring day.

Chapter Eight

"Sure and isn't the day a grand one—so blue and brawny? It was on such a May Day as this, or so it is said, that the Irish invented dancing."

Bria McKenna picked up her skirts and tried to do a little jig. But her big pregnant belly had her so front-heavy she teetered like a spent top.

She might have fallen if her daughter Noreen hadn't caught her with a thin but sturdy arm around her thighs. "Mam!" The girl gave Bria an imploring look, her face blushing fire and her words coming out in a strangled whisper. "Mam, what are you doing? Everybody's watching."

"And so what if they are, then?" Bria said, laughing so she was breathless with it.

She stopped her silliness, though, for she remembered what it was like to be ten years old and certain the whole world had nothing better to do than await the next moment when you and yours would be playing the fool.

She smoothed down her skirts. She gathered up her fly-away curls, trying to tuck them into the knot of twine at the back of her neck, but they only sprang out again. "There now," she said. "Sober as a magistrate's wife." She laughed and patted her protruding belly. "And big enough to shade an elephant."

She put her hands on her hips and looked down into her daughters' upturned faces. Noreen's mouth was so flat and tight it looked stitched shut. Little Merry wasn't smiling either; but then Merry rarely smiled anymore. Yet, Bria saw to her delight that the girl's blue eyes, usually so big and sad, were sparkling with silent laughter.

She pushed her fingers through her younger daughter's marigold curls. "Merry's not ashamed of her poor daft mother, are you, *m'eudail*?"

Merry shook her head and hummed a soft little note that was like the coo of a mourning dove.

Noreen whirled and stalked away from them, through the cotton mill's wide brick-arched gate, her tin lunch pail banging against her leg.

Bria swallowed down a sigh. She wanted to take Noreen by her shoulders and give her a little shake and *make* her look up at the big empty blue bowl of the sky, and all of it there for the sun to shine in. She wanted her daughter to suck the joy right out of the day, like you would a soda fountain drink. For so rare could they be, days such as this, moments such as this, and so precious, and you could never know when you'd see their like again.

Sweet mercy, it wasn't so often the girls were even able to turn their little faces up to the sunlight. Awakened by the shrill blast of the mill whistle and off to work they went before dawn, and not home again until after dark. Only one Saturday a month did they get a half day off, and for once it wasn't snowing or raining or blowing up a gale.

She felt a tug on her skirt, and she looked down. Merry slipped a sweaty hand into hers, and Bria smiled through a sudden prickling of tears.

They walked out the mill gate and down Thames Street, toward home. Laughter gusted out the open doors of the waterfront taverns. The tide was out, and the smell of the clam banks was strong on the breeze.

Merry began to hum, long and lilting, the way you do when you've forgotten the words to a song. Bria could only smile and nod and say, "Aye, m'love. You've the right of it there, m'love."

Once, the child had been so full of laughter and bright chatter, they had taken to calling her Merry. But then came that terrible day, the day the resident magistrate and his constables had paid the McKennas' poor stone cottage a visit and changed all their lives forever. That day Bria had warned her daughters to keep their mouths shut so tight not a peep could come out, no matter what happened—and what happened had been terrible indeed.

And little Merry McKenna had never spoken again.

She hummed all her words now instead, and the only one who could understand a bit of it was her sister. But as to whether Noreen always got it right, who was to really say? For sometimes the child would hum a long discourse and then her sister would say the most outlandish thing, such as: *Merry spoke to the elves that live in the coal box, and we're to be leaving them a bit of soda bread for supper every night.* Though sure enough Merry's solemn little face would nod, as if that truly was what all the humming had been about.

Well then, and who was to argue differently? Bria thought. For surely the world was full of miracles and mysteries, full of wondrous things.

Full of joyful things.

Before that day . . .

Before that day, their Noreen had been a brave, saucy lass, with the eyes of her always looking you over and the tongue on her bold as you please. She knew what she knew, did Noreen McKenna, and it didn't matter a jot what anyone said or thought. She would've danced a jig with her mam and laughed about it.

Before that day . . .

The baby gave a sudden kick and Bria grunted with surprise. She pressed her palm against her belly, feeling the life shift within her, but she didn't smile. Before that day, she thought, I was someone different as well.

A throbbing pain shot up Bria's arm, and she let go of Merry's hand to rub her shoulder, then rubbed her aching back while she was about it. Day after day of twelve hours working a spinning ring frame took its toll, it did, and there was another mixed blessing on this particular day. For when she went to punch out her time card this afternoon, Mr. Stipple told her she'd been given the sack. For deserting her post, he'd said.

Sure and she'd been bound to lose the job soon enough anyway, what with her belly getting so big it looked as though she'd swallowed not one pumpkin but the whole bloomin' patch. The trouble was, they would be having one more mouth to feed before long, and three dollars less a week coming in the door.

But she had a few coins making music in her pocket at the moment, and suddenly a euphoric recklessness seized her. She wanted to spend today in the belief that the heavens would be raining pennies tomorrow.

She spotted a girl selling ears of corn from a cast-iron pot of boiling water set up on the corner. She called her daughters over and bought a couple of the steaming treats.

"Let's take them on down to the bay shore to eat," she said. "We'll make a right little picnic out of it."

Merry wrapped her grimy fist around the ear of corn and ran ahead, down through an alley, toward the water. Noreen, after a moment's hesitation, ran after. Their tattered, feed-sack shifts slapped at their calves as their bare feet niftily dodged the geese droppings that littered the way.

A harbor gull swooped and dove at Noreen, trying to steal her corn, and though Bria would have thought she'd cringe in fear, she actually laughed. A glorious froggy belly laugh that made Bria's eyes fill up with tears again.

The girls sat down on the rocks to eat. Bria stood beside them, looking down at their bent heads. Merry's hair flaming and coiling wild, so like her mam's, and that would be a curse to her surely when she grew older. Noreen's darker, a leaf brown with only a bit of Irish red and curl in it. Bria looked at them, her darling girls, and felt such a love she hurt with it.

She blinked and looked up, out at the gilded waves. The air down here had a punch to it, full of salt and privet, and the stink of rotting fish shining in the sun on the mudflats. Far out on the bay a sailboat was on a last tack toward Poppasquash Point, its wake cutting a blue line through the silver water.

Bria felt the cough first as a tickle in her chest, and she tried to fight it by tamping down her breath. But there was never any stopping it, not anymore, and she couldn't hold her breath forever.

When she opened her mouth to pull in air, the coughs tore out of her and it felt as if they were ripping and pulling her chest inside out. Coughing, coughing, coughing until it seemed a giant's fist was squeezing her ribs and twisting all her bones.

She pressed one hand to her breast, right below her racing heart, while with the other she took a small brown glass bottle out of her pocket and drank from it, and after a moment the coughing eased.

Her lungs still felt thick and wet, but her chest would be quiet now. For a time it would be quiet. The patent medicine was a wonder, surely, although its cure lasted for only an hour or two.

Suddenly Merry stood up and began to dance from foot to foot, her humming high-pitched and excited. She pointed a finger, wet with corn juice, toward Poppasquash Point and the gray-shingled mansion that shone brightly beneath the sun.

Bria looked, squinting against the mirror dazzle of the water. With the white shimmer of sky and bay, the house seemed to be floating like a silver cloud. "Why, how like a fairy's castle it is, surely," she said.

But then she saw that Noreen was staring up at her little sister with dark brown eyes big as cartwheels in her face. "What?" Bria said. "What is she saying, then?"

Noreen turned those eyes onto her mother. "She . . . she says the angel who came to the mill today lives in that big silver house on the water and . . ."

Merry hummed, and nodded her head so hard her curls shook.

"And she's going to take you away with her, out to that house," Noreen finished in a rush, surging to her feet. "Mam, don't let her! Don't let the angel take you away from us!"

"What foolishness is this?" Bria tried to laugh, but her throat closed up. *I'll not be leaving you,* she wanted to promise. *Never, never would I leave you.* But the words got tangled up with the lie that lived inside of them.

"Foolishness," she said again instead, though she could understand what had started her fey daughter off on one of her wild imaginings. An angel . . . aye, an angel the girl had seemed, something magical and extraordinary, standing high above them all up there on the catwalk with the sun streaming down through the high windows, so that the very air around her had seemed to quiver and tremble with showered light.

Bria knelt on the shingled beach so that she could wrap an arm around each of her girls. "The lady who came to the mill today—it's no angel, she is. A very grand and pretty lady, surely. But no angel. And for certain she'll not be having anything to do with the likes of us."

Merry hummed a bright, sweet dreamsong. She began to sway, her eyes fluttering closed, and Noreen spoke for her, the words dreamy as well.

"She says it's not afraid we should be, for the angel will be making all our wishes come true."

Noreen turned pleading eyes onto her mother. She's like me, Bria thought, wanting the miracle, wanting it so very desperately, and yet unable to stop herself from looking always for the tarnish on the silver lining. While Merry took after her da, with the grand and impossible dreams in her.

"Come now, me darlin's," Bria said, her arms tightening around them, pulling them close. "We should be getting ourselves home."

Yet she stayed where she was, kneeling on the cool wet sand. They felt so small and fragile in her arms, her girls, and she wanted to hold them to her like this, safe against her breast, forever.

On the way home they crossed paths with the men who worked in the onion fields. The field hands all carried hoes on their shoulders, and ropes of the prized Bristol red onions swung from their fists. Bria looked for her man among them but he wasn't there.

As they walked past the Crow's Nest Saloon, she stopped to stand on tiptoe and peer above the slatted doors, searching for the big, brawny sight of him from among the b'hoys standing hipshot at the bar. But he wasn't there either.

Their house stood on the water side of Thames Street—a

two-room clapboard shack perched on stilts. It had a tarpaper roof, and its walls were stuffed with eelgrass for warmth against the New England winters. So different this house was from the thatched-roof *shibeen* she had lived in all of her life before this.

Some days she could shut her eyes and every stone hedge and potato ridge of her home in Ireland would rise vividly in her mind. She would feel the loss of her life, of herself, as big and gaping, and forever.

So she would make herself open her eyes wide and look at her girls and her man, all of them dear as God's breath to her, and she would make herself think of this country she had come to. This America, so big and grand, so full up to bursting with life and dreams and promise. *Och*, it could break your heart with its promises, this America.

By the time Bria turned up the dirt path, she was walking so fast the girls had to trot to keep up with her. She hardly felt the tired ache in her legs anymore as she climbed the steep stairs of the front stoop and threw open the door. But the kitchen was empty, and his name and the smile she always wore just for him died on her lips.

The house smelled of the bacon and cabbage she had cooked for supper last night, and so she left the door open to the salt breeze.

While the girls washed up, Bria put on her apron and made them soda bread and bacon sandwiches. "There now," she said as she set the heaping plates on the table. "You'll really have to use your jaws to get around that."

Noreen made a face at her, for she said that very same thing every Saturday-off when she made them sandwiches. But Bria only laughed.

She bent over and kissed the top of her daughter's head, where the part shone white in the brown hair. "Why don't you go on back outside and enjoy the rest of the day, what with the sun fit to burst in the sky?" She gave the girl's shoulder a gentle squeeze. "Go on, then, love, and take your supper with you."

Noreen cast a look full of yearning out the open door, yet leftover fears held her still. Then she snatched up the sandwich with both hands and ran out into the sunshine.

Bria followed her to the door, watching and smiling. But when she looked around for Merry a moment later, she saw that the child had sat down at the table and fallen asleep before she had taken the first bite from her sandwich. Sometimes the little ones fell asleep standing up at their ring spinners, they got that tired.

Bria gathered her up and carried her into the bedroom. So weightless did she feel in her arms, light as gossamer silk. And so heavy did Bria's heart feel at the sight of her darling baby's face, so thin and tired and pale.

Bria laid her down between the feed-sack sheets, which were rough but clean. She smoothed back Merry's bright curls and kissed her forehead. Tomorrow, Bria promised herself, she would take them for a proper picnic at Town Beach. She'd buy them a jelly roll as a treat, even though it would cost a whole nickel.

Tomorrow . . . She felt the despair smash into her like a breaking wave and she shook beneath the force of it. Tomorrow—what a grand and sad word that was. So full of hope and wonder and promise. But only if you were sure of having one, sure of having a tomorrow.

Bria gave her daughter another kiss, soft as a whisper, and went back out into the kitchen. She looked at the sandwich sitting there on the chipped enamel plate and thought she ought to eat it. It was just that she had so little appetite anymore, yet still the babe grew big and heavy in her belly, while the rest of her looked like a bundle of twigs tied together with string. And with herself out of a job now and her man back to working the onion fields, they would be living on carrots and turnips and swamp apples soon enough.

But even the smell of the bacon was making her ill. She wrapped the sandwich up in a scrap of paper and put it away in the pie cage for later.

She set about baking up a fresh batch of soda bread, pouring a scuttleful of coal into the potbelly of the black iron stove. In Ireland she had cooked over an open hearth, boiling potatoes and turnips in a big pot. She'd had no wood or coal to make a fire, but plenty of peat bog for digging up lay right outside the cottage door. No smell was so loamy sweet, she remembered with a sigh, as that of burning peat.

Bria shook her head hard, trying to tear her thoughts away from home. She might as well get her heart settled on it—she was never going to see Ireland again.

As she reached for the flour tin, Bria glanced out the window and caught sight of her daughter squatting in the dirt, playing jackstones against herself. A ragged bunch of mill boys had gathered around to watch in silent admiration as she tossed up four jacks and caught them all on the back of her hand.

Bria had to smile at the sight of it. You wouldn't think their Noreen, with her brown, pointy face and prickly ways, would be such a draw for the lads like she was.

"God save us!" Bria exclaimed aloud, for one of the boys had just offered her daughter a drag on his cigarette, and sure if the naughty child hadn't just taken him up on it. "Her da will be having to beat them off with a *shillelagh* afore long."

"You are speaking, maybe, to the fairies?"

Bria whirled so fast she nearly knocked over the open flour tin. "Donagh! You scared the breath right out of me."

The man who stood in the doorway gave her such a smile it outshone the sun. Laughing, she ran up to him and stood on tiptoe to plant a smacking kiss on his cheek. She smiled to herself at what the neighbors would say: Mrs. McKenna behaving so shamelessly forward with the Saint Mary's parish priest, and never mind that the brave and beautiful lad was her very own brother.

She took him by the arm, pulling him inside. "Set yourself down. I've just put a kettle on." She took his hat and hung it on a wall hook for him, then watched, smiling, while he settled the long length of him into one of her ladderback chairs. "You're looking fine, *mo bhriathair*."

Father Donagh O'Reilly was indeed a handsome man, with his thick, dark red hair and warm brown eyes, and the wide mouth on him that always seemed but a tickle away from a smile. God's gain had been some good woman's loss, surely.

Just then the kettle began to shriek and Bria went to set it on the hob, while she prepared the tea for steeping.

"I was pleased to see you at the five o'clock Mass this morning," her brother said over the dying whistle.

She cast a smile at him from over her shoulder. "Have you eyes in the back of your head, then?"

He grinned at her, but then his mouth took on a serious set. "Maybe not in the back of my head, but I've eyes. And ears. So faithful to the Mass every day, you are. Not one day have you missed in all the months you've been here. Yet not once have I heard your voice in the confessional box. Not once have I placed the sacred host between your lips."

Bria turned her back to him, pretending to be busy with fitting the teacups so carefully into their saucers. While her belly clenched with such a misery she feared she would be sick.

"Bria, lass . . . I may be God's anointed servant on earth, but I was your big brother before that, and I understand how you might . . ." His words trailed off, and she imagined he was looking at her now with the worry and the hurt plain in his eyes. "If it's a thing you can't say to me, there's a priest up in Warren, and a kind, understanding man he is. I can drive you up there in the cart, maybe?"

She resisted the urge to wrap her arms around the swell of her belly. "I can't," she nearly shouted. "I can't, I can't. So don't ask it of me, Donagh. Anything else, but not that."

She heard him get up and a moment later she felt the heavy warmth of his hand on her shoulder. "There's no sin greater than God's capacity to forgive," he said softly.

She wanted to lean back into the comfort he was offering, but she held herself still. Never would she go kneel in that golden oak box to beg forgiveness for something she wasn't sorry for.

He turned her around, trying to look into her face. But she pulled against him, averting her head, and so he let her go.

"I heard they've given you the sack up at the mill," he said after a moment.

"Hunh." She had meant it for a laugh, but it came out strangled. "I suppose your ears had the telling of the tale before the shift whistle had even finished its blowing."

He rubbed the back of his neck and cleared his throat. "Aye, well, that's the other reason you're being plagued with my company this day. Mrs. Daly—she who does the housekeeping for the rectory—has up and decided to go live with her daughter over t' Boston-way, and leaving my poor self with no one to dust the banisters and set out my slippers come an evening." He gave her chin a playful nudge with his curled knuckles. "So I'm here to say the tasks are yours for the doing, if you'll have them. Though I'll not be able to pay you mill wages, you mind."

The sobs thrust up in Bria's chest and burst out of her throat, shocking the both of them. He wrapped his arms around her, and she pressed her face hard into the black scratchy wool of his cassock, and still the tears came, while he stroked her back and said, "There now, there now," and she clung to him as if to let go were to drown.

When at last she quieted, he set her at arm's length from

him. He spoke as if his throat hurt. "Are you all right then, lass?"

She nodded and sniffled and scrubbed her nose with the back of her hand. "What will folk think? You giving such a plum job to your very own sister."

"They'll think: Better my sister than some pretty young colleen with designs on my priestly virtue."

She choked on a laugh, and then a fit of chest-racking coughs seized her. She bent over nearly double beneath the force of them, fumbling in her pocket for her handkerchief and the patent medicine.

She drank deep of the syrupy elixir and slowly the coughing eased. She dropped the bottle back into her pocket and tried to shove the handkerchief in there along with it without her brother seeing. But he had never been a fool. He took her wrist and pulled the hankie from her stiff fingers, and he saw the stains, dark rusty ones and the bright red fresh ones.

She couldn't bear to meet his eyes, but she could hear all that he was feeling in the way he said her name, "Ah, Bria, Bria . . ."

But he said nothing more, and neither did she.

Chapter Nine

They stood unmoving, not looking at each other, yet it was as if they were bound together anyway, by a rope made of those words not spoken.

Through the open door she heard the scrapings of a fiddler's bow, although she realized that the music must have been playing for quite some time. Bria's whole body jerked, as if she could break away by physical will from the thoughts that held them fast.

"Oh, listen!" she said. "They're having a bit of an Irish crack today. Somebody's playing 'The Wind That Shook the Barley,' and likely there'll be dancing."

"Bria . . ." He reached for her again, but she slipped past his outstretched hand and out into the street, where it seemed the whole of the ragtag waterfront neighborhood had begun to gather.

The Irish mill workers were there, of course, for it was a jig from the *ould* country that the fiddler played. But the *bravas* came as well, Portuguese from Cape Verde with their brass-colored skin and the stink of the rubber factory where they worked clinging to their clothes and hair. Even the swamp Yankees were being drawn out of doors by the lilting music—those Bristol natives who dug for clams and toiled in the onion fields and were poorer, maybe, even than the Irish.

The fiddler's fingers flew fast and nimble over the strings, setting everyone's feet to tapping. And when Colin the barber stepped out of his shop wearing his saffron kilt and with his uilleann pipes awailing bright and brawny, first one couple and then another and another linked arms and formed a square, heels and toes kicking high and fast.

Bria felt the touch of a man's lips on her ear. She was smiling even before the breath of his words fanned her cheek. "I'll be having both a dance and a kiss from you, *mo chridh*, before this day is through."

She was smiling still as she turned around and let her gaze move slowly up the long and splendid length of the man that was Seamus McKenna.

"What you'll be getting from me is a great clout on the ear, you cocky oaf," she said.

He threw back his head and laughed, and the sound of it was as elemental to Bria McKenna as the blood that beat through her veins.

Noreen appeared at her father's side. She grasped his big hand with both of hers. "Don't you dance with her, Da. She's too fat now and everyone will laugh."

Bria put her hands on her hips, pretending to be insulted. "Oh, so it's too fat, am I? Well then, it's you, my girl, who'd best be taking a turn with the poor man. For can't you see his feet are fairly itching to let fly?"

Shay didn't give the child a chance to protest. He swung her up into his arms and out among the whirling dancers. Soon their daughter's face was flushed and her mouth was smiling, and Bria's own eyes as she watched them blurred with love.

Donagh watched from beside her, making shoe music with his tapping toe and stirring up a cloud of dust. "He's still a handy man with his heels, is your Seamus. Quick enough to dance his way out of any trouble you might mention."

She gave her brother a sharp look. "And what sort of trouble ought you to be mentioning, Father O'Reilly?"

But just then the pipes and fiddle ended the jig with a wail and a flourish, and the dancers fell out, breathless and laughing. Shay's gaze met hers, and his smile, like the rest of him, was big and brash. He kept hold of Noreen's hand and slid his other arm around Bria's waist, and together they all began to walk back to the house.

Donagh fell into step beside them. "Would you just look at the man? Grinning like the miser squatting on his pot of gold."

"It's better than gold, I have," Shay said. "With two of the prettiest lasses in all of Rhode Island and her Providence Plantations, one on each arm."

Bria leaned in to him, rubbing her head against his shoulder, bumping hips. "What you have is a honey tongue in your head, Mr. McKenna."

Noreen giggled and looked up at her father with adoring eyes. But as they turned down the path to the front stoop, she slipped away to join some boys who were playing a game of stickball with a lopsided India rubber ball and a sawed-off broomstick.

The lads again, Bria thought with an inward sigh. Trouble was acoming from that quarter, surely.

As soon as they crossed the shack's threshold, Shay dug into the pocket of his worn corduroy britches and gave over to his wife the whole of his weekly wages, as he did every Saturday. But now that he was back to working in the onion fields, he was getting only a quarter a day. The coins looked few and small in her hand—scarce enough to buy food and coal and pay the rent.

She dropped them in her own apron pocket and looked up

at him, smiling, but he wasn't fooled. A red stain spread over his cheekbones, and he turned away from her.

Donagh brought his hands together in a loud clap, rubbing his palms. "Faith, I could use a bit of something wet. It's thirsty work, Seamus, watching you dance."

Shay went to the wall cupboard where the whiskey jug was kept. He yanked open the door so hard it banged.

"Hush now, the pair of you," Bria said. "Our Merry's tucked up in the bed, sleeping. The poor wee lass was so wore out, she couldn't keep her eyes open long enough to eat her supper . . ."

Bria's words fell into a heavy silence. Slowly, Shay's head came up and his gaze, bright and hard, locked with hers. But the anger, she knew, was all for himself. Other men, other women's husbands, sent their children off to the cotton mill and the rubber factory without a thought, but it chafed at her man fiercely. Shay's was a heart that felt things hard and deeply.

And later tonight she'd have to add to his burden and his worries by telling him she'd been given the sack herself, and though she'd be housekeeper now to the rectory, it would mean less money coming in.

As Bria turned away from him, her gaze fell on the table where there had suddenly appeared a string bag bursting at the seams with apples. With their shiny green skin, they looked made of wax they were so perfect.

"Oh, Shay," she exclaimed, her own voice too loud and bright now. "You've brought home some greening apples. How ever did you come by them?"

He didn't answer her at first, busying himself with pouring whiskey into a pair of tin cups. Then he lifted his head and met her eyes again, and his face softened. "I was walking by Mrs. Maguire's house, minding my own affairs, when out the door she came running, saying she bought too many and wouldn't I kindly take them off her hands, and she wouldn't take no thank you for an answer."

"Wouldn't she, then—the old man-hungry behemoth? Sure and if every spinster and widow in the county hasn't already got your fine self all measured out for a new wedding suit—"

Bria cut herself off again as soon as her ears caught up with her tongue, but it wasn't quick enough. She couldn't bear to look at Shay now, nor at her brother. The kitchen became so quiet she could hear the tick of the tin clock and the burning coals settling in the stove. And the merry fiddling and wail of the pipes coming from the street. They'd be out there dancing all night now, likely as not, she thought.

She felt a terrible urge to cough again but she held it down, although her chest burned fiercely with the effort it took. But she couldn't go hacking and spitting up blood now, after what she'd just said.

She gathered up the bag of apples, a bowl, and a paring knife and settled down in her straw-bottom rocking chair next to the stove. She would make a pie for tomorrow's picnic out of the greening apples. That was an American thing—an apple pie.

Shay and her brother sat at the table, elbows resting on the faded brown oilcloth, hands cradled around their cups of whiskey. She could feel their eyes on her, feel their aching thoughts, and the pain of it was worse by far than the pain in her chest.

Shay's cat, Gorgeous, came waddling through the open door and launched itself to land with a heavy plop on his lap. He claimed the beast had followed him home—huh, more likely it had been *carried* home. Starved and scrawny it had been then, with motley, dung-colored fur. And although it had fattened up a whole lot since fate had sent mush-hearted Shay McKenna to its rescue, it was still the ugliest cat God had ever created.

When she was sure he was no longer looking at her, she glanced up and let her gaze rest on him, her man. He sat with his spine dug deep into the chair, his legs stretched out long, his fingers restless on the cat's fur. In this mood he looked every bit the wild Irishman, brooding and dark. The love she bore for him lay both soft and heavy on her heart.

He stirred finally, raising his cup to her brother in an old Gaelic toast. "For the love of Ireland and the hate of England, God damn her."

Donagh touched his cup to Shay's. "Love of Ireland," he said, leaving off the curse in deference to the priest's collar he wore around his neck.

They fell into talking politics, as they usually did. Bria listened with half an ear as she peeled and sliced the apples. The old, familiar words about Ireland's troubles. They had drawn in a burning hatred of British rule with their mother's milk, and they nurtured it now with Irish whiskey, the *poitín* distilled illegally in the Crow's Nest cellars. To Bria, the whiskey smelled like the peat she'd burned in the hearth of her cottage back home.

Shay was talking about the Clan-na-Gael now. So that's where he was this afternoon, then, she thought. At another meeting of the clan, damning the English and singing rebel songs. Planning ways to raise money for the grand and glorious "rising," and never mind the mothers' sons who would die because of it, never mind the wives left behind to keen over their men's graves.

She rubbed her tired feet over the hooked-rag rug beneath the chair and let her thoughts wander to the picnic tomorrow. It would be fine to feel the sun hot in her hair and the sea spray in her face. She would spread a blanket out on the sand, and she would sit with Shay's head in her lap and watch the girls play tag with the waves, and her heart would swell near to bursting with joy for being with them. She would make it a savoring day, a day to tuck away in their hearts.

But for now she would sit listening to her men talk and watching the shiny green apple skin curl out from beneath her paring knife.

She caught the tail end of Shay saying, ". . . the best place for it would be the bay side of Poppasquash Point."

"Aye, that's as may be," Donagh said. "But trespassing on rich folk's land is no less a crime here than it was in Ireland, me boyo."

"And that puts me in mind of a thing that happened this morning," Bria said, then wished she hadn't. She felt strangely reluctant of a sudden to speak of the girl—the angel, Merry had called her, who would make all their wishes come true. She had stood up there on the catwalk, had that girl, looking as if she possessed the whole world, and Bria had felt both drawn to her and stricken to helpless stone beneath her eyes.

So she said instead, "That family what lives out on the point, the Tremaynes. They were telling tales about them at the mill."

"What tales would that be?" Donagh said. Shay was gently rubbing his cat's ears, but there was a hardness to his mouth and a tightness around his eyes.

"They call them the wild and wicked Tremaynes," Bria said. "The first of the lot came here from Cornwall over two hundred years ago. *Fled* Cornwall, so he did, and with a price for murder on his head. Then he went and made himself rich off the dark trades—slaving and piracy. And that's when the curse is supposed to've took hold."

"Didn't I know there'd be a curse in the story?" Donagh said. "There's always a curse."

"Aye, well the curse has surely hit them hard these last years. First the younger daughter was crippled in a sleighing accident. And then the boy, feeling the blame for it, took his boat out in the middle of a storm and was drowned. Or drowned himself, there's some as do say."

She craned her head around for a look through the bedroom door to be sure Merry was still sleeping. She could hear the grass growing, that child.

"Then shortly thereafter that tragedy," Bria went on, lowering her voice to a near whisper, "the father left. Sailed off on his yacht, he did, and there hasn't been a whisker of him seen since. But he wasn't lost at sea, not like the young Mr. Tremayne was. They say he's living high on his plantation house in Cuba with all his doxies."

Shay's head did come up at that, and Donagh sent a grin his way. "He's got more than the one doxy, do you say? Faith, what a fine thing it is to be a wealthy man."

"And to think," Shay said, heaving a mock sigh as he splashed more whiskey into Donagh's cup, "of your poor and chaste self never destined to know it."

He looked over at Bria and now deep laughter lit up his eyes. "It's a frightful lot of nattering you lasses must have been doing this day while at your spinning."

"Nattering, is it? And what do you call what you lads've been doing this night—grand philosophical discussions, I'll be supposing."

She had gotten up from her chair with the bowl of sliced apples, to sugar them, when she noticed a strange silence now seemed to be coming from the table where the men were. And when she turned around, she caught odd looks on their faces, as well, guilty looks. Or rather, her brother looked guilty. When Shay turned all stony-mouthed, as he was now, that was when she knew she should start to worry.

"What mischief are the pair of you up to?" she said.

Shay's answer was light and teasing, but there was an edge to his smile. "Sure and if I tell you, m'love, you'll give me a great clout on my ear."

Gorgeous chose that moment to break into a loud, raucous

purr as he kneaded Shay's thigh with his huge, soft paws. Shay lifted his hand to stroke the cat's head, and that was when Bria noticed for the first time the bloody scrapes and purpling bruises on his knuckles.

She set the bowl of apples carefully down on the slopstone and went to him. It wasn't in Shay's nature to get involved in a saloon brawl. But she knew of only one other thing that could do such damage to a man's fists—a punching bag filled with thirty pounds of sand.

She picked up his hand and he let her have it, and she thought she should be feeling angry or sad or disappointed, but all she had was this sick churning in the pit of her stomach, as if she'd eaten too much green fruit.

She pressed her lips to her man's bruised and bleeding flesh. Then threw his hand back down into his lap so hard it hit Gorgeous, and the cat jumped off with a squawk.

"You swore to me never again," she said. "On the grave of your mother, you swore."

He raised his head and met her eyes squarely, but he said nothing. All of their lives she had known him, and always he'd had a hardness buried in him, a place in him she could never reach and where he made his choices alone.

She jerked around to point a stiff finger at her brother. "And you, you've a part in this . . . this . . . whatever it is. Don't tell me you haven't, what with that devil of a look you're wearing all over the face of you—"

Donagh reached up and snagged her wrist. "Bria, for mercy's sake. Will you take hold of your temper and open your ears for a wee bit of a listen?"

She pulled free of him with such force she took a stumbling step backward. She crossed her arms tightly beneath her breasts. She couldn't look at Shay anymore. She wouldn't look at him.

"Tell me a tale then, Donagh, my brother."

He unbuttoned the front of his cassock and reached inside

to pull out a news sheet printed on pink-tinted paper. "You'll have heard of this scandal rag, the *Police Gazette*?"

Bria nodded stiffly. She'd heard of it, and seen it, and although she couldn't read, she knew the likes of it. The one her brother, the priest, now held in his hand sported a picture of a buxom showgirl wearing nothing but spangled tights and a cheesy smile.

"Aye, well . . ." Donagh said, flushing a little when he realized what she was looking at. He folded the paper so that the scandalous showgirl was tucked out of sight. "The publisher, a boyo by the name of Richard Fox—he's spent a good part of the last ten years looking for a challenger to beat John L. Sullivan, the great American fisticuffs champion. He's even put up a prize for the man who does so. A belt made all over of gold and silver and diamonds."

"Hunh. And why would a man want such a grand thing for holding up a pair of old worn-out corduroy britches?"

Donagh's gaze shifted from her to Shay, and a look passed between them charged with something she didn't understand. She thought she hated men sometimes, especially these two whom she loved most of all.

"This Mr. Fox," Donagh went on, "he already has a fellow he believes can win his prize—some blue-blooded Yankee, who attends Harvard University and wears trousers made of fine worsted and more suitable, surely, for a belt of diamonds. But before Sullivan will agree to fight him, the Yankee first needs to prove he's a serious contender by coming up to scratch against a worthy opponent . . ."

His voice trailed off, and again his gaze shifted over to Shay. But Bria wouldn't look at the man herself; maybe she'd never look at him again.

She stared hard at her brother, her eyes burning. "Would you pity the man, then—coming to the end of all his fine words and just when his tale was getting lively."

"Ah, Bria . . ." Donagh rubbed his hands over his face,

sighing. "Mr. Fox came to hear of how himself there"—he waved his hand at Shay—"was once the bare-knuckle champion of Ireland, and so a thought came into his head that Seamus and his Yankee boy could make a good match of it. They would be holding it here, during Bristol's famous Fourth of July celebration, and there you have it . . . Most of it."

Donagh snatched up the jug, emptied the whiskey into his cup, and downed nearly all of it in one swallow. His chin sank into his chest, as he pretended to give the bottom of his cup a deep study, and Bria realized that's all she would get from her brother.

Shay, of course, had given her nothing.

Slowly she turned to face him. He didn't flinch or look shamed before her, and whatever his thoughts were she couldn't see them on his face.

She wrapped her arms tighter around herself, as if she had to physically hold herself together. "Do you have a small dab of a word you want to say to me yourself, Seamus McKenna? Or did the fairies come and carry off your tongue when I wasn't looking?"

He reached up with both his hands to take her arms, unfolding them, pulling her to him, and she hated him for touching her because, God help her, she loved him so much.

He let go of her arms and cupped her hips in his big hands. He looked up at her, and his eyes burned fever bright. It had always hurt her to know that the fire in him had nothing to do with her.

"Maybe this word will please you, wife: *dollars.* One hundred of them to me, and the clan gets another one hundred for serving as my sponsor. And all I have to do for it is spar enough with this Yankee challenger to put on a good show and go down to the canvas sometime in the third or fourth round."

Somehow she was pressed against his thighs now, and her

hands were in his hair. His hair sprang soft and warm against her fingers, as if it had captured all of the shine from the day's sun.

"It's an outlaw sport," she said, hating the quaver she heard in her voice. The surrender. "You could be put into prison for it."

"They'll be calling it an exhibition of the science of bare-knuckle boxing," Donagh said from behind her. "Which are lawful things."

Her fingers tightened in Shay's hair, and she pushed herself away from him. "So they'll pay you to lose to this Yankee contender. And what honor will you have to call your own at the end of it?"

He'd always been able to move quickly, big as he was. He was up and standing at the open door, and all she'd felt was the breath of the air he stirred as he'd passed her. He leaned against the jamb, his hands stuffed deep in the pockets of his britches, his eyes on the world beyond. The fiddle and pipes were wailing fast and furious now.

She realized that shadows of dusk were lying long across the yard. The light beyond the door was the color of golden syrup, but inside their small house it was already growing dark. She thought she ought to light a lantern and yet she stood unmoving. His voice came to her, a rough whisper, like sand scraping over stone.

"There's a thing or two worse a man can suffer than the loss of his honor. Do I need to name them for you, Bria darlin'? Do I need to tell you of digging for potatoes in a stubble field and having them come up black and rotten, and your loved ones with the mouths on them stained green from the grass they're eating off the side of the road? Do I need to tell you of living in a stone hovel with a roof cut from the sod of a land that can never be yours, for all that it's been fed for centuries with the blood and bones of those who bore your name before you?"

He pushed off the wall and turned to her, lost still in the shadows just inside the door. But she didn't need to see his face, for she had known him all her life. Known the need in his eyes when he took her in bed, known the touch of his lips, urgent and hot on her bare skin. She knew his heart, so brave and defiant, so filled with that desperate dream of finding the great, good place and making it his own.

"Do I need to tell you," he said, "of the woman who kneels, keening, in dirt made into mud with the blood spilling from her man's guts? . . . Or the wife who is forced to watch her husband choke out his life at the end of a magistrate's rope?"

She pressed her fist hard to her mouth as if she would scream, though she made no sound. *Don't.*

"Do I need to tell you, Bria darlin'?"

She covered her ears with her hands and squeezed her eyes shut. *Don't. Don't. Don't.*

She didn't know he had come to her until she felt his fingers grasp her wrists to pull down her hands, and then he was spanning her neck with his fingers, his thumbs caressing her cheeks as if he would kiss her. He had never been anything but gentle to her with those hands.

He tilted her head back, forcing her to meet his eyes. "What should a man care for honor," he said, "when it can be sold to put food in the bellies of his wife and children and guns in the hands of his Irish brothers—"

She wrenched away from him, shouting, "Ah, *Dhia*, Ireland! It's always for Ireland!" Her voice quieted, thick now with tears held back. "There was never anything for us in Ireland. There's nothing there."

Shay swung his arm in a wide arc. "And is this so grand a place then? You think because the rich man gets ice in the summer and the poor man gets it in the winter, things are breaking even for us both, and we're all equal here in your America and in the sight of your God?"

Bria felt the anger drain from her and a dreadful tiredness take its place. She had never been able either to argue or woo him away from any of his grand and glorious causes. She'd always known he loved her, just as she knew he would never love her enough.

Her brother, the priest, scraped back his chair and got slowly to his feet. He went up to Shay, and his hand fell heavily on the other man's shoulder. "He's your God as well, Seamus."

Shay stared back at him, giving up nothing, this time not even a breath.

When Shay was born the only one of five sons to come out of the womb breathing, his mother had dedicated his life to God. Of the two friends, her brother had been the wild one in those early years, and in the later years, too—tippling and wenching and up to all manner of mischief. Even as a boy, Shay had been serious and intense, a fierce fanatic in his faith. He had been studying Latin at the knee of the village priest when the other lads in the *clachan* couldn't even write their own names.

But then life had happened to Seamus McKenna. *She* had happened to him one storm-tossed day on a rocky beach. The constables with their guns and hanging rope had happened.

And God, as if not to be denied, had sent His calling to Donagh instead. Or it was as if, Bria had often thought, her brother hadn't been able to compete against Shay for God's attention. Donagh hadn't been able to see what he was meant to do until Shay had gotten out of his way.

Donagh sighed now and gave the other man's shoulder a rough shake before letting him go. He went to the wall hook for his black priest's hat. He paused with it in his hands, shifting it around and around by the brim, then he turned to face her. The color was high in his face, his mouth set in a rueful slant. He couldn't quite meet her eyes.

Bria's voice shook with feelings she couldn't have described even to herself. "Was it not a miracle, Father—how this newspaper man came to hear of our Seamus once being the Irish champion? Or was it you who maybe put a bit of a word in his ear? Did you say to him how Shay McKenna wouldn't break a promise for himself, nor even for his wife and his wee little ones. But for Ireland and the clan . . . *och*, for Ireland the man would sell his very soul."

"Bria, don't . . ." Donagh pushed out a ragged sigh, shaking his head and studying the hat in his hands. "It's thinking, I am, that I should be getting on back to the rectory before Mrs. Daly loses her dear temper and serves me my slippers for supper."

He put on his hat and came up to her. He leaned over and kissed her on the forehead, then drew her against him and held her tightly for a moment. "*Dia is maire dhuit,*" he said.

She wrapped her arms around him and pressed her face into his chest. The wool of his cassock was rough beneath her cheek and smelled just a bit of incense and whiskey. *God and Mary be with you, too, Donagh.*

She went with her brother to the door, where he paused to bless himself at their little font of holy water. In the street, the frolic had indeed turned into a true bit of Irish crack as jugs of *poitín* were being passed from hand to hand. She watched Donagh make his way through the crowd, stopping to administer admonishments and blessings with equal measure. But she didn't think tomorrow's sermon would be on the evils of the devil's brew, for he'd tippled a bit of it himself this night.

She didn't hear Shay come up behind her, but she could feel him. If God had struck her blind she would have been able to find him still in a world of millions.

He wrapped his arms around her, fitting them under her breasts so that they rested on her swollen belly. Her breasts had grown large and heavy for the coming babe, and they ached sweetly.

"I'm asking you not to hold me to my promise," he said.

She said nothing, but she didn't see how she could deny him. A promise made to her and broken was nothing to the wrong she'd done him, the vow broken, the sin committed . . .

The sins.

She looked down at the arms that held her. He had his shirtsleeves rolled up to the elbows. His skin was brown, the dark hair bleached golden by the sun. The veins flowed in ridges over the hard muscle and sinew.

She lifted one of his hands, matching it to her own small one, letting his hand swallow hers up. She had always marveled at how his hands could be at once so tender and yet so brutal.

His fighter's hands.

"Have you forgotten," she said, "the terrible sin you made with these hands? The troubles they've brought upon us?"

"No," he said, and then nothing more.

"Why not go after it all, then? Why not fight for that diamond belt Donagh spoke of and keep your honor while you're about it?"

"Because I wouldn't have a prayer of beating the great John L. Neither does the Yankee fellow, but that's his lookout."

They fell into a silence that was neither easy nor hard, only familiar. His lips touched her in a familiar place, in the hollow of her flesh where her jaw bone met her ear.

"Why am I letting you kiss my neck," she said, and the words came out high and breathless, "when I ought to be giving you a desperate scold?"

His laugh blew hot against her skin. "God save us. And the tongue on you getting rusty from want of exercise." His arms tightened around her, pulling her closer against him. "Come here, *mo bhean.*"

She leaned back in to him, getting closer still, nestling her bottom into the cradle of his hips, rubbing against him.

She felt his lips move up gently into her hair.

Chapter Ten

That night she dreamed she had been sewn alive into her shroud, and the rough cotton filled her mouth and nose, smelling foully of death, tasting of despair.

She thrashed awake, choking, drowning in the wet swamp that lived swollen and thick and heavy inside her chest.

She lay back, gasping for air, sweating and shivering both at once. Slowly, her breathing eased, until all she could hear was the wind panting against the windowpanes.

She pushed herself up on her elbow and looked down on Shay's face. Moonlight glinted silver off the dried tears on his cheek. He must have been watching her again while she slept, watching over her while he still could. And grieving.

She leaned over and kissed the hollow in his throat, smelling his warmth, tasting the salt of his skin.

She eased out of bed, taking care not to wake him. In one corner of their tiny bedroom she had made a place to pray and say her beads. Donagh had given her a holy card of the Virgin Mary, stamped in gold and etched with a frame of floral wreaths. She'd hung it on the wall, and beneath it she'd set an old rickety tea table that she'd salvaged from the junk heap and covered with a cloth she'd embroidered herself.

When she could find them, she put wildflowers on the table. And burned a blessed candle when she could afford one.

There Bria would kneel and look up into the blessed Mother's face, into those knowing eyes, forgiving eyes, and the words would be sweet and desperate on her lips. *Holy Mary, Mother of God, pray for us sinners now and at the hour of our death . . .*

Mary, mother of Jesus, wife to Joseph, would understand the lengths a woman would go to, the sins she would commit, for those she loved.

Bria gathered up her rosary from off the table and knelt. She drew breath to begin the Apostle's Creed and coughed, hard, her chest bucking with the force of it. A deep, tearing sound, dreadful even to her own ears.

She smothered her mouth with her hands, her chest heaving, the blood pounding hot and fast in her ears, and then finally, after forever, the coughing quieted.

She lumbered to her feet, her pregnancy making her feel clumsy and heavy. She went into the kitchen to look at her girls, where they slept on a pallet spread out on the hooked-rag rug next to the stove. She knelt beside them and folded her hands together as if in prayer, though she said no words, either to God or to herself. She touched her daughters' faces only with her eyes. To feel their warm, living flesh would hurt too much.

She didn't know how long she stayed there, but when the need to cough began to burn again in her chest, she left the house so that she wouldn't wake them. The spring nights were cool, and she brought her old pumpkin-colored coat with her. She put it on, but she didn't button it; she couldn't anymore, she was getting that big.

She went around back and down to the shingled beach. She sat among the rocks. One minute it was silent and still; in the next, a rush of wind came up off the water, smelling of salt and seaweed.

She coughed and spit up bloody threads into her handkerchief. She drank more of the patent medicine, her false cure. False miracle.

Pray for us sinners . . .

Nights, when she couldn't sleep, she prayed and said her rosary. Some nights, like this, she remembered. When you died, did your memories seep away along with your life? She couldn't bear the thought. It seemed the whole of herself, of the woman who was Bria McKenna, was made of memories, and most of her memories, both cruel and sweet, were of Shay.

She had known him all her life, but she hadn't understood how she loved him until that summer's day of the crossroads dance. It wasn't the first time for her, going to the crossroads of a summer's Sunday afternoon. There'd been pipes and a fiddle there, much like today all the way over here in America. She and her girlfriends had danced mostly with each other then, though. The priest laid such a penance on them if they so much as smiled at a boy.

It was hard to keep yourself still even when you weren't dancing. Bria stood at the side of the road, her whole body swaying in tune with the music, when suddenly he was there, Seamus McKenna, planted before her and staring at her with such a fierceness in his eyes that she wanted to run away. Shay McKenna—her brother's friend more than hers, a boy who'd always seemed as if he didn't belong anywhere near their world of stone huts and rain-soaked potato fields.

Yet there he stood, so close to her it wouldn't have taken anything at all for her to lay her head on his chest and wrap her arms around his waist—a thought that frightened and intrigued and thrilled her.

He seemed to grow taller with every breath he took, all broad shoulders and long, ropy muscles even then. And too pretty for a boy, surely, with his full mouth and the hair on him the shiny dark color of wet slate.

He flustered her, too, the way he was staring, and she tried to hide it behind a tart tongue. "What are you doing here, Seamus McKenna?" she said, as she put her hands on her hips and gave him a look-over. "Haven't you prayers that need saying and holy books that need reading? Saintly deeds that need performing?"

His mouth softened, almost smiling. "Sure and I do, but maybe I wanted to indulge myself in a bit of wasteful wickedness by dancing with you."

"Hunh. As if I would." She turned and tried to flounce off, swiveling her hips the way she'd seen the older girls do.

He laid his hand on her arm with just enough force to stop her and no more, and he said, "I'll be having both a dance and a kiss from you, *mo chridh*, before this day is through."

She'd nearly given him everything he'd asked for, and more, right there at the crossroads—such was the way his words had gone like an arrow straight from his mouth and into her heart. For one of the first things you noticed about Shay McKenna, after you were struck by the grand size of him, was his voice. Even when his words were brash and cocky things, telling a girl what he would have from her, he sounded like an archangel singing.

He hadn't taken a kiss that day, but he'd had his dance. He'd simply come up to her and taken her hand and led her into the set that was forming, and she could have pulled away from him, walked away from him at any time, but she hadn't. She had sensed he could be pushed only so far, that with him she would only get so many dances, and so many chances.

She remembered that he spoke not another word and neither did she. But she looked at him, at the way the strong sinews in his throat stood out like ropes when he turned his head, and how his lower lip seemed to soften and grow fuller when he was on the verge of a smile. At the way his eyes squinted at the corners, as if he were used to looking beyond, to a place others couldn't see.

And she thought: I want him.

No, that wasn't quite the way it was. She hadn't *known* she wanted him. She had only felt the wanting, as a tightness in her chest, a breathlessness. A panic that was like a scream in her mind that if she couldn't be with him now, this very minute, and for every minute for forever after, she would die.

Shay's da had never been a steady worker, for he'd taken to the drink early in life. He spent his hours in the pubs, his favorite being the Three Hens, where he exercised his elbow by lifting glasses of whiskey and ale and his tongue by plotting rebellion. Shay and his mother were left to work the family's few scraggly potato ridges and the landlord's barley. When he could, Shay would take the curragh out to fish for cod along the rocky coast.

Bria was at the beach late the next afternoon, when he brought the curragh back to shore. It was a rare, grand day—the sky a clear, duck's-egg blue and a warm, steady wind to fill the sail.

She waded out into the surf to catch the mooring line he threw to her. She helped him tie the boat to the buoy and roll up the lug, and only when that was done did he look at her.

"What are you doing here?" he said.

She looked up at him, narrowing her eyes against the glare of sun on water. Nearly shivering at the rare beauty of him—his face, his body, his voice. He stood with his bare feet splayed wide on the deck, the sea breeze lifting his hair. The curragh's leather hull creaked in the tidewash. Overhead, a gull cawed, as if jeering at her.

"Waiting for you," she said.

She helped spread his seine nets out on the sand to dry and lay his catch on the flakes to cure in the sun. Once, she found herself standing so close to him that the wind sent a hank of her hair slapping across his mouth. He smelled faintly of the cod, but mostly of the sea. Sometimes she could remember every word they had said to each other that day and all the days to follow. Other times she could only remember how she had felt. That the air around them was about to catch fire from a glance, a touch, a sigh.

"Why do you want to be a priest?" she'd asked him.

He turned to look at her, and there was something so fiercely brave about him, standing in his bare feet and rags among a net full of fish, but with ink stains on his fingers and calluses on his knees that would do a scullery maid proud from so many hours of praying on a stone church floor.

"I want to *do* something with my life," he said. "To do . . ." He shrugged, flushing a little. "To do good."

She remembered that a lot, those words he'd said that day, in his angel's voice, with that mouth she had wanted so desperately to kiss. *To do good.*

"I think you'll be a fine priest," she said. She made herself smile, and stopped herself from running her finger along his lower lip . . . there, where it was the fullest. "A grand one."

She helped him with his fish and nets for many afternoons before he finally kissed her. And then it was only a soft brush of his lips against her cheekbone, as if he were whispering a secret. She remembered looking up afterward, into a sky milky with high clouds, and feeling watched.

Sometimes, before they parted, they would walk the beach together, climbing the rocks, exploring. One evening, when the setting sun was painting fiery splashes across the sky and the sea crinkled silver, they found a cave.

There, within the soft, hollow darkness, his kisses grew deeper, longer, bolder. One day his mouth left hers and moved lower, and he was kissing and licking her throat. Another day he pulled open her shawl and unlaced the neck of her dress, and brushed his lips across the hollow between her collarbones. And then somehow more laces were undone, and his lips and tongue were on the slopes of her breasts and then between them. She remembered hearing the sea pound on the rocks below them, and her fingers tangling in his sun-warmed hair, holding on to him, holding on.

"Bria," he said in his beautiful angel's voice, just her name and nothing more. It was one of the many discoveries she made that summer—how a boy, a man, revealed most what he was feeling in the way he said your name.

She remembered, too, how she had come to discover herself that summer, how she had learned all the soft and sweet and tender places of her body. And the dark, hungry, grasping places in her heart.

Because there had come that inevitable day when he had tried to turn away from her, and she hadn't the courage or the goodness to let him go. When he had rolled off her and onto his back, flinging his arm across his eyes, his chest heaving, and said, "*Dhia*," the word ripping out of him more curse than prayer. "We mustn't go no further. God save me . . . I am going to be a priest."

The cave smelled of both the sea and the warm, loamy earth. She'd always felt safe in the cave. Out of sight of heaven, where she could crawl inside of him and curl around his heart.

She lay in the dark with her body on fire, yearning and hungry, so hungry. Listening to his breathing, and to the water dancing and bubbling around the rocks below. She lay with her skirts rucked up around her waist, surrounded by the smell of the sea and the earth and of him.

She didn't know she was crying until she covered him, her bared breasts on his naked chest, and felt the tears splash onto the backs of her hands as she cupped his cheeks and pressed her mouth hard to his.

"Don't, Bria," he said into her open mouth, his breath hot, harsh. "Don't, don't . . ."

But she did, deliberately and wantonly. Although she still didn't own him at the end of it, not then. Not until the night of the storm did she truly own him.

But before the storm the land agent came, and he brought the constables with him. He came because the McKenna barley, meant for their English landlord, had gone into distilling illegal *poitín* instead.

Mrs. McKenna knelt in the barren yard and watched them cart away all she owned, which was precious little: a stool, straw ticking, an old iron stew pot. The constables had just put a torch to the roof when Mr. McKenna came running, on fire himself from an afternoon at the Three Hens. He tried to attack the land agent with a *shillelagh* and got shot in the belly before he'd taken two steps with the club in his hands. His blood spilled in a thick red pool and was soaked up by his wife's skirts, where she knelt in the dirt.

In the fields above the sea cliffs was a pagan place made of ancient stones with carved faces. All staring eyes and round, open mouths—the faces had always looked to Bria as if their souls had been stolen. Such was the way Shay looked to her as the two shrouded bodies were lowered into graves scratched out of bare Irish rock. There had been no wood to make coffins with, and no money to buy them. And there had been two graves to dig, for the night before, his mother had walked into the sea, and that morning the sea had given her back again.

And if Bria let herself look now, she could see the emptiness still, all these years later, living deep in his eyes, where once his faith had been.

He had gone out in his curragh, after the burial, even though the sky and seas were black and heaving. She waited on their beach for him while the gale shrieked around her and the clouds collapsed above her head. So afraid she would lose him, she was near blind with it.

He sailed home to her on a white froth of tumbling waves.

It seemed he was just suddenly there, bearing her down onto the sea-ravaged sand. The surf roared and slammed into them, pulling at her clothes . . . his hands were pulling at her clothes. His face loomed above hers, his eyes as broken and wild as the waves that crashed over them.

He shuddered, and a harsh sound tore from his throat. "Hold me, Bria," he said. He lowered himself over her, and his mouth was rough on hers, frantic and hot. The sea breathed around them, raucous and gasping. "Hold me. Please, just hold me."

Her hands and mouth moved over him, seeking the shape and taste of him. She wrapped her arms around his back, her nails gripping his wet fisherman's coat, holding him tightly. But she knew what he was really asking for.

"Hush, now, hush," she remembered herself saying, and the rain poured over her face and into her parted, panting mouth. "I'm holding you, m'love. I'll hold you forever . . ."

". . . Forever."

She hadn't realized she'd spoken aloud until the word echoed back at her from off the Bristol harbor water, still and black and empty in the night.

She felt suffocated with yearning for him, her man, even though in a moment she would get up and go in to him. She would curve her body around his and lay her head on his chest so she could fall back asleep listening to his heartbeat. Just as she had done that night of the storm eleven years ago, that night when she had given him her maidenhead and taken his innocence.

It was strange, she thought, how the memories could pile heavy on your heart like stones and yet be so warm and familiar and comforting anyway. She would make them all again, her memories. Every one of them.

She gathered her feet underneath her, to push her big-bellied, awkward self up, and the baby kicked. It was a hard kick, full of strength and life. She rubbed her hands over her taut, swollen flesh. The spinning calluses on her fingers snagged the cheap muslin of her night rail, but she didn't notice, for she'd never had a lady's hands.

She was sure this babe was a boy for she carried him high and forward. She had dangled her wedding ring from a cotton string over her belly, and the ring had circled to the left. And besides, she thought with a sweet-sad smile, Merry had hummed to Noreen, who had told it to her—the fairies had promised there'd be a baby brother in the house before long.

A son for Shay, her gift to him and a fine one it would be, as long as he never found out the whole truth of its conception. But for her this last child, she knew, was God's punishment. She just wasn't sure for which sin.

It was possible, she knew as well, to love both the sin and the fruit of it. She loved this babe already, as deeply and fiercely as she loved Shay and her girls. It was the first of May; by the end of this month he would be born. She would hold him in her arms and rock him, while she felt the sweet tug of his mouth suckling at her breasts.

But the days would come and go, and he would be changed by them. The way the beach was changed by the ebb and flow of the tide. By next summer he'd be playing patty-cake and peekaboo with his sisters. He'd have learned how to eat his porridge by then, although probably he'd still be wearing most of it in his hair. Maybe he'd even be walking a bit, as long as his father was there to catch him if he fell.

The days would have come and gone, and he would be doing all those things, their son. But she would never see any of it.

Because by next summer she would be dead.

Chapter Eleven

For so long Emma Tremayne had felt as if her life was being whittled down to a stick, smooth and straight. No notches would be etched upon it but those small ones she would put there herself, living through one day the same as another. Marking time.

On Monday she played whist with the Carter sisters. Geoffrey was there, and she kept looking at his mouth and imagining how it would feel to trace the shape of it with her tongue . . . there, where it peaked, then dipped, then peaked again. Twice she forgot what was trump.

On Tuesday evening she saw him again. In the basement of Saint Michael's, where the younger set had gathered to make crepe paper flags for Decoration Day. While the others pretended not to notice, they sneaked out for a walk alone through the graveyard. The moon spilled blue light onto the headstones, and the elms moaned in the sea wind, and this time she felt a roughness in his kiss, a desperation, shocking her so that she pulled out of his arms and ran back inside.

On Wednesday she took luncheon with her cousins out at Hope Farm. They ate turtle soup and scalloped oysters and asparagus, and afterward she walked out to the kennels even though it was raining. But a different man was there handling the hounds.

Thursday evening she attended a lecture at the Lyceum on "Man as Artist, Michelangelo." When she returned home she went out to the orangery, and she thought of the morning she'd come here to find that Mama had smashed to ruination her latest work in progress, her "Adam in the Garden Before the Fall"—that morning she had felt as though she'd been smashed as well. She had been so sure that with her "Adam" she'd at last been on the verge of something grand, real, only to lose it.

But she knew now she'd been on the verge of nothing but mediocrity. She was glad her work had been destroyed, for it had been no good, not fit to be. She felt as an aching hole in her soul all of what she did not know about life, what she would never come to know. And she wondered how anyone but a god found the courage to try to create truth out of clay.

She promised herself she would never sculpt again.

Now it was Sunday morning, and as she did on the third Sunday of every month, she was delivering food baskets to the poor who lived in Goree. It was the back end of town, a place far from the harbor breezes, of wooden row houses, trampled grass, and wash-hung alleys. On hot days like today, smoke smudged the sky yellow and stank of burnt rubber from the nearby factory.

Someone had told her once that the factory turned out five thousand pairs of boots a year. As she drove past the place in her little black shay, it occurred to Emma that she had never even set eyes on, let alone owned, a pair of Bristol-made boots.

The baskets she gave out were filled with fishballs, brown bread, and beans baked in brown crocks. Molasses oozed out from under the lids of the crocks, and the women held them in their brown, callused hands and looked up at her with faded eyes. "No, no, please don't," she would say every time they thanked her. The food came from the church kitchens and she never had any part in its making.

It was unseasonably warm for the first week in May. By the time Emma finished delivering the baskets, the sun beat down on her shoulders, hot and stinging. She was supposed to meet her mother at Saint Michael's for the late service, but instead she drove out of town and down the Ferry Road toward Tanyard Woods.

It was cooler beneath the trees. Feathery hemlock boughs weaved a lacy arbor above her head. Mayflowers blushed pink among the curling fronds of tobacco ferns. The trees were up to their shins in the ferns.

At the end of the road, the woods opened up and the bay blazed blue. The ferry landing was deserted. A pair of iron jockey hitching posts stood next to the docks. She tied up the shay and walked along the boardwalk that crossed the mudflats.

She paused to watch a pair of snipes peck and stir the mud, their white-striped feathers flashing in the sun. A gust of wind flapped the brim of her plumed hat, startling the birds into flight.

They zigged and zagged across the blue horizon, wing to wing. Until two rifle shots cracked through the air, one almost an echo of the other, and the birds plunged from the sky.

A man came out of the woods and walked across the flats. She knew who it was from the size of him, and the loose and arrogant way he had of moving. He carried a rifle in one hand, and another swung by a strap across his shoulder.

When he reached the place where the birds had fallen, he stopped. She didn't actually think through the act of putting one foot in front of the other—suddenly she was just there, standing before him.

She looked up at his rugged face with its shattered nose and scarred cheek and startling eyes, then down at the dead birds. Snipes didn't make much of a meal, but their swift, erratic, dipping flight made them targets that only an expert could hope to hit.

And he had shot off their heads.

Emma's gaze went slowly from his boots, up the long length of him, back to his face. He smiled, and it was like lightning, his smile—quick and stark.

"If you could just bring those birds along with us, then, I and certain wee friends of mine would be most grateful," he said, in his harsh voice that was part growl, part whisper.

"What?" Emma looked from her silk-gloved hands to the dead birds, then back up to him. But he was already striding away from her, back across the mudflats toward the woods from where he had come.

She picked the snipes up by their feet, both in one hand. With the other hand she lifted the skirt of her lemon-yellow organdy dress, then stepped off the boardwalk and into the mud. Only later, when she looked back on this moment, would she wonder what wild and alien courage had possessed her.

They followed an old, crumbling stone wall that ran its lonely, broken course through the woods. Great oaks threw tangles of light and shade across their path. Their shoes crunched on the gray moss.

They came to a spring stream blanketed with skunk cabbage. He splashed right through it. "Wait," Emma called after him, but he didn't slow or look back.

She lifted her skirts higher and waded into the stream. The icy water soaked right through her kid shoes, which had once been white but were now the brown-gray color of salt mud.

"This is madness," she said aloud to herself. "You are a

madman," she said to the back of him that was fast walking away from her down the trail. "I am following a mad Irishman, who shoots the heads off birds, following him to God knows where, and I don't even know his name."

A gentleman, when first introduced to a lady, was supposed to bow without extending his hand. He hadn't bowed to her; he had touched her ankle without even a by-your-leave and said mocking things to her. But he hadn't bowed to her and he wasn't a gentleman, and they hadn't been introduced, and she thought she was rather glad she didn't know his name. It made her feel safe to think of him as nameless, a nobody.

He stopped at the edge of a small meadow where a giant white pine straddled a rock. He turned and put a finger to his lips. He laid down his guns, squatted on his haunches behind the rock, and motioned for her to come.

She came and knelt beside him, and her organdy skirts—not nearly so crisp as they'd been earlier that morning—still crackled like tissue paper.

"God save us," he said beneath his breath.

It was an ordinary clearing, and empty from what she could see. Red deer grass with clumps of scarlet pimpernel. Cattails and sedges that danced in the fitful breeze. A hedge of mountain laurel grew together to form a canopy over the entrance to an old woodchuck burrow.

He took the birds from her hand and threw them, one at a time, out into the clearing, about ten feet from the burrow. She wondered at the why behind what he had done, but she didn't ask. She felt so intensely alive just to be where she was in this one moment out of time, and she didn't want to think about the why of that either.

They were very close to each other. So close that part of her skirt fell in a soft fold over his thigh, and the shadow of his shoulders lay across her breast.

She didn't know how long they knelt there behind the

rock at the edge of the clearing. Long enough for the dampness in the ground to soak through her skirts. Long enough for a black-capped chickadee to decide they were part of the scenery and flit from branch to branch above their heads.

Her breath left her in a soft rush when he took her chin and turned her head slightly, so that she was looking not across the clearing but into it.

A fox's head had poked out of the burrow, ears perked, nose quivering. The fox was very patient; an eternity passed before it darted out of its earth. It paused to listen again, ears straight up, nose in the air, then it trotted dainty and light-footed, long tail floating proudly, out to where the dead snipes lay in the grass. It circled and sniffed, cocked its head, sniffed and circled.

The fox barked, and four kits came tumbling out of the burrow, all gangly legs and huge ears. They fell on the birds, whining and yipping, tearing into flesh and feathers with their sharp little teeth. Except for one of the kits, which fancied itself a hunter. It crouched down, its plump and fluffy body wiggling and twitching, then it pounced. And Emma smiled.

She turned her head and caught him staring at her, and she found it odd that for once she didn't mind. "Thank you," she said, "for . . . this." She waved her hand, encompassing the meadow and the foxes and all of the brave, strange world he was showing her, although he couldn't know . . . How could he possibly know? "But why did you bring me here?"

He held her gaze a moment longer, then looked away. "Now as to that I am not sure. Haven't you ever just done a thing without having a reason?"

"No, never. Why, if it isn't a tradition backed by at least four generations of practice, it isn't a done thing at all."

He surprised her by laughing. People so rarely laughed at her little jokes that she'd begun to think her sense of humor was perverse. And then it was the strangest thing—she suddenly felt as though she could have talked to him, laughed with him, for a long time. Yet no sooner did the thought enter her head, than she was unable to come up with the first word to get started.

He picked up his guns and pushed to his feet. He walked back down the way they had come and he didn't look to see if she followed after.

Back across the stream, he stopped at a place where a felled tree trunk lay across a gap in the stone wall. He sat down on the log and worked the lever on one of his rifles, ejecting an empty shell casing. He broke the gun open and peered into the breech.

Emma didn't know if she was meant to go on her way, now that he no longer seemed to have a use for her, or if he wanted her to stay . . . Or if she wanted herself to stay. For the first time in her life, she knew of no rule that could tell her how to behave.

The fallen stones made something of a chair. She settled gracefully down upon them and folded her hands in her lap, as if she'd suddenly found herself in someone's best parlor. Yet, the way she felt inside—it was like the shock of silence before the onslaught of a storm. That taut, breath-held moment just before the clouds opened up and the first raindrops fell.

He snapped the breech closed, cocked and pulled the trigger. The hammer fell on the empty chamber with a loud click. She was fascinated with his hands, with the size and shape of them and the way they moved. The way the sinews flexed, and the veins and bones stood out in stark relief against his skin.

"Why," she said, her voice cracking a little, "do you need so many guns just to slaughter a few of our native waterfowl?"

He lifted the rifle and sighted along the barrel. "They're just old Spencer repeaters left over from your great war that

I've managed to rebuild with bits and pieces I've cadged here and there. I'm trying them out, so to speak, to make certain they won't be misfiring and blowing off the hand of the first man to use them."

Emma jerked back in alarm and then had to laugh at herself. "Isn't that rather dangerous? What if one does misfire and yours is the hand that gets blown off?"

"Then it would be my own bloody fault, wouldn't it?"

"What will you do with them?" she said. "Discarded old rifles put back together again with bits and pieces."

"Smuggle them into Ireland." He slanted a look up at her, his eyes taunting. "Where maybe they'll be used to shoot spoiled little rich British lasses who ask too many questions."

He made her smile, the way he talked. "I might be spoiled and rich, but I beg to inform you, sir, that I am not British."

"Hunh. The airs and graces you Rhode Island Yankees put on could give the *ould* queen herself a proper scare."

She'd noticed that the thickness of his brogue had a tendency to ebb and flow depending on his mood and the subject. But whether he was putting on the Irish or not, his voice always sounded tortured when he spoke. As if his throat had rusted shut and he had to grate the words out by force. She wanted to ask him how he had come by the scar on his neck, but that was too much. Even for this strange, brave new Emma that she had become.

Her gaze fell to her lap. She put a pleat in her skirt with her fingers, then smoothed it out with her palm. "That . . ." She saw that she'd gotten the snipes' blood on her gloves—another pair ruined. "That vixen and her kits, they belonged to the fox that died."

She didn't say it as a question. Sometimes, when she really made herself, she could speak the truth.

"Ah, but that poor fox didn't just die. Your lot ran him down and tore him to pieces," he said, and she knew then that that was the real reason he'd brought her to the meadow.

He swung the rifle up to his shoulder and pulled the trigger. She heard the hammer fall on the empty chamber, again and then again, and each time she flinched. "They mate for life, do foxes," he said. "I wonder, Miss Tremayne, do you think they feel love?"

She made herself look up again and meet his eyes. "I don't know."

"I found them a couple of days after the hunt, your fox's vixen and their kits. She had ripped at her own fur with her teeth until it tore off in great bloody patches, and she'd paced back and forth in front of their earth until she'd worn a path, waiting for him to come home. Only he wasn't ever coming and she might've just quit eating and drinking and died herself, but she has the four wee little ones to care for and there's only herself now to hunt for them and so she had to go on."

Emma lowered her head so that he couldn't see the tears she was holding back, for she knew he would think they had come too easily.

She pushed the dead leaves and pine needles around with the mud-smeared patent toe of her shoe. A single tear fell, leaving a dark stain, like another drop of blood, on her lemon-yellow skirt. "I didn't want . . . what happened."

"You didn't want it, so you say, and yet yon vixen's mate still died and her loss hasn't kept the wind from blowing through these trees or the sun from shining bright upon the harbor, or her kits from needing to be fed. And you were there, were you not?"

Her head came up proud. "So were you. And besides, we Tremaynes always attend the last hunt of the season."

"Do you now?"

"I can't help that," she said. "I can't help who I am."

He looked back at her, saying nothing. In the tree-shadowed gloom his eyes glinted like broken beach glass.

She turned away from him. He was rude, hateful. An ignorant, bog-trotting, Irish smuggler who shot the heads off innocent birds and then had the brass to look down his broken nose at her for riding on a fox hunt. She would get up and leave him without even a see-you-later, and that would show him . . . show him . . .

She saw an aster blooming among the spill of rocks from the broken wall and she bent over to pick it. She twirled the stem, and the golden petals fluttered like a pinwheel. "Why do you dislike me so?"

"It's flattering yourself, you are, to think I have any thoughts about you at all."

"And it's lying, you are, sir, to try and tell me otherwise," she said, trying to mimic the Irish in his talk.

He laughed. "Lying—now there's a word. Sure and you would never think of telling lies, would you? Especially to the likes of me. But you've spent all of your young life running away from the truth, and you are crushing that poor wee flower to bits in your hand."

She opened her clenched fist and the aster fell, to lie broken among the leaves and pine needles.

"The other day," she said, "while at my cousin's farm, I went out to the kennels. A man there told me you had been dismissed."

"Aye, I'm back to toiling in the onion fields again. Terrrrrible work, it is," he said, rolling out the word with a flourish and laughing at her with his eyes. "The hoe gives you bloody blisters on your hands, and your back feels as if it's going to break in two. Now, does it please you to hear of my suffering, Miss Tremayne?"

"You flatter yourself, sir, if you think I have any feelings about you at all."

His face broke into a smile, and she couldn't help smiling

in return. The moment seemed to last forever, then ended abruptly when he stretched to his feet. He took her by the arm, helping her to stand.

"It's time you were getting on home, Miss Tremayne," he said in his raw, cracked voice. "Before someone thinks you've lost your way."

She turned and walked away from him. The wind suddenly swirled through the treetops, pelting her with a hail of pine needles that smelled incredibly sweet. If she had any pride at all, she thought, she would not look back to see if he watched her.

She had no pride.

She whirled, but the path behind her was empty. The felled tree trunk was there, as was the gap in the stone wall, but he was gone. So completely had he vanished that she felt compelled to go back, to seek some evidence that he had been there.

And, yes, the leaf mulch was trampled flat where he'd planted his boots. A single shell casing glinted in the sun, and the air smelled faintly of gun oil.

But for the rest of that day her throat felt tight and her chest was weighted with a strange sadness, as if she were grieving for something she had never seen. A thing that never even was, never imagined.

Chapter Twelve

Emma forgot that she was never going to sculpt again.

After that day in the woods, she spent hours in the old orangery. She would shape the clay, smash it, then shape it again.

It was deep into the night, in the glow of a kerosene lantern, when she finally stopped and stared at what she had done, and her hands began to tremble. Because for the first time she understood that there was an artery leading from her heart to her hands and those things that she would create with them. She knew that someday she would find that artery, and when she did she would open it and bleed, and perhaps she would die. But she would have made a thing that was real.

She stared at it, this thing that had come from her own hands, and saw not a clay model but living bone and skin and sinew. A man's hands reaching for the sky.

His hands.

She had chosen to end the sculpture at the wrists. She wanted nothing more of him than that—only his hands.

The rest of Emma's life dissolved into a merry-go-round of teas and soirees, charity functions and whist parties. Except for one memorable morning, when the ball gowns that they had ordered last winter from Maison Worth arrived from Paris.

When the package came, the Tremayne women were all in the morning room, arranging flower bouquets for the children's ward at the hospital. Emma, in a flurry of excitement, fell upon the distinctive silk-covered box that proclaimed to the world that it was from Worth's, and thus expensive and exclusive, and beautiful.

"This is like having Christmas in May," Maddie said, laughing with delight.

"And it'll be Christmas before we see them, if I can't get this wretched knot undone. I'm going to need a knife—no, there it is." Emma sneaked a quick peek under the box's lid. "I believe yours is the one on top, Maddie. Shut your eyes while I lift it out."

Emma looked up, smiling, her hands still now, prolonging the moment.

Maddie closed her eyes, smiling herself in sweet anticipation. Even their mother's face, Emma saw, had taken on a shine of excitement. Mama had been so irritable that morning, finding fault with everything they did. But then lately she had taken to bathing in cold water every day upon rising, to dull her appetite, and she claimed the baths made her bones and joints ache.

Emma looked at her mother now, where she stood before a glass and white wire table, surrounded by lilies and tulips and sheathed in a mauve watered-silk morning dress. The morning room glowed like the heart of a rose with the way the sun shone through the leaded glass windows to caper on the pink silk walls. Bathed in a pink blush of light, Bethel Tremayne looked young and willowy, and beautiful.

"You're looking especially pretty this morning, Mama," Emma said.

Bethel's smooth, pale cheeks flushed with pleasure, although she shook her head. "How kind of you to think so, my dear, but I can hardly believe it, for I feel positively haggard. I declare, the *suffering* I have endured. I only hope your father . . ." Her voice trailed off as her blush deepened. "Oh, do open the box, for heaven's sake. Your poor sister is about to expire from excitement."

The ball gown rustled like a flock of doves taking wing as Emma lifted it from the box. It was made of yards and yards of magenta lamé silk threaded with silver that flashed and shimmered rainbows in the rosy light.

Maddie, unable to wait any longer, opened her eyes and uttered a soft gasp of joy. "Oh, my . . . !"

Emma held the dress up to her breast with one hand and spread open the skirts with the other. She did a slow dip and turn, humming the lilt of a waltz. She danced once around the room and then stopped to lay the gown gently, reverently, across her sister's lap, and Maddie sighed with happiness.

"Oh, it's so beautiful. It is just so beautiful, don't you think so, Mama?"

"If only you could wear it to my betrothal ball," Emma said, although she knew it was a vain hope. It was considered extremely unrefined to dress in the latest fashions. The rule was generally to pack away Paris dresses in a trunk to season for two years, New York dresses for one.

"Still, Maddie, it is such a pity we can't break the rules just this once," she said aloud. "All Stuart Alcott would need would be one look at you in that dress and he'd be a goner."

Maddie started to laugh, but their mother's sharp voice cut her off abruptly.

"Emmaline Tremayne!" Bethel turned on her daughter

her deepest blue frown. "I will not allow such . . . such words of *slang* uttered in my house."

Emma bit her lip, and her gaze fell to the plush, floral carpet. "I'm sorry, Mama," she said, but a moment later she looked up and met Maddie's eyes, and they exchanged smiles.

"What is more," their mama was saying, "and though it pains me to have to do this, still there is nothing for it, it must be done, for it will not do . . ." She fingered the stiff lace at her throat. The color receded from her face and then flooded back again. "Madeleine will not be attending your betrothal ball."

"Mama . . ." Emma sat slowly down on a blue and green porcelain stool. "You cannot possibly be so mean, so cruel, so heartless . . ."

Bethel waved her hand through the air as if she were flourishing a palmetto fan. "Oh, do cease your melodramatic nonsense, Emma. Why have all my children always persisted in embarrassing me with displays of vulgar feelings? I'm certain the predilection for it must be a Tremayne trait, for it certainly doesn't come from my family."

She picked up one of the lilies, then set it back down on the table. "I intend for my decision to be a kindness to Maddie as well as to our guests. What is the point of allowing her to attend such an event when she cannot dance? To see her sitting there like a pitiable wallflower, through set after set, confined to her chair—why, it would put a damper on everyone's own enjoyment of the evening." She picked up the lily again and this time thrust it into the middle of a sheaf of ruby red tulips. "And which would show a want of delicacy on our part that I cannot allow."

Emma dared a look at her sister. Maddie usually shriveled down in her chair when their mama turned mean like that, but now she was sitting tall and stiff, her mouth slanted up in a funny, twisted way. Yet the blood had drained completely from her face, as if her heart had been cut open.

Suddenly she began to rip and pull at the beautiful ball gown she still held in her lap. And she was crying now, choking, heaving sobs. "Why do you buy me these things if I'm never allowed to go anywhere? I can't walk, I can't dance, and I can't bear it, I can't bear it!"

She clutched the dress in her fists and buried her face in the shimmering, purple-red silk. "I want to die. Oh, God, please just let me die . . ."

Emma rushed to her sister's side and, kneeling, tried to wrap her arms around her. But Maddie put the butts of her hands on Emma's shoulders and shoved her away. She pounded her thighs with her fists. "Let me alone. I want to be let alone, alone, alone!"

Bethel went to the bell rope and gave it a sharp pull. Maddie's sobs ended suddenly, as if someone had choked them off. She rocked back and forth, moaning, the dress gripped tightly in her hands. A few moments later a servant entered and, without being told, wheeled Maddie's chair from the room.

Emma stayed where she was, kneeling on the floor. There was such a savage shaking going on inside of her she felt as though a wild and angry wind were blowing through her. She wanted to scream, but she was afraid that if she started she might not be able to stop. That she would become like Maddie, ripping into things, trying to destroy their world with her bare hands.

"I declare," her mother was saying, and she'd gone back to arranging the flowers as if the interruption had been a mere trifle. "Sometimes I fear that the accident damaged our poor Maddie's mind as well as her legs. I know it's unsettling to think of, but perhaps I really ought to speak to your uncle Stanton about having her committed for a time to the asylum at Warren. To cure her of this unreasonable hysteria that seems to overtake her when one least expects it."

Emma bit down on her fist to stifle a cry, and she closed her eyes against a scalding rush of tears. It was a threat their mama had been making for years, ever since she'd seen old Mr. Alcott use the punishment on his son Stu. And she could manage it so easily, too—all she need do was persuade Uncle Stanton, who was a doctor, to declare Maddie to be suffering from a temporary loss of her reason, and then to have their cousin, who was a judge, sign the commitment papers.

A girl, a woman, Emma had learned, could legally be sent against her will to a madhouse at any time by her father or husband or guardian, even her son. All that was needed were the proper documents.

"She's understandably upset," Emma said, trying to make her voice sound calm, reasonable. "We've all done nothing but talk about the betrothal ball and now you say she cannot attend, so she is bound to be terribly disappointed."

She got stiffly to her feet and went to her mother facing her across a table strewn with lilies and tulips and pink ribbon. "Mama, please. Don't do this to Maddie. I won't be able to bear it if you do this."

Bethel didn't look up from the ribbon she was tying around a milk-glass vase. "You must learn to put aside your own personal feelings on such matters, Emma. Family dignity and good form should always come first."

"No, not this time," Emma said, although afterward she would wonder where she'd found the courage. Perhaps there was a certain power, she thought, in being the family's only hope. "This time Maddie comes first. Otherwise, I'll . . . I'll do something outrageous and spoil it all for you, Mama. I swear I will."

Bethel gave the ribbon ends a sharp tug, ruining the bow. She heaved a deep, long-suffering sigh. "If one didn't know better, one would think the pair of you had been brought up in a shanty. It shows an indelicacy of breeding that certainly doesn't come from *my* family."

She turned abruptly and headed for the door, abandoning the flowers for charity, abandoning the argument.

"I meant what I said," Emma declared, her voice quavering only a little.

Her mother pulled the door shut behind her without another word, but Emma knew she had won.

When she went up to her sister's room, though, she found Maddie lying on her bed, deep in a fevered sleep, and the air shrouded and reeking of chloral hydrate.

Emma sat down on the bed and smoothed the sweat-damp hair off her sister's flushed forehead. Maddie's lips were dry and cracked, but she was smiling.

"Look, Stu," Maddie whispered, lost and yet happy, so happy, in her dreams. "I'm dancing, I'm dancing . . ."

On the twelfth of May, they gave a ball at The Birches to celebrate the official announcement of Emma's engagement to Geoffrey Alcott. The ballroom was decorated on the theme of an English garden, with potted shrubs clipped to look like topiary animals and real nightingales let loose to sing in gilded rose bushes. Not everyone in Bristol was invited, only those who were anyone.

It pleased Emma perversely to think a certain Irish immigrant would never be invited. That no one would even think to invite him.

She danced with Geoffrey, and sometimes when he looked at her he made her feel beautiful and fragile, and a little breathless. Once, he led her out of the ballroom garden, through the French doors, and into the real garden. Wind rustled through the birches, and she could smell the sea.

They walked down the piazza steps and out onto the lawn, and they danced a waltz to music she could barely hear above the pounding of her heart.

But when she came back inside she found Maddie huddled in her chair in the alcove beneath the stairs. Her sister's eyes were wide and purple, the color of a bruise, and glassy from the chloral hydrate she had taken. "He didn't come," she said, over and over. "He's never coming."

Maddie had been allowed to attend the ball, and Stu Alcott had been invited. But he hadn't come. His brother said that he had gone to New York for a time, but he would be back when he ran out of money.

The next morning Emma's mother gave her paper and pen and told her she must write her father and beg him to come home, and this she did.

Afterward, she went down to the dock, where her sloop rocked in its slip and Willie's boat was no longer. She sat down on the gray, warped boards and wrapped her arms around her bent legs. She pressed her eyes hard into the bones of her knees, but she couldn't stop herself from weeping.

The night after the ball, the wind blew wild and blustery, and Emma came suddenly awake, restless and excited.

The wind and the night drew her outside. The wrought-iron gates cast barred and scrolled shadows on the quahog-shell drive. The dark branches of the birches shook against the sky, the ferns and sedges shuddered in the dark. There was mystery in the air, but somehow still she knew what she would find when she got to the bay.

She smelled the water before she came in sight of it, heard its endless soft sighing. The moon was coming up pale and white over the surf.

In the distance, where the bay lapped black and oily in the dark, she saw a fishing dory's running lights. And coming from it, a dinghy carrying the silhouettes of two men.

Standing there, where the birches met the beach, waiting for him to come, she felt like someone else.

She heard the slap of oars and the tap of the gunwale lightly hitting a piling. One of the men climbed out of the dinghy, then pushed it off. He was tall, and his shoulders blocked out the moon and most of the stars, and the wind caught at his black pea coat, making it flare darkly.

He walked light-footed down the dock, jumped off it, and strolled right up to her. The moonlight made a silver slash of the scar on his cheek.

She thought, for just the torn half of an instant, that he could hurt her. But she didn't run or make a sound, not even when he took her hand and pulled her deeper into the birches. His palm was warm and rough, callused from an onion hoe.

Once they were enshrouded by the shadows of the trees, he let her go. He shoved his hands deep into his pockets. She could see nothing of his face. It was only another shadow in a night full of shadows.

"Why," he said, "are you running around these woods in the middle of the bloody night and wearing nothing but your night rail?"

She looked down at her bare feet and then back up at him. She wrapped her arms around herself and shivered, pretending to be cold, although what she really felt was disgraced and exposed. She was swaddled from neck to ankle in yards of linen and lace, but she might as well have been naked.

"Sweet saints," he said. "How old are you?"

The question surprised her, coming out of nowhere. "Twenty-two. Don't say that's too young."

He didn't; he didn't say anything. She wished she could

see his face, but she liked the anonymity of the darkness for herself. It made her feel rather bold and daring, even though she was wearing only her night rail. "How old are you?" she said.

"Twenty-seven."

"I thought you older."

"We Irish are born old. And poor."

"And proud of it, apparently." She allowed herself to smile, since he wouldn't be able to see it in the dark.

"Miss Tremayne, Miss Tremayne . . . What am I going to do with you?" he said, almost singing, and she thought he might have been smiling as well. "Out here where you don't belong, seeing things you shouldn't."

"You could murder me, cut out my heart, and bury me deep in these woods where no one will ever find me."

He laughed at that, which made her feel absurdly pleased with herself—that she seemed to have a talent for making him laugh.

"But then," she went on, "you'd run the risk that my ghost would haunt you forever. Wherever you go, I'd be following in your wake with my head tucked underneath my arm, dripping blood, and howling at the full moon."

"I thought it was your heart I was going to cut out, not your head. *Dhia*, what a gruesome little miss you are."

"If you're going to turn all faint and squeamish at the least little mention of violence, you could simply extract a promise from me not to tell anyone about your nefarious activities."

"Aye? And what nefarious activities might those be?"

"Why, gun smuggling, of course."

"Shipping. It's not called smuggling until they're brought into Ireland, God save her."

"Nevertheless, I'll not tell on you, if you won't tell on me."

"What would I be telling?"

"My going out alone after dark, and without the proper accompaniments in either chaperons or wraps."

"Ah, that," he said.

"A heinous crime. And on a scale of wickedness, heinous must rank well above nefarious, surely."

He laughed again, then took a swift and sudden step, bringing himself right up next to her. "There's nothing for it," he said, a smile lingering in his voice. "If we're to be partners in our crimes, then we'll have to swear a blood oath on it."

He brought his hand out of his pocket, and she saw that he held a knife when he pressed a latch on the handle and the blade snapped open.

"Give me your hand," he said.

She held her hand out to him as if she were presenting it to a gentleman to be bowed over, and it trembled only a little.

He pressed the edge of the knife blade to the heel of his palm, then he did it to hers. She flinched, more at the thought, for it was a small cut and she felt no pain. Her blood welled up shiny and black.

He pressed his bleeding palm against hers, flesh to flesh. It seemed as if her blood flowed into him and his into her.

"Now, we swear," he said.

"What . . . what do we swear?"

"That we'll never tell."

We'll never speak of it again.

She wondered if there was a meaning in his words beyond what was happening on this night, but if so she had no hope of understanding it, and for once she relished her ignorance.

Her lips formed the words before she spoke them. "I swear," they said together, and this time her voice grated as roughly as his.

She didn't remember parting from him. Suddenly she was standing before The Birches' iron gates, looking through them to the scrolled and barred shadows that stretched far and deep across the lawn. The moon had risen and filled the night. Inside she felt sizzling and full of fire, as if she'd swallowed a bolt of lightning whole.

Chapter Thirteen

Bristolians loved to tell a story on themselves and their hidebound ways—about a young man who left home for the California gold fields in the middle of a Sunday sermon in Saint Michael's Episcopalian Church. When his fortune was made he came back to Bristol, walked into Saint Michael's of another Sunday, and picked up the sermon in the exact same sentence where he'd left it all those many years before.

And things, Emma thought with a sigh she could feel all the way down to her toes, surely hadn't changed in the years that had passed since. Well, the rector had changed, of course—the Reverend Shrewsbury having died of apoplexy some while ago. The Reverend Peele shepherded the flock now. He was considered a newcomer to Bristol, having lived and preached here for only the last fifteen years.

The rector, besides his having chosen somewhere else to be born, was faulted for his whiskers, which splayed out from his cheeks in a rather unruly fashion, like an untrimmed hedge. His loose, dewlapped cheeks flapped when he preached, punctuating his words. The essence of which, on this Sunday, appeared to be that God was an Episcopalian.

Emma wasn't listening to the particulars, having heard

them all before. She had just noticed how her Sunday dress, a lush shade of cranberry velour frappé, clashed to an eye-watering degree with the turkey-red pew cushions. It wasn't at all like her not to have been thinking that morning of where she was going, when she decided upon what she would be wearing.

Yet, the more she thought about it now, Emma felt perversely pleased with her faux pas. She saw the same people Sunday after Sunday, month after month, year after year. Indeed, she spent most of her hours doing the same things with the same people. If she never once did anything the least bit extraordinary and unexpected, then her life would become whittled down so smooth and straight there'd be nothing left of it.

She looked down at her right hand. Her pearl-button silk jersey glove fit smooth and tight, hiding the mark that man had put on her palm. It had been a small cut, only a nick really, and already it had healed. But she often thought she could feel her heart beating there, pulsing hard and fast, as if it lived right beneath her skin and struggled to get out.

She clenched her hand into a fist, then opened it again. She rubbed her palm on her knee and then looked up to find that the Carter sisters were watching her, and so she made herself be still.

At least no one sat beside her in the Tremayne box pew to take especial note of the flaws in her good form. Maddie hadn't once left The Birches since the accident—not even to come to church, although she used to love singing in the choir. But her appearance at Saint Michael's in her wheelchair would have called undue attention to herself and her unfortunate affliction and drawn shame upon the family, or so their mama had said, and so it would not do.

That morning, Mama herself had stayed in bed with a sick headache. Last week the Wilbur Nortons had returned home from a cruise to Florida full of stories about William

Tremayne and the parties on his yacht with his latest mistress. In the past, Mama had always confronted her husband's peccadilloes by refusing to acknowledge that they existed. But this latest shame had been too much for her.

"It is your duty to put in an appearance in our pew," she had said to Emma earlier that morning, as she lay in bed in a cascade of Brussels lace, propped up by silk pillows and surrounded by bottles of laudanum and smelling salts. "For the sake of our family's dignity and good form. You are our only hope."

You are our only hope . . .

Once Emma married, she would sit with Geoffrey and his grandmother in their family pew. At least, she thought, the view would be different from across the aisle, even if the sermons remained the same.

She glanced over at her intended now. He held his fine, narrow head erect on his shoulders, and the candleshine reflecting off the glazed cathedral glass made his face and hair look gilded. His gaze was fixed on the rector as if he hung on every word, but perhaps he was only absorbed by the man's flapping dewlaps. Geoffrey wore a gardenia in the buttonhole of his gray frock coat, but then he had always been a dapper dresser. He'd probably never clashed with anything in his life.

Emma walked through Saint Michael's polished ash doors and breathed deeply of the wet, gray air. She buttoned her long sealskin coat up under her chin and thrust her hands into a small, round ermine muff. After such a warm early spring the weather had turned chilly and unsettling again.

And thus providing, she thought with another small sigh, ample fodder for Great Folk conversation.

Geoffrey came up to her, setting his top hat squarely on

his head and adjusting the cuffs of his gray gloves. He smiled broadly, showing off his long teeth. She used to think she liked his smile . . . and she still did. Yes, she did. She was only irritated with him for some reason she couldn't fathom.

"A splendid sermon today, wasn't it, my dear?" he said. "Very uplifting."

"It's the same sermon he gives every year at this time."

Emma felt as though she were being smothered by a wet wool blanket. He was going to be her husband, and she wanted to ask him what he had really spent the last hour thinking. But the social conventions didn't allow them to speak of intimate things, such as thoughts and feelings.

"Geoffrey," she said, "do you believe in God?"

He took her arm, his fingers grasping her elbow just a little too tightly as he led her over to the side portal and out of the way of listening ears. "What kind of a thing is that to say right here on the steps of Saint Michael's on a Sunday morning?"

"Yes, you're right. Of course you believe, otherwise you wouldn't be here. You certainly wouldn't be here simply because this is where everyone else is, would you, Geoffrey? I suppose the more appropriate question is: How can you be so certain that He's Episcopalian?"

A gust of wind blew down Church Street, ruffling the ivy that climbed the stone wall at their backs. And carrying with it the sounds of Gregorian chanting, shuffling feet, and ringing bells. It must be, Emma thought, that Sunday in May when the Catholic girls of Saint Mary's dressed up all in white and paraded a plaster statue of their Virgin around the common and down to the bay. When she was a little girl, Emma had always wanted to join in the procession, but of course it was unthinkable.

Saint Michael's, as if not to be outdone, began to toll its big copper bell. Geoffrey tugged on the gold chain that swagged his stomach, pulling out his hunter's watch. He flipped open the lid and studied its face a moment, then glanced back up, giving Emma a scattered look. "Am I certain who's Episcopalian?"

"God."

"Of course He's Episcopalian," Geoffrey protested, although he did smile.

The procession rounded the corner coming into view. A strikingly handsome young priest led the way, swinging a bowl of smoking incense and chanting Latin phrases in a beautiful tenor voice. He was flanked on both sides by a bevy of nuns in their starched white cowls and stiff black habits. Their skirts flared like the lips of the bells they rang in rhythm with the priest's chanting.

Six men followed more slowly, dressed like pallbearers and carrying a wooden platform that supported the plaster Virgin. The statue was surrounded by shocks of white lilies and burning votive candles, and Emma thought it a pretty thing. The Virgin wore a crown woven of tiny pink rosebuds and blue forget-me-nots. She had a pink, smiling mouth that gave her an air of coquettish mystery. Her blue-painted robe was only a little chipped at the hem.

The young girls came after her, in their white dresses with blue sashes. And with wreaths on their heads like the Virgin's. Many carried baskets of flowers, and some waved large green and white banners decorated with harps and shamrocks. They sang, "Oh, Mary, we cover you with blossoms today, Queen of the Angels, Queen of the May . . ."

"Well, they," Emma said, nodding at the procession, since pointing was not good form, "probably think He's both Catholic and Irish."

"Emma!" Geoffrey exclaimed, genuine shock in his voice. He looked around to make certain no one had heard her. And Emma, having at last gotten what she wanted out of him, now for some strange reason felt like crying.

"You're funning with me again, aren't you?" he said, but

now he wasn't smiling. Apparently funning too much with one's fiancé was not good form either.

Emma blinked tears out of her eyes. She looked up at a sky clotted with clouds that were gray as pewter. "I do believe it's going to rain today. Dark clouds always bring wet weather."

Geoffrey made a sound that was halfway between a laugh and a sigh, but he was clearly pleased to be back on familiar conversational ground. "You're beginning to sound like my grandmother," he said, "always predicting rain."

"Clear skies, on the other hand, often mean the sun will shine."

He wasn't really listening to her, of course. He often didn't, as long as she spoke as she ought to and looked out for her good form. "Speaking of Grandmama," he said, "she's gone to inspect the cemetery to see which families are tending properly to their plots and which are being sadly neglectful. And if there is so much as a stray leaf or frayed blade of grass on Grandpapa's final resting place, I'll be hearing about it all through luncheon."

He took Emma's arm again and began to lead her down the church steps. "Would you be a darling and distract the old dear for a moment, while I have a quick word with my banker."

Geoffrey's grandmother was indeed walking among the gravestones and crypts, and peering at them through a pearl-rimmed lorgnette. Although she used a cane, she was not bent over. Perhaps it was her regal but diminutive size and the pale blue coat she wore, but she reminded Emma of the plaster Virgin. Except that instead of a flower crown she sported a hat with a long black feather that stabbed at the sky.

Emma had always sought out the company of Geoffrey's grandmother while out in society, mainly because she'd never felt scrutinized and judged in the old woman's presence. Eunice Alcott wasn't interested in anyone under the age of sixty.

"Good morning, ma'am," Emma said with a shy smile as she joined her. "You are looking well."

The old woman drew in such a deep breath she snorted. "Certainly I am looking well. One can't, however, say the same about Gladys Longworth." Geoffrey's grandmother had a nose that turned up on the end like a slipper and she pointed it at a well-padded matron who leaned heavily on a pair of canes as she made her laborious way down Saint Michael's granite steps. "Will you just look at her? Wasted down to skin and bones, she is. Not enough left of her to make a shadow. You mark if she isn't lying in her coffin, cold and shriveled as a dead cod, before the end of summer."

"We can only hope not, Mrs. Alcott."

"*You* might hope not, my dear. I, on the other hand, have learned to bow to the inevitable." She peered around Emma's shoulder to shoot a deadly glare at the stout, gray-haired man who had just offered his arm as support for the tottering old lady. "And there's that boy of Gladys's, hounding her into her grave so's he can get his paws on her money, and she's letting him do it, the mewly hearted fool. Gladys never did have gumption enough to spit in a privy."

The Catholic procession was passing the church now. The incense smoke eddied and swirled, its exotic scent following the wind. The Virgin Mary seemed to be floating above the heads of the people, on a cloud of lilies and dancing candle flames. Someone had begun to play the pipes—wailing, mournful music.

Geoffrey and his banker were walking toward them, and Emma heard the banker say, "The Irish are the scum of creation. I say the solution to the problem of this country's deserving poor is obvious. Encourage every Irishman to kill a Negro and then hang him for it."

Geoffrey's high-arched nose sniffed as if offended. But

whether at the sight of the procession or at the other man's words, she wasn't sure which.

Just then Emma picked out the fiery-haired mill woman in her pumpkin-colored coat from among the crowd watching the procession. She stood at the curb, in front of Pardon Hardy's Drugstore, waving to one of the young girls in white dresses and blue sashes. The woman had another, smaller child by the hand. The little girl's own curls, bright as a new copper penny, danced and swirled around her flushed face. She seemed excited or angry about something, for even as Emma watched, she jerked free of the woman and ran to join the tag end of the older girls who followed the floating Virgin.

The woman tried to go after her, but she had to stop and grab on to a lamppost as a fit of coughing seized her.

"Please excuse me, Mrs. Alcott," Emma said, although she was already walking away. "I see a . . . friend."

Then she heard Geoffrey call her name. She almost kept going, but she was afraid he'd come after her, so she turned and went back. She made herself smile, although she could feel her pulse beating hard and fast in her neck. She didn't know what was compelling her to do this. It was as if she had suddenly become someone else.

"I thought to visit a sick friend this afternoon," she said to her betrothed. "But you needn't concern yourself, for I've my carriage and a driver to see me home."

Geoffrey's mouth tightened a little at the corners. "But I had hoped you would join Grandmama and me for luncheon. I realize I haven't issued you a formal invitation, but I'd supposed . . ." He lifted his hand, then let it fall.

"That's very kind of you, Geoffrey. It's just that she's had so little company this past week . . . my friend."

"It's not Judith Patterson, is it?" His frown deepened. "I heard she was struck with a particularly virulent form of measles. Are you certain—"

She leaned in to him and patted the lapel of his frock coat, then smoothed its nap, surprising them both, for she had never before deliberately and so intimately touched him first. "I've already had the measles, Geoffrey. I can only catch them once."

He gave her one of his wistful smiles and took the hand that still rested on his coat, bringing it up to his lips. "Of course you must pay your call on a sick, and doubtless lonely, friend. And never mind my abominable selfishness. There'll be many a luncheon in our future. After all, we have the rest of our lives to spend together."

Guilt sent the color rushing hot to her face, and her hand trembled in his. She wondered what kind of terrible person she was, for she had never been more fond of him than during this very moment when she was deceiving him.

"Yes, we do, don't we—have the rest of our lives? Geoffrey, I . . . Thank you," she said, and left him quickly, before she could say more.

She cut across the cemetery, wending her way through the tall elms and crumbling old gravestones. She shook inside with fear and shame, and a wonder at herself. What am I doing? she thought. *Oh, mercy, Emma Tremayne, what are you doing?*

The Queen of May procession had passed by, turning the corner and going out of sight up Thames Street. Most of the crowd had followed after it, and Emma easily spotted the woman on the nearly empty sidewalk. She had let go of the lamppost and stood now in front of the drugstore window, with her forehead pressed against the glass, as if she were trying to read the ads there for digestive tablets and hair dye. But then she started coughing again, bending over almost double, and her back shook as if it were being pummeled with fists. When she straightened up, she swayed heavily, nearly falling.

She was leaning with her shoulder up against the drugstore window by the time Emma got to her side. The woman turned to face her and her dark eyes widened, as if in fear. Then they glazed over, and she slid slowly to the sidewalk, a heap of orange wool and wild, flaming hair.

Emma knelt beside her. The woman's face was sheened with sweat and unearthly pale. Her breath came in soggy, shallow gasps. She had a bloody handkerchief and a small brown bottle clutched tightly in her hand.

"Well, of all things!"

Emma looked around behind her. A man was there, a tubby little man with a face plump and soft as a bun and two black raisins for eyes. He looked familiar to her although she couldn't place his name. He wasn't one of the Great Folk.

"Please, sir," she said. "Will you be so kind as to help me? This woman appears to have—"

"Miss Tremayne!" the man exclaimed. He leaned over, peering into her face, as if he couldn't quite believe the evidence of his own eyes. "You shouldn't be concerning yourself with some little no-'count mill chit. Inebriated, she is. And on a Sunday. The very shame of it."

"She's not drunk. She's ill."

"All the worse, then. No telling what infectious diseases she might be carrying." And as if suddenly reminded of his own mortality, the man stepped quickly backward, pulling out a handkerchief to cover his face.

The skies chose that moment to crack open and pour rain. The fat man and the few other passersby who had stopped to watch now hurried off with umbrellas and newspapers held over their heads.

The woman groaned and stirred, then fell into a deeper faint. Emma's carriage and driver were waiting back at Saint Michael's, but she didn't want to go fetch them and leave the woman here alone, lying on the sidewalk with the rain pouring over her as if she were only so much rubbish.

The rain sliced down on them in wind-driven sheets. The woman shivered so hard her teeth rattled, although her eyes were sunken into her face in a deathlike sleep. Emma put her ermine muff beneath the woman's head and then took off her own sealskin coat and laid it over her.

The rain flowed over the drugstore awning, so that it seemed to Emma she looked out at the now-deserted street through a waterfall. Strangely, she thought she heard humming.

Something moved beyond the curtain of rain . . . the child. She came closer, and Emma saw that she was smiling, although her copper curls were now soaked dark and plastered to her head, and the frayed ragwool sweater she wore streamed water.

The child reached out and touched Emma's cheek with her small, chilled hand. Then she rocked from foot to foot, humming loudly and fiercely, like a bee swarm.

If it weren't for the woman's wet, shuddering breaths, Emma would have thought her dead. Her flesh was white and cold—what there was of it. She was pathetically thin, except for her enormously distended belly.

Emma had bathed her in steaming hot towels, then dressed her in one of her own tatted lace and fine woolen night shifts. Only after the woman was seen to had Emma changed out of her own soaked dress and into a simple black skirt and white shirtwaist. Now the woman slept in Emma's bed, between Swiss embroidered linen sheets that had been sprinkled with lavender water, and Emma paced the room.

The lamps had been lit for over an hour when the woman finally woke. She lay in utter stillness, staring up at the starched muslin canopy of the bed. While Emma watched from the shadows, feeling self-conscious and awkward.

The woman's bright hair whispered over the silk-slipped pillows as she looked around the room, taking in the gaslights with their Tiffany glass globes, the marble fireplace with its coal fire burning hot in the grate. The yellow silk-papered walls, and the Chinese vases of hothouse roses that spilled their oily perfume into the air.

"Oh, my . . ." she said on a soft sigh, and Emma felt embarrassed, as if she'd just been caught putting on airs.

Emma cleared her throat and tried for a smile as she approached the bed. "You're at The Birches, if you were wondering. You took ill during the Virgin statue's procession." She swallowed, breathed. "I saw you because I . . ." But she couldn't really explain, even to herself, what impulse had driven her to seek out this woman.

"Look," she said instead and made a nervous, jerking movement toward a Hepplewhite table that bore a silver tea service swaddled in a quilted cozy. "I've been keeping the tea hot for when you awakened."

The woman was staring at her with eyes as deep and dark and still as wells. "You brought me here, to your house?"

"I didn't know what else to do. My uncle, Stanton Albertson? He's a doctor. After you fainted in the street and your little girl fetched my carriage and driver, I took you straight to him, but he was out on another call, and his housekeeper was making such a fuss about it being Sunday, as if one is supposed to choose a more convenient and proper day of the week to fall ill . . ."

She gripped her hands together at her waist, then pulled them apart. She realized she'd neglected to pour the tea after making such a fuss about it, yet she remained standing where she was, in the middle of the Aubusson carpet.

The woman was trying frantically to push herself upright against the mound of pillows at her back. "Please, you mustn't—" She coughed, her chest heaving. "I don't need to see a doctor. It's only a spring sickness I have."

Emma's gaze went to the bedstand, where lay a crumpled, bloodstained handkerchief and a brown bottle whose label read: DR. KING'S NEW DISCOVERY FOR CONSUMPTION.

The woman saw what Emma was looking at and she collapsed back against the pillows. Her breathing sawed raw and harsh in her throat. "*Dhia*, please, please don't be telling any doctors about me. They'll be sending me back to Ireland, tearing me away from my loved ones and sending me off to die alone. Or they'll be making me drink from the black bottle, and I'll die before my time." She shut her eyes, but tears escaped from beneath her clenched eyelids to roll down the side of her face and into her hair. "I don't want to die alone. I don't want to die . . ."

Her voice trailed off. Hard rain clattered like fistfuls of pebbles against the windowpanes. The wind cried and moaned.

Emma had heard the rumor of the "black bottle," from which physicians were supposed to administer the coup de grâce to hopeless consumptives. And she'd had an aunt who'd died of the disease, her father's younger sister. Charlotte Tremayne's death hadn't come from a bottle, though, but rather in a private sanitarium near Providence. Only once had they gone to visit her there. Emma remembered the curtainless windows and the empty white walls, the plain iron cots. "It's the finest blossoms," Mama had said, as she blotted up a single, perfect tear with her handkerchief, "that are nipped in the bud."

But Emma had thought her aunt looked nothing like a blossom, but rather pale and wasted, and so very lonely. Only the rich could afford to die in the bare isolation of a sanitarium. The poor stayed home and passed the disease on to their loved ones.

Lightning flashed blue, and Emma found herself waiting for the thunder, which came much later. A low, slow rumble.

"I . . . I'll not summon the doctor," she finally said. "Or tell anyone. I promise."

The woman's thin chest rose and fell in a silent sigh.

"I don't—" Emma's voice cracked and she had to start over. "I don't know where my manners are. I haven't even introduced myself. I'm Emma Tremayne."

The woman opened her eyes, and she stared so hard and long that Emma flushed. "Aye, I know," she said. But then her mouth trembled at the corners, creasing into something close to a smile. "Though I'm pleased to be making your proper acquaintance, Miss Tremayne. And my name is Bria. Bria McKenna." The smile widened, became real, lighting up her eyes. "It's Mrs. McKenna, rather, and I should surely hope to say so—what with two little ones near to half grown already and another on the way."

She started to laugh but it turned into a cough. She put her fist to her mouth, her shoulders shaking.

At last Emma got her legs to move, although they felt stiff as stilts. "Let me pour that tea. It's red clover. And I had Cook steep it with linseed oil and honey. That's supposed to be soothing to one who suffers from consu—the spring croup."

She filled a rose-patterned Sèvres cup with the brew. But when she turned back to the woman in the bed, Emma saw that her eyes had grown wide and even darker. Her gaze went from the bone china cup to the canopy that spread, delicate and sheer as an angel's wings above her head, and then back to Emma's face. Her hands, lying flat and small on the silk counterpane, trembled.

And Emma knew the woman's thoughts, for she'd had them so many times herself. It was as if you had suddenly stepped through the looking glass, and not only was your world not as it should be, but neither were you. You found yourself uneasy, even with the beat of your own heart.

Emma could feel her mouth smiling, yet there was a hollowness inside her, a yearning for something she couldn't name. Maybe she simply wanted to say to this woman: *I know.* And then to have the words said back to her.

"I could hold the cup and saucer for you," she said instead. "If you'd like."

The woman swallowed, nodded, then let her eyes drift closed.

Emma sat on the bed. Her black taffeta skirts rustled, and the goose-down mattress softly sighed. The woman—Bria McKenna—was running her hand over and over her swollen belly. Emma knew little about babies and birthing, but she thought this one would be coming soon.

It seemed to Emma a sorrow too heavy to be borne. To bring a child into the world knowing you would soon be leaving it, to miss all those wondrous years of watching him grow. And knowing he was destined never to have the one thing he would need most—you.

The only pain worse, perhaps, would be to watch him grow old enough to be chewed up by a monstrous mill machine and then to watch him die, bleeding in your arms.

Emma's throat hurt and her eyes burned, and she felt ashamed of her feelings. She hadn't earned the right to feel pity.

She reached out to touch Bria McKenna's hand, pulled back, then did it after all. Their fingers entwined like the strands of a rope, and Emma felt the fragility of the woman's bones beneath the thin, white skin.

"I'm sorry about your boy," Emma said, so softly it was nearly a whisper.

The woman's eyes flew open, and her face bled so pale it seemed transparent. Her fingers tightened around Emma's, gripping hard. "But how . . . how could you know about him?"

"You brought him to us and he was dead. Padraic, you said his name was—so we would . . . know."

The woman's chest lifted as if she were suddenly drawing back in all the breath she had lost. "*Och*, no, no, that one wasn't mine. Poor Mrs. Cartwright, widowed and losing a son all in the one year and in no fit state even to see to the wake and the burying. He just as easily could have been, though. I mean to say it just as easily could've been one of my girls."

She brought their entwined hands up to her breast and struggled to sit up. A blue vein beat wildly in her temple. "That woman who carried poor wee Padraic's dead body to the hunt—she wasn't me. It was a momentary madness, born of despair, you understand? She wasn't . . ." She stared hard into Emma's face, searching. "It wasn't myself doing that."

"No, it wasn't," Emma said. "I understand. I . . ." *Know.*

Bria McKenna fell back, her breaths coming hard and shallow, and she let go of Emma's hand. "I'd like that tea now, if you would be so kind."

Emma wasn't sure why she smiled just then, but she did. And when Bria McKenna smiled back at her, the warmth of it spread down deep inside her. "My mother once spent an entire summer training me how to properly serve tea," she said, "and now here I can't seem to get it done when it's needed the most."

Yet, she was surprised at her own efficiency and the ease she felt inside herself, the lack of shyness, as she stacked the pillows up under the woman's back. It did cross her mind that the woman's disease was supposed to be contagious, but she couldn't very well behave as though it were and still be mannerly. And good manners, Emma's mother had taught her, were to be valued above all things.

Emma poured a fresh cup of the tea, holding it so that it could be drunk with only a slight tip of the head. Bria McKenna took a small, careful sip, then looked up to stare for the longest time at Emma with eyes that seemed at once both sweet and sad. And Emma stared back. For the first time in her life, she stared back.

"It's sorry I am now for what I said to you that day," Bria finally said. "I was sorely wrong, for you've a kindness in your heart. Taking me in and caring for me like you've done."

Emma flushed a little, and her gaze fell to her lap. "I saw you fall, so I could hardly leave you lying there. Then, too, some of the credit must go to your little girl. I was all for driving you all the way up to the doctor in Warren, but she insisted I was to take you home with me instead—to my silver house, she called it. She said the fairies wanted it done that way."

"Where—" Bria coughed, her whole body jerking violently. A trickle of blood leaked from one corner of her mouth. "She . . ."

"She isn't here with us now, your little girl," Emma said as she set down the cup and saucer. She handed Bria a fresh handkerchief and helped her settle back into the pillows. "But you needn't fret over her. She said she had to tell her father where I'd taken you and she ran off to find him, I suspect."

Bria sighed. Her eyelids drooped heavily and then closed, and Emma thought she slept.

But then she lifted her hand, though she did so slowly and with effort, as if it bore the weight of the world. "The fairies again . . ." And she made a sound that began as a laugh and ended in another chest-rattling cough. "Only fancy our Noreen saying and doing such a thing."

Emma stood up, smoothing the sheet, tucking in pillows, wanting to brush the bright hair off Bria McKenna's forehead and not daring to, for that was the sort of thing one did for a friend, not a stranger.

"A pretty child with copper-colored curls? She told me her name was Merry."

"Not our Merry, surely." Bria's eyes opened, dark and blurred, then drifted closed again. "Merry doesn't talk."

Emma watched the woman sleep. Bria McKenna . . . Emma liked the name, for it had a brave, ringing sound to it. A brightness, like her hair.

Bria McKenna. Her dark red eyebrows were thick and uncompromising. Her mouth was wide and too full. She wasn't beautiful, but she had a striking face. It was her bones, what one saw in her bones—raw strength tempered by suffering. Hers was a warrior's face.

Emma's fingers trembled with the need to sculpt those bones. She would do a model in clay first, only of the front of the head. Then when she had that right she would cast just the face in the thinnest sheet of copper, like a mask. So that the bones would forever be hidden from the eye and yet felt with the heart.

But in the meantime, when Bria McKenna awoke again, she would need something more substantial than tea. Chicken soup was supposed to be good. They'd had pheasant consommé for dinner yesterday, Emma remembered—there had been a whole tureen of it. Perhaps the soup didn't have to be made with a chicken precisely, she thought. Perhaps any manner of fowl would do.

She started to ring the bell for a servant and then decided she would go down to the kitchen and fetch it herself.

The hall below was dark, lit only by a pair of gas sconces that flanked the enormous, fluted gold-framed mirror hanging on the back wall. Years ago, in the last century, the great sweeping double oak staircase had been illuminated by hundreds of burning tapers. One night, a Tremayne daughter had tripped and fallen into the tapers, setting herself on fire. The fashionable steel panniers she wore beneath her raw silk skirts had prevented her frantic father from smothering the flames, and she had burned to death. She wasn't the first, or the last, to add to the Tremayne legend of a curse, and it was said that her ghost still haunted the great hall. But no one in Emma's memory had claimed to have seen her.

Emma got as far as the middle landing of the staircase when she stopped. The house did have a strange feel to it tonight. But more than ghostly, it felt empty, abandoned. As if of all the wild and wicked and cursed Tremaynes who had lived and died here, not even a scrap of their souls was left to haunt the place. Not even the memories that they had been.

Emma shook her head. She was imagining things only because it was a stormy night, all the servants were below-stairs, and both her mother and sister slept, lost in laudanum dreams.

Her kid slippers moved silently down the polished oak treads. Shadows writhed up the stairwell. Lightning flashed and was broken into a million shards by the beveled glass panes of the fanlight above the door.

Emma stopped again, her hand gripping the banister, waiting. But she barely had time to draw a breath before the thunder cracked open the night, and rolled and rolled and rolled, seeming to last forever.

And then Emma realized she was no longer hearing thunder, but someone lifting and pounding the brass lion's head knocker onto the doors' thick ebony panels.

She stepped down another tread.

The doors burst open, slamming against the marble-faced walls. The crash rebounded around the domed ceiling, louder than any clap of thunder. Wind gusted into the hall. The gas jets in the sconces wavered and dimmed, nearly going out. But not before she saw his reflection in the mirror.

His black pea coat flared open, his slouch hat and hair

dripped water. Behind him, in the lantern-shine out on the piazza, the rain slashed like silver knives.

He must have seen the flash of her white shirtwaist in the mirror, for his gaze went there first and locked with hers. They stared at each other across a world of marble and silvered glass and fractured gaslight.

He has come, she thought

He had come. For her. He wanted her, and so he had come for her. He was her infinite possibility and he had come to tear her life out by the roots, and this time she would let it happen.

He took a step toward her, and she moaned. A moan filled with fear and wonder and expectation.

"I've come," he said, "for my wife."

Chapter Fourteen

Emma Tremayne sat on the maroon leather seat of her black-lacquered shay. She was properly attired for paying a morning call, in a French promenade dress of moiré taffeta the colors of a pigeon's wing, trimmed with a cascade of Belgian lace at the throat and a broad white satin ribbon at the waist. Her accessories were proper as well: doeskin driving gloves, a taffeta and lace parasol, and a hat of reseda straw trimmed with satin roses and a tuft of ostrich feathers.

Yet she couldn't have felt more conspicuous and out of place.

She didn't come often to this end of Thames Street. Indeed, she couldn't remember ever having driven past here, let alone pulling up alongside the weathered boardwalk to stop among steaming piles of horse droppings beneath a listing lamppost.

Not many people were out and about at this time of morning, this being a working neighborhood. But the two who were—a fisherman sitting on his front stoop mending a lobster trap and a ragpicker pushing his cart home from the rubbish heap—had stopped to gape and stare.

She was in plain view because she had the top of the shay folded down, but then everything wouldn't have fit into it otherwise. On the seat next to her was a calico-lined picnic basket filled with tongue sandwiches, delicate fillets of beef, terrapin, pâté de foie gras, and truffled turkey. Stuffed in the back were carpetbags and striped bandboxes overflowing with clothes she'd never worn. And wedged next to her feet was a steamer trunk packed with dolls and other toys she'd found in The Birches' attics but couldn't remember ever playing with.

Indeed, the shay was so crowded she had to stand up for a better look at the house she was visiting, a tiny clapboard shack perched high on stilts at the edge of a gray shingle beach.

Emma alighted from the shay and walked toward the house on a path that was really nothing more than a bald rut worn into a patch of cattails and asters. With each step her courage nearly failed her. She had never done this before, never sought out another's company. People had always courted her.

The front door opened and Bria McKenna stepped out onto the tall front stoop, wiping her hands on her apron. Her gaze went from Emma out to the street, where the shay waited, stuffed with the picnic basket and bandboxes and trunk. Anger flared deep and bright in the woman's eyes.

And Emma knew instantly her mistake.

"Good morning!" she exclaimed, her voice sounding breathy, as if she'd swallowed too much air. "I was . . ." She waved her hand back at the overflowing carriage. "I was on my way to drop off some charitable donations to Saint Michael's and I thought, as I was passing, that I would call first and see how you were faring."

A flush slowly suffused Bria's face. She nodded stiffly and stepped to the side of the oak plank door. "Won't you come in, then, Miss Tremayne. I was just about to put the kettle on."

Emma picked up her skirts and climbed the steep steps,

with legs that shook so she nearly stumbled. The kitchen smelled wonderful, of fresh baking bread and the wild buttercups that filled a tomato can set in the middle of the table. The bird-of-paradise wallpaper might have been faded and watermarked, but its orange and blue flowers gave the room a cheerful air. The cracked linoleum floor, once a dark brown, had been bleached nearly white by a scrub brush and was covered in one corner with a colorful hooked-rag rug.

Emma stood in the middle of the floor, uncertain of what to do with herself.

"It's lucky you are you caught me t'home," Bria said as she set a battered copper kettle onto the stove. "I'm supposed to be housekeeping for my brother at the rectory—he's the priest to Saint Mary's parish. But why he ever took me on I don't know, since he won't let me do a thing. I spend more time in my own kitchen these days than in his."

She turned from the stove, a smile breaking wide across her mouth. "Why don't you set yourself down and— Oh, shoo away, you old lazy cat!" She waved her arms, advancing on one of the ladderback chairs whose woven seat was filled with a huge, shaggy brown creature. "You! You get on outside, Gorgeous. Go catch yourself some mice like you're supposed to be doing."

The cat sprang off the chair with a hiss. But then it sauntered slowly, very slowly, out the open door.

Emma stared after the creature. Its ears were chewed at the ends, its tail was bent in three places like a corkscrew, and it appeared to be molting. " 'Gorgeous?' "

Bria laughed, surprising Emma, for her laugh was all cinnamon and spice, and it didn't go at all with those oh-so-solemn eyes.

"Shay named him that because he's so bloomin' ugly. Myself, I'd have named him Brilliant, since near as I can tell he hasn't got the smarts to scratch an itch."

Bria laughed again and turned around to the stove to take

off the kettle, a lightness to her step. She wasn't coughing today. Life bloomed deep pink like late summer roses in her cheeks.

Emma sat down in the chair left warm by Gorgeous. It felt strange yet rather pleasant to be doing this. As if she were a neighbor—no, a friend, who often dropped by of a morning to share a cup of tea and a bit of a gossip. After the initial awkwardness, Bria McKenna now seemed totally at ease with her unexpected visitor. Emma wished she could be that way, because her own tongue was sticking to the roof of her mouth and her palms were growing hot and wet inside her doeskin driving gloves.

Bria fell into a silence, though, while she prepared the tea things. Emma tried not to notice that the patterns on the clayware cups didn't match their saucers. That the spoons were made of tin, and the milk came from one, and molasses would be the sweetener instead of sugar.

By the time Bria had poured the tea, put a plate of sliced brown bread and a crock of oleo on the table, and sat down across from her, Emma was feeling such a pressing obligation to say something, anything, that she was nearly choking with it.

"There's not a cloud in the sky today," she said, "and the sun is already quite warm. Perhaps spring has finally settled in."

"Why, so it has," Bria said. She craned her head to peer out the open door, as if the sun shining in a clear blue sky warranted a look. "A lot different, surely, than Sunday last, when I played the fool, fainting in front of Pardon Hardy's Drugstore."

Emma spread the thin cotton blue-checkered napkin across her lap and drank a swallow of tea. She broke a slice of the brown bread into four proper pieces, but then didn't eat it. When she caught herself tracing a pattern on the table's brown oilcloth, she made herself stop and pull in a deep breath.

"On this day six years ago," she said, "there was another terrible lightning and thunder storm. My brother, Willie, took his sloop out onto the bay and he never came back."

She heard Bria's sharp, sucked-in breath, and she pressed her fingers to her own lips as if she were stopping a scream. The words had come blurting out of her, exploded out of her like a cork out of a champagne bottle. She thought the words must have been stuck right there in her throat for years, fermenting, waiting for a chance to blow.

They weren't to speak of it, though, not even amongst themselves, not even to their own grieving hearts . . . Willie's death. Such an embarrassment to the family, such a scandal. Such an unpleasantness to have brought up over tea.

But she wanted to speak of it—she had to or she would go mad. *An act born of madness and despair.*

She felt Bria move, heard the dull ring of clayware, and then their fingers were curling together, resting a moment on the table's shiny brown oilcloth.

"Oh, Miss Tremayne. It's that sorry I am."

"Something like that happens," Emma said into the kitchen with its faded wallpaper and cracked linoleum, "and it leaves a well of pain that goes down deep inside you, deep where your heart is, I suppose. A well that feels so wretchedly empty. And whenever anything else bad happens to you, even things that are just a little hurtful, it always seems to lead right to that well that's just sitting there waiting."

Emma thought she probably wasn't making a lot of sense, but she wasn't going to stop until she got to the end of it. "For the longest time after . . . after it happened, I used to think: If he's not around then why should I live, why should I matter? Why should anything matter?"

All the while she spoke she hadn't been able to look at

Bria, but now she did. Bria's eyes were so full up with pain they glittered from it, and Emma felt ashamed.

"Forgive me," she said. "I shouldn't be speaking to you of such things."

"Why should you not? Because I'm dying myself?"

"Oh, no, no—I only meant one doesn't talk of such things. It isn't done. At least in my world it isn't done."

"It isn't done much down here on Thames Street either."

What they shared then wasn't a smile, for what they spoke of cut too deeply. It was a quiet and profound understanding: *I know*.

"Dying." Bria said it flat out and simply, and Emma thought it was a word she'd been living with for quite some time now. "It's a journey each of us has to make alone when the time comes, and sure if that doesn't scare us silly. Maybe because we've just spent all our lives doing everything possible not to be alone. Though it's strange that we should feel such a way, since it's what we are from our very first breath—alone."

"I think there was no one more alone than Willie that day he sailed off into the storm."

Bria breathed and the sound of it was like a sigh, only deeper. "Most times it's worse, I think, for us who're left behind. Left alone to endure life without the one we love above all others."

For the first time since she had stepped through the door into this kitchen with its flowered wallpaper and smells of baking bread and buttercups, Emma allowed herself to think of him—Bria McKenna's husband.

That night, that night, that night . . . Waiting for him there on the stairs, she had thought he was going to carry her off to a life of danger and adventure. But what she'd been was carried away by her own wild imaginings.

That night he had walked past her and up the stairs without another word. And she had stayed where she was, caught fast within the hall's shrouded silence. Her thoughts had been caught fast, as well. Caught up still in those wild imaginings that he had come for her, when instead he had come for . . . come for . . .

She had waited, unmoving. When at last he emerged from the dark upper reaches of the house, Emma had started, as if she would run. But it was too late for that, and she might as well not have been there anyway, for he didn't seem to see her. His eyes, full of love and anguish, were riveted on the woman he carried in his arms.

But at the bottom of the stairs he had paused and looked up. Bria McKenna's head stirred against his chest, and his arms tightened their grip around her, although she didn't waken. His eyes glittered up at Emma like shards of fallen, shattered stars.

"She is my wife," he had said. "And I'm taking her home."

That night, that night . . . She had felt like such a fool. She couldn't blame him, though, for she'd done it all to herself. She hadn't even bothered to find out his name, let alone other simple details of his life, such as whether he was married. He had treated her differently than anyone else ever had before. He'd laughed with her and been a little cruel to her. He had treated her as a person, not some fragile figurine to be kept away from life, safe in a bell jar. She had become intrigued by him, and so she'd assumed he'd found her intriguing in turn.

And she had wanted him to remain a stranger, because it had been safer that way.

Yet he probably hadn't thought of her from their one meeting to the next. He'd only wanted to distract her, the way one would a child, perhaps charm her a little, so that he could use her dock for his gunrunning without being arrested for trespassing. And that time in the meadow—that had been merely a whim; he'd said so himself. An opportunity to teach a spoiled little rich girl that foxes had families.

A child. A spoiled little rich girl. That was how he'd seen her, how he'd thought of her, if he'd thought of her at all. And as for what she had ever wanted from him . . . that she couldn't even formulate into a thought, let alone put into words to describe as something real. What was real was what she'd seen in his face that night when he walked past her down the stairs, carrying Bria McKenna in his arms.

She had seen the look of a man who was watching his beloved wife die before his eyes, slowly, breath by breath.

Emma stood among the cattails and asters in the yard, with the cat Gorgeous curling around her legs. "Thank you for inviting me into your home," she said to Bria McKenna.

But when she held out her hand, the other woman didn't take it.

"Those things in your carriage," Bria said. "I know they were meant for us. You meant to bring them here as charity for us."

Emma's hand fell to her side, and a warmth spread up her neck. "I intended no insult, truly. I only thought . . ." Her mouth twisted a little. "I guess I didn't think."

Bria searched her face until Emma wanted to look away, although she didn't. "I'm mindful of your kindness in the offering, you understand," Bria said.

"You don't have to explain." Emma waved her hand, her flush deepening.

"It's my Shay. It would hurt him so if he thought I don't trust that he can provide for me and the girls."

"Of course. I mean, I do understand."

"But I don't want you to think it's all about pride, mine and his. He *does* provide for us. It's just that money and

Shay haven't always had an easy time of it. Oh, he makes certain to take care of me and the girls when the shillings and pennies are rolling in, but he's forever giving such a good bit of it away. To the church, and to charities—orphans and widows and pretty much anyone who needs it more than we. And he gives to the cause, of course. Him being such the Irishman and not happy unless he's dabbling one way or t'other in the rebellion." She stopped to draw in a breath. "I don't want you to think ill of him, of my Shay."

As she spoke her man's name, Bria's mouth softened and a lightness suffused her face, as if a thousand candles had suddenly flared into life behind her eyes. Why, she loves him, Emma thought, she loves him desperately. And she didn't know why this should startle her so. Had she assumed that a woman who worked in a cotton mill and lived in a clapboard shack wouldn't know of love?

The shack was on the water side of Thames Street. Behind it stretched the bay, shining flat and silvery like a pewter platter beneath the noon sun. Emma stared at it a moment, and then her gaze shifted back to Bria's face. "Mrs. McKenna . . . would it be an imposition if I called on you again?"

She saw surprise come into the other woman's face, and a certain wariness. "You're welcome to," Bria said after a moment, although unspoken was the thought: *But why ever should you want to?*

"I do," Emma said, smiling suddenly without calculation, and without feeling shy about it. "I do and I will."

And she did. Not waiting until a week later, as was proper, but coming the very next day.

That time she found Bria on her knees at the bottom of the

front stoop, stabbing a spade into the dirt. Bria had pulled out the cattails and asters and was now planting violets.

She tilted her head back, squinting against the sun, as Emma came toward her up the path. "I've time now to do this," she said, as if she wasn't at all surprised to see Miss Emma Tremayne coming to pay another call, and so soon. As if she was glad to see her. "Now that I'm no longer working in the mill and my brother's idea of housekeeping seems to be to pat me on the head and tell me to go put my feet up."

That morning Emma wore a dress of pink taffeta and lace, but she didn't spare it a thought as she knelt beside Bria in the dirt. "What can I do?" she said.

Bria pointed to a clump of fleshy chickweed. Deep laughter lightened her dark eyes. "You could wrap your hands around that big boyo over yonder and give him a good yank. Pull him up by the roots."

Emma looked at the weed as if she feared it would bite her. "Very well," she said. "I'll do it." But before she did it, she took off her gloves and plunged her hands into the freshly turned flower bed. The feel of it, warm and moist, thrilled her.

The feeling stayed with her well into the afternoon, when she was scrubbing the dirt out from beneath her nails in her private bathroom with its stenciled tile walls and fixtures of sterling silver. It was almost, she thought, as though she'd done something a little wicked, pushing her naked hands through moist, warm earth.

When she walked from the bathroom into her bedroom, she was startled to find her mother standing before the lacquered peacock dressing screen. Startled and a little frightened, as though she'd been caught out in her wickedness.

"Where," her mama said in a drawl that was slow and thick, "have you been?" They were due for tea at Mrs. Hamilton's in less than an hour, and Bethel was already dressed in a midnight-blue broché satin gown encrusted with thousands of shiny jet bugle beads.

Emma sat on the velvet plush stool before her dressing table. The red silk kimono-style dressing gown she wore gaped open, and she quickly pulled it closed. She felt strangely vulnerable, as if she were about to be stripped naked.

Bethel came up behind her in a rustle of stiff satin, and for a moment Emma's gaze met her mother's in the mirror, then veered away.

"You will give me the courtesy of an answer," Bethel said.

Emma reached for her silver-backed hairbrush, but her hand shook and so she let it fall to her lap. She stared down at the dresser's linen runner with its tiny embroidered primroses.

"I've been calling on a new friend of mine . . . a Mrs. McKenna."

She wasn't surprised to hear her mother gasp at that very Irish of names. They were considered a lower form of life, the Irish. Violent drunkards and lazy scalawags. One hired them to scrub one's floors and to muck out one's stables. One did not pay them visits and call them friends.

"She's the woman I cared for here after she fell ill during the Queen of May procession," Emma hurried on in the face of her mother's shocked silence. "You know, Sunday last when you were so under the weather yourself and Uncle Stanton was nowhere to be found? I'm sure Carrews must have told you about it." Carrews was their butler and he told Mama everything, even though she sometimes pretended not to hear.

Bethel waved away this explanation with a flutter of her white-gloved hand. "Are you telling me that you have paid a call on that—that . . ."

"Oh, well!" Emma said on a bright gust of breath. She

traced the *E* engraved in the silver of her brush with one clean fingernail. "One sees the same people day after day and it can get to be so tiresome. It's diverting to pass the time occasionally with someone not of our set."

Her stomach felt heavy and queasy, as if she'd suddenly taken seasick. She knew that if her mother were to forbid her to pay any more calls on Bria McKenna, she would be defiant and do it anyway.

"We shared a rather pleasant conversation over tea, Mrs. McKenna and I. She was telling me about the weather in Ireland. It rains a lot." She snatched up the brush and began to pull it through her hair. "Rather dreary, I should think, but at least there are few surprises in it."

Her mother paced from the peacock screen to the marble fireplace, kicking at her skirts with the satin toes of her slippers. "You can get such strange notions at times, I swear you must be a changeling, for you can't possibly be a child of mine. A woman faints in the street and you stop to assist her, and that is one thing—although, why . . . But still . . . And yet it is quite another thing to take that same woman up as an acquaintance. You deliver charity baskets to the poor coloreds in Goree every third Sunday, but they would never think to invite you into their homes. It just isn't done."

"Why isn't it done?"

Bethel turned, her face bearing a strangely haunted look. "It isn't done," she finally said, "because the lower races have learned to keep their humble distance from us Great Folk, as well they should."

"Perhaps it's never done because they believe us to be a bunch of boring snobs, and they are right in their assumption. But Mrs. McKenna has twice graciously asked me into her home, and I have accepted. She is a respectable married woman—"

"Respectable! She is *Irish*."

Emma set down the hairbrush and opened a tortoiseshell

hairpin box. She gathered up her hair and began to arrange it in a smooth seashell pouf. But there was such a trembling going on inside her, the loose bodice of her kimono quivered with it.

"I shall ask Geoffrey what he thinks," she said, calling once again on her newfound power as Geoffrey Alcott's betrothed and the Tremayne family's only, and soon-to-be-realized, hope. "He, at least, seems to approve of the things I do."

He wouldn't approve of this thing, though. As little as she thought she knew of him at times, that much she did know. Geoffrey had strong feelings about one's place in the world and the proper order of things, and he did not like them questioned or disturbed.

Emma braved a glance at her mother in the mirror. Bethel had tangled her fingers in her jet necklace and was staring hard at the cabbage roses on the carpet. She spoke as though to herself, "Whispers . . . there'll be whispering again, like at the ball. And what if we're found out? We can't be found out."

"What? Find out what?" Emma had never seen her mother in such a distracted state, but then she had lately taken to dosing herself not only with laudanum but with Maddie's chloral hydrate. She claimed it dulled her appetite. "Mama? Are you . . . are you feeling well?"

Bethel jerked, swinging around. "Never mind, then," she said, waving a trembling hand through the air. "Never mind."

Emma let out a deep, shaky breath. She wasn't sure herself just how much she'd been bluffing, but she wouldn't have to find out yet, because her mama wasn't going to call it.

Bethel thrust her shoulders back and marched toward her daughter. "Here, let me do that, for heaven's sake," she said, taking the ivory hairpins from Emma's hand. "You are making an utter mess of it. You don't know how fortunate you are to have such long, thick hair to work with, when the rest of us must make do with rats and switches and falls."

She stabbed the pins so hard into Emma's hair she pricked the scalp. "Poor Mr. Alcott might be besotted with you for the moment, but he can hardly be expected to indulge your eccentricities indefinitely, and neither can society. I declare, Emma, it has always been a struggle to get you to conduct yourself appropriately to your station in life. You go out sailing by yourself for hours at a time, and never mind that you're a Bristolian and a Tremayne, it is still hoydenish behavior for a girl of twenty-two. And what you do out in the old orangery—I'll not call it art, for it certainly is not. Disgraceful is what it is. But this latest. Befriending this nonperson—an *Irish*woman. It is so . . . so undignified."

"It is a kindness," Emma said, and she felt a twinge of shame. For if anyone was being kind and indulgent it was Bria McKenna. "Mrs. McKenna is new to Bristol and so she has few friends. What's more, she can't go out much, for she is in a delicate condition."

"She sounds as common as clay." Her mama's hands fell onto Emma's shoulders and she gripped them hard, twisting Emma around on the stool. "Why are you doing this to me? It's because of what happened that night, isn't it? You're trying to punish me like your father is punishing me."

Her mother's words so shocked Emma that for a moment she couldn't speak. "I'm not trying to punish you, Mama," she finally said, her voice breaking at the edges. Because maybe she did want her mother punished, and herself punished as well. "You . . . you said we are not to talk about it."

Her mother's fingers dug into her shoulders, hard, and then she pushed away. She pressed the back of her hand against her forehead. "I don't know how I shall survive these months until you are safely married."

"If I really wanted to be a trial to you, I could become one of those 'new women' the newspapers and magazines have been going on about. I could take up smoking cigarettes and bicycling. Or I could organize a girl's baseball team right here in Bristol and we could all wear bloomers. Do you think Monsieur Worth would design me a pair?"

Bethel shuddered, and the face she turned to her daughter was soft and yellow as old wax. Emma felt mean for having done that, tormenting her mother with words even if she hadn't meant them. Mama had always been as scared of scandal as people used to be afraid of catching smallpox.

Emma's gaze fell to the fingers she had clutched in her lap. "I was only joking, Mama."

"I do not find you the least bit amusing in such a mood, Emma." Her mother turned on her heel and walked stiffly to the door. "You hurry up and finish dressing. We're going to be unpardonably late as it is."

Emma watched the door close behind her mother's back. She was a tumble of feelings: guilt and fear, and a wild sort of excitement. She might not be a new woman, but she felt like a new Emma.

She heard the hum and click of Maddie's wheelchair and she looked around to find that her sister was being pushed through the door by her maid from the sitting room they shared.

The maid guided the chair up onto the plush carpet and over next to the big tester bed. Maddie dismissed the girl with a nod and a quiet thank-you and then cocked her head, pretending to study her sister carefully. "You are a paradox, Emma Tremayne. I've seen you blush six shades of violet when someone you've known for twenty years so much as wishes you a good morning. Yet you just stood up to our formidable mama without turning an eyelash."

"That's because my eyelashes were too frozen with fear to turn," Emma said. They shared a smile, then, although Emma's lips trembled.

She wondered how much Maddie had heard, if she'd understood what their mama had meant when she'd spoken of punishment. Willie and what had happened the night he drowned was a subject she and her sister had never broached. Maddie never spoke of Willie at all, for he had been responsible for the accident that had put her in a wheelchair. And Emma thought that even with him dead, Maddie had yet to forgive him.

Maddie leaned over to touch the white lace and crepe bib on the lilac muslin tea dress that was laid out on the bed, along with a fresh set of silk and lace underthings. "You and Mama are going out?"

"To tea at Mrs. Hamilton's."

Emma got up and went to sit on the bed, facing her sister's chair. She picked up a sheer lisle stocking and leaned back to pull it onto her leg. "And, oh, I do so not want to go. She will serve day-old pastries, even though she's rich enough to buy the contents of a dozen bakeries. And she'll entertain us, as she does every time, by playing the same Chopin interlude on a piano that hasn't been tuned in forty years. We'll be seeing the same people we saw yesterday and the day before that . . ." Emma rolled the top of the stocking down over a pink silk garter. "You would hate it, Maddie."

At the silence that followed this pronouncement, Emma looked up. Although Maddie had averted her face, Emma thought she saw a sheen of tears in her sister's eyes.

"No, I wouldn't," Maddie said softly.

Emma's gaze fell back to her lap. She put a pleat in her kimono robe, then smoothed it out again. "No, probably not." She pushed her breath out in a small sigh. "It's just me being foolish, I suppose. And it's gotten worse since I've become engaged to Geoffrey. I feel on display everywhere I go, like some butterfly on a pin. Everyone always stares so, and you know how I hate that."

"They stare because you're beautiful, Emma, and you seem to have grown more so ever since you and Geoffrey proclaimed your devotion to the world. You can quite take one's breath away when one glances up to catch you in certain poses—"

"I don't *pose*," Emma protested, her cheeks flaming.

"Perhaps not consciously. But no matter what you're doing, all your limbs somehow manage to arrange themselves in the most graceful way possible. And there's always such a play of feelings on your face—it's as though one were watching a rose burst into blossom all at once, from bud to full and glorious bloom." Maddie's mouth curved into an impish smile. "Having said that, I now expect you to go to Mrs. Hamilton's and behave the whole afternoon in a perfectly ordinary manner."

Emma couldn't help smiling as well, although her face still burned with embarrassment. "Perhaps I'll do something audacious and outrageous instead," she said. "Perhaps I'll beg Mrs. Hamilton for some fresh cream to go along with my stale scone."

They laughed together, but Maddie was the first to fall quiet. She cocked her head to stare at Emma again.

"You're changing, Em. I do believe it must come from being so much in love."

It was a startling thought to Emma—that Geoffrey had done this to her. That her feelings for him could be so powerful that they would change what she was inside herself.

"I wish I knew for certain what it felt like to be in love," she said. "There are moments when I feel so lighthearted and giddy, and I smile for no reason, and I want to twirl around and around until I make myself dizzy, except that I'm already dizzy. And then there are other moments when there's such a fierce and lonely ache in my chest, and I find myself mourning things I can't even name, and wishing for things that seem wild and crazy and impossible . . ."

She leaned forward and seized Maddie's hands, which were clasped together on her lap rug. "Oh, Maddie, do you think that's love?"

Maddie's gaze fell away from Emma. She looked down at their entwined fingers, hiding her thoughts. "Yes," she said. "I do."

~

As if to establish her privilege to do so, Emma paid another visit to the house on Thames Street the very next day—the third in a row. But this time Bria wasn't at home.

As a matter of habit, Emma opened her black lizard chatelaine bag and took out one of her gilt-edged, embossed calling cards. It was only when she was looking around for a place to put it that Emma had to laugh at herself. As if there would be a silver tray sitting on Bria McKenna's front stoop where one could leave a bit of pasteboard as proof of one's proper intentions.

She came calling again, though, late the very next afternoon. On her way home from a couple of hours spent with Geoffrey attending a travelogue at the lyceum on the wonders of Indonesia. She hadn't realized it was an off-Saturday, when the day shift ended early at the mill, until the door opened at her knock and she was looking down into a bright, smiling face framed by orange curls.

"Why, hello, Merry," Emma said. "We meet again."

The little girl's smile widened, and two round dimples the size of pennies indented her cheeks. She hummed fiercely and spun around on one foot in a circle.

A little alarmed at these strange antics, Emma peered around the jamb to look for Bria just as an older girl came to the door. She had skinny, awkward limbs that seemed all elbows and knees, and her brown hair was twisted into such tight braids they stuck out from the sides of her face like jug handles.

"What do you keep coming around here for?" she said.

"Noreen!" Bria appeared in the doorway, her hands falling on the older girl's shoulders. "Shame on you, lass," she scolded, giving her a little shake. "Show Miss Tremayne you've been taught proper manners."

The girl dropped into a stiff curtsey. But then she jerked her pointed chin into the air and scowled at Emma as if challenging her to find anything the least bit likable around her. Emma responded by loving her instantly.

"How do you do, Noreen," Emma said, giving the girl her brightest smile.

The girl turned to her mother, and Emma caught the sparkle of angry tears held back in her eyes. "Merry *said* the angel would be coming today."

Bria tucked loose wisps of hair back into one of her daughter's braids. Both girls were covered with the sooty grime and lint from the cotton mill. "Did she, then?" Bria said. "And I suppose the fairies told her as much?"

Merry hummed loudly, shaking her head so hard her curls bounced.

Noreen watched her sister's face intently, listening. She turned back to her mother again and shrugged. "She just knew."

Bria caught Emma's eye, giving a little shrug herself. "They think you're an angel."

"Oh, surely not," Emma protested, flushing.

"Better than being mistaken for the devil, I suppose," Bria said, and her eyes squinted with such teasing laughter that Emma couldn't help smiling.

Bria smiled back at her, then she gave Noreen a little nudge. "You girls wash up now." She linked arms with Emma, pulling her into the kitchen. "I'm making *colcannon* for supper. That's a good Irish dish if ever there was one, and sure, then, if it isn't my Shay's favorite. It's made of mashed potato and cabbage, which is fried in milk and butter with a wee bit of nutmeg added. Why don't you share a bite with us?"

Emma suddenly couldn't get a deep breath or control the curious racing of her heart. It was the off-Saturday, which meant short shifts for the mill and rubber factory and the onion fields, and that meant families would be gathering to share the afternoon meal, and that meant . . .

"Thank you," she said. "I'm sure it's delicious, but I really shouldn't stay. No doubt your . . . Mr. McKenna will be coming home shortly, and I . . ."

She didn't want to come face to face with Bria's husband, not that she thought about him much anymore. She'd decided that she couldn't have been infatuated with the man, because she was going to marry Geoffrey. She was in love with Geoffrey; everybody said so. They could see it on her face.

As for the Irishman—she might allow that what she'd felt for him had been a certain *interest.* It was just that she still felt such shame when she remembered the thoughts that had leaped into her head that night.

She would never have gone off with him into the storm, though, not even if she really had been the one he'd come for. She'd never been the brave Emma of her imaginings.

"Oh, Shay won't be home till long after sunset this day, because the striped bass are running," Bria was saying. She had let go of Emma's arm to go stir a pot on the stove. "He's just bought himself a fishing dory with money borrowed from Mr. Delaney, who owns the Crow's Nest. He don't like owing to a saloonkeeper, does Shay, but he was that desperate to get out of the onion fields. And sure if no Yankee bank is going to be throwing money at the head of an Irishman—"

Bria dropped the ladle into the pot, splattering gravy, and

her hands flew up to her flaming cheeks. "*Dhia*, what've I said?" She whirled and looked at Emma with stricken eyes. "Oh, Miss Tremayne. Don't you be telling me the banker's an uncle, or some such."

Emma sucked on the inside of her lower lip to hide a smile. "Well, he's a cousin. Once removed. And he's rather reluctant to throw money at anyone's head, I'm afraid. My father once accused him of sitting on his investments and trying to hatch them like a brood hen."

Bria sputtered a little laugh. "*Och*, still you'd think I'd learn to mind me tongue." She pointed a stiff finger at her daughters, who still stood just inside the front door, their eyes riveted on Emma. "And didn't I just tell you girls to do something?"

Merry ran to Emma and held up her hands, humming a tune that was sweet and pleading.

Emma looked at Noreen, who seemed to be the interpreter for her sister's strange way of communicating. A wariness lingered in Noreen's pinched face. She stood braced, with her hands clenched at her sides, as if expecting a fight. She'll not be won over easily, Emma thought, and loved her all the more for it.

Meanwhile, Merry's humming had reached the crescendo of a shriek.

"Nory," Bria said. "Have some mercy on our ears and tell us what your sister wants, then."

A challenge flashed in Noreen's eyes as she looked at Emma, but she answered her mother readily enough. "She's saying she wants the lady to wash her hands for her."

"Me?" Emma looked behind her, as if someone else had suddenly appeared in the kitchen.

Merry hummed and nodded and spun once around on one foot.

The shack, Emma discovered, didn't have either a bathing room or a water closet; it had no hot-water pipes. What it did have was a washstand with curtains of patterned cretonne, and a chipped white enameled basin and pitcher.

While Bria filled the basin, Emma cupped the little girl's hands between her own and dipped them into the water. She gathered up a dab of soap in her palms and ever so gently rubbed those hands, so small in hers. Merry hummed, a gentle lullaby that quivered into a bright, excited trill.

The water was cold. The soap, rough with pumice and lye, stung Emma's pampered skin. The huck towel Bria handed her was stiff from having been dried before the stove and smelled of coal dust. But all Emma knew was a sense of wonderment that such a small thing as washing a little girl's hands could make her feel so full up inside with happiness.

Chapter Fifteen

She was a wonder to herself when she was at the house on Thames Street. And when she left there and went back to her other life, her Great Folk life, she carried with her a lingering sense of unease. The faintest conviction that she had known what it was like for a time to be someone else.

She brought the children little presents, lemon balls and hair ribbons. She brought Bria a box of petit-point handkerchiefs, and a Currier and Ives lithograph of a thatch-roofed village nestled among green rolling hills. It was called *Life in the Old Country*, and the look of real joy on Bria's face as she held it in her hands made Emma feel as though she'd just given her friend the world.

Her friend. Emma wasn't sure when that, too, had become real. Perhaps it had always been so, and they had only needed the courage to discover each other.

She came every day that week, in between Great Folk garden parties and teas and afternoon at-homes. Most times she came openly, but other times she was at the Thames Street house when Mama thought she was sailing, or sculpting in the old orangery.

On Sunday she sat at the table in the kitchen with the flowered wallpaper and scrubbed linoleum floor, watching

Bria comb kerosene through Merry's hair to get rid of the lice. The kitchen smelled of steam and soft soap, for Bria had a copper full of linens on to boil.

"They pick them up at the mill," Bria said, her mouth and nose wrinkling with disgust. "No matter how hard and often I scrub their heads." She pointed the comb's tail at Emma. "You Americans, always bragging on your land of milk and honey. I say better you should call it the land of cattails and cooties."

Emma looked down at the pattern she was tracing in the brown oilcloth so that Bria couldn't see her smile. "There aren't any cooties in Ireland?"

"*Cooties* in Ireland? Go on with you!"

Merry hummed, a long, flat tune that lilted up on the end like a question. But Noreen wasn't around to tell them what she'd said.

Earlier, Bria had confided that little Merry hadn't spoken a word in almost three years, since "some troubles" back in Ireland. But Emma knew she hadn't imagined the child speaking real words that day in front of Pardon Hardy's Drugstore. She kept it to herself, though. She understood a little girl's need to keep some things secret, even from those you love.

So while Merry hummed, Emma leaned forward to rearrange the flowers in the tomato can that sat in the middle of the table. They were white daisies and wild irises this time. "I think she's trying to ask you something about Ireland. Was it so long ago that you left there?"

Bria patted the mound of her belly. "Sure and I should always be able to remember the day I first set foot in America, what with this one about to be making his appearance now these nine months later," she said. But then the smile that had started to pull at her mouth seemed to catch, twisting it. Shadows moved, like clouds, over her eyes.

She grew quiet after that, and Emma thought she could almost see the memories come over her and settle deep.

"Will you tell me a little of your life there?" Emma said. "Can you bear to?"

Bria gave a little shrug with her shoulders, as if to throw off the weight of any sadness. "*A mhuire*. I could numb your ears with the stories I could tell of the *ould* country," she said, the Irish brogue curling thick now on her tongue. "My own birth, you mind, was not regarded as a blessing in my family, what with my father dying three weeks before of the sweating sickness. There was only the three of us, after that: my mother and my brother and myself. We worked for Squire Varney, any farm work he'd give us, but mostly breaking up clods in a potato bed with a spade."

She paused in the combing of her daughter's hair and looked around her, her mouth curling into a wry smile. "And our *shibeen* now—*och*, it would make this house look like a palace. Just the four stone walls thatched with straw, with a hole cut in it for a chimney and no windows so it was always dark. For a time we had us a pig and he lived in the house along with us."

Emma caught a startled laugh with her hand. "Surely not."

"Aye, and he ate better than we did, too. Mam was always saying that pig was worth a sight more than Donagh and me since we couldn't be slaughtered and made into bacon."

Emma laughed again and this time Bria joined her. And Merry, her humming swelling into happy shrieks. They laughed together, loud whoops that filled the kitchen and felt good.

Bria ended her laughter with a gentle sigh, and Emma thought she'd become caught up in sweeter memories now. She looked up, her gaze going to the lithograph Emma had given her, where it hung now in a position of honor above the holy water font.

"The place you came from," Emma said, "does it look like that?"

"As sweetly green, surely. But it's a wilder land. Our village, or *clachan*, as we say, is called Gortadoo, which means 'black fields' in English. It's on the tip of county Kerry, where the land gives way to the sea. The fishing isn't so good as you might think, though, but you won't starve long as you have a boat and a net. The land itself is poor, rocky and rain-soaked, and good for little else than growing a few potatoes. But, oh, is it green. And every shade of it from dark to light. A rainbow of green . . ."

Bria's shoulders jerked, as if she'd suddenly come awake from a deep sleep. "Will you listen to myself describe the place. You'd wonder why I wept so when I left it."

"Why did you leave?"

It was a moment before Emma realized that her question had been met with silence. That Merry, standing between her mother's knees, with her hair dripping kerosene, had gone utterly still with the kind of quiet that wells up from a place deep within. That Bria's face shone pale and was sheened with sweat.

Then Bria coughed, a harsh, ragged sound. She took out her handkerchief and coughed into it again, covering her whole face with the cloth, and Emma thought she might have been hiding tears, as well.

Emma looked carefully away. "Forgive me for prying into your troubles."

Bria stuffed the handkerchief back into the sleeve of her butternut shirtwaist. "Prying? God save us," she said on an expulsion of breath that was close to a laugh. "Nobody can talk like we Irish can, and trouble is the subject dearest to our hearts."

Emma's gaze came back to Bria, and they shared a smile. A smile that deepened, altered, and became something more.

Became an understanding that Emma *felt*, as surely as if they'd reached across the table and clasped hands.

"God save us," Bria said again, after a long and tender silence had passed between them. "I've got to get this child's head washed."

She stood up and steered Merry by her shoulders over to the washstand. "Would you mind giving those sheets a stir?"

After a moment Emma realized with a start that Bria had been speaking to her. She didn't even try to hold back the smile that broke across her face as she got up from the table and went to the stove. If Bria could ask her to share in the chores, then it must mean they were becoming true friends.

Emma felt some trepidation, though, as she folded back the cover of the steaming copper cauldron, for she'd never done such a thing before. She picked up the wooden paddle and began to stir, or rather she tried to. She was surprised at how difficult a task it was; the water-logged linens were heavy and hard to push around.

Blinking against the lye fumes that stung her eyes, she looked up and out the window . . . and saw Shay McKenna come into the yard. *Run* into the yard, where he stopped, his chest heaving. He wasn't wearing a shirt, and even from where she was, here in the kitchen, she could see how the sweat gleamed on his bare skin. His chest and shoulders were sun-browned and strapped with muscle.

She looked away from him, and her hands that gripped the paddle grew still. She felt so strange, her skin tight all over, too small for her body. It was the memory of that night, of her secret and foolish imaginings, she thought. It made her uncomfortable with herself.

She felt Bria come up behind her to look out the window, as well. "He's been running," Bria said.

He'd been standing with his hands on his hips, watching the road while he got his breath back, but now he turned around and looked toward the house.

Emma jerked back out of sight behind the yellow gingham curtains, a blush stinging her cheeks. "But what is he running from?"

"Just running in circles and getting nowhere. Typical man."

Bria drew closer to the window and touched the glass pane. Touched it gently with her fingers, as she would touch the man, and Emma was caught up in the change that came over her friend's face. Love shone from it, as blinding as a white desert sun.

Emma wondered if she had ever looked at Geoffrey in such a way. She doubted so, because she already knew that never in her life had her heart felt a thing that deeply.

"He's in training, as he calls it," Bria said. "Building his wind up for an exhibition of the science of bare-knuckle boxing. He'll be doing it here in Bristol on your Fourth of July."

"But why?" Emma exclaimed, horrified by the very thought. She knew it for a barbaric sport, violent and lawless and patronized only by the dregs of society.

"For the prize money, of course. Or so he says." Bria lifted her fingers off the glass. She curled her hand into a fist before she brought it back down to her side. "Always fighting something, is Seamus McKenna, one way or t'other. I sometimes wonder if men don't just fight for the love of it."

She turned to the washstand where little Merry waited, still caught fast in that odd stillness, her hair dripping water now instead of kerosene. Bria wrapped a towel around the child's head, rubbing it dry.

Emma was drawn to look back out the window, at the man in the yard. He had put on a blue chambray shirt that was worn thin from repeated washings. Already he'd sweated through it, so that it clung to his back and shoulders. He does have a brawler's body, she thought, hardened, battered . . . brutal.

"Prizefighting," she said aloud. "Imagine such a thing."

"He once was bare-knuckle champion of Ireland, was my Shay," Bria said, pride coloring her voice a bit.

She had gone to sit in her rocking chair so that she could put Merry between her splayed knees and comb out the damp, tangled curls. But the child squirmed loose and ran out the door, banging it hard behind her.

Bria stared at the closed door, but Emma thought she was seeing beyond it, to the man outside. "For a lark one morning, at the horse fair over t' Shannon way, he stepped into a ring to go a round with some fellow who was being billed as the champion of Dublin. Shay laid him out flat with his second punch, and the next thing we knew he was being paid good coin to take on any and all contenders himself."

Her gaze fell to the comb she still held in her hand, gripped so tightly now that the teeth bit into her flesh. "Paid to get his poor self pounded bloody every summer's Sunday afternoon." Sighing, she dropped the comb into her big apron pocket and pushed heavily to her feet. "But then as Shay himself used to say, a champion is only the poor *slieveen* who's left standing at the end of it."

Bria came back to the window again. She looked at him, at her man, and she touched him with her eyes the way she'd touched the glass a moment before.

"At every fair and race day throughout Ireland he fought, until that sorrow's own day when he killed a man with those fists of his."

Emma nearly gasped aloud. Her eyes, of their own accord, searched for Shay McKenna out in the yard. But he was gone now.

"He kept getting back up, you see," Bria went on, although her voice was strangely flat now, as if she were reading the words from a newspaper account. "Shay would knock him down, and he would get back up, and so Shay would hit him again, hurt him bad, and so down he would go, and back up he would come, again and again, until Shay hit him one time too many or one time too hard, and then he didn't get back up. And maybe Shay hadn't set out to kill him, but surely at the end of it the poor fool of a man was still stone dead."

She looked around at Emma, and the pain in her eyes seemed to have swallowed the world. "We are all of us both light and dark, do you not find it so, Miss Tremayne? Wanting in our hearts to do right and able to do wrong. And so it's the choices we've made, surely, that make of us what we are—"

Bria's last word broke apart as a thick, ragged cough tore out of her chest, then another and another and another. Emma wrapped her arm around Bria's waist, taking her weight while her shoulders shook and heaved.

And when the coughing finally subsided, she brushed the fever-damp hair off Bria's forehead and held her closer.

The door opened, and they pulled slowly apart.

Shay McKenna stood at the threshold with Merry in the crook of one arm, her legs wrapped around his hips. Noreen held on tight to his other hand, and she was looking up at him as if he'd just hung the moon and the stars.

Merry hummed a bright little tune. She tugged at her father's ear, turning his head so that she could plant a loud, smacking kiss on his cheek.

"Just look at who I found hanging around our front yard, Mam," Noreen said, her dark eyes shining with laughter. "He says he's hungry enough to eat a bear, tooth and claws and hair!"

Bria thrust her handkerchief with its bloody smears into her apron pocket, but not before her husband saw it. His face seemed to turn darker, harder, and his eyes grew shadowed.

Bria averted her head, as though she couldn't bear to meet those eyes.

And Emma, standing there watching them, wondered how they could bear it.

"Oh, mercy," Bria said, trying to tuck flyaway curls back into the thick roll of hair at the nape of her neck. "You've gone and caught me with the wash on to boil, instead of the tea."

"Neverrr you be minding that," Shay McKenna said, lapsing into his stage Irish brogue. He came all the way inside, leaving the door open. He set Merry on her feet and herded the girls toward the washstand. "You lot scrub up and have a sit down, and I'll be seeing if I can't put me hands around a kettle without burnin' all ten of me thumbs."

Both the girls giggled, and he flashed a grin at them. Then his gaze went back to his wife and he smiled at her, as well, and Emma saw how his eyes burned with love and a sweet tenderness. She wondered if Geoffrey had ever looked at her like that. She thought she would give up all she had in the world to have a man look at her like that.

He passed by Emma on his way to the stove. "Good day to you, Miss Tremayne," he said. She realized he had yet to look at her, and he didn't do so now.

"Good afternoon, Mr. McKenna," she said in her drawing-room voice, though she found it odd to say his name.

He was only an ordinary man; she knew that now. An immigrant fisherman with a wife and two little girls and another babe on the way. She knew him for what he was, so she couldn't understand why her heart was beating so crazily, as if he'd come to her again from out of her own wild imaginings.

"I . . . I really ought to be leaving," Emma said.

Bria linked arms with her, pulling her over to the table. "No, you really ought not to. You'll come take tea with us. All of us."

Emma would think about it often in the days to come. While playing tennis with Geoffrey on his court at the Hope Street mansion, and going with Miss Liluth on Tuesday to wait for the train to Providence. While dining alone at The Birches with only the clink of sterling silver against bone china for company . . . She would think about that hour she'd spent having tea with the McKenna family. All of the McKennas.

She sat with Bria and the girls at the table, watching him put the kettle on to boil. When he brought a loaf of brown bread to the table he stopped to rub Merry's marigold curls. When he laid out the cups and saucers he paused to squeeze his wife's shoulder and lean over to whisper something in her ear that made her smile. He teased Noreen about her giving some boy named Rory a bloody nose, and then gave the girl's own nose a playful pinch as they laughed together. Emma had never known a man, never known anyone, for laughing and teasing and touching the way he did.

She wondered if Geoffrey would ever behave in such a way with her and their children; but of course he would not. It wasn't done—to display your feelings so openly before the world. Not even your own heart was allowed to know the secrets of its deep affections and fond hopes. Its dark desires.

She tried to remember if she'd ever felt the touch of her own father's hand in her hair. When she shut her eyes she saw only a tall man in an elegant black frock coat and top hat. To Emma, her father's eyes had always seemed focused on exotic distances no one else could see, on dreams no one else could share. Except . . . except for that one magical summer when he'd taught her to sail. Only then had he seemed of this world, and she had been there with him. Those rare blue days on the little racing sloop he'd had built especially for her, running before the wind. They had been happy together in those moments, the two of them. She could remember that.

And her own father had never sent her to work in a mill.

She looked at Shay McKenna, at his scarred and battered face, at his eyes so startling in their intensity. He still looked like the dark marauder of her wild imaginings, but he was not that man. She understood that now.

This was a man who had to watch his wife die a little more with her every breath and his children go off to toil in a cotton mill, and yet he still gave to those he believed needed it more. A rebel who fought on for a land, a place of black rock and bogs and thatched-roofed hovels, that he would likely never see again. A man of violence who had once killed with his bare hands, the same hands that so tenderly touched his daughter's hair.

This man she had come to know through Bria's eyes, through Bria's words:

"I was wild for the lad, and him forever with his nose in a book and the love of every other girl in the breast of his shirt."

"It was how he earned our living back home in Ireland—with a curragh and a string of nets."

"It's not happy, he is, if he's not living with his heart in his throat and the wild words always on the tip of his tongue."

"He has fists the size of pie plates, but he's never raised them in anger to me or the girls. Not even when he has the drop in him."

"The dog's leg was hopelessly caught in the rocks and Squire Varney was all for shooting it, when my Shay opens his mouth and next I know we've a three-legged hound taking up the warmest spot in front of our fire."

"He could've forgiven God his father's death, but not hers. I sometimes fear that when he put her in that black hole, he buried his faith in there along with her."

Only an ordinary man.

But not to Bria.

These last days, the hours and moments of talk and sharing, and still Emma hadn't truly understood until now. How Bria's love for her man, her need for him, pumped like life blood through the whole of her—elemental, essential, eternal. Shay McKenna was the sun of her world. And when she spoke of him, her face blossomed like a flower.

Emma wondered what her own face looked like when she spoke of Geoffrey. But then she thought: I have never spoken of Geoffrey in this house. Not once had she talked with Bria about the man she would marry and the life they would have together and the dreams they would share, and she wondered now why this was so.

Tea splashed into the cup in front of her, releasing a pungent steam that bathed her face. Lost in her thoughts, she looked up and into Shay McKenna's face. For the length of a breath, he smiled at her.

"Th-thank you," she said. "I mean, for the tea," she added, flushing.

"You are welcome," he said. "For the tea."

Her gaze fell away from his, down to the blue-checked napkin spread across her lap. His smile had disturbed her. She couldn't measure its meaning or her reaction to it. It had soothed and frightened her at the same time.

Shay sat down at the table, which he'd laid out with a simple meal of brown bread, head cheese, and *chourice*—the spicy sausage the *bravas* sold from their dimly lit stores smelling of olive oil.

The kitchen fell into a moment of quiet, and then Merry's hum tinkled brightly, like silver chimes.

Noreen covered her mouth with her hand, catching a giggle. "She says Da's been boxing shadows."

Their father leaned over the table to aim a mock blow at Merry's face, his knuckles brushing her nose as gently as a kiss, and the little girl squirmed in her chair and hummed in delight. "It's a thing called shadowboxing, Nory," he said.

"And who is the better pugilist, Mr. McKenna—yourself or your shadow?" Emma said.

She saw him go still for the briefest of moments, as though he were as surprised as she was that she had spoken up. Then he leaned back in his chair and hooked his thumbs in the pockets of his corduroy britches, and she knew he'd put on the Irish even before he opened his mouth.

"The better pugilist, do you ask, Miss Tremayne? Why, 'tis meself, of course, and it's mortally offended I am that you would be suspecting otherwise. For sure if I didn't give that shadow of mine such a proper belting, it's hard set he was to go slinking out the door ahead of me."

"Hunh," Bria sniffed. "It's surprised I am you made it out the door at all, Shay McKenna, what with the head on you being another of the great wonders of the world, so big is it."

Shay clutched at his heart as if he'd been mortally wounded, and his wife and daughters all laughed. Even Emma had to smile. Although she was just now getting her breath back, she'd been that shocked by her own boldness. Her remark had been the sort of "smart talk" she always imagined making while out in company but rarely dared to.

But then it had been a long time since she'd felt the pains of shyness in Bria's kitchen. This was a familiar place to her, a safe place. In the same way that the birch woods near home and the glass walls of the old orangery and the bay waters all held her safely.

She looked around the kitchen with its faded wallpaper and worn linoleum. With its touches peculiar to Bria: the tomato can always full of wildflowers, the hooked-rag rug and rush-seat rocking chair, the font of holy water next to the door. Emma realized with a small sense of wonder that she had been happy in this place, and the thought made her smile.

"Don't. Don't do that, Miss Tremayne."

Her name, spoken so harshly in that shattered voice, skated along her flesh, and stung. She swung her head around, back to him, and slammed into the blazing anger in his eyes.

"Wh-what?" she said. "Don't do what?"

"Be looking around my Bria's kitchen with your nose in the air, sneering. You're spoiled and you're bored and you think playing peasant is an amusing way to pass a free afternoon. It gives you a chance to display your superiority, surely, and practice all your fine manners, splendid little miss that you are, but—"

"Shay!"

Bria's cry cut across his words, stopping them, but his eyes stayed hard on Emma.

You are wrong about me, she wanted to say to him. But the words got caught up somewhere in her throat, because for all that it was untrue now, there had been an element of truth there in the beginning, at the heart of it. And he was looking at her as if he knew it.

"Oh, Shay," Bria cried again, his name tearing out of her on a ragged cough. "How could you say such a thing, and Miss Tremayne a guest in our house?"

"Our house, aye." He laid his hands flat on the table, as if he would push himself to his feet, although he stayed seated, and his gaze remained fastened on Emma's face. "You could be saying that, since we pay the rent on it. Or you could be saying she's a guest in Mr. Geoffrey Alcott's house, as he owns the title on it. And as she's soon to be Mr. Alcott's wife, that almost makes us a guest of hers, does it not?"

Emma hadn't known that Geoffrey owned this house, although she realized she should have. Alcott Textiles probably held title to almost all the property around the mill. Just as the Tremaynes owned most of the shacks and tenements in Goree.

"And you," Bria was saying to her man, her voice roughened from her coughing and her anger, "are behaving as though Miss Tremayne was someone we ought to despise just for being who she is. God save us, we're not in Ireland anymore."

"Landlords are the same the world over, is that not so, Miss Tremayne? Only here in America you've added a new twist on how you go about bleeding your tenants: grading a family's rent on the number of its wee ones that're sent to slave in the mills for your profits. The more children, the less the rent. Isn't that how it is, Miss Tremayne?"

She shook her head, her gaze falling away from his. She hadn't known that, either.

"It's a cruel practice, would you not say so, Miss Tremayne? To force a man to choose between putting his daughters into the spinning room or watching them starve in the gutter."

His eyes were hard on her, judging her. She felt as she had every other time she'd been near him, that he was testing her with rules from a world she didn't know.

Bria pressed a wadded-up handkerchief to her mouth, stifling another cough. She gripped her man's arm, her fingers digging into the flesh bared by his rolled-up sleeve. "Do you mean to be teaching your daughters tinkers' manners by your own bad example, Seamus McKenna? No matter who has the owning of this house, Miss Tremayne is a guest at our table, and you will tell her now that you're sorry."

He let a long, edgy moment pass before he said, "If the truth offends you, Miss Tremayne, then I do humbly beg your pardon."

Emma lifted her head, her gaze locking now head-on with his. "You've a rare knack, Mr. McKenna, for inserting insults into your apologies."

She saw his eyes tighten a little at the corners, and then his mouth opened into something that was not quite a smile.

She thought he was going to say something more, when Merry erupted into a shrill, excited humming.

Noreen had been watching her father the whole time, with a worried frown pinching her face. But now she fastened her attention on to her sister, and her mouth twisted as if pulled between smiling and weeping.

"Merry says there's no need to be making such a fuss." She pointed at Emma, her cheeks flushing brightly. " 'Cause *she's* going to be buying us all a brand-new house someday. Merry says she's got lots and lots of money." Her gaze went from Emma to her father and then back to Emma again, and her eyes turned wary. "Just how much money have you got anyways?"

Emma was taken aback. It wasn't the sort of question anyone of her set would have dared to ask. Yet the girls, Mr. McKenna, and even Bria were all looking at her as if they expected an answer.

She lifted her chin. They expected pride—well, then, she would show them pride. "There is the Tremayne family fortune, of course, which will come to Maddie and me upon my father's death. It's mostly in interest- and dividend-bearing securities, although I've no earthly idea how much it amounts to. And then I've a trust fund that comes to me upon my marriage, or when I turn twenty-five. It's only a million."

"Mother Mary," Shay McKenna exclaimed, rolling his eyes in exaggerated wonder. " 'Only a million,' she says." He waved his arm in a wide sweep around the room. "And how many flowers are papered on our kitchen walls—only a thousand, would you say?" He picked up the small blue shaker of Morton's salt that always sat in the middle of the table, next to the can of wildflowers. "And how many grains of salt in this here—only a hundred thousand? Yet our dear Miss Tremayne has this thing called a trust fund and only a million dollars are in it, and she speaks of it as if it were such an inconsequential thing."

"Oh, Shay . . ." Bria said on a long sigh.

Emma carefully folded her napkin and laid it out beside the teacup and saucer. "Please forgive me," she said in her genteelest of voices, "but I'm afraid I must be leaving now." She came gracefully to her feet with the barest rustle of silken petticoats. If he was going to accuse her of coming here to practice her fine manners, then she would practice them.

"Thank you for your generous hospitality." She gave him a small but gracious nod. "Good day, Mr. McKenna. Noreen, Merry . . ." She nearly faltered at the stricken look that darkened Bria's eyes. "Mrs. McKenna," she said, her voice breaking a little.

She walked through the door and down the steep steps and out to Thames Street, to where her little carriage waited for her at the hitching post next to the boardwalk. She had just unlooped the reins from around the iron ring when she heard the door bang behind her.

"Miss Tremayne, I'd like a further word with you."

Slowly, she turned and waited for him. He walked down the dirt path toward her, the path lined with the blue and yellow violets she had helped to plant.

He brought himself right up to her. Close enough for her to watch a bead of sweat form below his ear and run down the pulsing vein in his neck. He unnerved her, the way he was looking at her, the intensity of his stare.

Her throat had grown so tight, she could barely speak. "Do you wish to berate me more, Mr. McKenna? Or perhaps you want to forbid my spoiled self from setting foot inside your house again."

He shook his head slowly. "No, I'll not be doing that. Only I'll be asking you . . ." For the flash of an instant she saw a vulnerability in his eyes, as if a brittle shell had cracked to reveal a part of his soul. "Don't hurt them," he said.

Her breath gusted out in a small gasp. "I would never!"

He searched her face, as though weighing the truth of her words. His eyes had turned brittle again, hard, his mouth unrelenting.

"You don't understand," she said. "Bria is my friend."

"Your friend, is she? And what's going to happen, then, when your other 'friends' learn about your visits here? When that man whose ring you're wearing, and whose life you're going to be sharing, comes to know of it? I can give you a Yankee guarantee they won't like it, and before long they won't like you for doing it. And you can't tell me that won't matter to you."

"That won't matter to me," she said, although even she could hear the lie in her words. She didn't *want* it to matter, but she had never before braved the censure of the whole of society. And she knew it could be brutal.

"You could as easily pull a fish out of the bay and ask it to take up living on the land," he said, echoing her unwanted thoughts, "than to build a bridge between our two worlds."

"I only . . ." She stopped, unable to go on. She didn't want to build any bridges. She only wanted to be Bria McKenna's friend.

He drew in a deep breath, easing it out again slowly. She thought his mouth might have softened a little, although his eyes remained hard. "It's such a grand life you've had up until now, Emma Tremayne. You've never had to look ahead to the end of things, to their cost."

She tried to force a smile but her lips were too stiff. "Surely you're exaggerating. It might be unusual, but it's hardly a crime against either God or man for a Yankee blue blood and an Irish immigrant woman to share a bit of friendship."

"Oh, so it's down to a 'bit' of friendship now, is it?" He

leaned in to her, his voice growing even rougher. "My Bria doesn't give of her heart easily, and so it's a fragile thing. Whereas you . . . *Dhia*, your sort breaks hearts as easily as most folk break bread."

His words hurt, surprisingly so. Her throat thickened, and hot tears pricked at the back of her eyes. She was going to start crying in front of him at any moment now, and she didn't think she could bear that. "You really do despise me, don't you?"

His laugh was low and ragged. "Now, there's the Great Folk for you, always looking at the world from how it touches upon yourselves. It's nearly down on my knees I am, begging you to spare my wife the pain I know you're going to bring her, and all you're caring about is that I might not be holding you in the grand esteem that you think is your due."

She tightened the whole of her face against the tears. She lifted her head and turned away from him to climb into her carriage with all the dignity she could muster from two hundred years' worth of Great Folk breeding.

But then she heard his frayed voice follow her as she drove away. "I don't despise you," he said.

He didn't despise her.

He watched her drive down the road, her carriage wheels rattling on the packed, oiled dirt. The wide straw brim of her hat shadowed her face, and the lace jabot at her throat fluttered in the bay breeze. She looked haughty and unapproachable, and expensive, and he had thought her to be all of those things the first time he'd seen her, that day of the fox hunt. Later, he had thought her a bravehearted child, hungering for adventure. An innocent being pulled apart by her own painful shyness and a wild daring.

He didn't despise her. God save us all, but if she hadn't

been who she was he might have come to like her. Even so, he did feel something for her, although he couldn't for the life of him have explained what it was. Oddly, the word that came to his mind was *admiration.*

Maybe that was what had driven him to . . . Well, he hadn't exactly sought her out. He'd lingered with her awhile, when the opportunity had been there, and now, surely, he wished it all undone. For although his mind told him she hadn't come to his Bria through anything he had done, still his heart insisted it was all his fault. He didn't want her in his life, in their lives.

And yet, and yet . . . there was something about her, something that made him want to get a deeper glimpse into her heart. And in that he was behaving just as foolishly as he'd accused her—not understanding how glimpses into the human heart came at such a cost.

He watched her until a beer wagon and horse ambulance had turned onto the street behind her, and all but the bobbing white ostrich feathers of her hat had disappeared from his view. But even after she was long gone her image stayed on his eyes like sunspots. In the air was the faintest whiff of lilac toilet water.

He walked back to the house, climbed the steep steps of the stoop, and pushed open the door. His wife stood at the slopstone with the shard of a broken tea saucer in one hand, and in the other a bloodstained handkerchief that she had pressed to her mouth to stifle the wet, chest-tearing coughs that were killing her.

He looked at her, at her bent head and her thin, heaving shoulders, and his heart broke again for the thousandth time.

"Bria," he said.

She coughed—one last harsh, ragged cough. She looked down at the piece of broken clayware in her hand, then dropped it onto the slopstone and turned. She held out her hand, but not to him.

"Nory, come here," she said softly.

Their daughters still sat at the table, caught up in the tension that twanged in the air, quiet in their fear. Noreen's face washed even paler as she jerked to her feet and went to her mother. "Mam?" she said.

Bria pressed a couple of pennies into the child's hand. "Take your sister and go up to Pardon Hardy's and buy yourselves some peppermint sticks."

Noreen cast a panicked look at her father, but she said nothing more. She went to the table and took Merry's hand.

Shay waited until the door had closed behind them. "Am I in for a scolding?" he said, struggling for the smile that just wouldn't come.

She stared at him for forever, and then her face seemed to crumble in upon itself; all of her crumbled, and she wrapped her arms around the slope of her belly, hugging herself and the babe.

"She won't be coming here no more," she said, and her shoulders shook so hard he thought she was coughing again, but then he realized that she was crying.

"Ah, Bria, darlin' . . ." He went to her and gathered her to him. She tried to snuggle into him, to press her face deep into his chest, but their baby was in the way.

"I never had such a friend before," he heard her say through her crying. "You don't understand . . . It's a rare thing to touch and be touched in that way."

He did understand, and the understanding brought him such pain it was as though he'd tried to swallow a knife and it had gotten caught in his throat. He had wanted to believe that he was all she needed, all she would ever need. And once, that might have been true. But such a need had to be answered, fulfilled, and he had always known deep in some small dark corner of his heart that he had failed her in that way. That as much as he loved her, he hadn't loved her enough.

He rubbed his hands over the bowed curve of her back,

over and over. There was hardly any flesh to her anymore, only fragile, wasted bones, and he couldn't bear it. God, God, she was dying. He was losing her, losing her . . . had lost her.

"Your Emma Tremayne is no coward," he said around the hurt, the knife, in his throat, "so she'll be coming back if she wants. And you'll be knowing then, surely, how much of a true friend she means to be to you."

She leaned back within the circle of his arms to look up at him. Her cheeks bore the roses of death and her eyes were black pools of hurt and loss. . . . Losing her, he was losing her.

"You don't think any good'll come of it, do you?" she said.

He smoothed the hair back from her wet face. She'd always had the most beautiful hair of any woman he'd ever known. Irish hair, fiery and temperamental, and red as the sun rising over the thatched roofs of Gortadoo.

He lowered his head and spoke into her hair, his lips brushing against its softness. "No good at all. But then maybe that's because I've always seen miracles as coming from God. Whilst you, m'love, see them as coming from ourselves."

Chapter Sixteen

The late May skies waxed bluer and the marsh grass grew thick and green, and Emma Tremayne went back to the house on Thames Street.

She didn't know whether it was pride that drove her to go there again, or a lack of pride that kept her from staying away. She went back because it seemed she had no choice, or every choice. She couldn't decide.

Choices. The idea of choices held such a compelling interest for her now. How people led their lives and the choices they made and why. There were the things that just weren't done, and the things one did anyway. The human heart, she was coming to understand, could not be ruled by any other. Only itself.

One night, at the Pattersons' soiree, she said to Geoffrey, "Why do you hire mostly little children to work in your mills?"

He looked taken aback—that she would bring up an unpleasantness over champagne and brandy cocktails, she supposed—but he answered her readily enough. "Because their smaller fingers can catch the looping threads more easily. I once stood through the day's shift at a ring spinner. It's not as easily managed as one might think."

She hadn't known he'd done such a thing—taken on, if only for one day, the tasks of one of his commonest laborers. She thought it showed that he must have a care for them, and it nearly stopped her from saying what she said next. "But you're not obliged to pay a child as much as you would a grown man, is that not so, Geoffrey?"

His smile slipped a little, the smile she thought she liked. "There are such things as profits and losses and bottom lines, dearest Emma. I have a living to make. *Our* living."

"But so do they. And—"

"Emma." Her mama's voice cut across the length of the drawing room. "Mrs. Patterson wishes to know if you and Mr. Alcott are planning to honeymoon in Vienna or Paris."

Later, when they were home again at The Birches, her mama said, "You have grown too bold in your questions, Emma. How many times must I remind you that it is better not to say anything at all than to say one wrong thing?"

And the worried, haunted look that she saw lurking deep in her mother's eyes reminded Emma that they lived in a world that discouraged questions and choices of any kind.

The next afternoon while playing whist with the Carter sisters, Miss Carter said, "We'll not be seeing dear Mrs. Oliver out in society for a goodly while."

"Why not?" Emma said, forgetting already how she was not to be so bold in her questions. Mrs. Oliver was a new bride, and Emma had also taken an interest lately in new brides.

"Because she is going to be indisposed," Miss Carter said.

"For seven more months," said Miss Liluth with a soft giggle.

"Liluth!" Miss Carter gasped. "For shame."

"Emma," Emma's mama said, "have you forgotten that hearts are trump?"

When the whist game ended, Emma told her mother she was taking the sloop out for a sail, but she went to the house on Thames Street.

Bria had the door open to the May sunshine, and Emma found her sitting in her rocker, darning one of her man's big socks. Her hands rested on her round, thrusting belly while she worked.

Bria McKenna, Emma thought, had gone everywhere—although perhaps not to all the best places—with her pregnancy plainly on view. She carried the child in her womb as a burden not of shame but of glory.

Bria looked up as Emma's shadow fell across her light. Her mouth, beginning to smile, opened wider with a shocked little squeal. She looked down at her stomach. It was, Emma could see even from where she was in the doorway, literally dancing with the force of the baby's kicking.

"Oooh! He'll be making his appearance in the world any day now, he's gotten that active," Bria said, the words coming out in bright little gasps. "And he's his father's son, sure as I'm sitting here and suffering his pummels."

Emma went to her and knelt at her feet. She reached out, her hand hovering over Bria's quivering belly. "May I?" she said.

Smiling and panting both at once, Bria took Emma's hand and laid it on the swelling, pulsing life that was inside her. "Oh, my!" Emma exclaimed. "He's so strong."

"Aye, a brave, brawny Irish lad he'll be."

But then a cry cracked in Bria's throat, and she fell into such a fit of weeping, Emma could barely make out what she was saying. Only that her brave, brawny Irish lad would likely never set his shamrock-green eyes on the rainswept green hills of Ireland.

"Don't you go paying me no mind," Bria said as she

gulped down a final sob, scrubbing her face with the sleeve of her shirtwaist. "When I get scared, I get weepy."

"Don't be scared," Emma said. "The baby will be fine." She didn't say, And you will be fine—for that was too obvious a lie. And maybe the other was a lie as well. She wondered if a babe could catch its mother's sickness through the womb.

Once, Emma had wondered if she, too, could catch the disease by coming into this house, wondered enough that she feared it even though she refused to let it keep her away. Now, she didn't even think of it as she leaned in to Bria and wrapped her arms around her waist, and Bria bent forward in the rocker and rested her chin on Emma's head. It was awkward this way, but somehow comforting to both of them.

"Why did you leave Ireland, if you loved it so?" she said, and she felt Bria stiffen beneath her hands.

She sat back on her heels and looked up. The sunlight pouring through the open door had set fire to Bria's hair. "Forgive me," Emma said. "I asked you that before. I don't mean to pry."

But she had very much meant to pry. She wanted to crack open the world that existed inside this kitchen, this shack on stilts, crack open Bria's world like a walnut shell and taste the meat within.

Bria had taken the wooden darning egg out of the heel of the sock and she was rubbing it now, over and over, between her palms. "In Ireland, girls aren't so modern as they are here, marrying where they fancy. In Ireland, we have matchmakers, and sure no one was ever going to match me up with any boy, being as how I had no dowry or hope of one."

Bria drew in a deep, shaky breath as her gaze drifted away into the past. "But I wanted Shay McKenna, you see. I was that wild for the lad. So I set out to get him in the way every girl who's ever wanted a boy has gotten him since time began. He was going to be a priest, and at sixteen he finds himself instead with a wife and a babe on the way, and only a curragh and a few nets to make a living with."

A priest, Emma thought. That man, that man . . . that man had nearly been a priest, and she almost laughed. But then something caught at her chest, something that hurt and made a curious melting feeling.

"He wanted to be a priest," Bria was saying. "And I stole him away from God, which is a mortal sin, surely. But not nearly so terrible a sin as stealing him away from himself, from what he might have been."

"Bria . . ." Emma reached out to touch her hand, pulled back, then did it after all. Bria let go of the wooden egg and their fingers curled together, holding on. "I don't know Mr. McKenna all that well," Emma said. "But a blind stranger could see in an instant that he loves you desperately."

Bria's eyes filled with tears, and her mouth trembled into a hurting smile. "He'd always had such grand dreams, though, even as a boy. Whilst mine were small, ordinary things: a man to call my own, children to raise up bright and strong, maybe a house and a few potato fields. Whenever troubles came, I never wanted to fight them. I only wanted for them to be over."

Emma gave her hand a squeeze of understanding, and Bria fell into a silence, then swallowed as if she were choking back a rock. "I'll be telling you what happened," she said. "In a wee moment."

"There's no need, Bria. No need, no need."

"There is, surely. Like yourself, I've been feeling the urge to tell someone for a long time now."

The face Bria turned to her was suffused with both a haunting strength and a tender innocence. "I told you before how Shay's mam came to die, and how the faith died in his heart that day he buried her. But I didn't tell you how, when the faith passed on, there came such a hate to take its place . . .

"He had joined the Fenians after that. And the Land Leaguers, a group of violent rebels that harassed and terrorized the landowners and their agents, even killing them when the opportunity presented itself.

"He waited eight years for a chance to do for the land agent who'd driven his mam into the sea. Leastways I think it was Shay who did that cold-blooded killing. He's never admitted so to me, and that's one thing I'll never be asking him. But the resident magistrate had a warrant that said he'd done it, all the same."

She was gripping so tightly to Emma's hand now that she was crushing flesh to bone, but Emma didn't make a sound. She could barely breathe, for the sick bucking of her heart.

Shay was out in his curragh when the resident magistrate came for him. Sir Michael Barnes had come riding into Gortadoo on his blood bay horse, wearing the scarlet coat of the master of the hunt, as if he'd only had to take a pause in doing that more important thing to round up a common Irish criminal. He'd been accompanied by a full complement of the Royal Irish Constabulary, though, in their smart green uniforms.

Bria had had some warning, enough to hide the girls. She put them in the pigsty and covered them with the wet, stinking slop. She made them swear to keep out of sight and silent, no matter what happened.

"The magistrate said Shay was to turn himself in, and to make certain he got the message, the magistrate, he . . . he raped me. He bent me over a stone wall and took me like a dog, outside, where all the neighbors could see . . . where my girls could see. And Shay would be sure to hear of it."

"Dear God, no," Emma whispered.

"Only Shay didn't have to hear of it," Bria went on. She was crying now, big, silent tears that coursed in streams down her cheeks. "Because he came home in time to see it, to see the last of it. He tried to kill the man who . . . the magistrate, with his fists, and he would have if the constables hadn't been there to pull him off. They were supposed to take him to Kilmainham Jail for trial, but they set out to hang him right there in Gortadoo, for attempting to murder an officer of the Crown, they said. It was the only tree to be had for twenty miles. A yew tree."

"Oh, Bria . . ." Emma could feel the wetness of tears on her own face. She came up onto her knees and wrapped her free arm around Bria's back while still holding on to her hand. For she wasn't going to let Bria go; never would she let her go.

"They made me watch it," Bria said. "And the girls—they made them watch it, too."

Emma moaned and held her tighter.

"He took a long time at dying, Shay did, strangling at the end of that rope. When my brother, Donagh, cut him down his face was all black, and there was the hangman's bloody rope burn around his neck. There was a trickle of breath still in him, too, though, only I didn't know it was so at the time."

Emma tried to stop the sounds of her crying by pressing her mouth into Bria's shoulder, but she couldn't, and it didn't matter. They cried together for a while, and then slowly grew quiet.

"I don't know how you bore it," Emma said into the kitchen's soft silence.

Bria shrugged and swiped at her cheeks with the back of her free hand. Her other hand still held on tightly to Emma's. She was breathing hard and shallow, almost panting.

"I bore it in the only way I could. I held a wake for him and buried him, and it wasn't until he was already on a ship bound for America that my brother told me I'd put a coffin full of stones into the ground instead of my man. Donagh said they were afraid I'd let on, that I wouldn't seem sorrowful enough." A ragged laugh tore hard from Bria's chest. "I suffered through three days of thinking he was dead, and weeping enough rivers of sorrow to drown the world, and sure I'll never forgive either one of them for that."

She took such a breath now, as if there were no air left in all the world. "When I thought he was dead . . . Oh, Miss Tremayne, when I thought he was dead, when I put him in the ground—I didn't know heart and soul could hurt like that, and now I'm doing it to him. Now he'll be burying me."

Emma stayed with Bria until the shadows grew long and lavender across the open door, and the girls came home from the mill. And then she went with them to the back end of town to pick raspberries from the bushes that grew wild along Ferry Road.

The sun began to sink into the bay, turning it to melted gold. The breeze had a floating lightness to it, like feathers. Bria sang beneath her breath while she picked, stopping from time to time to pop a berry into her mouth. " 'If maidens could sing like blackbirds and thrushes . . . How many young men would hide in the bushes . . .' "

Her song trailed off and she looked around her. "Where did those girls disappear to, did you see?"

Emma didn't answer, for she was lost herself in looking at Bria's face. At the sharp curve of a cheekbone, the high ridge of her brow, the proud thrust of her chin. She had made many sketches of that face. She wanted desperately, hungrily, to try molding that face in clay, but she was also afraid to. As if the instant she tried to create it, she would lose it.

"Are we friends, Bria?" she said, as they kneeled together at the side of the dusty road, among fringes of goldenrod and Queen Anne's lace, holding baskets in the shallows of their laps, and with the tangy kiss of raspberries lingering on their lips.

Bria turned to face her. Her mouth, Emma saw, was stained red with juice. "If we aren't friends after all that has passed between us, then what would you call us?"

"I want," Emma said, "to invent another name for what we are." She looked away, down the road that led through the woods to The Ferry, where she knew from experience that snipes pecked through the mudflats and occasionally died. "There are many people I call friends, but I know they're not. I'm beginning to think that nothing in my life is real."

"That's a *real* nice dress you have on, surely. *Real* expensive too, I shouldn't wonder."

Emma's sigh was colored with laughter. "Am I behaving foolishly?"

"Aye. And a little pridefully, too."

"There, you see, that's why I need you in my life. To keep me humble and wise."

They shared a smile. Bria plucked a raspberry off the bush and put it to Emma's lips. Emma opened her mouth and sucked it in, and the fruit exploded on her tongue, warm and sweet.

"I am your friend, Emma," Bria said, using her given name for the first time in all their moments and hours together. The color was high in her cheeks, giving them life. Her smile was real. "I've come to love you dearly."

Emma knew her own face revealed the force of all she was feeling. "I always thought that when I found a friend, a *real* friend, it would be like discovering the missing half of myself. But I was wrong. A real friend isn't your other half, she's the whole of you, of your soul. She's the reflection you see in the mirror."

Emma lifted her hand, palm out, and then Bria did the same. They touched fingertips, the way they would touch their images in a sheet of silvered glass. Then they both blinked and looked away, as if they had suddenly become blinded by the mirror's reflection.

And they both realized that the girls were running toward them down the road, running hard as if they were being chased. Merry was humming so wildly they could hear her from all that way, humming as loudly as the whir of a hummingbird's wing. Then Noreen began to shout.

"Da's fighting!"

The swinging doors of the Crow's Nest Saloon slapped together behind their backs. It was like a cave inside, dim and dank, thick with the yeasty smell of beer and the tang of whiskey. A haze of tobacco smoke floated through the air, stinging Emma's eyes.

She had never been inside a place that sold the devil's brew. A couple of years ago some daughters of the Great Folk had joined the Women's Temperance. They had knelt in the rain and the mud outside the Crow's Nest, praying loudly for God to bring the drunkards to the light and handing out white ribbons as pledges of purity against alcoholic drink. Emma, of course, hadn't been allowed to take part. Mama frowned on public displays of any sort, even righteous ones.

Emma wasn't sure what she was expecting now, but what she first saw was disappointing in its very ordinariness. A crude plank bar rested atop stacks of barrels; sawdust lay damp and greasy on the floor. In the middle of the bar stood a wash boiler full of chowder, but the saloon had no tables and chairs, only boxes and stools and a few wobbly benches leaning up against the rough, knotholed walls. None of it looked as if it had been cleaned in the memory of man.

A few men stood around, drinking from tin pails and

tomato cans. On the wall in back of the bar hung a sign offering beer for three cents—all you could drink without breathing.

Emma read the sign twice and still couldn't imagine what it meant. Until she noticed a man lying on the floor beneath one of the barrels, with a rubber hose running from it into his mouth. His chest heaved and his throat worked furiously, while another man in a long leather apron stood over him, his hand on the barrel's tap. Ready to shut it off, no doubt, as soon as his customer took a breath.

As for Bria, she had barely given the bar or its offerings a glance. She was heading for a back room. Shouts and whistles spilled out from behind the glass-beaded curtain that covered the doorway. And smacking noises that sounded like a cleaver hitting meat.

Blocking the way, with his long legs and broad shoulders, was a man wearing a priest's robe and collar. Emma didn't have to be told who he was. The proud bones that gave Bria's face its strength made of her brother an extraordinarily handsome man.

His gaze went from Bria to Emma, and his eyes widened. "Bria, what in heaven's holy name—"

"Are you doing here, Father O'Reilly?" Bria shot back. She gave a long, angry look up and down the length of him. "Sweet saints. And why am I not surprised? Don't tell me you've come to the Crow's Nest to give the *poitín* your blessing and turn it into holy water."

"Aw, Bria." He reached up to brush away the curls that were always clinging to her cheek. "It's only a wee bit of a sparring he's doing. The sandbag is all well and good, but it doesn't hit back. The lad needs to get his feet wet."

She knocked his hand away. "The lad needs a great clout on his ear, and so do you." She pushed past him, aiming for the beaded curtain. "You'll be stepping out of our way, Donagh, if you know what's good for you."

Within the back room, two circus lamps cast arcs of ghostly, flickering light through a blue fog of tobacco smoke. A rude and boisterous crowd of men and a few women pushed and jostled elbows for space in front of an area that had been roped off to form a ring around two brawling, panting men: Shay McKenna, and a man with lumpy ears and thick, dark eyebrows that bristled across his forehead like a hedge.

Both men were stripped to the waist, and their flesh bore the marks of their violence. Chests and shoulders were blistered and crisscrossed with red welts raised by the bare-knuckle blows. Blood oozed from a cut above Shay's eye. His opponent's nose had swelled up purple as an overripe plum.

Emma stifled a gasp with her hands, but Bria didn't make a sound. She was looking at her man, and her face, as always, showed her love for him. But her eyes had clouded with fearful memories. There could be, Emma had come to understand earlier that day, a terrible cost you paid for loving.

Shay must have felt his wife's sudden presence, for his gaze flashed to her. His guard dropped for an instant, and the hedge-browed man unleashed a terrific blow to his jaw. Shay's head snapped back with a crack you could hear as he reeled and staggered down onto one knee.

Emma gave a little cry and started forward, as if she could help him. It was Bria who stopped her, by grabbing her arm. But Emma could feel a fine trembling going on inside the other woman. She remembered the pain in Bria's voice and on her face as she'd spoken of watching him be beaten bloody every summer Sunday, and she thought again how loving a man, loving some men, could be so very hard.

A man who appeared to be serving as a referee stepped between the fighting men, ringing a cowbell. The hedge-browed man backed into a corner of the ring and squatted down on a barrel. Shay stayed kneeling a moment, one arm resting on his thigh, his chest shuddering as he shook his head and gulped in air. Then he pushed to his feet and went to his own corner.

Bria's brother was there to hand him a wet towel. The priest worked his hands into Shay's powerful shoulder muscles while he whispered encouragement into his ear. Shay's nostrils flared and his chest rose and fell with his labored breathing. His skin was slick with sweat and smeared with blood. He stared across the ring at his opponent, his eyes burning.

It seemed less than a minute had passed before the referee stepped up and rang the bell again, pointing to a line of chalk drawn down the center of the ring.

For a moment it was quiet enough to hear the squeak of the men's shoes on the rosin-coated floor as they closed, grappling, each getting in quick shots to the ribs and stomach. Then a great roar erupted as Shay threw a smoking, smashing punch to the mouth that sent the hedge-browed man flying against the rope.

The man bounced back fast, though, onto his feet, shaking his head, spittle and blood splattering. His mashed lips pulled back in a snarl as he rushed at Shay, fists flailing. But Shay dodged and weaved, easily avoiding the man's wild swings.

Shay delivered a solid shot to the mouth again. Blood spurted, and the crowd screamed. The muscles in his back and shoulders flexed and bulged as he sank a flurry of punches into his opponent's stomach. Another punch, hard and smacking, to the ear this time, and the man swayed, his arms weakening, lowering, his knees sagging. Shay's fists were hammering now, like a blacksmith forging a piece of iron. Hammering, hammering, hammering, muscles thrusting, punching, chest grunting, breathing out his open mouth in quick, hard pants.

Slowly, as if all his strength had run out of his legs like water, the man sank to his knees. His eyes rolled back in his head and he keeled over sideways to lie on the floor as if he were sleeping. He even began to snore. And standing over him, standing over this man he had beaten bloody, Shay McKenna seemed suddenly to go quiet all over.

He tossed his head, flicking the hair and sweat out of his eyes. His gaze searched out Bria, and he cast a brash, white grin her way, and then his face softened. And his eyes, as he looked at his wife, seemed to be glowing with an inner fire that was all wanting and need, and love.

Emma stood still, waiting for him to notice her, to look at her, and then he did, and there was nothing on his face at all, nothing, but it didn't matter, it didn't matter, because . . .

I love him.

One moment the world had been too bright and sharp, full of shouts and screams and the stench of sweat and blood. Then everything turned thick and queer and soundless.

Emma stood with her back pressed hard into the rough pine wall in the rear room of the Crow's Nest Saloon, and she couldn't take her eyes off him. Bria, crying, was kissing his bloody, shredded, swollen hands. Father O'Reilly was rubbing his hair with a towel. The eye below the cut was beginning to swell shut. A bruise purpled the bridge of his nose.

The man in the leather apron stood up on one of the barrels and proclaimed that the drinks were on Seamus McKenna, the great Irish fisticuffs champion. The back room began to empty, but Emma couldn't move away from the wall. Her legs and arms were heavy and weak. Her throat felt frayed and bloodied, as if she'd been screaming, only she hadn't made a sound.

She laid her hands flat on the wall as if she would push herself away, push herself out of her body. She wanted to be away from here, away from herself, away from the thought that kept circling through her, through every part of her.

I love him.

She looked through the swaying, glass-beaded curtain into the barroom. A man played the hornpipes. Another danced a jig while balancing a glass of beer on his head.

At last she took a step and then another, and it was a tremendous relief to her that she could do this.

She pushed through the curtain, beads clacking, and into the crowded barroom. An elbow jabbed her in the belly, and someone stepped on her foot with his hobnailed boot. A jetted stream of tobacco juice barely missed her cheek on its way to the floor. She became vaguely irritated that it was so hard to get where she wanted to be. But she stopped when she did get there—to the swinging, louvered doors that opened onto Thames Street.

She didn't mean to look around for him. She was looking for Bria instead, but Bria was with him. Of course they would be together.

He sat on a stool in the middle of the barroom, and Father O'Reilly sat on an upturned barrel across from him, laughing, excited, punching the air with his fists and reliving the fight. Merry straddled her father's knee and Noreen leaned against his side, within the circle of his right arm. And Bria . . .

Bria, Bria, I am so sorry. I didn't know it was going to happen, I never meant for it to happen. But I'll make it stop, don't worry. In a minute I can make it stop.

Bria was standing behind him. He was leaning back against her, rubbing his head against the swell of her belly, and her hands were in his hair.

Emma looked away from them, out at a twilight sky strafed with deep purple clouds, and she was shocked to discover that time hadn't lost its way, the world hadn't come to an end.

Leaving, she thought, would simply require going out these doors. But leaving the Crow's Nest, leaving town, leaving the world, had nothing to do with the kind of leaving she had to do.

I love him.

Chapter Seventeen

In her dreams, Maddie Tremayne was always running.

It was always summer in her dreams. Summer on a beach of white sand and foam-stippled waves. And oh how she'd run, run flat out, stretching her legs, straining her lungs. Running, running, running with the wind blowing in her hair, knees pumping high, the sand oozing around her toes and the waves slapping at her heels. Running until she thought that maybe she wasn't touching the beach at all but flying above it.

But no matter how long and sweet the dreams, they always ended. And when she awakened, no matter what the season, it was always winter.

It had been winter the day the accident happened. An ice storm had blown through the night before, sheathing the birches with millions of icicle droplets, so that their branches clicked together like beads when the wind blew. The harbor had frozen into thick yellow curls.

And Willie had offered to take her sledding.

They were always competing for his attention, she and Emma. Their adorable and adoring big brother, with his laughing blue eyes and teasing ways. So that winter's day, when he had snubbed Emma because they'd been squabbling over a chess game and he'd said to Maddie instead, "Come on, sport. Grab your sled and I'll give you a push down the hill," Maddie thought she'd been offered the world.

The harness bells jangled as the sleigh crunched and squeaked over the snow on the way to Fort Hill. Once, Lafayette had fought the British troops there. Now the children of Bristol slid down its smooth, steep slopes, fast as the wind on waxed ash runners, the tassels of their stocking caps flying behind them.

But that day the snow on the hill was slick and ice crusted and sculpted into windblown drifts in places. Blue and purple shadows lay in the hollows. Watery winter sunlight glinted off the rime-whitened oak trees and rocks that lined the sled run.

Maddie looked down the long, steep run and felt a shudder of fear. Willie had thought he was giving her a treat, and now she didn't want it. But she didn't know how to tell him that. Words had never come easily, not among any of them.

Her knees cracked as she sat down on her sled. Her fingers, stuffed deep into her wool mittens, still felt stiff and frozen. The wind suddenly gusted. Ice crystals swirled and sparkled and flashed in the air.

She craned her head around to look up at her brother. His breath trailed across his face in thin clouds, and his gaze was on a place only he could see. It was a thing Willie often did—he would go away from wherever he was and into a place where no one could find him.

She had to say his name twice, had to shout it, before he blinked and looked down at her. "What?" he said, impatient with her now.

Her teeth were chattering so, and her lips were so blue-cold she could barely talk. "I—I don't want to d-do it, after all. The snow's t-too packed and icy."

"Oh, don't be such a little scaredy-cat," he said, curling his lip at her, acting a little mean as he sometimes could. He bent over and gripped the side rails. "Come on—I'll give you a good push, and see if you don't fly."

"Noooo!" she wailed, but he had already pushed.

The ash runners shot out over the glazed snow. Maddie screamed and groped for the steering rope but couldn't find it. The wind drove stinging icy needles into her face and eyes. The sled dipped and rocked over the ruts and crests, veering off the run. She leaned over, trying to grab the steering bar, but her mittens slid off the slick wood.

She looked up and saw trees and rocks flying at her from out of a coiling swirl of whiteness. But she never saw the rock she hit. One instant she was flying through the world on a sled, and in the next the bumper hit something hard. The sled shot straight up on its end, flipping her as if off the end of a seesaw.

She spun end over end through the air and landed on her back among the rocks. She lay there, looking up at a blue, ice-spangled sky, feeling nothing. The wind blew, ringing the icicles in the trees. She watched one break into pieces and fall like shattered teardrops into the snow. Then the trees blurred into the gauzy white haze of a dream.

And in her dreams she was always running.

Maddie saw his shadow first, stretching long and lean on the glossy parquet floor.

She was in the library, she and her chair tucked into the large, oval bay window that looked out on the garden. Warm early-summer evening as it was now, she could almost imagine herself truly out there on the wide rolling lawns, running like a wild deer among the Greek statues and stone geranium urns.

The library's heavy walnut doors opened with a soft click, and there he was—tall and lean, elegant in a black silk-faced, four-button cutaway. The light from the wall sconces, with their shades of yellow silk, gilded his hair and cast his shadow out long in front of him.

Maddie hunched down in her chair, hoping he wouldn't see her hiding among the books and wine velvet curtains. If only, if only, if only she could still run.

But his eyes had always been sharp. His gray-water eyes. "Why are you hiding away in here?" he said.

He came right up to her, moving with the prowling grace that had always been the way of him. He'd been home, on and off, since the last fox hunt of the season, and yet this was the first visit he'd paid to The Birches. She had been wanting him to come and not wanting him to come and now he was here. She waited for him to say something about her chair, about her crippled body and ruined life, but he didn't.

The last time she'd seen him was at a garden party at the mansion on Hope Street. She'd been twelve at the time and still able to run. She was also Bethel Tremayne's daughter and able to recognize a Disgraceful Scene when it was being created before her eyes. Stu Alcott, inebriated on brandy and champagne cocktails, had sailed the ice sculpture across the lawn—it happened to be a swan boat that summer. He'd sailed it across the lawn, and then launched it and himself into the fountain.

His father and brother had said not a word—indeed, they'd behaved as if they weren't aware of his bad form. For such public breaches of etiquette were best ignored, as all unpleasantnesses were to be ignored. Recriminations would come later, in private.

Stu had stood in the middle of the fountain with the water lapping around the tails of his frock coat and his finely checked trousers. His hair dripping, his face white, and a queer look in his eyes that were for once fixed on her. "Maddie?" he'd said, and there'd been something desperate in his voice. "*You* are angry with me, aren't you, Maddie?"

"Of course I'm angry with you, Stuart Alcott," she'd shouted at him, not understanding why he was asking her such a thing. Why he seemed to be *wanting* her disapproval. "You are wicked and nasty, and I hate you."

Tears of shame had burned hot in her eyes, shame and disappointment. She felt shame for him, for his behavior, and she was disappointed in herself. For a part of her had understood already that the kind of girl he would one day come to love would have waded right into the fountain to join him, and Maddie Tremayne was never going to be that kind of girl.

The very next day his father had had him carried by force up to the insane asylum in Warren, and there he'd been locked up for nearly a year. And when they let him out, he had not come home.

He'd been nineteen that year of his disgrace. She had thought him a man at the time, but she understood now that in many ways he'd still been a boy. A boy crying out, so desperate just to be *noticed* by someone, anyone, that he'd even sought that attention from a twelve-year-old child.

She looked up at him now. He was taller than she remembered, his chest deeper, his shoulders broader. The caring had been stamped out of his narrow face, along with the laughter. But the wildness was still there.

She realized that not only was she staring at him but he was returning the compliment. Her gaze fell to her lap, where she gripped her hands together in a tight fist. She knew he was looking at the whole of her now, her wasted legs and the chair, and still he said nothing.

When she dared at last to look up at him again, she saw no pity in his eyes. Only a weariness, and a tender wariness, that he seemed to be trying hard not to show.

"Well, if I'm doing it," she said, "then so are you."

A dazzling smile flashed across his face. "Really?" He flipped up the tails of his coat and sat down on the window seat. Leaning back, he rested one arm on the sill and crossed his legs. "Enlighten me, dear child. What precisely are we doing? And please tell me that we're having fun at it."

"Hiding away in here."

He pretended to be disappointed. "Oh, that . . . The thing is, I seem to have committed the unpardonable sins of not only arriving late but without the pearl-gray gloves requisite for attending a dinner party."

He lifted his hands to show her that they were indeed gloveless. But although he might have left them off deliberately, just to be perverse, she doubted he had forgotten them.

"Geoffrey was scowling so fiercely at me," he elaborated, "that he was not only endangering his handsome features, but my tender feelings were taking quite a bruising as well, and so . . ." He sent another grin her way that was all boyish wickedness. "Here I am."

"Here you are," she echoed, trying to sound bright and cheerful, trying to smile, and no doubt impressing him as a pathetic fool instead. So now here he was, here she was, and here they were all back together again. Of them all, she was the one who'd changed the most. And Willie. Willie had changed by disappearing entirely.

As for Stu and Geoffrey—they had never gotten along as boys, and things were hardly likely to improve between them now that they were men and their papa had left Geoffrey all the money.

She'd heard that Stu wasn't living at the Hope Street mansion but rather at the Belvedere Hotel. Maddie's memories of the place were of crumbling brick steps and a pair of green-lacquered doors that were buckling and peeling and smelled of stale beer. But perhaps she didn't remember it right. She never left home now. At first she hadn't been allowed to leave. She still wasn't allowed to leave, but she no longer wanted to.

"Well," he said. "You've had your vulgar curiosity satisfied. Now it's my turn."

She jerked hard in her chair, as if he'd reached over and slapped her awake. Her mind had wandered. That seemed to be happening more and more often lately. The white gauze of her dreams slipped over her eyes sometimes, even when she was awake.

She could feel herself staring at him now, wide-eyed and blinking, like an owl caught in a wash of light.

"Why are you skulking here in the library?" he repeated.

She gripped the edges of the rug that covered her lap. "Mama says my wheelchair calls undue attention to me and my unfortunate affliction and draws shame down upon the family." She lifted a hand out of her lap, then let it fall back down, helplessly. "Hence, the guests are made to feel uncomfortable . . . by being party to our own discomfort, I suppose. Anyway, it won't do."

He seemed to go strangely tight and still, and she realized she had committed a social error by mentioning her unfortunate affliction at all.

"Won't it do?" he said, his voice tight as well. His boiled shirtfront crackled as he leaned back, the better to survey her. He raised one pale eyebrow. "Yet I had no trouble securing an invitation. For certain, then, I shall have to test the bounds of their comfort tonight—indeed, it has now become my veritable obligation. I believe I will get pie-eyed drunk, throw up into the Roman punch, and pee on the piano."

"And afterward?"

"After what?"

"After you ruin Mama's dinner party by making her guests uncomfortable, will you go away again?"

"As soon as I can pry more money out of my parsimonious brother I will indeed go away again." He waved his hand, fluttering it like a bird's wing. "Far, far away."

A movement through the windows caught Maddie's eye. Emma and Geoffrey walked together along the flagstone garden path, her arm linked with his. Light from the drawing-room doors fell across them in a wash of gold. Trellises of Chinese wisteria framed them like a wedding bower.

Then, as Maddie watched, Geoffrey took Emma's hand off his arm and turned so that they were face to face and he was holding her hand in both of his. He was looking down at her, and she was looking up at him, and although all Maddie could really see was the white oval of her sister's face, she was sure it was filled with adoration. And, as always, was stunningly beautiful.

A burning envy spread through Maddie and ate at her like acid. She wanted, wanted, wanted . . . She wanted Emma's face and Emma's legs. Oh, especially Emma's legs, which could still stroll with a man through a garden of a summer's evening, still dance with him at a betrothal ball, still walk down the church aisle to meet him at the altar as his bride. She wanted the life Emma would have: the mansion on Hope Street, the adoring, wealthy husband, Society breathless with admiration and prostrate at her feet.

It didn't matter that she loved her sister—and she did, truly she did. But her love didn't stop the consuming, burning envy. She wanted all that Emma had, and she could have none of it.

Stu had turned his head to look at them as well, at Emma and his brother. She wondered what he felt at seeing them together, so blissful in their perfect lives. If he was envious, or resigned, or pleased.

But then he took his attention off of the adoring couple and turned back to her, and Maddie was suddenly afraid he could read her bitter and aching heart.

"They look made for each other, don't they?" she said,

her voice a little too loud, so that it echoed in the wood-paneled room.

He widened his eyes in mock wonderment. "Ah, but are they mad for each other?"

"They love each other, surely?"

"He loves her, or so he says, and for once I do believe him." This time the smile he gave her had a touch of boyish whimsicality about it, and Maddie's eyes blurred with a wash of tears. "Indeed, his love appears to be very much of the maddening variety, both literally and figuratively."

He fell quiet a moment, then he lifted his shoulders in an elegant shrug. "But does *she* love him—desperately, wantonly, passionately? Because if you can't inspire passion in the woman you are mad for, then that is a killing thing for the both of you."

But not, Maddie thought, as killing a thing as possessing a wasted, useless body that could inspire the man you loved to nothing but pity. Or perhaps, if you'd ever mattered to him at all, a touch of regret.

More tears crowded her eyes. She averted her face from him and looked down at the toes of her kid slippers peeking out from under her lap rug. She felt the gauzy white haze begin to settle over her mind again, and this time she welcomed it.

She came back to herself with another start when he leaned forward with his elbows on his knees, leaned quite close to her, so that their faces were nearly touching. "Have you been smoking dry booze?" he said.

"What?"

"Your eyes are nothing but two black holes, as if they've been swallowed up. And you keep nodding off, drifting."

He leaned farther in to her, so close now his hair brushed her cheek. He sniffed. "Chloral hydrate, by Christ. I suppose that quack Uncle Stanton of yours doles it out to you like candy pills."

She tried to pull away from him but she was pinned to the back of her chair. "It's the medicine I take for the pain in my legs," she said, her voice breaking. "You make it sound as though . . . There's nothing wrong with it."

He shook his head. "I know all about chloral hydrate, Maddie child. They gave it to me when I was in the madhouse." He pulled back from her a little, then, but he still kept her pinned in place with his hard-edged gaze. "And such is its nature that when I left that place I graduated to finer and sweeter dreams. Perhaps next time I come visit you, I'll bring along my pipe and we can float away together on clouds of white joy."

She wasn't sure what he was talking about, except that it was certainly something wicked. She looked up at him, frightened of him, loving him. And then, for just an instant, she saw a break in the shadows that hovered within the pale gray flatness of his eyes, and her own heart broke all over again to see what lived inside Stu Alcott. The hurt and emptiness and defeat.

It was the same look she'd seen in Willie's eyes before he'd killed himself, before she had *driven* him to kill himself. Because they hadn't ever been able to speak aloud of what had happened that terrible icy winter's day. Because, although they hadn't spoken of it, still Willie must have looked into her heart and seen the ugly truth: that she couldn't forgive him for what he'd done to her.

Willie was gone, lost to her forever, but Stu was close enough to touch, and so she did. She laid her hand on his thigh. She could feel the hardness of his flesh, his manly heat, through the fine material of his trousers.

"Why are you this way? What's happened, Stu?" she said, not sure of what she was asking him. If she wasn't really asking him what had happened to her, what had happened to them all.

His hand covered hers. She felt her own hand tremble as

if it were something separate from her, with a will of its own. He gave it a gentle squeeze. "I fell down, Maddie, just like you. I fell down and hurt myself very, very badly."

"You . . ." The tears were coming now. She felt them, warm like summer raindrops, on her cheeks. "But you could try getting back up."

He stood and started to walk past her, but he stopped next to her chair. His hand hovered over her head for a moment, as if he would touch her hair, then it drifted lower and he brushed, lightly, ever so lightly, the tips of his fingers across her cheek.

"Some of us can't get back up," he said, so softly she barely heard him. "Some of us will never walk again."

Dinner that night at The Birches was a formal affair.

The table was set with a Roman punch, a centerpiece of jacqueminot roses and maidenhair, and bonbons in open silverwork baskets between the George III candelabra. The party favors were sterling silver roses from Tiffany's. The menu was printed on gilt-edged cards, two dishes for each course. And these delicacies—oysters, partridge, lobster, roast chicken with caper sauce, and twelve-egg soufflés—were being washed down with White Seal champagne and wine bottled before the French Revolution.

The feast was being presented on a banquet table that had once belonged to a Tudor king of England, in a room with silken walls and fluted columns embellished with gold leaf. A massive bronze chandelier hung from a ceiling festooned like a wedding cake.

The room did have one peculiarity, which every guest, out of deference to the hostess and general good form, was careful to ignore. Above the black walnut mantelpiece hung an enormous oil painting of the family's Cuban plantation house—the very house where William Tremayne now lived with his mistress du jour. When he wasn't giving wild parties on his yacht.

The painting could have been replaced with a barroom's naked lady and Geoffrey Alcott wouldn't have noticed. He had eyes only for the woman who would be his wife. His Emma had never seemed finer or fairer to him than she did that night, and he felt a warm glow of proprietorship as he watched the other men's glances seek her out again and again.

Tonight she looked particularly fetching in a pale green gown that was all silk and lace and that bared her neck and shoulders . . . and perhaps a bit more of her bosom than he would have allowed as her husband. The other women at the table dripped jewels, but she wore only the betrothal ring he had given her. It flashed on her finger quick and bright as a falling star.

She brought her wineglass to her lips, and he watched her drink. Watched as her head fell back to expose her impossibly long white neck, and the round bared slopes of her breasts lifted as she swallowed.

He wanted her. God, how he wanted her. So desperately he sometimes forgot himself when he was alone with her. He always seemed on the verge of frightening her with his kisses, but then that was to be expected. A man should know that his wife's desires and passions would never be as strong as his.

He looked at her again, his Emma, and this time their gazes met across the table. Geoffrey felt his smile tighten a little. Her eyes seemed even more changeling than usual tonight, like dark and restless seas.

It always worried him when she became like this, for then he couldn't know what she was thinking. He couldn't predict what she would do or say, and so he always felt as though he were out of tune with her, thinking black when she meant white, hearing yes when she'd said no.

He loved her so much; he wanted nothing more than to make her happy. But lately . . . lately, he'd had this terrible lost feeling that he was forever disappointing her.

Emma watched her intended sip his consommé doublé out of the white Sèvres soup plate. Watched his lips open and pucker slightly, just the way they did when he kissed her.

He had kissed her earlier, when they had gone for a walk in the garden. When he'd wrapped his arm around her waist and pulled her hard against him, and covered her mouth with his, she had wanted to stop breathing, to surrender. She wanted desperately to believe she had everything she wanted, that *he* could be everything she wanted. That he could be . . . someone else.

Shay.

And Bria.

She should never have allowed them to become separate in her mind, for they had become separate in her heart as well. And she had been left smashed and feeling sick and hollow with longing and a terrible, terrible guilt.

I love him.

I will love him not.

She couldn't allow this wrong, impossible love. This betrayal of the one person who mattered most to her in this world. She would have to stay far, far away from him, and then no one would ever know. It would be her secret to keep, another one of those things she couldn't speak of, or think about. Or feel.

It had been nearly a week since she'd been to the house on Thames Street. She would never be able to go there again. Bria would be hurt by that alone, at first, but eventually she would decide that Emma Tremayne had simply become bored with playing peasant after all.

But how could she go to Bria and say: *I can't be near you anymore, dearest, and only, friend, because where you are, so is Shay, and I have fallen in love with him. I am in love with your husband.*

She looked again at Geoffrey Alcott. Her intended. He was impeccably dressed tonight as always. His black cutaway managed somehow to be both understated and yet obviously expensive. His matching black pearl vest buttons, cuff links, and tie pin were elegant but didn't attract undue attention. Geoffrey, she'd heard her mother say to her uncle the doctor just moments before, was as solid as the bricks on the mills he owned.

But she was behaving unfairly, she knew, blaming Geoffrey for being exactly the sort of man he was meant to be.

Emma reached for her wine, caught her mother's frown, and so she set the glass back down. Good form dictated that she take two sips per course and no more, and tonight Mama was apparently counting.

Her mother was so encrusted with diamonds she glittered white like the Milky Way. Diamond rings, diamond bracelets, a diamond-studded brooch, a diamond tiara. And the biggest sparkler of all—a twelve-strand diamond necklace cascading over her bosom. Perhaps, Emma thought with a tinge of weary sadness, Mama was hoping all that dazzle would hide the holes in the family left by those who had run away. Or been made to stay away.

But she would as always do her duty, would Mama, no matter who was hurt by it, no matter what the cost. Emma had heard Geoffrey's grandmother whisper to Mrs. Longworth that duty was preserving Bethel Tremayne like a salt mackerel, and so she was likely to outlive them all.

Her own duty, Emma knew, was to marry well, to marry

money, to be the sort of wife a brick-solid gentleman like Geoffrey Alcott would be proud to have on his arm. To have the kind of life with him that she was meant to have.

She could hear Geoffrey talking now in his soft flat voice to the man seated next to him, about how he would be spending the summer up in Maine, building a foundry. Had he told her that? She couldn't remember. She had found during the course of this spring that they could be in the same room for hours on end, she and Geoffrey, without exchanging a word. Of course, no one when out in society spoke with one's husband or intended. Like laughing at one's own little jokes, or yawning in church, or staring at strangers—it simply wasn't done.

They would live in the same house, she and Geoffrey. They would go to soirees and garden parties together, and to church of a Sunday, and never would they speak about the things that really mattered. She would watch him carefully, but silently, to see what choices he made, since his choices would determine the whole of her life. He would expect her to be content with his choices, as long as he kept her properly adorned in Worth gowns and Fabergé jewels.

And so she would be on a glittering carousel, going round and round, unable to get off and yet going nowhere, and always knowing exactly how her life would unfold. No one would expect them to be passionately in love, she and Geoffrey. It simply wasn't done.

Chapter Eighteen

Bria's shoes crunched on the shingled sand as she walked along the beach. It was a sweet May night, with the breeze blowing warm and soft. And not nearly loud enough to drown out her own labored breathing.

She'd been walking here for the last hour, back and forth over her little patch of the world. From time to time she would stop and look out across the harbor to Poppasquash Point. Tonight the silver house was ablaze with lights.

It seemed a wonder to think of Emma in that place, dancing in a gilded ballroom with diamonds in her hair. Not the Emma she knew, who'd boiled sheets with her and picked raspberries. Who had spoken of mirrored hearts and held her hand when she'd cried.

She hadn't seen Emma in over a week, and she wondered some why this was so. But then Emma did have another life, her *real* life, as she liked to call it. A life of duties and social obligations. Of dances in gilded ballrooms with diamonds in her hair.

It was just . . . just that she wished Emma was here with her now, this very moment. To hold her hand if she should have to cry.

As soon as Bria thought this, the pains came again, gripping her lower back and spreading around to clench her belly. She paused in her walking, her breath going shallower.

It would come tonight, this babe of hers.

This babe. What a strange thing it was, Bria thought, that the acts of love and passion and rape and whoring could all end the same—with a babe growing big and full of life in your belly.

After the resident magistrate had taken her like a dog, bent over a stone wall, she had made a pilgrimage to the shrine at Slea Head. There she drank from the holy well and prayed, begging God to make her bleed. She tied her rosary to the fairy thorn and walked three times around the cross toward the sunrise, and begged God to make her bleed. She did this for three days, and on the last day she bled, and so she knew there would be no child of rape. That time.

Now, three years later, she prayed for something else. She prayed that God would give this babe she carried the black hair and green eyes of his father . . . who might not be his father.

His father—the man who might be his father—had had fair hair and gray eyes. She could remember that much about him, but nothing of his face. Whenever she made herself try to picture his face, all she could see was the smiling white-lipped face of a clown. A clown's face on a vaudeville calendar, hanging on a door in Castle Garden.

Castle Garden—the place where the immigrants passed through into New York, into America. Such a stewpot of smells it had been. The spice of an old woman's garlic sausage poking out the top of her string bag. The sweet milky smell of a new mother putting her babe to her breast. The stink of a toddler with soiled drawers.

And such a tumult of noise. Bells and whistles and horns. Shouts of anger, fear, and joy, all in a babel of tongues. All echoing through the open rafters of the huge round brownstone fort. And everywhere there were men in blue serge suits, pushing and pointing them into lines.

So many lines and questions. Where are you from? Where are you going? Have you family here? Do you have work waiting for you?

She'd felt smug for having all the right answers. She had a husband and a brother who were Americans already, and a home waiting for her in a place called Bristol, Rhode Island. For two years her husband had worked in the onion fields there, and then a month ago he'd sent her an American ticket, a paper with an eagle on it that was as good as money, and she'd used it to pay for their ship's passage, for her and her two girls, and now here they were. In America.

Bria had begun to feel confident with all her right answers, until she got into the line for the medical examination.

The physicians thumped people's chests and listened to their lungs with instruments that had small metal ear trumpets and rubber tubes. They made the women open their shawls and dresses. Though some women were shy and others mortified, still they made them do it.

The line was an eternity long. They would all stand, shuffle forward a few feet, and stand again. Noreen held Bria's hand, gripping it so hard it hurt down to the bone. Merry wrapped her fist up tightly in Bria's skirt. She hummed constantly, a high-pitched, worried buzz.

Eventually they got close enough to the front of the line to see better what was happening. The physicians were examining a family someone said was from Russia. The women were wrapped in large fringed shawls and had kerchiefs tied over their heads. The men wore vests decorated with braids and big frog buttons. One of the women had the letter *E* chalked on her shoulder. She seemed to have drawn one doctor's particular attention.

Suddenly the woman let out a loud wail and began to

weep, wringing her hands and pulling at her clothes. Horrified whispers skittered up and down the line in a swirl of languages.

She's being rejected. . . . She's blind. . . . She's an undesirable. . . .

Fear clutched at Bria's belly so strongly she nearly vomited. They would listen to her chest and hear the swamp that lived inside her lungs, and she would be declared rejected, an undesirable. Her children would be wrenched from her arms, and she would be put on a boat back to Ireland, she and Shay would be parted forever, and she would die alone.

She was dizzy and nearly blind herself with fear by the time it became her turn. When one of the physicians checked her eyes for some disease by turning her eyelids inside out—a thing that hurt terribly—Bria was sure he would say, *Rejected, rejected, rejected.* . . . And then he picked up his chest-listening instrument.

"Unfasten your bodice. Shirtwaist and shift, and your corset if you're wearing one," he said in the coldest voice she'd ever heard. They hadn't asked the other women to open their underthings, which meant, she thought, that they probably already suspected her of having the wasting disease. The way they had suspected that old Russian woman of being blind.

Bria's hands shook so, she could barely manage the hooks and laces. But the man didn't put his instrument to her chest, he put his hand. He rubbed the backs of his knuckles under the round sloping moons of her breasts, following their shape.

Bria looked up and met his eyes and saw what he wanted, even before he spoke.

"Is it true what they say about you Irish lasses?" he said. The chest-listening instrument dangled from his other hand, the little ear trumpet swinging like a pendulum, back and forth, back and forth. "Have you a fire in your belly to match the fire on your head?"

Bria could hear her own breath rattling wet and thick in her throat. A cough tore out of her chest, loud and racking, sounding horrible even to her own ears.

The metal ear trumpet swung again, back and forth. "Do you have consumption?" He said it as a question, but it was meant as an accusation.

Bria undid another button on her shirtwaist. She turned slightly so that her breast filled the whole of his palm. But when her nipple tightened and hardened against his fingers, she shuddered and jerked away from him.

He sighed and let his hand fall to his side. "Consumption is a contagious disease," he said. "I'm supposed to report all cases of contagious diseases to the Department of Health. Likely you will be deported."

"But what—" Her voice cracked roughly as she picked up his hand and put it back on her breast. "But what if you don't report it?"

"Come with me," he said then, simply that and no more. But then it was all he needed to say.

"My girls," she did manage to whisper back to him, so choked with fear and shame now that she could barely breathe.

The physician turned to a woman who stood beside a desk, writing things in a big black leather registry. Bria, looking down at the floor, saw only the woman's black button shoes and the hem of her navy serge skirt. "Miss Spencer," he said, "this woman warrants a more thorough examination. Give her two little Irish lasses a peppermint stick and see to it that they don't wander off."

Bria followed him into a small room that was crowded with desks and wooden crates, but empty of people. She turned around and faced the open door, wanting to run back through it and knowing she would not.

She looked out on the line where they combed your hair, checking for head lice. One woman, her hair newly cropped close to her pink scalp, her face raw with shame, stood quivering with her eyes squeezed shut, and as Bria watched, a man lifted a bucket of sulfur water and poured it over the woman's head.

A hand touched the back of Bria's neck.

"I hope you catch it from me," she said to him. "I hope you rot from it."

He laughed. "Lassie, the only thing I can catch from the part of you I'll be fucking is the pox." He laughed again and pushed the door shut with a soft click, and the immigrant woman's face was replaced with that of a smiling, white-lipped clown on a vaudeville calendar.

When Bria walked back through that door again, she knew that she would never speak of what had been done to her, of what she had allowed to be done. Not to Shay, who was staggering already from the burden of shame he felt for all he'd put her through. And not to God, whose commandment she had broken.

For a woman to lie with a man not her husband, whether for money or an immigrant document—in the eyes of Mother Church it was all the same. Bria McKenna had played the part of a whore.

Bria had that document clutched tightly in her hand when she and the girls walked through the big columned entrance of Castle Garden and out into streets swarming with shouting people, pushcarts, and wagons. She didn't see how she would ever find Shay in such a crush of humanity, and suddenly she was sure that it had all been for nothing—her sin and her shame. That God's terrible and swift sword of retribution would keep them forever apart by not letting her find him in this America that she had given up so much to enter.

She turned around and around in a circle, making herself dizzy, wanting to scream. She kept thinking she heard someone shout her name, but every time she whirled in that direction, all she saw were strangers' faces. Then she spotted Donagh, his black priest's cassock standing out in the colorful crowd. And suddenly Shay was there, and she was in his arms, and she heard him say her name, just her name, but he didn't sound like himself. The hanging rope had stolen away his beautiful voice.

His mouth came down hard on hers, and for one fierce and terrible moment she thought she would be sick. But then she was clinging to him, clinging desperately, and she clung to him all through their first night together after so long apart, as if she would never let him go.

The doctor's touch had been crude and rough and taking, where Shay's was all tender and giving. But the ending had been the same, both men had spilled their seed inside her.

And she had conceived a child her first day in America.

A child that would soon be drawing its first breath, here in this America.

Bria sucked in a sharp breath of her own as another pain wrapped around her back and belly, squeezing hard. But the pains weren't as strong as they would be later and they hadn't shown a close pattern as yet. He would be a while in coming, their son.

Still, the hurting was fierce enough that she had to stop her pacing and lean against a pier piling. She closed her eyes, rubbing the small of her back.

When she opened her eyes again, she was looking into her husband's white face.

"Shay," she said, gasping a little. "The baby's coming."

"Aye, I can see that." He smiled and there was only the weeist bit of a tremble to it. "Were you thinking, maybe, of telling me soon?"

"*Och.* It's hours off yet."

He slid his arm around her waist, taking her weight, and began to lead her back to the house. "That's as may be, but my heart would be beating some easier if you were inside and tucked up safe in our bed. A fisherman's babe it might be, but dropping the little darlin' here on the beach is carrying things a wee bit too far, surely?"

A fisherman's babe.

"Shay." She grasped his arm, pulling him hard around to face her. "Promise me you'll love this babe no matter what happens."

"Bria . . ." Her name came out almost as a sob, but he caught it. He cupped her face with his big hand, brushing his mouth across hers, sweetly, tenderly.

She leaned in to him, nestling her face into the curve of his neck. She breathed against his warm skin, smelling sea salt and that male smell that was uniquely his. "Promise me," she said.

His hand came up, his fingers tangling in her hair, pulling her head back so that she could see his promise in his eyes. "I'll love the babe. I love it already."

"And will you do something else for me, then?"

He dipped his head to lean his forehead against hers, rubbing noses. "You're a fine one, you are, for hoarding all your requests and then spending them so freely just when I would sprout wings like an angel and fly to the heavens to bring you back the moon should you be asking for it."

"You'd look a sight odd in angel's wings, Seamus McKenna—you've too much of the devil about you. And whatever would I want with the moon?"

He laughed again and kissed her hard on the mouth. "I love you, wife."

He began to walk with her again, arm in arm, slowly, for she was so big and clumsy now, and the shingled sand, wet from the tide, slid slick beneath their feet. She felt another pain coming, spiraling out from someplace deep, deep inside her.

"Then will you go and fetch Miss Tremayne," she said, "and bring her here to be with me for the birthing?"

His arm tightened around her waist, and to her surprise the pain subsided. "Isn't she a thought too grand for it?" he said. "Of what use would she be to you?"

No, the pain was coming after all, and it would be worse than before. "She is my particular woman friend. This is her place to be on this night. With me."

"Aye, so particular a friend is she that you call her Miss Tremayne."

The pain crashed over her, out of her, through her, strong and violent like a hurricane wave. She wanted Emma to hold her hand, to keep the tears at bay.

"Bring her to me, Shay. Please . . . I need her."

Emma Tremayne walked out of the dining room feeling stifled. As if she'd just spent the evening locked up in a clothes press, being smothered by yards and yards of silk and satin and taffeta, and all of it smelling powerfully of stale perfume and camphor balls.

The men had been left to their cigars and brandy. The women were retiring to the drawing room, where they would engage in more conversation, and Emma didn't think she could bear it.

Afterward, when the men rejoined them, she would be expected to play the piano and sing a lover's duet with Geoffrey, although she was not particularly skillful at either singing or playing, and everyone would of course be staring, and she really didn't think she could bear that at all.

Emma stopped suddenly just inside the drawing room, unable to go one step farther, to take one breath more. She gripped her green chiffon skirts so hard she trembled and her hands made tight fists.

"Emma? What is the matter?"

Her mother's face wavered before her. Emma closed her eyes and put the back of her hand against her cheek. "I feel faint," she said, trying to sound weak and trembly. Ladies were supposed to feel faint on occasion; it showed a certain delicacy on their part and encouraged men to feel protective. Mama was always fainting. "I . . . I think I ought to go lie down for a while."

"Oh, very well, if you must. We can't have you making a scene," Bethel said. She sounded peevish, but not, to Emma's relief, disbelieving. "I'll make your excuses."

"Thank you, Mama," Emma said, letting her voice trail off into a sigh.

She turned and made herself walk slowly through the velvet-swagged doorway. But she wanted to run.

She was halfway up the oak stairs when the knocking began. She spun around again, nearly falling. She grabbed the banister tightly with a silk-gloved hand. She had no reason to believe it was he, yet she knew, she knew.

She went back down the stairs, but slowly, for her legs felt as stiff as old leather, and her heart thumped unevenly. She stared at the big coffered ebony doors a long time before she jerked them open, and then she was looking at his face, into his eyes, looking at him.

At first he said nothing, then his ruined voice came in a whisper. "My wife . . ." The words were so much an echo of that other night, she was almost shocked to see a clear, star-filled sky at his back. "Bria's having the baby and she's asking for you."

Such a freight of feeling came over Emma that she couldn't move or speak. Bria was having the baby. Bria had asked for her, for *her.* It didn't matter that for honor's sake she had decided to stay away. If Bria needed her, then she would come. For tonight she would come.

Emma heard voices coming from the direction of the drawing room. She took a step nearer to him, pulling the door shut behind her. A balmy sea breeze caressed her bared skin. She heard the bay lapping at the rocks on the shore. His chest was heaving; the sweat was rank on him.

"Oh, God, is it happening now? Did you run all this way?"

"Sure and what was I thinking, awearin' out my poor shoes, when I could've ridden here in my coach with its team of four matching bays to pull it and the gilded crest painted on its doors." He snatched off his hat and thrust his fingers through his hair. "The worst pains've only just started, but she's not known for taking her sweet time at it, so are you coming, or no?"

"But shouldn't we . . . My uncle's here tonight. He's a doctor and—"

He gripped her arm just above the pearl-beaded cuff of her evening glove. As if he would keep her from turning around and going back inside, although she hadn't moved. His hand was rough with calluses.

"No, no doctor," he said. "Bria has such a mortal fear of them, and she doesn't need any more upset. You don't think I'd be here to fetch you otherwise, do you? Except to make her happy?" He let her go and took a step back. "But if you can't be bothered to come, then just be saying so, and I'll be taking myself off."

"Do you expect me to run the three miles back with you, or may we take my carriage? It hasn't got a crest, though, so you'll have to slum it."

She thought he almost smiled at her then, that he thought about smiling. "Ah, *Dhia*, what a strange little miss you are. Just when I think you—" He stopped, shook his head. "I didn't run here, I borrowed Paddy O'Donahue's milk wagon. It awaits beyond your castle gates, Miss Tremayne," he said, and he held out his hand to her.

She put her hand into his, and they walked together down the piazza steps. She hadn't known it could be such an intimate thing, going hand in hand. How it could make you tremble and your heart beat fast and your breath go away entirely.

At the bottom of the steps, he said, "Can you manage a wee bit of a run after all?" And then they were running hand in hand along the quahog-shell drive and through the scrolled iron gates, to where indeed a milk wagon waited.

The wagon smelled of soured milk and was full of empty bottles that rattled in their metal cages as they bounced over the road. He drove recklessly, wildly.

In the wagon's close darkness, she breathed him in, although she was careful not to brush against him or touch him in any way. She thought he must be able to hear her heart beating for him, but she could hide everything else. Her life had made her a master at hiding things.

The wagon swayed as he took the corner onto Hope Street too fast. Emma clutched at the seat, and the frothy chiffon skirts of her evening dress rustled like dry grass in the wind. She wondered what one normally wore to attend a birthing.

She smoothed down her skirts, making them rustle some more. She hugged herself, gripping her elbows, suddenly feeling cold.

He turned to look at her, his face flashing white in the glare of a passing street lamp. "You'll not be having to do anything, you know. The midwife'll be there."

She breathed, swallowed, nodded.

The wagon swayed, the milk bottles rattled, and Bria's husband said, "For two weeks you're there to see her near every day, regular as a cuckoo out of a clock, you are. And then you disappear. Do you think she hasn't noticed?"

Emma swallowed again, breathed again. "I've been busy."

"Have you, then? Bria's been busy herself. Busy dying."

Tears clawed, hot and salty, at Emma's eyes. She turned her head away from him, toward the dark of the passing night.

But when he pulled up to the house on Thames Street, beneath the listing lamppost, he reached across and gripped her chin, turning her face to the white light spilling out from beneath the lamp's cracked globe. She could feel the tears wet on her cheeks; she hadn't been able to stop them.

He said nothing, though, only looked at her, and then he let her go and jumped out of the wagon. He helped her down with a hand under her elbow, turned, and walked away from her up the path, not waiting to see if she followed.

Noreen was sitting on the front stoop, with her arms wrapped around her legs and her shoulders hunched. At the sight of her father, she jumped up and ran into the house ahead of him, through the open door.

Emma stood where she was, among the violets she and Bria had planted. She felt disjointed all over, like a marionette dangling loose on its strings.

She heard a loud humming from behind the milk wagon and she turned. Merry crawled out from between the wagon's large rear wheels. She stood beneath the street lamp, within the circle of its stark light, and stared at Emma with wide, solemn eyes.

"Mam needs you," she said, and it took a moment for Emma to understand that she'd actually spoken real words.

Emma gathered up the chiffon silk skirt of her evening dress and knelt, sitting back on her heels, so that they were eye to eye. Her tongue felt so thick and uncertain. She'd just spent the last hours engaged in endless small talk. Now, when it mattered so much, she seemed to have no words to say, or even breath to speak them with. All her life she'd always had such trouble with words: finding them and losing them, hoarding them and wasting them.

"And so I'm here," she finally said. "Though I'm not sure what good I'll be. You could put what I know about birthing babies into a thimble and still have room left over for a thumb."

Merry's laugh rang pure and bright. She skipped up to Emma and grabbed her hand. "We should go in the house now, 'cause the baby's coming. Noreen says the fairies are going to bring him, but that's silly. He'll be coming out of Mam's tummy, from between her legs."

She tugged on Emma's hand, helping her up, and once Emma was standing, she wrapped both of her hands around Emma's and began swinging their arms back and forth. Her hands were sweaty and sticky, in need of a good washing.

I can do that. I can wash a little girl's hands. At the thought, a warm, elusive feeling swelled inside Emma—an unfamiliar thing, it was. A feeling of belonging, of being needed.

Merry stopped swinging their arms and looked up at her. "You musn't leave us ever again."

Emma didn't know she was crying until she felt the seep of tears on her eyelids. "No, I . . . I won't."

Merry let go of her hand and ran up the path. She hopped onto the stoop with both feet like a rabbit, then looked back at Emma, waiting.

"Merry?" Emma said, her voice pitched low and breaking. "You can talk."

The child rocked once, from one foot to the other. She hummed a long, flat note that could have meant anything, then she disappeared inside the house.

It was bright inside the kitchen with the kerosene lamps all lit. But it was empty. Emma walked slowly into the bedroom as she had walked into so many rooms in her life, feeling shy and self-conscious and unsure.

Bria lay in a white iron bed, with her knees up and bent and spread wide beneath a sheet, and her hands stretched high over her head, gripping the pipe railings. Her back was arched into a taut bow, and she was so drenched with sweat that her thin cotton night rail clung, soaking, to her wasted flesh. Her breathing blew hard in and out her open mouth, sucking and rasping in her chest.

Shay stood at the washstand. He had his coat off and his shirtsleeves rolled up and he was scrubbing his hands in a speckled blue enamel basin. Emma had stopped just inside the door, and he turned to look at her. Taut, white lines bracketed his mouth, and a muscle ticked in his cheek, alongside the scar.

"The midwife hasn't come," he said.

"She's afraid Mam's going to give her the wasting sickness," Noreen said. "No one ever comes to see Mam anymore because they're all afraid she'll give them the sickness." She stood next to the door, her back and hands flat against the wall like a soldier at attention. Merry stood next to her, mute and still.

But Bria had turned her head at the sound of their voices. It seemed there was no flesh left on her face, only pale, thin skin pulled tight over the beautiful, strong bones of her skull.

"Emma, *mo bhanacharaid* . . ." She drew in another shallow, rattling breath. "I was so afraid you . . . wouldn't come."

"What, not come and miss *the* premier blessed event of the season?" A strange sound came out of Emma's tight throat, that was both a laugh and a sob. It hurt so sweetly, the love she felt for this woman, her friend.

One of the kitchen's ladderback chairs had been pulled up next to the bed. Emma went to it and sat, her chiffon skirts rustling. "I must make mention, Mrs. McKenna," she drawled in an exaggerated Great Folk drawing-room voice, "that you've chosen a nice night for it, for there's not a cloud in the sky. However, the wind is coming from the southwest, and that always brings wet weather by morning."

Bria's ravaged mouth parted into a smile, and then her whole body lurched in a jolting cramp and her mouth pulled wider into a silent scream. The cramping pain seemed to last forever, and when it ended it left Bria exhausted and trembling. Her blue-tinged lips were marked white where her teeth had bitten. But her dark eyes burned with fierce, brave life as she looked at Emma.

"Will you . . . hold my hand," she said.

Emma took off her evening gloves and let them fall to the floor. She picked up Bria's hand from where it lay limply on the sheet. She had never felt anything so cold as Bria's hand. It was as if all the life had left her body, to live only in her extraordinary eyes.

"You've been . . . dancing," Bria said.

Emma smiled. "And a sad, dull affair it was, too. The violinist forgot his bow and had to pluck at the strings with his nose, the cello was forever missing his cue, and I kept treading on poor Mr. Alcott's toes."

Bria breathed a laugh, and then another shuddering, racking contraction seized her, and she was lost to the long, dark pain of it. When it was over she said, between hard gasps for breath, "I might be . . . having to hang on a wee bit too tightly . . . from time to time."

Emma pushed the wet hair off Bria's forehead with her other hand. "Never you mind that. That's what a friend is for, after all—to lend one a hand when it is needed."

Shay appeared on the other side of the bed with a basin full of water and rags in his hands, and Emma felt a shudder of fear as she suddenly realized the full import of the words: *The midwife hasn't come.*

"I've had me some practice at this," he said to Emma, as if reading her thoughts. "Last time our Merry came so fast there wasn't a moment for taking a breath, let alone sending for anyone."

He bent over and said something to his wife in Gaelic, and though the words were spoken in his harsh, shattered voice, Emma knew they were tender, for their love was, as always, like a living thing in the room.

With amazing gentleness for having such big hands, he lifted the sheet off his wife's spread thighs. Bria's night rail was rucked up around her waist, and runnels of sweat coursed down her legs. Her distended belly quivered and jumped, then suddenly contracted and squeezed like an enormous fist.

As Shay washed between his wife's legs, Emma looked around the bedroom, noticing its clean shabbiness. There was little furniture: only the bed, with a crucifix hanging on the wall above it, the washstand, and a small bureau with chipped varnish. And something that looked to be an altar set up beneath a postcard of the Virgin Mary. Then she realized that at some point Shay must have sent the girls back into the kitchen, and she wondered if that meant that whatever was to happen would happen soon.

Whatever was to happen . . . Her own ignorance frightened her. She could recite all the rules of etiquette for presenting a formal dinner for thirty-four. But a seven-year-old child knew more than she did about such an elemental part of life as childbirth.

But then it didn't come soon, after all—whatever was to happen.

Bria clung to Emma's hand, squeezing hard, crushing flesh and bone, while the cramping pains came and went, came and went, on and on, through the night's long hours. The newspapers that had been slipped between Bria's hips and the sheets became soaked with watery blood and the smell of it filled the room, rank as spoiled fruit, and still the babe didn't come. And the waiting for it to end, and the fear that it would end badly, became like a scream in Emma's mind.

Then at last, at last, she heard Shay say, "If you could push just a wee bit more now, darlin'. Its head is showing."

Huffing and panting, Bria was trying to push herself up on her elbows, as if she would look between her legs to see what was happening. "Emma, tell me . . . what color hair does he have?"

Emma looked between Bria's legs. The baby's head was indeed emerging out of Bria's womb. A real baby's head with hair and skin and veins, wet with mucus and blood, moving with life. Never had Emma seen such an awesome, frightening, beautiful thing.

"It's red, I think. It's red and curly and there's lots of it . . . Oh, Bria, he'll be having your hair!"

Bria fell back against the pillows, laughing, gasping. "*Och*, the poor wee lad . . . to come into the world with such an affliction."

Emma watched in wonder and awe as the baby was born from his mother's body, first his head and then one shoulder and an arm, and then all of him was there, cradled in his father's waiting hands, while Emma laughed and wept and stared at them with heartaching joy, and Bria's new son squawked as he took his first breaths of life.

Bria lay on the white iron bed, so drained of strength she looked shrunken. Her hair was plastered to her head in wet, sticky strands. Her face was drawn and impossibly pale. But as she lay gazing up at her husband and their newborn child, there was still all that fire, all that life in her dark eyes.

"Does he have all his bits and pieces, Shay?" she said, and her voice matched what was in her eyes.

His smile was like hot sunshine, breaking across his face.

And even though it wasn't meant for her, it plucked at Emma's soul and cracked open her heart.

"He's perfection itself, m'love. You've given me a fine son."

"Let me see him, let me see— No, wait. Give him to Emma first."

"Oh, no, I shouldn't . . . I might drop him," Emma said, but Shay was already putting the baby into her arms. He was wet with the birth blood, his skin all wrinkled and purple, his tiny face scrunched up tight as an angry fist. "Oh, my," she whispered, as more tears mingled with her smile.

Her arms trembled as she oh-so carefully laid the baby onto her friend's breast. Bria's mouth broke open into a smile of her own that went from her man to Emma and then widened to embrace the whole world.

"He's beautiful," she said.

Shay McKenna dropped onto his knees beside the bed. His back bowed and his head came down and he pressed his face into his wife's breast, next to his squirming son. "Ah, darlin', darlin' . . ."

Slowly, Emma got up from the chair and left them alone with their son, and their love.

The girls were sitting together on the front stoop. Merry had fallen asleep with her head in her sister's lap, and she didn't wake when Emma opened the door. Noreen looked up, fear and hope warring it out in her eyes.

"You have a new baby brother and your mama is just fine," Emma said. Her voice sounded strange to her own ears, too stiff and formal. She tried to make her mouth smile. "You should wait a few minutes before you go in and see them, though. Your papa will be needing to make him all nice for company."

She left them then, walking down the path to the street. But when she saw the milk wagon she realized she had no way of getting herself home, so she walked around the house and down to the rocky, shingled beach.

The moonlight on the bay had grown old. The tide slept, caught between the old night and the new day. She stood alone at the water's edge. It was so still, all she could hear was the ocean noises of her own heart.

Dawn was just beginning to leach the dark out of the sky when she heard the scraping of a shoe on the rocks behind her. She turned and watched him come.

He stopped before her and searched her face, and she searched his.

"She's sleeping," he finally said. "They're both sleeping, her and the babe."

So many things to say to him . . . She had a lifetime of things to say, and so few were allowed. Even fewer would be welcome.

"Later," he said, "when she comes awake, she'll be wanting to thank you."

"But I didn't do anything."

He took her by the wrist, lifting her hand. Even in the pale light, the bruises and nail marks were livid on her flesh. "You came," he said.

He let go of her, and her hand floated down to her side as if weightless. It was as if her hand suddenly didn't feel a part of her at all, but rather a thing disconnected from herself.

He looked away from her, toward the bay. The rising sun was painting watercolor splashes of red and yellow across the sky. "It can be a joyous thing, sometimes, to see the sun rise up on a new day." His gaze came back to meet hers, and his smile broke across his face brighter than any sunrise. "Would you not say so, Miss Tremayne?"

She knew his smile for the gift that it was, no more and no less, and so she gave it back to him. "I would say, Mr.

McKenna, that a new day can be the most joyous thing in the world."

The sun was rising golden and voluptuous over the gabled roofs of The Birches by the time Emma climbed the piazza steps and walked through the coffered ebony doors. The house was hushed in an early-morning stillness, the marbled hall gray and cold as a mausoleum.

Emma closed the heavy doors gently behind her and walked on light feet across the hall toward the oak staircase. But as she passed the great mirror, she caught the flashing reflection of a pale wraith floating next to the white jade newel post, where the Tremayne daughter had burned to death so many years ago.

"Mama?" Emma said, fear putting a creak in her voice. She would rather have faced a dozen ghosts than be caught out in an impropriety by her mother.

"How could you, Emma? How could you do this to me?"

Emma's steps had faltered at seeing her mother, but now she made herself go on, all the way to the foot of the staircase. I'm not a child anymore, she thought. I can't be beaten, or locked up in the cellars, and this time I know in my heart I've done nothing wrong.

"Didn't I tell you to keep your drawers buttoned and your knees together until after a ring was on your finger?" her mother was saying in a Georgia drawl so thick Emma could barely understand it.

"Mama, you never . . . What are you saying?"

"You are ruined, disgraced. The entire family is ruined. You've up and given him just what he wanted, haven't you? He'll never marry you now. You—" Bethel's face suddenly blanched white and haggard. "God in heaven, did he force you?"

Emma looked down at herself, following the direction of her mother's horrified stare. Her green silk chiffon evening gown was streaked rusty red in the front with dried blood. For a moment she couldn't think how Bria's blood had come to be on her, and then she remembered that she'd held the baby just after he was born.

"Oh!" Emma exclaimed, flushing hot, as the full implication of her mother's words finally struck her. "It's not what you're thinking at all, not at all. Mrs. McKenna had her baby tonight. I've been with her, not Geoffrey."

Her mother staggered forward and then she swayed, collapsing onto the wide bottom tread of the sweeping stairs. She hugged her knees and rocked once, twice. When she looked up again at Emma, tears silvered wetly on her face. The blue of her eyes, Emma saw, was nearly swallowed up by the black centers.

"Not what I think, not what I think . . . What else was I *supposed* to think?" Bethel said, a shudder in her voice. "I discover your bed empty in the dead of night, and you're nowhere to be found. You say you're feeling faint and must leave the party early, and then Mr. Alcott suddenly discovers he has pressing business and must leave as well, and naturally the first thought that leaps to one's mind is . . . Why, by this afternoon the whole of society will be talking about your little 'fainting spell.' There'll be whispers and sly innuendos bantered about for weeks. We'll be watched carefully—oh yes, we'll all be watched. And it won't let up, not even when it becomes obvious that their worst suspicions won't be realized. They *won't* be realized, will they, Emma?"

"No, Mama," Emma said, flushing again, for surely this was one of those things they ought never to be talking about.

But then she had never seen her mother like this. She looked like a child awakened from a bad dream, shaking, hugging herself and rocking back and forth, wrapped up in a white quilted robe and with her hair up in pins. Her eyes so wide and staring and dark.

Emma sat on the stairs beside her. She almost laid her arm across her mother's shoulders, but in the end she didn't. She was too afraid it wouldn't be welcome. She was sitting close enough, though, to feel the fine trembling going on inside the other woman.

"Mama, have you been taking Maddie's medicine?"

Bethel gave a hard shudder and gripped her knees tighter. "My nerves have been so frazzled lately. You can't appreciate what it's like, the constant *vigilance* . . . I've always had such a delicate constitution, you know that, and yet still you're cruel to me, to have given me such a scare. All of my children have always been so cruel to me."

"I'm sorry, Mama. I would've told you where I was going, but . . ." *You would have tried to stop me, and I would have had to defy you, and there would have been one of those scenes you dread so much.* "But there wasn't time."

Bethel lifted her head and stiffened her shoulders, for a moment more of her old self. "That woman is a bad influence on you, Emma. I knew no good would come of it."

"It was all my own fault—I should have told you . . . Here, let me help you up to your room," Emma said. But she hesitated a moment before wrapping her arm around her mother's waist and half-lifting her to her feet. They began to climb the stairs slowly. Her mother leaned in to her for the first two steps and then began to pull away.

"Shall I send Jewell up with some breakfast?" Emma said. "You need to eat something. All those lovely courses at dinner last night and you didn't have more than a bite from any of them."

Bethel shook her head so hard her whole body shuddered. "No, no. No more eating. I'm too fat, and you know how your father cannot abide fat women. He'll be coming home for your wedding, and I'll have my slender figure back by then. He'll be able to see that I've changed, and then he'll stay. You watch and see if he doesn't stay."

"Yes, Mama," Emma said, fighting back a sudden need to cry. Tears. It seemed she had shed so many of them lately, both happy and sad, and yet the well seemed never to empty.

Mama was looking up at her, a raw hope burning in her face, brightening it like candleglow. "He loves me, Emma," she said. "He's only forgotten it. But when he sees me, he'll remember. It will be like that night of the Sparta ball, and he will love me again. He'll love me forever this time. See if he doesn't love me forever."

Chapter Nineteen

It began as a day of high sun and a crisp starboard wind. A perfect sailing day, or so Emma had told her.

It had been Bria's idea to go on a clambake, her first outing since little Jacko's birth. It was Emma, though, who suggested that they sail her sloop over to Town Beach, which lay around The Ferry, on the west shore of Mount Hope Bay.

"Father O'Reilly can bring the baby and the girls in the tea cart and meet us there," Emma said. "Just think what fun it will be, just the two of us. We can pretend we're lady pirates at sail on the high seas."

"Sweet saints," Bria said. "You've a queer notion of what's fun, Emma Tremayne."

Emma laughed, sounding happy. "Please say yes, Bria. It will be a short little sail—with this wind, only a half hour at the most. And we'll be in sight of the shore the whole way."

"Hunh," Bria said, fighting back a smile. "It's relieved I am, to know I'll be having a scenic view to look at whilst I'm drowning."

Although born and raised within a high tide's reach of the sea, Bria had never been on a boat in her life, except for the big steamship that had brought her to America. Fishing was men's work, and surely no one in Gortadoo had ever sailed a sleek little racing sloop just for the pure joy of it.

This particular racing sloop was named *Icarus*, after some daft Greek who flew too close to the sun with wings made of wax, or so Emma had told her. Not a thing, surely, Bria thought as she climbed aboard with quaking legs, to inspire confidence in a landlubber like herself.

No sooner did they cast off from shore than Bria wanted off. The wind bellied the sails, and the boat canted so steeply its deck rail sliced the water. Bria's heart was flopping in her chest like a netted fish, and she went through two dozen Hail Marys before she believed Emma's laughing promise that the sloop wouldn't tip all the way over and dump them both in the drink.

She liked the music sailing made, though. The rush of the wind pushing over the sails, the spill and splash of water over the bow. She let her head fall back, and the sun poured over her face like wild honey. She licked her lips, enjoying the taste of the salt.

She smiled as she listened to Emma explain how the sails worked with the wind to make the boat go so fast through the water, although she made little sense of it. She felt so full up inside with happiness, and the day would have been perfect if only Shay could have been there. But it seemed as if he'd been trying to catch all the fish in the sea lately, so that he could pay back the money he owed on the dory.

They turned toward shore and Town Beach, and Bria watched the flat white swatch of sand grow larger, sparkling in the sun. The sails went slack and began to flap as they coasted up to a barnacle-studded pier. Emma picked up a mooring line and lifted her skirts, but instead of jumping out onto the dock she went utterly still, as if she'd just been winded.

"What is it?" Bria said, standing up on shaky legs, for the boat never seemed to feel quite steady beneath her feet. She didn't see how Emma managed, especially in skirts, climbing all over to adjust this or that rope—or "sheets" as Emma insisted they were called.

"It's nothing," Emma was saying. "Only, Mr. . . . Mr. McKenna has come after all."

"Shay?" Bria's face broke into a beaming smile as she spotted the cart that had just turned onto the beach road. She waved so hard the boat rocked and she had to grab on to the boom to keep from falling.

"Mother Mary, I nearly went for a swim!" she exclaimed, laughing at herself. But when she looked up at Emma, she saw that the other woman was still standing with the mooring line forgotten in her hands, her face pale and tight. It all had to do with Shay, Bria knew. Emma had never been at ease in his company and she did everything she could, short of outright rudeness, to avoid it, and Bria supposed she couldn't blame her. Not after those mean things he'd said to her that one day.

Bria never would have said so to Emma, not wanting to hurt her feelings, but she was that happy to be setting foot on firm land. Her legs felt funny for a bit, as if things were still rocking beneath her. But then the girls came running across the white sand, Merry so full of excited hums she was fairly vibrating with them. Laughing, Bria looked around. It was a pretty spot for a clambake. Little sea meadows encroached on the sandy beach, thick with wildflowers and rimmed with black-green firs and stately maples and elms.

"Where's my scamp of a brother?" she said to Shay, standing on tiptoe to kiss him on the mouth. He carried little Jacko, wrapped like a cocoon, in a straw basket.

Bria peeled back the edge of the blanket and saw the baby was sleeping. Shay raised a hand to wave at Emma, but she was on the sloop, folding the sails, and didn't see him.

"The good father got a summons from his bishop this

mornin'," Shay was saying, "and it seems 'I'll be along later' wasn't to be allowed as an answer."

"*Och*, the poor lad. He's in trouble again, sure as I'm saying it." Her brother had ever been the one for not following all the rules, and even the priesthood hadn't completely cured him of his wildness.

Shay huffed a laugh as he handed her the baby. "Well, as Donagh himself did put it: 'Likely he hasn't asked me to drop around so's he can hang a halo on my head.' "

While Shay and the girls gathered driftwood to build a fire for the clambake, and little Jacko lay sleeping in his basket, Bria helped Emma to spread out a blanket and unpack the hamper of food she'd brought along. "Just a little something to nibble on," Emma had said, "while we wait for the clams to steam."

Emma's idea of a little something to nibble on was deviled eggs, lobster sandwiches, champagne, peaches, and coconut meringues. She'd even brought along plates and silverware to eat her little somethings with, Bria discovered as she dug deeper into the hamper. Plates that were so thin she could see her hand right through them. And four different kinds of forks.

She held up one of the forks so she could see it better—a small, skinny, two-pronged thing that looked to be about as much use as a three-legged mule. "Whatever good is this for?" she asked.

Emma's mouth curved into one of her shy smiles. "That's an oyster fork. For just in case."

"In case of what?"

She shrugged prettily. "In case we find some oysters and decide to eat them."

Just then a gull flew by to drop an oyster on some nearby rocks. The oyster split open and the gull dove at the broken shell, plucking out the succulent treat.

"Faith," Bria said. "We should be giving that bird one of your forks."

Emma caught a laugh with her hand, and then she laughed outright, laughed hard, so that Bria was soon laughing with her, even though she was still some sore from the birthing. She found it hilarious that the Great Folk needed special forks to eat oysters with, when the gulls did not. Yet she found it splendid to know that such a thing as an oyster fork existed in this strange and marvelous world.

"And what is there about this day that has the pair of you laughing so?" Shay said as he and the girls came up to dump armloads of wood onto the sand. But when Bria tried to explain it to them, Shay looked at her as if she'd been out in the sun too long. While Noreen and Merry shared secret smiles.

Emma held one of the peaches out to Bria on the palm of her hand. "Have one of these," she said, and there was laughter all over her, on her mouth, in her eyes. "Only you might be obliged to go break it open on those rocks over yonder . . . since I forgot the fruit knives." Which set them to laughing again.

And when Bria was finished clutching her aching belly and wiping the tears off her cheeks, she looked at Shay and saw him smiling, deep in his eyes.

Bria laughed again and bit into the peach. The juice ran out the corners of her mouth, dripping off her chin, and it was so delicious she shivered with the wonder of it.

She turned to say as much to Emma, and she was struck, as she so often was, even after all this time of knowing her, by the girl's breathtaking beauty. She looked posed for a portrait in a white dress of some silky-crisp stuff sprigged with roses and leaves, and a pale straw hat, its brim weighted with daisies. All the light that was in the world seemed to have gathered around her, thick as cream.

Little Jacko began fussing then, so Bria took him out of

his basket to nurse. Shay began to tell the girls a story while he made the clambake fire, laying stones in a circle and putting kindling on top.

"Once there were two princes, one Irish and the other a Scot, who wanted to rule over the same grand island, itself a great wonder of the world—"

Merry spun around, red curls flying, humming loudly.

"She wants to know," Noreen said, "what the Irish prince's name was, and if he was handsome."

"His name was Ivor the Brave, and sure if he wasn't one of the handsomest men born to woman, being Irish and a McKenna by way of his mother's father."

Bria snorted. "Likely a great liar he was, too. Being both Irish and a McKenna."

"And wasn't it the lucky thing, then," Shay said, "that the man didn't have a wife always ready and willing to point out his faults. . . . As I was saying, the two princes, they held a boat race, you see, for it was agreed that the first of the princes to touch the island would be wearing the island's crown for all the days to come thereafter. Now the Irish prince, when he saw he was losing the race, he took out his sword and cut off his hand and threw it onto the island's shore—"

Merry hummed and jumped up and down.

"She wants to know," Noreen said, "why he cut off his whole hand. Why didn't he just do the one finger?"

"Aye, well . . ." Shay sucked on his cheek. He shoved his fingers through his hair. "Because . . . because he couldn't throw a finger that far. He needed a thing a sight heftier. He needed a whole hand."

"Hunh," Bria said. "Will you listen to the man with the words always ready and willing on the tip of his tongue, and sounding fine, they do, until you realize there's no sense to be made to a bit of it."

"There's sense to it if the lot of you would only let me get to the end of my tale. . . . In his haste to lay claim to the island, the Irish prince forgot he would need his two strong hands to protect it with. He managed fine with the one hand, building his house and planting his potato fields, but then along came the thieving English, and sure if the prince didn't see it all pass into their own greedy hands—the house, the fields, and the grand little island itself."

Merry hummed a sad little tune.

"She wants to know," Noreen said, "if Miss Emma could buy the island from the thieving English and give it back to the prince so's he can live happily ever after."

Shay sighed and shook his head. "An island such as that one is only bought with the blood of a brave warrior, or a full and honest heart. And sure if there hasn't been some question of whether, when you crack open a New England Yankee, there's a heart to be found at all. Or only a black and shriveled bit of stone."

"Seamus McKenna, for shame!" Bria looked at Emma, afraid that she'd been hurt once again, even though this time he'd only been teasing. Yet Emma was staring right back at him, and with an impish look on her face.

Emma stretched out her arm to him. The lace fell away from her sleeve, revealing a pale wrist streaked with blue veins, and in her hand a perfect peach, round and rosy, and she said in her haughtiest Great Folk voice, "Would you like to have a bite of my peach, Mr. McKenna? Only, please, do have a care for the stone. For one can so easily break one's teeth on it . . . can't one?"

Shay's mouth lifted in a loose smile. He looked down the beach where the sloop rocked in its mooring, then back at Emma. "You've a wicked tongue on you, child."

"And quicker than yours, surely," Bria said, "by a New England mile." Little Jacko was done with his suckling. He lay in the curve of her arm with his fists clenched on either side of his fat cheeks and his open mouth gulping air. "Here, take hold of your son and give him a burp, and if you're going to be telling any more stories, leave the blood and politics out of it."

Shay took the baby from her and laid him on his broad shoulder. He cradled little Jacko's tiny bottom in one big hand, while the other gently patted the baby's back. Love for his child softened his hard man's mouth and made his eyes go dark and heavy lidded.

If wasn't for any particular reason that Bria turned to look at Emma then. But once she did, she sat still as a stone and emptied of air, as if she had been kicked in the chest.

For Emma was looking at Shay, and on her beautiful face was pure and naked longing.

She watched them after that; she couldn't help herself.

She sat on the blanket, holding little Jacko in her arms while he slept, and watched them while they raked clams out of the sand and dropped them into buckets.

She could see Emma trying so hard, pretending so hard, but then Shay would laugh, or say some silly, teasing thing to one of the girls, and she would look. Only for a moment would she look, but Bria would catch that sudden burst of longing on her face, like a flash of light under the skin.

She watched to see if Shay did any looking back.

When Emma sat down on a rock to take off her shoes and stockings, he said to her, "You've Yankee feet. Long and skinny."

"And you've Irish feet," she said, right back at him. "Big and always in your mouth."

Even Bria had to smile at that. But she thought also of how Emma's voice sounded different when she spoke to him, as if there wasn't enough breath to push the words out.

Once, the wind caught the brim of Emma's straw hat, knocking it askew. It was a simple thing what she did, very much a woman thing—she raised her arms to take the hat off and put it on again. The wide lace at her sleeves fell away to reveal her bare white arms, and her breasts lifted with a rustle of silk. And then she cocked her head just a little, as she stabbed the hat pins back through the straw. It was a simple thing, but Shay's face changed as he looked at her. Only a little, the barest echo of an echo, but it had changed.

And Bria felt as if a hole opened up inside her heart.

She went on sitting, still as a stone, unable to think, unable to breathe. The wind plucked at her hair and at the pine boughs and maple leaves. The sky was blue, and the bay was bluer, and the sun shone warm on the white sand. And Bria saw none of it, felt none of it.

She jumped when something heavy landed in her lap. She looked up into Noreen's face, she saw Noreen's mouth moving, but it was as if all life had been washed out of the world.

Then Noreen's words came rushing at her in a swell of sound, as if blown to her on the wind. "Mam, look at what I found buried in the sand."

Bria picked up the thing in her lap. "Why, it's some sort of a pipe, I believe."

"It's an Indian soapstone pipe," Emma said. Her dear friend Emma, who had looked at Shay McKenna with such a hunger in her eyes. Bria knew what it was like, though, to have the wildness inside your heart for him, the burning up. She knew what it was to feel your will dissolve when you looked at him.

"That pipe could have belonged to the great King Philip himself," Emma was saying. "Philip was the grand sachem of the Wampanoag, and they owned all this land before the settlers came and took it away from them."

"And isn't that always the way of it," Shay said.

This time Emma looked at him squarely and smiled. "It so happens that King Philip was ambushed and killed by a member of his own race. It's a tale you would appreciate, Mr. McKenna, as it involves blood and politics."

Emma told a story, then, about how this King Philip was killed by an Indian whose brother he had tomahawked, and as a reward that man got Philip's hand, which he carried around in a bucket of rum. Noreen, always the strange one for liking to have herself scared silly with gruesome tales, listened with wide eyes and excited little shivers. While Merry hummed questions faster than Noreen could ask them.

Bria looked at her girls and she saw how young they were and how little they knew. And she thought of how alone they were going to be, her soon-to-be-motherless girls, and she wanted to weep.

She laid her face against the baby's head, his hair so soft against her cheek. He wasn't born so long ago that she couldn't remember the fierce pain of his birthing, that price a woman paid for giving life, and that terrible, glorious moment when he had been torn from her body and he was no longer hers alone.

He was going to be so lost without her, this brand-new son of hers, without even a memory of her and her mother's love to comfort him during the bad and empty times.

She looked at Shay, her man, and love and pain twisted inside her, from her throat to the pit of her stomach. Surely it had only been a moment of manly appreciation that she had seen in his eyes, nothing more. Emma was beautiful beyond a man's dreams, and Shay was every bit of a man. But what if, what if . . .

Not, What if it had been something more?

But, What if it could *become* something more?

She waited until the clams were all gathered, and the fire had burned down to hot embers, and the stones were swept off with a fir limb, and the buckets of clams were dumped on top of the stones and covered with rockweed to hold in the steam.

She waited until all that was done and then she said, "It's a grand day, it is, to be out on the water, what with the way the wind is blowing so. Would you be willing, Emma, to take Shay out for a wee little sail while the clams're steaming? For all the boats he's been on, I doubt one's ever been as fine as your racing sloop."

Her words seemed to echo in the small silence that followed. A flush blossomed over Emma's cheeks, as pink as cabbage roses, and Bria saw her swallow hard. But of course she wouldn't refuse a request put to her like that, from her dearest friend. Emma Tremayne had impeccable manners.

Bria's gaze went from Emma to Shay. A look of raw hunger and yearning had come over his face, but he was looking at the sloop.

Bria watched them walk together down to the little weathered dock where the sloop was moored. They walked close enough that the wind was able to snatch at Emma's skirt and slap it against Shay's legs. But they both looked straight ahead, as if all the world's answers could be found in that sharp white line where blue salt water met bluer sky.

If they spoke at all while they hoisted the sails and cast off, Bria couldn't tell. She buried her face in the bundle of baby in her arms, smelled his warm breath, and brushed her nose against his cheek.

When next she looked up, all she could see of the sloop was its white sails flitting sharply like a butterfly's wings over the blue bay water.

Shay hauled hard on the jibsheet as the sloop came about, cleating the line fast with expert hitches. The wind blew strong and steady, and they sailed up into her, close hauled and nicely trimmed.

The *Icarus* made music to his ears, like the finely tuned instrument that she was. The creak of her hull, the tap of her shrouds on the mast, the flutter of the mainsail's leech when she turned up too close to the wind.

He let his head fall back and closed his eyes, felt the sun burn deep into his eyelids, deep inside him. He felt the tilt and pitch of the deck beneath his feet, heard the suck and splash of the water over the bow, and he knew a moment of pure, unadulterated happiness.

He opened his eyes and turned his head and saw Emma's eyes look quickly away, as if she didn't want to be caught looking at him. She sat in the cockpit with her hand on the tiller. The sinews and bones of her wrist flexed starkly against the skin. It took strength, he knew, to hold the rudder steady in such a wind.

"She's a saucy little craft, Miss Tremayne," he said. And that she was. There would never be any salt pocks on her brass or stains on the glossy teak deck. She also cost more money to buy than he could even dream of. "And you're a deft hand at sailing her."

A smile stole over her face, although she carefully kept that face turned away from him. She'd had to take her hat off because of the wind, and most of her hair had come loose to blow about her, wild and free.

"We Tremaynes like to claim we have salt water in our veins," she said. "My father taught me how to sail. He had me out on the water as soon as I could walk, and by the time I was six I'd already capsized my first boat, a little ten-foot dagger board. I own the distinction of being the youngest Tremayne ever to have manufactured and survived her own shipwreck."

He couldn't help laughing. She surprised him sometimes, the things she said. "I have you beat there, Miss Tremayne. It so happens my mam set out to sea one day, looking for pilchards, and brought me back instead."

She had a way about her, he'd discovered. Her mouth would dimple just at one corner when she was about to say or do something she thought rather daring. "I suppose you're going to tell me the fairies delivered you to your parents in a reed boat, rather like an Irish Moses."

"Not so miraculous as that," he said, shaking his head, smiling. "My mother had taken the curragh out herself that day, my old man having drunk himself under the table the night before. I came early and sudden, or so I was told. She was too far out to turn about, and so there was only herself to take care of herself, and then me."

She looked at him then. He hadn't quite been able to decide what color her eyes were, whether gray or blue or green. They changed the way the sea did on an unsettled day. "She must have been a very brave woman."

"I don't remember her being brave so much as . . ." He shrugged. "As desperate," he finished, and then wondered where that revelation had come from. He didn't often admit such thoughts, even to himself.

He pulled his gaze away from her, from those eyes, and it was almost a physical wrenching, although he couldn't have said why. He studied the sails, in hope that they needed trimming, but they didn't. Suddenly he didn't know what to do with his hands.

"I imagine those clams are about done," he heard her say. "Would you take over the helm and sail her back to shore, Mr. McKenna?"

He gave her a mock salute. "Aye-aye, Captain."

He reached for the tiller just as the wind gusted hard and the boat heeled smartly into it. Emma, in the act of shifting out of his way, grabbed the tiller again herself, to steady her balance, and her hand came down on top of his.

He allowed his hand to feel her hand, just for a moment. And then he slipped his hand out from underneath hers, and that was the end of it.

It wasn't lust, he told himself. Because he couldn't imagine laying her down and taking her the way a man took a woman he wanted, hard and rough and hungry. And it wasn't love—he was sure of that. Love was what he felt for Bria. It was laughing and dancing and working and worrying and fighting and making up and making babies. It wasn't this . . . whatever this was.

Chapter Twenty

"We've a wee bit of time left," Bria said, "before the parade. Why don't we stop off at the gymnasium and see if Shay wants to come along with us?"

She pretended not to notice the dismay that flashed across Emma's face. Instead, she bent over little Jacko's pram and fussed some with the blankets. The shellacked reed pram was upholstered in blue silk plush and lined with woven cane webbing. It was topped with a silk-fringed, satin-lined parasol and rode splendidly along on nickel springs and steel wheels. It had been a christening gift from Emma, and surely no Gortadoo baby had ever been paraded through the world in such style.

"It's not proper," Emma said, after a moment of silence had passed between them, "for a lady to be seen entering such a place."

Bria slanted a teasing smile up at her. "And I suppose it's afraid, the world is, that the sight of a few sweaty, winded, flab-bellied men will be turning us into a pair of wild-eyed, drooling, lust-crazed jezebels."

"Oh, Bria." Emma actually managed a laugh, although it did quiver a little at the edges. "It's just that . . ."

It's just that, Bria thought, you are finding it harder and

harder, *mo bhanacharaid*, to be near him, to be within sight and touch of him. To be within loving distance of him, and yet unable to let yourself love him.

Bria straightened up and laid her hand on Emma's arm. She made her eyes go all soft and pleading, although inside she felt so ill she couldn't get the words out. It seemed such a sly thing, what she was doing, and it was hard. It was too hard.

But then Noreen, bless her, said, "Let's please go get Da, Miss Emma." And Merry chimed in with a mewling hum.

Emma bit her lip and looked down at the hands she had clasped together at her waist. "Well . . ."

Bria let a long trembling breath go and looped her arm through Emma's. "That's settled, then. Noreen, love, you can push the pram for me. Here, Merry, you take hold of my hand." And they all walked together down the violet-bordered path of the Thames Street house, turning uptown.

It had been a week since the clambake, a week since Bria had waited for them on the beach, waited with her feet wedged in the sand, braced against the push of the wind.

It had frightened her when the wind began to gust so. She could see the sloop; she'd been watching it the whole time. But suddenly it had tilted so far over, the sails seemed to be skimming along the white-capped water.

Bria had held little Jacko so tightly in her arms he began to cry, and Merry had stood beside her, humming madly. Noreen was on the dock, jumping up and down and waving as the sloop dropped her sails and drifted toward the pilings.

"Da!" she shouted, her voice rising shrilly above the wind. "We've been watching you sail. Once the wind came up you went so fast! But Mam said there was no one as good a sailor as yourself."

"And there's not," Bria heard him say. "Except maybe for Miss Tremayne, who has sea water for blood and the wind for a kind lover."

Bria had watched Shay jump out and make the boat fast, had heard the squeak of a pulley and the slap of a rope on canvas. Emma stood on deck, hanging on to the shrouds. Her cheeks were flushed, but that could have been from the wind.

Shay walked off the dock and came up to Bria and he kissed her on the mouth, kissed her hard and hungrily. "What are these for?" he said, rubbing his thumbs over her cheeks as if he would gather up all her tears for safekeeping.

"It got so windy and I was afraid. I was afraid I'd lose you both."

She thought she'd seen something shift deep in his eyes then, but it was there and gone so fast she knew she would never be sure. "Well, you didn't," he said. "You haven't."

"No, I haven't, have I?"

She knew him so well, knew them both so well. She had known when she sent them out alone together that nothing would happen.

And that someday everything could happen.

The gymnasium had been a Quaker meetinghouse long ago. But instead of praises sung to the Lord that Sunday afternoon, the massive cross-timbered ceiling echoed with the smack of a fist hitting leather, the slap of a jumping rope on the old puncheon floor, the clatter-clang of dropped barbells. The cavernous old meeting hall was hazy with cigar smoke and reeked of male sweat.

They found Shay working on the punching bag, his feet dancing, his shoulders bobbing and weaving, muscles flexing and bunching. His fists hammered like pistons, faster than the eye could follow, making a *tha-thumping* sound that mimicked the heartbeat of life.

"He's not flab bellied," Bria said.

"No," Emma said, but she wasn't looking at him.

Shay finished with his punching and grabbed the bag with his leather-wrapped hands to stop it from swinging. He was breathing hard and deep, the way he did sometimes, Bria thought, when they made love. Sweat gleamed on his skin, matting his dark chest hair into swirls around his nipples and trickling in slow rivulets down his shuddering belly to disappear into the wet patch on the waistband of his britches.

"Bria, darlin'," he said. He'd been glaring so ugly at the punching bag, as if it were an enemy he had to pummel into submission, but now his face lightened and he smiled. "What are you doing here?"

She smiled back at him, although her eyes surprised her by blurring with tears. It was just that she loved him so much, so much. "Myself, I've turned into a lust-crazed jezebel what's going to ravish you. Afterward, though, we'll all be taking you with us to the minstrels' parade."

"Ravish me, you do say?" He advanced on her, screwing his face into a particularly lecherous leer. "Kiss me instead."

Bria put her hands up in front of her face and pretended to reel back in horror. "Faith, he'll have everyone thinking I'm in love with the man."

Shay turned to his girls instead, smothering them with sweaty hugs that had them squealing and laughing. And that was when Emma looked at him.

She looked at him for only a moment.

But in that one moment she wrote a love song with her eyes. And then Bria was the one who had to turn away.

The pain, *Dhia*, it was like sticking your hand in a fire, almost on a dare, to see if you could feel it, to see if you could bear it. But then she thought it must be hard for Emma as well. Poor Emma's heart, to have been snared by this unasked-for love.

As for Shay—whatever he was feeling, Bria doubted she would ever come to know, not for a certainty. His deepest feelings had always lived behind the hardness that was buried inside him, the place she had never been able to reach. Sometimes he would take such care, as Emma did with him, not to look, holding his head stiff the way he did the morning after he drank too much *poitín.* But at other times he would be all friendly like and teasing, treating her as he would one of his daughters, or a favorite sister.

He never touched her, though, not even in any innocent way.

And so Bria thought that for as long as she lived, he would bend all of his considerable will toward feeling nothing at all. But afterward . . . Oh, it was thinking of the afterward, of what might become, that always brought her such hope, and such pain.

"Hurry up, Da," Noreen said. "We'll be missing the parade."

Shay rested his hand on his daughter's head, and Bria saw that it was badly swollen. "Why don't you go on out and wait for it, and I'll be catching up to you soon as I've washed up."

He scooped a towel off a wooden folding chair and draped it over his bare shoulders. "And a good afternoon to you, too, Miss Tremayne," he said with a grin, then he walked off in that sauntering, lean-hipped way of his, and they all watched him go. Even Emma watched him, and it was as if her beautiful self had been turned to marble.

They went back out onto Thames Street then, for the parade was supposed to be passing by that way from the railroad depot. Already they could hear fiddle music and hornpipes and the rapid, rhythmic heel-toe tapping of Irish step dancing.

The sun beat down hot on the bay, turning it to steam, and heat shimmered in waves off the packed dirt. A man pushed a cart through the crowd, selling salted Spanish peanuts and popcorn balls, and filling the air with wonderful smells.

The parade had just come into view when Shay joined them. He was in shirtsleeves, with his coat hooked over one shoulder, but he'd put on a collar and tie in honor of it being Sunday. The ends of his hair were wet, and his cheeks shone ruddy from a fresh shave. He looked so fine when he came up beside her and wrapped his arm around her waist that Bria wanted to stop breathing, to stop the world altogether.

The parade was little more than a way for the Primrose Minstrels—who would be performing on the common during tomorrow's Fourth of July celebration—to show off their dancing skills. And show them off they did: tapping their way down the street with their faces shining black with burnt cork, the metal caps on their shoes beating out a rhythm to stir the blood of the Irish.

So it wasn't long before the Irish in the crowd had joined the Irish vaudeville act, dancing to the wail of the pipes and scrape of the fiddle, and Shay tossed his coat at Bria and joined them.

He held his back straight and still, his arms close to his sides, while his feet flashed high and fast, clicking, tapping, heel and toe, heel and toe, making shoe music that was as old as Ireland herself. Noreen's eyes fairly sparkled with delight to see him, Merry hummed and tried to do a jig of her own, and little Jacko crowed and pumped his legs in the air.

Too soon the minstrels had danced on by, and Shay fell out, laughing and breathless. They all were laughing, even Emma.

The crowd began to spill into the middle of the street, following in the minstrels' wake. The whole town was already taking on the atmosphere of the next day's holiday. Bristolians, it seemed, had begun celebrating Independence Day before it was even won, back in 1777, and they took pride in putting on the grandest Fourth in the country. Bria overheard many say how tomorrow's parade would be the most spectacular show they were ever likely to see.

Somehow they found themselves strolling out into the countryside, down the Ferry Road. Shay pushed the pram, and Bria put her arm around his waist, feeling the movement of his hips as she walked beside him. She liked this New England custom of these long Sunday-afternoon walks. In Ireland, a wife and her man walked together only once—to church on the day they got married.

Sunshine beat down on their heads from a hazy sky. The air was thick and still, the few sailboats out on the bay bobbing like fishing corks.

Emma walked ahead of them with the girls on either side of her. She looked like a baker's spun-sugar confection in a white dress with big puffy leg-of-mutton sleeves and a big, square collar of crocheted lace. Her white straw hat was decorated with red, white, and blue plumes and long, trailing blue ribbons. Her white lace parasol freckled her back and shoulders with stipples of light and shadow.

Bria was just about to point out to Shay what a stunning picture her friend made, when he reached over to cup the back of her neck with his hand and, lightly, sweetly, caressed the lobe of her ear with his thumb. "Have I told you," he said, "how lovely you are looking today, Bria McKenna? Like a field of blooming heather."

Bria wondered if the man was uncanny, sensing somehow her wounded, tender heart. Or if he truly did have eyes only for her. She did feel pretty herself, in her new lilac muslin. But then her brother, Donagh, was often saying how Shay had such a gift of the blarney he could negotiate with God and get the best share.

Bria could hear Noreen's chatter and Merry's bright humming, and she smiled to think of how at ease her girls were with Emma now. Emma seemed to have a gift with them, a way of listening that made them feel special and chosen.

Just then Noreen grabbed Emma's hand and pointed into the thicket of elms and birches that lined the road. "Look, Miss Emma, there's a toadstool ring. Come along, let's see if we can catch ourselves a leprechaun."

"If you catch one," Bria called out, "don't let him go until he shows you his treasure."

Emma had started to follow Noreen into the trees, but she turned around, one hand lifting her skirts, the other tilting back her lace-scalloped parasol to reveal her smiling face. "I fear I'm more likely to catch a bad case of poison ivy," she said with such a sweet laugh it caught at Bria's heart.

Emma followed the girls into the woods, bending over to watch while Noreen peered under each toadstool. Noreen kept up a bit of blarney herself on the living habits of leprechauns. Merry kept her mouth closed, as usual, but happiness curled her lips at the corners.

If you catch a leprechaun . . . But Emma Tremayne already had herself so many treasures, what would she need with another one? It was when she remembered Emma's money, when she remembered her position in Great Folk society, that Bria understood what wild things were her thoughts. How foolish were the dreams that lurked and trembled in her heart.

Emma marrying Shay and making him happy in the way a woman who loves a man, desperately and exclusively, can make him happy. Emma being a mother to her girls, taking them out of the mill and sending them to school, dressing them in lace and satin and finding decent, well-to-do young men for them to marry. Emma raising little Jacko in her place, raising him up to be a gentleman, with all of a gentleman's fine ways and manners, and all of a gentleman's advantages in the world.

For Emma to marry Shay and be a mother to her girls, her son . . . But for Emma Tremayne to marry an Irish fisherman would be as disgraceful a thing as marrying a tinker's son would have been a disgrace for Bria O'Reilly. It would mean for Emma the loss of everything in her world. It would take a powerful love to bear such a cost for its own fulfillment. But Emma had such a love, Bria was sure of it. She had seen it in Emma's eyes.

For Emma to marry Shay . . . It hurt to think of it—how could it not? But all Bria had to do was think of him, of their children, and a fierce and terrible love would seize her heart. A love that was as strong and as old as the earth itself, and would go on long after her dying was a finished thing. It was hard, hard, sometimes, to think of them living on without her. But to know that someday they all could find happiness again, to be assured of that, she would do anything, bear anything.

They had been walking for a good ways now and Bria was finding it harder and harder to hide how weak she was feeling of a sudden, how her breath had grown so short and ragged.

The cardinal flowers that blazed among the trees blurred dizzily before her eyes. Shay pointed out a black porcupine with white-tipped quills that lay dozing on a rock, making the most of the sun, and Bria nodded and smiled, and clenched her teeth to keep them from rattling. She could see the sun blazing white upon the water, and she knew it was hot, but she felt cold, so cold.

The coughs came tearing up her chest and out her mouth—wet, gurgling coughs, laced with blood. She hunched over beneath the force of them, trying to stop them with her handkerchief. When she was done, she looked up and saw those she loved staring back at her with fear and pain etched starkly on their faces.

Shay and Emma stood next to each other, too far apart to touch. While she lived they would always stand apart, but she was dying, soon she would be dead, and they would need each other to see them through it.

In Ireland, it was said that a dying bard could pass on the gift of his music. But only to a beloved friend.

A gang of ragged and rowdy boys ran across the sun-parched grass of the Bristol Common, blowing on fish horns and conch shells. One of them threw a lit lady cracker underneath the bandstand. It went off with a loud and smoky bang, shredding the red, white, and blue bunting.

Emma jumped at the noise it made, and then laughed at herself.

"My poor darling," Geoffrey said, giving the hand she had placed on his arm a solicitous pat. "Were you frightened badly?"

He glared at the wrecked bandstand. Judging from its condition, the lady cracker wasn't the first attack it had suffered that day. "These wretched mill rats—such is what comes of giving them a holiday off from work. There ought to be a law against setting off firecrackers where they can endanger public property and frighten the ladies."

"Oh, Geoffrey, you would spoil all the fun." Emma laughed again as she tilted back her head to watch a red balloon float up into a white bronze sky and entangle itself in the branches of a big lofty elm. "Would you buy me one of those big cannon crackers, please? I should like to set it off during the mayor's speech. When he gets to that part where the cannons of freedom are booming down through the ages—that would be the perfect time to do it, don't you think?"

"You are funning with me again," Geoffrey said after a moment of silence.

"Yes, Geoffrey."

She leaned in to him to straighten his blue and white polka-dot tie, even though it would never have dared to be crooked while around Geoffrey Alcott's neck. She smiled at the very thought and would have kissed his cheek, but he frowned on public displays of affection.

"Geoffrey, are you enjoying the day?" she said. "Really enjoying it?"

"Of course I'm enjoying the day. It's the Bristol Fourth—why wouldn't I enjoy the day?"

"Indeed, it is a Bristolian's veritable *duty* to enjoy his Fourth, and you, my dearest Geoffrey, would never shirk your duty," she said, smiling at him so that he would know she was funning.

After all, he had come all this way from his new foundry in Maine, just to be with her on this day. She wondered if she enjoyed Geoffrey's company better now that she wasn't seeing so much of him. It was not a comfortable thought. But then there were other times when she could make herself believe they would be happy, she and Geoffrey, as man and wife. She knew what to expect from him now, and so she would be wise enough not to expect him to be something he was not.

Because the kind of man she wanted, the kind of man she could love with *all* her heart, instead of just a part of it—that man didn't exist in her world.

Because that man, the man she loved, was Seamus McKenna, and she could never have him.

There, it was said, said flat out in all its wrongness. She loved him, even though she didn't want to, had tried so hard not to. But wanting and trying hadn't changed what was. And she sometimes feared what harm such a secret love, even buried deep, would one day do to Geoffrey and their marriage.

Geoffrey placed her hand back on his arm and they resumed their stroll, stopping from time to time to greet people they had seen just moments before while watching the parade.

Every Fourth, for as long as anyone could remember, the Alcotts had held open house during the parade, although nobody but other Great Folk would have dared to walk in without an invitation. They would all stroll out to the street with punch glass and orange cake in hand to watch the brass bands, the war veterans, and fire engines go marching by. Then they would all stroll back inside again to discuss what they had seen and what the weather had been like while they were seeing it.

Like holding the last fox hunt of the season at Hope Farm, watching the Fourth of July parade from the marble piazza of the Alcotts' Hope Street mansion was a Great Folk tradition.

And the weather was providing even more than usual conversational interest this year, for it was so hot the air seemed to be crackling. The sun had pounded hard on the common all morning, and now the yellow dust was rising to settle over the tables loaded with baked beans, clam chowder, codfish cakes, johnnycake, and apple pie.

When you are in love with a man, Emma thought as she walked arm in arm with Geoffrey, you see him everywhere. You see him in a pair of broad shoulders walking away from you. In the hair sliding black and too long from beneath an Irish tweed scally cap. In the flash of white teeth in a brash smile.

That day she thought she saw him coming out of a yellow-striped tent with an ice cream cone in his hand. She thought she saw him among the crowd that was cheering on a boy chasing a greased pig. She thought she saw him carrying a basket of oysters to the shucking contest.

And each time she saw him, in that caught-breath instant before she realized that it wasn't he, after all, her face would flush and her heart would feel all fat and warm and heavy in her chest.

And then she did see him, for real.

He was lifting Merry onto the back of a dragon, a carousel dragon with green scales and orange fire coming out its flared nostrils. Noreen was already mounted on a camel wearing a red fez.

As Emma watched, he grabbed a pole and swung off the platform, laughing. Music spilled out of the steam calliope, and the carousel began to turn, and Emma's own head began to spin, sun motes dancing before her eyes.

She looked for Bria and found her, holding little Jacko in one arm and waving at the whirling menagerie. But Bria must have sensed her presence, for she turned and their gazes met, and the smile of joy and welcome she gave to Emma came from the heart.

Emma would never have gone up to Shay alone, for so many reasons. But with Bria there, she had no thought now of not going. She would never cut her friend—not in front of Geoffrey, not in front of the world.

Emma slid her hand down Geoffrey's arm to take his hand and pull him along after her. "Geoffrey, here is Mrs. McKenna, whom I've told you about—my new friend who just had a baby? It's about time the two of you met, don't you think?"

Geoffrey looked around in obvious bewilderment before he noticed the woman with the baby, who was smiling and holding out her hand to Emma. And the giant of a man in shirtsleeves and worn corduroy britches who had just come up to put his arm around the woman's waist.

"*She* is your friend?" Geoffrey said. "I had somehow thought . . ." He didn't finish, but Emma knew what he had somehow thought: that the Mrs. McKenna he'd heard about was lace, not shanty, Irish.

"My dearest, best friend in the world," Emma said, as she took Bria's hand, their fingers entwining. She leaned forward to press her cheek against Bria's and kiss the baby's forehead. Bria's dark eyes were bright and laughing. Her cheeks glowed like dew-kissed roses, but Emma knew they were blossoms of a false health. Only yesterday Shay had had to carry her home from their walk. They'd never known her to cough up so much blood before.

"Bria," Emma said, giving her friend's hand a gentle squeeze. "I would like for you to meet my fiancé, Geoffrey Alcott. Geoffrey, these are the McKennas, Bria and her husband, Seamus. And this," she said, peeling the blanket back from the baby's face so that he could have a better look, "is little Jacko, over a month old now and thriving."

"It is a pleasure to make your acquaintance, madam," Geoffrey said, bowing in Bria's direction. If he recognized her as the mill woman who had brought a dead child to the last fox hunt of the season, he wasn't letting on. "Sir," he said to Shay. "And little sir," he said, bestowing a small smile on the sleeping Jacko.

"How d'you do, Mr. Alcott," Bria said, looking him over with a forthright curiosity in turn, and Emma suddenly found herself a little embarrassed on behalf of her intended husband, although she could not for the life of her have said why. He cut a fine figure as usual in his white linen suit and straw boater. His behavior was, as always, the epitome of Great Folk propriety.

"It's rather warm today, is it not?" Geoffrey said, to fill the small silence that had fallen after the introductions.

"Terrrribly warm," Shay said, his stage Irish brogue turning thick as mulligan stew. "But it would be queer if it wasn't, what with the sun shining in an empty sky and nary a breath of wind to be had for a prayer." His face was set serious, but for the quickest of moments his gaze met hers, and Emma saw the laughter lurking there.

"McKenna, McKenna," she heard Geoffrey say. "Ah, yes. You're the Irish fellow who's going to be fighting James Parker, our Harvard champion, later this evening."

"Aye, that I am." Shay hooked his thumb in his pocket

and cocked his hip in a bit of a masculine pose. "I hope to be making a decent match of it."

Geoffrey's lips pulled back in a long-toothed smile. "I understand you won a few prizefights during your heyday, some while back." He looked Shay slowly up and down, as if the Irishman had long ago gone to seed. "But you'll have your hands full taking on our Harvard champ. He's captain of the football team and rows number seven on the crew. It's a matter of racial stock and breeding, you understand. A matter of the keener eye, the steadier hand, in riding, shooting, boxing—whatever. The man of pure Yankee stock is simply the better animal."

"*Och*, the better animal, do you say?" Bria had planted onto her hip the hand that wasn't full of baby, and she was making her eyes go round with mock surprise. "And silly me, with the notion that having a soul was what made all of us, no matter what the breeding, rise above the beasts. Now you're telling me it is only we Irish who've been blessed with such a thing."

The carousel's calliope wound down into a silence that was raucously broken by a string of popping firecrackers. A man walked past, carrying a big pail with a dipper in the middle and a half dozen tin cups hanging on the rim, and chanting: "Cold lemonade, made in the shade, stirred with a stick by an ugly old maid."

"Mrs. McKenna," Shay said, "has always been the one for having the keen and steady tongue on her."

"Indeed," Geoffrey said, forcing a smile that made his mouth pull white at the corners. He bowed and tipped his hat at Bria. "Regretfully, we are expected momentarily in the mayor's tent, and so we must bid you a good day and a happy Fourth."

Afterward, Emma was to wonder why she had done nothing, said nothing, been nothing. She'd simply let Geoffrey lead her away. She'd felt so empty, as if a great airy space had blown up inside her. Blown her all away.

The sun had slipped behind the birches on Poppasquash Point when the referee drew a line in chalk down the center of the ring and summoned the pugilists to scratch in the Bristol Fourth of July's First Annual Prizefighting Exhibition.

A cloud of smoke from the flaring, oil-soaked torches already thickened the air over the ring, which had been pitched in the center of the common. The ring was made of stakes hewn from pines out of the Tanyard Woods and ropes from a ship's rigging. A canvas flooring sewn of old sails had been stretched over the grass.

The fighters had already tossed their hats into the ring and tossed a coin for the corners, and now Shay was standing in his corner, shaking his arms and legs to loosen the muscles, breathing deeply to stretch his lungs. And his gaze searching the milling, shifting crowd for his wife, and not certain that it would find her.

Though they hadn't spoken much of it, he knew she was some bitter in her heart for what he was about to do. For breaking the promise he had once made to her, and for breaking the promise a man should always be making to himself: to behave honorably in all things.

There—he'd found her after all, standing next to the bandstand with its shredded bunting. So she'd come, then. But she was alone.

She'd said she was going to ask their neighbor, the widow Mrs. Hale, who was a swamp Yankee but a kindly woman for all that, to help the girls watch over the baby back at the Thames Street house. She'd told him flat out that she wouldn't be allowing their children to watch the prizefighting exhibition.

"There would be no shame coming to them or to you," she'd said, "for watching you lose a match fairly fought. But to see their father sell his honor for money, that I could not be bearing."

"It's the children I am doing this for," he'd said back to her.

He'd thought for a moment that she was going to hit him, such was her anger. "Don't you lie to me, Seamus McKenna," she'd said, her words all the more cutting because they'd been spoken softly, not shouted. "You're doing it for Ireland, and what is Ireland to your son who wasn't even born there, to your girls who barely remember it? Ireland is only a place on the map to them. When are you going to put them first above Ireland, Shay? When are you going to put me first? Will you finally be thinking of it, maybe, after I am dead?"

He'd wrapped his arms around her then, trying to hold her close. "Bria, sweet Jesus. Don't say that. You know I love you above all else."

She'd held herself stiffly but a moment longer, before her arms were around him and she was laying her head on his chest, giving him the sweet comfort of her body as she always had. "I never said you didn't love me."

He'd felt a weighty shame to hear her words then, and he felt that shame still. Shame and a sorrow at knowing how sorely he was disappointing her. Honor was everything to his Bria. Maybe the only thing she valued more than honor was the love she bore for him and their children.

Although at the moment she wasn't giving him much of a loving look. He could intimidate most men with his size alone, but his wife had always stood up to him, matched him toe to toe and word for word. Bria O'Reilly McKenna had the fear of the Lord, but Shay doubted she had any other fear in her.

So when he caught her eye he smiled at her. The smile he'd often used on her when he'd get a sudden hankering for some bed play, and she busy with her endless women's chores and not in the mood . . . until he would hit her with his roundhouse punch of a smile.

But maybe this time his smile wasn't going to work. Then, as he watched, her whole body seemed to soften. Though he couldn't see her that well, with all the space and people that separated them, he thought that a warmth would be coming into her eyes, the welcoming warmth of a well-fed fire on a bitter night. That a smile would be curving the edges of her mouth, the kind of smile a man would want to capture with a kiss. That her face would be wearing the look of a woman who went on loving and forgiving her man even when she knew she shouldn't.

And Shay's throat suddenly felt tight and scratchy, the way it had as a boy when he'd needed to cry but known he was too old.

It had been a long time since he'd thought of those early days on the beaches of Gortadoo. But he thought of them now. Of how he had admired the strength he found in her, even before he'd come to know the true depths of that strength. Admired the play of muscles in her back as she spread his heavy nets out over the rocks, the way she would splay her bare feet wide and dig them deep into the sand, plant them in the sand. All of her always planted firmly, not caught up in foolish dreams as he had been.

Of how his body had felt, the hunger in his body, standing with his chest against her back and his hands laced under her breasts, while they watched the sun sink slowly into a purple sea, and the wind would blow her hair into his face and he would smell her and his heart would lose its sense of direction, forget to beat.

Of how her face had looked floating above his in the dark and secret cave of their desires, while her thighs gripped his hips and her breasts pressed against his chest, and her tears fell salty and warm on his cheeks, and himself saying, "I am going to be a priest." He had been lying even then.

A hand slapped him hard on the back, jerking his gaze and his thoughts off his wife with a wrench that was physical. And he found himself looking into his brother-in-law's frowning face.

"I don't know," Donagh was saying, "down what roads your thoughts had gone a-wandering, boyo. But you'd better give them a whistle on back, or you'll be finding yourself knocked flat on your arse ten seconds into the first round."

"You look to your own end of things," Shay said, "and leave me to deal with mine."

Donagh's chin shot into the air. "Sure I've me sponges all nicely soaking in their bucket and me towels all handy, and myself playing second to a man who's forgotten how to be the champion that he is."

A flush rose high and hot in Shay's face. "Ah, *Dhia*, Donagh. What I should've said is that you're a good man for being in a fellow's corner. And it's grateful I am to have you there."

Donagh sighed and shrugged, flushing a little. "Aye, well . . . we've the bishop, wise man that he is, to be thanking for that."

Father O'Reilly's bishop hadn't been at all pleased to hear that one of his priests was going to be serving as second at a boxing exhibition. Until he'd heard as well that more than a wee bit of the prize money would be finding its way into the Saint Mary's poor box.

Just then the referee called the combatants into the center of the ring to shake hands. Both men would fight stripped to the waist and clad in ankle-length white tights and leather shoes. But the Harvard champ trotted into the middle of the ring wrapped up in a green and blue Turkish silk bathrobe that drew from Father O'Reilly a most unpriestly remark.

Shay looked his opponent full in the face for the first time. James Parker was a fine-boned young man with large, widely spaced eyes and one of those long and narrow Yankee noses. The nose was a little too straight in that pampered, trust-fund face, and Shay vowed right then to break it for the lad. Before he himself went down for Ireland, God bless her, in the fourth round.

Then as they shook hands, Shay looked deeply into the other man's eyes and saw his fear.

There was always fear in the ring. Fear you could taste, as bitter and sharp as acid on your tongue. Fear you could smell rank in your own sweat. The secret to winning was to hurl yourself at the fear. To hate the fear you found inside you more than you hated the man who faced you across the ring.

The referee broke apart their clasped hands, and they retired to their respective corners. Shay held his hands out to Donagh so that the priest could tighten the laces on the thin leather coaching gloves that bound his knuckles.

The gloves were being worn to give lip service to the law that required such things even in exhibition fights and public sparring matches. In Ireland he'd fought with bare fists that he'd soaked in walnut juice. In those days, his hands had been as tough and hard as tree burls. They weren't in such condition now, and he knew that even with wearing the gloves, by the end of the night his hands would be a swollen, shredded mess.

Donagh knotted the last of the laces and looked up at him. "You've a plan, then," he said, keeping his voice low, "for how you're going to do it."

"Aye." Shay would fight hard for three rounds, to give the

crowd the exhibition it was expecting. They would be fighting under the Marquess of Queensberry Rules, which disqualified any boxer who went down without being hit, even if he only slipped. By the fourth round the canvas would be wet enough with blood and sweat for Shay to make a "slip" convincing.

"I'll be making it—" *Convincing*, he was about to say. Except he never got the word out, for out of the mass of Fourth of July revelers surrounding the ring, he'd suddenly seen Emma.

She stood with her hand on the arm of her intended husband, the handsome and wealthy Geoffrey Alcott. But even from this distance he could tell that her gaze was riveted on the ring, and he wondered what she saw. If she saw Shay McKenna as the Irish brawler who conquered men with his fists, or the knight-errant he fancied himself to be. He wondered if she would care whether he fought tough and fair or threw away his honor for the money to buy guns for Ireland and the rising.

God above . . . It was hard enough having to bear the sore knowledge that his wife thought less of him for what he was about to do, without having to fret over the likes of Miss Emma Tremayne's thoughts. Yet to his surprise, he realized that he did care. He didn't like to think he'd be shaming himself, shaming his honor, in front of her.

Donagh startled him by shoving a leather mouthpiece hard between his teeth. "It would be nice, Seamus lad, if you'd be putting your mind to the business at hand," he said, and he gave Shay a stinging slap on his shoulder, and a shove, sending him out into the middle of the ring to toe the scratch line with the Harvard boy.

The crowd grew breathlessly silent, then exploded into a cheer that was as loud as any cannon cracker when Shay sent a whistling right cross into Parker's neck, smashing him just behind the ear, and knocking him so hard into the ropes the hemp stripped the skin off his back.

The men fought evenly matched for seven brutal minutes after that, before Shay let loose with a clubbing right that landed smack in the middle of Parker's face. The man went down onto one knee, just as the bell sounded, ending the round.

Shay allowed himself a smile, for he had broken the Harvard champ's perfect nose.

But Shay had taken punishment as well. His lip was split, and his upper chest was bruised and welted. Donagh dabbed at the cut lip with a sponge, and his face screwed into a grimace as he looked over at the enemy's corner. Parker's second was sucking blood from the smashed nose and spitting it out onto the canvas.

"Sweet saints," Donagh said, shaking his head. "You know that I love you dearly, Seamus lad. But I don't think I could do that. And you with a honker on you that's such a grand target it fairly begs for a belting."

Shay's laughter was cut short by the ringing of the bell. "Keep your guard tight and your elbows close to your ribs," Donagh shouted after him, as he propelled himself out of his corner, charging. Parker came out fast as well, but Shay could see within the first minute that his opponent's punches now lacked snap and timing. He began to flinch even at the blows that didn't land.

A man fought as much with his head as with his hands. For although the fear was always with him, he couldn't let it out. He couldn't let himself know the fear of getting hurt, for as soon as he did, he would be hurt for certain. And he would lose.

James Parker smelled his own defeat in the sweat of his fear and so he began to cheat. He flailed all over the ring, trying to trip up Shay's feet to bring him down. He landed two under-the-belt blows that drew boos from the crowd.

Shay began to think he was going to have to start pulling some of his own punches, otherwise he wouldn't be able to make the fight last until the fourth round.

Then Parker feinted and let fly with a left that Shay easily ducked. But Shay slipped on a clot of blood, and although he didn't go down then, his guard dropped long enough for him to be clubbed down by a blow to his neck. His legs felt as loose as Italian noodles as he staggered upright, and it was all he could do to keep bobbing and weaving and ducking punches until the bell rang.

"Myself," Donagh said as he pushed a water siphon between Shay's battered lips, "I do not like the fellow. Myself, I think the fellow needs teaching a lesson."

Shay smiled, and then winced as he pulled open the cut on his mouth. "And what of Saint Mary's poor box, then?"

Donagh grinned back at him. "God, being such the fellow himself for giving a man his just deserts, would understand."

"And the clan's guns?"

"The clan, being made up of proud Irish fighting men, would understand as well."

The bell rang and Shay bounced to his feet. But he didn't leave his corner just yet. He looked at his wife and thought that what he was about to do, he'd probably been intending to do all along, in his heart. Because of her . . . She always made him better than he was, did his Bria.

A man fought with his heart as much as with his head and his hands. Fought with the hate and fire that he carried in his heart. To beat another man to the ground with your bare fists you needed to fight utterly without mercy or pity. And to do that, you had to hate.

Shay landed a tremendous right jab that smashed what was left of Parker's nose, but he wasn't seeing the face of the man he was hitting. He saw his mother's wave-battered body lying broken on a rocky beach. He saw his wife's thin white body lying beneath a rutting bastard, who wore a coat that was as red as the blood between her thighs.

Shay sliced at the man's face with short, sharp jabs and landed crunching blows to his chest and belly, forcing him across the ring into the ropes. Parker held his arms up in front of him in a futile attempt to ward off Shay's punches. He quit even trying to hit back, except for one dazed poke at Shay's face with an unsteady left.

Shay sent several left shots of his own to the other man's face, then feinted with a right for the jaw. Parker flinched, raising his arms again, and Shay shifted the whole of his considerable weight, bringing his right foot forward, slamming his right fist into Parker's heart, and his left into the man's stomach.

Shay heard and felt his own thumb pop loose from the joint in the same second that he saw the light fade out of Parker's eyes, and the Harvard champ fell to the canvas, sprawling senseless.

Parker's second took a sponge from the water pail and threw it into the middle of the ring, while the crowd screamed, "Knocked out! Knocked out!" and rushed the ropes.

Shay looked for his wife and found her. She was pushing her way toward him through the mob of people, and she was smiling. He thought she looked so young and pretty, with her cheeks blooming pink and the torchlights setting ablaze her glorious hair.

But then she coughed hard, and pressed her fist to her breast, and he thought he could almost see her heart bucking like a wild thing in her chest.

She opened her mouth, and he thought he heard her call his name. And then the blood gushed out of her mouth, bright red and so much blood, so much, spilling all down the front of her, as if her throat had been cut.

"Bria!" he screamed, shoving, pushing, leaping over the ropes to get to her, while rockets suddenly shot into the air, and the sky rained stars.

Chapter Twenty-one

Bria turned her head on the pillow and looked at her own hair lying on the sheet, dull and faded to rust like old blood. And her hand, curled next to her cheek, bleached the color of long-dried bone.

A spill of the most beautiful lace she could imagine fell over her wrist. She felt the luscious softness of the night rail she wore caressing what was left of her flesh. Emma, she thought, dear Emma must have dressed her in one of her own fine things.

She wished she could see how she looked in it, but it was probably just as well. She was nothing but a bundle of bones now, seemingly tied together with string.

She was alone for once. The other times when she'd awakened, someone had been in the room with her. Emma usually during the day, and Shay at night, and sometimes the two of them together. The girls, from time to time, with their frightened, knowing eyes that always broke her heart. Her brother, Donagh, wearing his green sacramental stole, for the giving of the last rites. Which she would be needing soon.

And once Mrs. Hale had brought little Jacko in for her to

see, although she no longer had the strength to nurse or even hold him.

Even to breathe took more strength than she had anymore. With each breath it felt as though a stone was being put on her chest, one stone for each breath, one by heavy, crushing one. One day soon there would be one stone too many, and that breath would be her last.

Poor Shay and Emma, always with smiles on their faces and soothing words, gentle touches. Pretending to her that they couldn't see the stones stacking up on her chest one by one. But sometimes . . . oh, sometimes she would awaken before they had realized it and catch them unawares, and she would see on their faces how their hearts were breaking.

She heard a step in the kitchen now, and the whistle of the teakettle. She heard voices, Shay and Emma talking together. Already, she thought, they are seeing each other through this, taking comfort from each other, even if they don't know it yet.

And as she let her heavy eyelids fall closed and struggled to pull in just one more swampy breath, Bria McKenna planned how she would say her goodbyes.

She began with her brother.

Each time he came he would ask her if she was sorry for her sins, and she would answer in her voice that had grown so thin and slow and strange to her own ears: "All but the one, and that one I'll not ever be confessing to any man or priest, Donagh, so don't you be asking me."

But in the end she couldn't bear to think of her brother being left in torment after she was gone, worrying about the state of her immortal soul and feeling as though he had failed her, and failed God, as her priest.

So the next time he came she told him about that day at Castle Garden, and she made him believe she was confessing the sin of her shame, although in her heart she would never be contrite.

And yet, as she saw her brother's gentle hand make the sign of the cross over her face, as she heard him say the words, *Ego te absolvo . . .* deep in Bria's soul she felt forgiven.

Donagh wept when he put the sacred host, dry and sweet, on her tongue, restoring her soul to a state of grace. But as he was leaving he leaned over and whispered in her ear, "And doesn't God understand easier the sins that are born of love?"

It was a terrible thing to say goodbye to her girls.

If she'd been more like Shay—him forever reading his books and pondering the meaning of things—perhaps she would have acquired enough wisdom to pass it on to them to see them through their motherless years. But she knew that in the end, little of her own wisdom would matter. They would have to grow up wise from life, or not at all.

She wanted to say something that would make it so they would never forget her. But she was afraid that if she dwelled on it too long and hard, what they would remember most about her was her dying, and that she couldn't bear.

Then there was her poor little Jacko, who would have no memories of her at all.

So in the end, each time she saw them, she simply asked them to lie down beside her so that she could put her arms around them and hold them and tell them that she loved them.

At least they would get this from her—a knowing in their hearts that they were loved.

To Emma, her dear friend, her mirrored heart, she said, "You gave me one of your beautiful night rails when I wasn't looking."

She saw Emma's throat work as she swallowed, saw how the smile came hard. "I always wanted to give you so much," Emma said, "and you would never let me."

"You gave me more than you can ever imagine. And you can give me something now. A promise that after I am gone you will still come a-calling on the girls, on Shay."

She saw Emma's eyes widen with something, surprise perhaps, and fear. She wasn't sure how close either of them had come to admitting to their own hearts that they were falling in love. But she was certain they had never once gone so far as to admit it to each other. For they both loved her far too much, and they would never want to hurt her.

But after she was gone, she would be beyond hurt. They could never tarnish the love they bore for her by loving each other.

Yet, she couldn't speak of this too plainly, not with Emma as she would with Shay. Words frightened Emma. The girl who lived in the silver house and danced in gilded ballrooms with diamonds in her hair had always grown uneasy when looking too closely at her heart.

So Bria said, "Promise me you'll come for the sake of the girls. They've grown to love you so. To lose you, too, would be more than heart and soul should have to bear."

And Emma said, with the tears held back, choking her voice, "Of course I will come. I will come for as long as they want me."

Then, once she had Emma's promise, Bria spent the hours when she was awake, and had the strength, talking of her man, and no Irish warrior hero ever had such songs sung of him as had Seamus McKenna.

Once, she said, "I do believe he actually likes living with his heart in his mouth, does my Shay. But maybe men are just easier at that, at living and loving in the moment. We women . . . we tend to dwell more on yesterdays and tomorrows."

And Emma asked, "But when you dwell on your yesterdays, Bria—do you ever wonder what your life would've been like if you hadn't gone to the beach to wait for him that day after the crossroads dance? Have you ever once thought you could have made a different choice?"

And she answered, "Aye, maybe I could've chosen differently. Chosen not to love him at all. Or chosen to look deeper inside of me for that kind of brave love that would've let him go. But then, when I dwell on my tomorrows, I see that loving him will've been worth it all, no matter how it ends."

That day ended with Bria coughing up such a gush of blood it splattered everywhere—on the walls and the floor, even on the postcard of the Virgin Mary. And Emma, with her lady's hands and lady's clothes, cleaned it up.

When it was over, Bria laid back against the pillows, straining, grasping desperately for the breath to tell Emma all that was in her heart.

"*Mo bhanacharaid* . . ." she wheezed, and the air sucked wetly in her chest. "That means 'my particular woman friend' in Irish, did I ever tell you that? And it is a grand, true friend you are—"

Emma, who had been bent over the bed, tucking in the clean sheet, suddenly seized Bria's hand with both of hers and brought it up to her cheek. "Oh, God, God. I don't know how I'll live without you."

Bria felt the weakness seeping over her, the stones building, building, one by one. But she managed a smile. "Remember . . . ? All you need do is look in the mirror."

"No, no." Emma shook her head so hard the tears splashed from her eyes and onto their clasped hands. "I was wrong, wrong. You aren't the mirror side of me, you're the best of me. You taught me how I should be. You've given me a glimpse of the life I should live for myself, and now you are leaving me to live it alone."

No, Bria thought, I am leaving you to live it with my Shay.

Shay . . .

She was wildly in love with him still, now as much as ever.

Those times when she came awake at night and found him in the chair next to the bed, watching over her, she wished his last memories of her wouldn't be these. But rather of those other times, when she had been young and pretty and full of life.

One night she asked him to lie down on the bed with her. With him stretched out beside her in the dark, face turned to face, his arm lying heavily on her waist—it reminded her of those times in the cave, when they had been so young and had lain like this, just lain together, holding each other close, holding on.

She put her palms against his chest and felt the tension in him—he was a man ready to fly into a thousand pieces. She thought of that time in Ireland when for three days she'd believed he was dead, and the pain of it had been truly beyond what she could bear. She wondered how he was standing this, how he had stood it all these months, watching her die breath by breath. Or if, somewhere deep inside himself, he had prepared his heart for her passing a long time ago.

Shay's heart had so often been mysterious to her. But she thought that if she asked him for a moment's truth this night, to tell her what was his heart's desire, he would say, "For you to live."

And that was the one thing she could not give. So she would give him instead his heart's other desire, even if he didn't know yet what that was.

So she laid her hands on his chest and felt his heart beat. "Will you do a wee thing for me, m'love?" she said. "After I am gone. I want for you to mourn me, weep for me, and miss me sorely. But after a time I want you to ask our Emma to be your wife."

Moonlight shining blue through the window showed her the shock on his face, and underneath the shock a tinge of hurt and guilt. And one other feeling she had hoped not to see—resistance.

"That is not a wee thing, Bria," he said.

"A grand thing, then." She moved one hand up to grasp his neck and pull herself closer against him. She felt his pulse leap and throb against her hand, felt his heart beat against her hand.

"A daft, impossible thing," he was saying, his voice roughened with pain. "You can't will her into taking your place. Not in my heart and not in the hearts of our children. You can't just be telling me to love her and be thinking I'll marry her after you are gone."

"But she loves the girls and they love her, and at the age they are, they sorely need a mother. And our Jacko, wee little thing that he is—he'll be needing a mother most of all. And she would be a good wife to you. She would follow you to the end of the world."

His laugh was ragged, broken. "Darlin', she has money enough to buy the world. What would she need with me?"

"There is the need born of love. She *loves* you, Shay. I know this, for I've seen it on her face, and I know her as well as I know myself, for we are the same in our deepest places. She loves you for the fine, brave, dreaming man that you are."

She felt his chest move in a hard breath. "*A mhuire*, Bria. You're my wife. You're the only wife I want."

So she laid her head against his chest, her cheek nestling into the hollow above his heart. She could hear it beating. "Let your heart find its way," she said.

It could have been hours later or only moments when she said, "I did wrong to you, Shay . . . that night on the beach in Gortadoo, seducing you away from God."

He rubbed his open mouth over her cheek and nose and lips. "*Mo chridh, mo chridh* . . . I wanted you for my wife then, and I want you still, and I don't know how I'm going to live through your dying."

On those evenings when she had the strength, she asked to be carried outside to watch the day end. They would bundle her up in quilts and sit her in her straw-bottomed rocker, and she would watch the sun slip away, slowly and silently, behind Poppasquash Point.

On this evening the setting sun was trailing gold ribbons across the sky. The air was soft and still and full of promise.

Evenings like this, she remembered . . .

A Saturday-off afternoon, picnicking at Town Beach. She sitting with her back against an elm's gnarly trunk. Shay's head lying in her lap and her playing with his hair, so warm from the sun and soft it was, sliding through her fingers. The girls studying a tidal pool, squatting in the sand, knees spread wide, two heads bent together, red and brown. Their darling girls . . . And then Bria looking from the two heads, red and brown, down to her husband's face and seeing that he was sleeping.

Such an ordinary day it had been, an ordinary moment, and yet suddenly she had realized that she was happy. Not ordinarily happy, but savagely happy. So full up to bursting with a pure and violent joy that she could have screamed with it.

And the happiness she'd felt then, she thought, was sweetness itself now in this remembering.

She opened her eyes and found herself alone. No, not alone . . . They thought she slept, Emma and Shay, and so they had gone to stand at the water's edge side by side, talking quietly. Once she heard Shay laugh.

Then perhaps she did sleep, for when she opened her eyes the sun was shrunken and orange on the horizon. Shay and Emma were still where they had been, and they appeared outlined in a golden light, as things do when the sun first comes out after a storm.

And it was the strangest thing, for she could hear Shay's voice, not ruined as it was now, but beautiful as it once had been, and it was in her blood, his voice, a part of her blood, pulsing strong and full of life, pulsing hot through her veins.

She heard him as well as if he stood beside her, yet she knew for certain that he was speaking to Emma, speaking to Emma now, saying to Emma, "An evening like this . . . it seems as though the sun is clinging to the edge of the world, and so the day is going to last forever, and in the next instant the sun goes and loses its grip and the day is over after all. But the promise of it stays with you somehow, into the night. The promise and the memory."

Yes, Bria thought, the memory lives on.

She opened her mouth to say his name and felt her breath leave her body, and she couldn't seem to get it back.

For a moment she thought it had grown dark. But then she saw that she was wrong, for the sun was shining brighter than ever now, and Shay was coming toward her. A Shay without shadows, all light and youth, joyous and burning, and he said to her, "Will you dance with me, *mo chridh*?"

So she went into his arms, and they were dancing and laughing and loving in the sun of an enchanted day.

Chapter Twenty-two

Bria McKenna's black lacquered coffin sat on a pair of stools in the middle of the kitchen with the faded bird-of-paradise wallpaper and the cracked linoleum floor.

At her head rested a horseshoe of wax flowers set in a silk frame. At her feet, tall candles and a holy lamp burned. Their flames flickered in the draft coming through the door that was open to a night of summer fog.

The holy card of the Virgin Mary that had once hung on her bedroom wall now lay on her chest. She held her brown wooden rosary beads in her hands, as though she were praying. Everyone said what a beautiful corpse she made.

Bria's husband stood next to the coffin, dressed in a pallbearer's black cloth suit. He shook hands with the men and accepted kisses on his cheek from the women who came to offer condolences and give him Mass cards for the repose of Bria's soul. His mouth spoke soft words of gratitude, but his eyes were two flat, smooth stones.

His daughters sat on chairs beside him, their hands folded in the laps of their purple mourning dresses. Noreen answered everyone who spoke to her in a polite, subdued voice. Merry was silent, not even humming, but from time to time she would draw in such a shuddering breath that the holy medal she wore around her neck would jump on her chest.

Bria's son, who would never know her, lay sleeping in his cradle by the stove.

Earlier—before Bria's neighbors and fellow mill workers came to pay her their last respects—the kitchen had been so quiet, Emma could hear the ice melt dripping into the catch basin beneath the icebox. She had helped the girls hang black crepe paper over the door, and she'd heard only the mewl of the harbor gulls and the moan of a buoy out in the fog-shrouded bay.

She'd put cans of wildflowers all over the kitchen, and made pots of tea and coffee, and filled platters with cheese and corned beef and soda bread, and all the while she'd listened for his step on the stoop. But he'd stayed out back, on the beach where Bria had died.

They had thought she was sleeping. They had been standing together watching the sunset and talking. Not about anything of great importance, just talking in the easy way that had grown between them during these last weeks of Bria's illness.

They'd talked until the sun had melted into a copper-colored bay, and then they had turned around to carry Bria inside and they'd seen she was gone. That was what he'd said, Emma remembered: "Ah, Bria darlin'. You're gone."

He went and knelt beside the rocking chair and kissed her cold lips, and then he had picked her up and carried her inside the house.

Emma had stayed on the beach until the mill's shift whistle blew, then she went in to help him tell the girls. She hugged Noreen while they cried together. Merry didn't cry. She sat on her father's lap and curled her body around him, and her humming was the sweetest, saddest music that Emma had ever heard.

She'd stayed with the girls for a while after that, and

she'd fed the baby his pap bottle when Mrs. Hale brought him over. But Shay had been the one to bathe and dress Bria's body for the waking party, and he had done it alone.

The waking party began somberly enough, with Bria's brother leading them all in saying the rosary. His priest's voice chanted the prayers, slow and deep, making of them a glorious chorus of hope and faith. But his face had taken on the ashen-gray color of a dead fire.

Emma knelt with the others and closed her eyes, listening to the clicking beads count off the Hail Marys and Our Fathers. Bria, she knew, would have loved the beautiful music the rosaries made. And she would have loved what came after as well.

Colin, the barber, put wind in his bag and his mouth to the blowpipe, and filled the night with wails so harsh and rich and sad they pulled at the sinews of the soul. But then out came a fiddle and an accordion. The music turned loud and joyous, and it wasn't long before shoes began tapping and the kerosene ceiling lamp swayed as if the little shack were dancing on its stilts.

Someone said something that caused someone else to laugh, and then the talk grew as lively as the music. Father O'Reilly handed around a plate of clay pipes and a bowl of tobacco. The men dipped mugs into the beer bucket in the sink and passed around jars of *poitín.* Soon the kitchen grew hot with the press of bodies and the burning candles, the air thick with tobacco smoke and the malty smell of beer.

The women gathered around the table and drank endless cups of tea. Emma stood on their fringes, listening but not belonging. They weren't being rude, she knew. They didn't know what to make of her, and so they made nothing at all.

"He took right to the pap bottle, God bless him," Mrs. Hale was saying. As the caretaker of little Jacko, she was commanding most of the attention. "After she couldn't nurse him no more, the poor dear. And you wouldn't live so long as to see a sweeter babe. He never fusses. Just lays in his cradle for hours on end, blowing spit bubbles and practicing his smile."

"He's got his father's smile, he does," someone said.

"And his mother's hair, God bless him."

They all looked over at Bria lying in her coffin with her hair spread in a scarlet fan on the white satin pillow.

All but Emma, who walked out the open door and stood alone on the tall front stoop. But the night offered no comfort. The whole world was blurred in a thick white salt cloud. It muffled some sounds and magnified others. She could hear the small sucking rattle of the tide on the beach around back.

The beach where Bria had died.

Emma's head fell back and she looked up, into a white infinity. She had thought she hadn't any more tears inside her, yet they came again, overflowing her eyes and rolling across her cheekbones and into her hair.

I can't bear this, she thought. God must end this now, for I can't bear another moment of it.

Tomorrow would be the funeral Mass and then they would bury Bria in the Saint Mary's cemetery, among the tumbled old monuments whose weathered faces were furred with moss. Her grave would be a fresh scar on the earth for a while, but within weeks the grass would begin to grow there again, and come winter, the snow and rain would begin to scour the new stone. And in the spring, Emma would plant violets, and they would bloom.

Eventually, Emma knew, her tears would stop coming so easily, and what seemed so unbearable now would become bearable almost without her realizing it. But her heart would hold on to her grief forever, would hold on like a lover. Because her heart knew there were some losses you never got over.

The fog had turned as thick as buttermilk by the time the

waking party came to an end. In groups of twos and threes, by families and alone, the guests dipped their fingers in the holy-water font and received Father O'Reilly's blessing of *Dia is Maire Dhuit* before disappearing into the white-shrouded night.

And the house grew silent once again.

Emma helped the girls to undress and saw them settled for the rest of the night in the white iron bed. She leaned over and brushed the red curls off Merry's forehead and kissed the soft, pink skin.

Merry hummed.

"She says Mam doesn't want to leave us," Noreen said.

Emma cupped Merry's face. The little girl's cheeks were wet and sticky with tears. "Of course she didn't, honey, because she loved you all so very, very much. But she's at peace now, in heaven."

Merry's hum took on an angry tone, and she shook her head, hard, but this time Noreen only shrugged.

Emma tucked the sheet more snugly under Merry's round, dimpled chin. "Good night, girls," she said, although she could barely get the words out her throat had grown so sore. All of her had grown so sore. But as she turned to leave, Noreen said in a small, tight voice, "Miss Emma, will you lay by us for a time?"

So she turned down the lamp and stretched out beside them on top of the diamond-patterned quilt, lay beside Bria's daughters in the dark on this, the second night they would spend without her. Through the open bedroom door she heard Shay and Bria's brother talking. Rather, the priest was talking; there were no answering words from Bria's husband. And when the girls finally slept and she went out into the kitchen, she found him alone, standing in the middle of the worn brown linoleum floor as if he weren't quite sure how he'd come to be there.

The black taffeta skirts of her mourning dress rustled as

she came up to him. She laid her hand on his back. He turned, slowly, so that for a moment her hand seemed to cling to the black cloth of his coat before it fell to her side.

She stood before him, bleeding inside for him. He looked as though someone had wrenched his heart out of his breast and wrung it empty. She wanted to comfort him, to take comfort from him, but she couldn't think how to begin to do either one.

"If there's anything else I can do . . ."

She watched him try to smile and fail. "No, thank you. You've done so much already." His gaze went back to the casket on the table as though pulled there. He looked at it as if he waited for the woman inside to get up and come to him. "I'd like to be alone, please," he said.

He'd said it gently, almost sweetly, but it hurt.

She turned and left him then. But when she was through the door, she paused and looked back, although afterward she wished she hadn't. He had gone to the coffin and stood looking down on his dead wife's face, and in that silent kitchen she heard him speak such broken, desperate words.

"And how am I supposed to go on living without you, Bria darlin'? Will you be telling me that, then, *mo bhean*?"

In the days that followed his wife's death, Shay McKenna took his fishing dory out on the water at dawn and stayed there until it grew dark.

The hours of daylight were long in August, and they were easily filled up with dragging nets, harvesting traps, and baiting lines. On days when the wind blew strong, he sailed up into it and let the wind beat on his face and body as if it had fists. On days when there was no wind, he rowed. Those were the best days, when he made himself so tired he couldn't think, and the only pain he felt was the ache in his muscles and joints and bones.

But sometimes . . . Sometimes the setting sun would turn the clouds the color of her hair, and the water spilling over the bow would sound like her laugh. Or the evening breeze would make the same little sighing sound she'd always made when he entered her, and he would know the soul-scouring pain of loss and never-again.

Sometimes, thought Shay McKenna, it felt as though he'd taken a gun and shot a hole in his heart.

She'd been gone over two weeks when he came home one day a little earlier than usual. Even so, the sun had set, leaving the sky an ashen gray with puffs of charcoal here and there. He took his time putting up the dory, delaying that moment when he would have to walk into the house and she wouldn't be there.

By the time he made himself climb the stoop and open the door, the lamps had been lit against the falling darkness. The kitchen smelled good, he thought, of supper cooking on the stove. He started into his bedroom, then stopped dead on the threshold.

Miss Emma Tremayne was bent over his bed, changing his son's soiled nappy. As he watched, she pushed her face into Jacko's belly, nuzzling him with her nose, and the little fellow waved his fisted hands and laughed—that deep, gurgling chortle babies made.

And tears stung Shay McKenna's eyes.

She must have sensed his presence, for she straightened and turned. She uttered a small exclamation of surprise, and the blood rushed pink over her cheeks. "Mr. McKenna! I thought you were . . . I hope you don't mind. He needed changing."

He nodded and waved his hand, as if giving her permission to carry on. But he couldn't seem to say anything, and he backed out of the doorway, feeling hulking and clumsy and too big for his skin.

He sat down at the kitchen table, and the cat Gorgeous jumped into his lap. He fondled the cat's chewed ears while it kneaded his thighs with its huge paws. There was a peaceful, homey silence to the house. He could hear the rattle of potatoes simmering on the stove. And from the bedroom, the rustle of silk, the whisper of a kid slipper across the floor.

He was just wondering where his daughters were when her voice came floating out to him. "I sent the girls over to Mrs. Hale's with the leftover poppyseed cake we had for tea . . . She's been so kind, Mrs. Hale has."

He knew Emma Tremayne had been coming here often in the weeks since Bria's death. The girls told him of those afternoons when she met them at the mill gates, with a hamper full of food. They would collect little Jacko from Mrs. Hale, and then Emma would put on tea parties for them all. Proper, Great Folk–type tea parties that would have made Bria smile.

He looked around him. The flowers on the table sure hadn't been put there by him. He'd left the breakfast dishes on the slopstone, but they'd been washed and put away. Yet even without all that, he knew those days when she came because he could smell the traces of her presence that she left behind. A hint of lilacs that always made him think of warm spring afternoons, when the whole world seemed full of expectation and promise.

He noticed an unfamiliar book on the table and he picked it up. It was a gold-leafed, satin-bound volume titled *The Lives of the Presidents.* He opened it up to the flyleaf and read: "To Emmaline Tremayne, for excellence in spelling."

Excellence in spelling . . . The thought made him smile. He tried to imagine her as a child. She probably wore white pinafores so starched they crackled when she walked. Surely she'd never gone around with holes in her stockings and skinned knees and straw in her hair.

She came out of the bedroom with little Jacko in her arms,

not crackling, maybe, but rustling, surely. That silky whisper of a rustle that she seemed to make even when she was standing still. He watched her lay his son in his cradle, watched how she smoothed the hair down over the soft spot on his head with her finger, and he thought of how Bria had always done that, and his throat tightened with longing for something that was never again to be.

He looked away from her, out the window that framed a sky that was now the deep, dark blue of summer twilight. When he looked back, he realized she had come to stand at the table, with her hand on the back of a chair, and she was staring at the book he held. A worried frown had put a little crease between her dark eyebrows.

"Noreen told me you've been teaching her how to read," she said, "and I thought . . . Well, as she's interested in American history, and there're a few deliciously gory parts in there to give her the shivers, I thought she might like . . ." Her hand tightened its grip on the chair. "I did say she had to ask you first, though, before she could keep it. I hope you don't mind."

He wanted to tell her he was that desperate for his girls to learn to read, to be educated. He was that desperate to get them out of the mill, he would have sold whatever he had left of his soul. But he couldn't seem to get any air or words past his throat.

He laid the book down carefully on the table. He spread his hand out flat on the oilcloth. Spread his fingers out wide, until the veins and bones of his hand pushed against the skin.

He glanced up and saw that she, too, was looking at his hand. His big, brutish, scarred, and callused hand.

Her gaze jerked up, met his, and then pulled hard away.

The skin on her forehead was so translucent he could see the blue veins, see them pulse. He wondered what had her so skittish around him tonight. He never knew which Emma she would be. The daring, rebellious child with the mouth on her saucy and quirky as an Irish riddle. Or the shy society miss who behaved as if she wouldn't say boo to a mouse.

And then there was the young woman he had come to know and like during those final weeks of his wife's life. That Emma was a generous, kind, and loyal friend.

The Emma of this evening had retreated across the kitchen, to the stove. She used a red-striped huck towel to lift the lid off the black pot that steamed on the fire, and the earthy smell of boiling potatoes filled the air. It was a strange sight she made there in his kitchen, in her dress that seemed all lace and satin bows, the pale yellow of fresh cream.

"Father O'Reilly stopped by for tea with us today," she was saying. "He was telling us such stories of Bria, about when she was a girl in Gortadoo. He had us laughing so, and it seemed such a good thing—to give the girls memories of their mama to tuck away in their hearts." She glanced back at him over her shoulder. She had twisted the towel up into a knot in her hands. "I hope you don't mind."

"Stop saying that."

The words had come out harsher than he'd meant them. He drew in a deep breath and cleared his throat. "Stop saying you hope I don't mind, because I don't."

She had turned her back to him and was laying the towel on the slopstone, folding it carefully. "It's only that I promised Bria I would . . ."

He stood up, spilling Gorgeous onto the floor. The cat streaked off into the bedroom with an aggrieved yowl and a flash of its tail. Emma spun back around, her eyes wide and luminous.

"Sweet saints, Miss Tremayne," he said. "Why shouldn't you come as often as you like?"

She backed up as if she expected him to spring at her, although he hadn't taken a step. "Thank you," she said. "I—

I should be leaving now, though." She cast a look out the window. "It's grown quite dark."

She had set her hat and gloves on the small table next to the holy-water font. He watched her put them on. A white straw hat with a wide yellow ribbon that she tied at a jaunty angle under her chin. Gloves of so delicate a lace he could see through it to the pale skin of her hands.

She put her lace-gloved palm on the latch and opened the door, but before she walked on through it, she turned and gave him a sweet, tremulous smile. "Good evening, Mr. McKenna."

"Good evening, Miss Tremayne," he said. But she was already gone.

Slowly, he sat back down. He picked up the book that she had given to Noreen, then he set it down again. He thought he should get up and take the potatoes off the fire before they boiled to mush. He thought about going to the cupboard and taking out the jar of *poitín.* His mouth was as dry as thatch.

"*Dhia.* What a grand sort of liar you are, Seamus McKenna. Tellin' her, and tellin' yourself, that you don't mind."

It was hard for Emma, coming back to the house on Thames Street, knowing now that he might be there. For she could no longer separate herself from how she felt about him, and he would always belong to Bria.

She nearly stayed away after that, would have stayed away if not for the promise she had made.

Even so, she let some time pass before she came again, and she chose a day of little wind, when she knew it would take him some hours to sail home. It had been a hot day, of brassy yellow sunshine and moist, hazy air. One of those

Bristol summer days when Emma thought she could almost hear the heat, sweating and panting and dripping.

It was hot inside the house that evening. Emma left the door open, remembering how Bria had always craved the light so.

She had just taken off her hat and gloves and set them on the table when it happened: She looked up and saw Bria standing at the stove.

Standing at the stove with her hand on the teakettle. With her hand wrapped up in a huck towel, as though she feared the handle would be too hot, for steam was coming out the kettle's spout.

She had on the batiste night rail that Emma had given her, the one with the spills of lace at the wrists. She was wearing her riotous hair as she often did, tied back with a piece of twine, but tendrils of it had pulled loose and were sticking to her damp cheeks. Ribbons of sunlight unfurled from the open door across the floor to wrap around her bare feet. The night rail was too short; Emma could see the white, knobby bones of her ankles.

"Bria . . ." Emma whispered, aching.

Bria, the Bria at the stove, turned and smiled, her dark eyes lighting up as she saw Emma.

And then she disappeared.

"That was Mam."

Emma whirled so fast she had to grasp the back of the ladderback chair to keep from falling. Her heart pounded hard and violently in her ears, like a hurricane surf.

Merry stood in the doorway. She looked every bit the mill rat with cotton lint and threads clinging to her clothes and hair, her bare feet black and greasy.

"You saw her," Emma said, or thought she said. She couldn't get her lungs to work.

Merry hummed and nodded.

Emma turned back to the stove. She took a step toward it,

her legs trembling. No one was there. The kettle sat on the hob, and the fire was out.

But Bria had been so real standing there at the stove; in that one white flash of an instant she had been real. A woman wearing a night rail that was too short for her, holding a steaming teakettle in her towel-wrapped hand. Not some amorphous, gauzy figure floating in the air. She'd been sweating.

Emma swallowed, breathed. She closed her eyes and opened them again. There was still no woman standing at the stove. Merry came up to her and took her hand.

Emma's hand trembled. She tried to stop it, but she couldn't. And she couldn't stop her voice from trembling, either. "Have you seen her . . . seen your mama before this?"

"Sometimes," Merry said, talking the word, not humming it. "She comes when Da is crying for her. He sits here at the table real late at night sometimes, not doing anything, just sitting. And he talks to her, talks to Mam. He says, 'Bria darlin', why did you go and leave me?' and then he cries. That's when she comes and stands behind him and touches his hair."

"Does . . . does your father see her?"

Merry hummed a *no.* She drew in a deep breath and hummed again, loud and long. Then her mouth opened, and Emma thought she would speak in words again, but Noreen came bursting into the kitchen just then, chattering like a magpie and carrying little Jacko in her arms.

"Mrs. Hale said he was sweet as a sugar tit today, and I said, 'When is he never?' Like the o'erseer was mean as a polecat today, and when is he never? He whipped Nate O'Hara's legs with a rope 'cause he spilled his bobbins, so Merry's gone and put a fairy's curse on him, on the o'erseer, and now his weenie's gonna fall off. Only he don't know it yet. Do you want for me to fire up the kettle, Miss Emma?"

"What? Oh, no, it's much too hot today," Emma said, her voice still quavering a little. "I'll make us some effervescent lemon instead." She took the baby from his sister's arms. She hugged him tightly to her breast, breathing in his baby smell of talcum and milk. She rubbed her cheek against his soft red hair, his mother's hair.

A foot landed on the wooden stoop, making it creak. A shadow fell across the sun-washed floor. She looked up as Shay McKenna filled the doorway. Their gazes held for one taut moment, then he took a step back and looked away.

"There's work that needs doing out on the dory," he said. "I thought I'd let you . . . let the girls know where I am."

Emma laid her cheek against the baby's head and listened to Shay walk away. The baby's back rose and fell beneath her hand with his breathing. He made soft suckling sounds against her shoulder.

Emma rubbed her mouth over his hair in a soft kiss and then she gave him back to Noreen and went after his father.

He wasn't working on his dory. He was on the gray shingled beach, sitting among the rocks and rubbery strands of seaweed, in the place where Bria had died. Emma gathered up the skirt of her white muslin summer dress and sat down next to him.

He kept his face averted from hers, watching a pair of tongers rake the deep water for quahogs. Grief and the wind had etched the lines deeper at the corners of his eyes. A jar of *poitín* dangled from the fingers of one hand, but he didn't seem to be drinking from it.

He smelled of the sea and summer wind, and she wanted to touch him. Simply touch him.

"Merry talks to me," she said.

"Merry hasn't spoken a word in three years."

"She does to me."

He turned his head to look at her. She saw pain and a raw guilt, but no disbelief in his eyes. "But why? Why you?" His mouth twisted down at one corner. "I didn't mean that how it sounded. I only—"

"You meant why me, and not Bria." Emma shook her head, shrugging a little. "That I can't tell you. It's a strange thing when it happens. It's as though she suddenly finds her words and then loses them again."

He turned away from her. He looked down between his spread knees; he pushed at a wet clump of rockweed with his boot. "And did Bria tell you how it came to be, how it was my daughter lost her words?"

She wanted to tell him that such was the way she had fallen in love with him. Through Bria's telling her. "Yes," she said.

He lifted the jar as though he would drink from it, but then he didn't. "There's some as say that God gave the Irish whiskey to keep them from ruling the world."

The wind came up suddenly, spangling the harbor into a million diamonds and lifting his hair where it lay long on the back of his neck. She wanted to tangle her fingers in his hair and pull his head to her until it lay against her breast.

"I fancied myself man enough to rule the world, surely. I fancied myself the brave and brawny lad, living for Ireland, fighting for Ireland, dreaming always of the grand and glorious day when the rising would come. And my Bria, she used to say to me that I spent precious little time thinking of what would come after. Of what me and Ireland would do with our freedom once we had it."

His mouth had gone hard and gaunt. She wanted to press her lips fiercely against that mouth, press until the kiss became painful.

"I killed the land agent who drove my mother into the sea, and like a fool I didn't plan for what would come after. *Dhia*, there was myself, behaving as though it were all a music-hall farce, all the way down to the martyred hero who gets up and walks off the stage at the end. And leaving my wife and girls to pay the bitter price of it."

She sensed a hard trembling going on deep inside him, and she wanted to wrap her arms around him and hold him until it stopped.

"I know what you think of me," she said. "That I am young and pampered and ignorant of the real world, and you would be right. But I know how Bria died and some of how she lived, and she did both as though she believed that honor is what shapes our souls. You wouldn't be who you are, Shay McKenna, if you didn't fight for Ireland and yourself. And you wouldn't be the man that Bria loved."

He had fallen silent and wasn't looking at her, but she didn't care. She listened to the gentle slap of the water against the pier pilings and the whir of the mill spindles in the distance. She watched a seagull feed off the leftovers of someone's corned beef sandwich.

She wanted to tell him that he was the man she loved. She wanted to tell him that he was her first thought in the morning and the last before she slept. That because of him, and Bria before him, her whole life had come undone.

"Mother of God!"

The words came out of him on a tearing gasp, as if something had broken inside him. His head bowed, and the jar of whiskey fell from his hands, and his back shuddered, hard. Shuddered with harsh, silent, wrenching sobs.

She wanted to . . .

Her hand hovered over his hair, and then she touched him. And then he turned in to her, and her arms went around him, and she was holding him, holding him close while he wept.

Chapter Twenty-three

"Aaaagh . . . Go chase yerself!"

Father Donagh O'Reilly snatched the hat off his head and slapped it against his thigh. "He goes and lays such a fat one right over the plate, the blessed Saint Patrick himself could've sent it for a ride on a straw. I'm tellin' you, Miss Tremayne, that lad couldn't pitch his way out of a wet sack."

He jammed his hat back on his head and resumed his seat on the bottom row of the makeshift bleachers, while the batter trotted around the diamond that had been scratched into the dun-colored grass of the Bristol Common. The Philadelphia Athletics were playing the New York Mutuals in an exhibition of professional baseball, and the crowd had adopted the Mutuals as their home team. The Mutuals were losing eight runs to two.

The Athletic batter was taking his sweet time touring the bases, accompanied by hoots and birdcalls. Merry jumped up and began dancing from foot to foot, humming fiercely.

"She's laying a fairy curse on him," Noreen said. "So's his—"

"Teeth and hair will fall out by morning," Emma quickly put in. She was careful not to look Father O'Reilly's way, but from his knowing chuckle she suspected he had a good idea of the true nature of Merry McKenna's curses.

Emma flapped her palmetto fan so hard it lifted the brim of her white leghorn straw hat. Although the sky was clotted with clouds as gray as pewter, it was hot. A pall hung over the common, thick with the smells of summer-scorched grass and burnt rubber from the nearby factory. The lofty elms drooped heavy in the steamy air.

A *brava* strolled past the bleachers, selling *chourice* on strings. Father O'Reilly was up and after him, taking the girls with him. He'd already treated them all to watermelon slices, roasted peanuts, buttered popcorn, and pickles on a stick. She would have to remind him that when they had hatched the plan of making this off-Saturday a special one for the girls, it hadn't included eating their way into a bellyache.

The Mutual pitcher finally made an out, and the crowd gave him a derisive ovation. Emma spotted Judith Patterson and Grace Attwater strolling arm in arm around the edge of the outfield. She waved at them, but they didn't seem to see her. She waited a moment and waved again. That time she was sure they saw her, but they slowly turned their backs to her and walked away.

Emma bit her lip and looked off toward the empty bandstand, blinking against a sting of tears. She should have been able to predict this moment. She had become used to the Great Folk thinking of her friendship with an Irish immigrant family as a peculiar form of Tremayne wildness, rather like her sculpting. But now, apparently, some invisible line had been crossed, and she had ventured into the realm of bad form.

Emma told herself she didn't care, but the truth was she did. Much as she had always hated going out in society, at least she had been welcomed and accepted there. The stares she'd received had been ones of admiration, not of censure and disgust. Now only the awesome weight of her name and Mr. Geoffrey Alcott's ring on her finger would keep her from being ostracized permanently and completely.

And lately her mother's tolerance had been wearing thin as well. This morning, when Emma had mentioned she was taking the McKenna children to the baseball game, that haunted look had come into Mama's eyes, and her hand had shaken so that she'd spilled coffee onto her slice of dry toast, which was all she allowed herself anymore for breakfast.

"I can't help worrying," Bethel had said, "how your turning those Irish waifs into your pet charity project will be received, Emma. Such a *personal* involvement on your part can hardly be the done thing."

Emma passed her mother the tray of toast, hoping to distract her. "Did you notice, Mama, that you've spilled coffee on your plate? Have another—"

Bethel pushed the toast away. "You know I cannot, when every bite I eat shows itself upon my person. You have no appreciation, Emma, of the sacrifices I am making on your behalf . . ." Then her mother had gone on to enumerate those sacrifices, and the baseball game was forgotten about.

It was just as well, Emma thought, that she hadn't mentioned an Irish Catholic priest would be rounding out the party. Yet she'd felt a shiver of apprehension even then. She wasn't going to be able to go on living in two worlds indefinitely. Someday, someone—Mama, Geoffrey, or the likes of Judith Patterson and Grace Attwater—would make her choose. Between the Emma who dwelled in straitlaced luxury at The Birches and was the family's only hope, and the Emma who had been Bria McKenna's *banacharaid*.

The elms sighed and dipped their heads now in the hot, damp wind. She was thinking how lonely a bandstand could look, empty on a cloudy summer's day, when she saw Shay McKenna come walking around it, cutting across the sunbrowned grass of the common.

He was dressed as if he'd just come off his dory, with his shirtsleeves rolled up to his elbows and no collar on his shirt. She watched him walk toward her in the loose, confident way he had. She watched him walk toward her, and her heart seemed to leap in expectation.

He touched his finger to the brim of his scally cap as he came up to her. "Good day to you, Miss Tremayne," he said, taking Father O'Reilly's seat next to her on the bleachers. He waved to his daughters, who had gotten sidetracked by a group of boys trading baseball cards.

Sometimes she felt as though her skin would catch fire if only he would touch her, but of course he never touched her. She hadn't even seen him since that evening on the beach, when she'd held him while he cried for the wife he had lost.

He caught Father O'Reilly's eyes, over by the *chourice* man, and pointed to a red-and-white-striped tent that was selling buckets of beer. To Emma, he said, "The good father hasn't been trying to convert you, has he?"

She gave him a shy smile and shook her head. "He's a quiet man. When he's not shouting at the ballplayers."

Shay widened his eyes a little. Eyes that were the deep green of sunlight on marsh water. "Quiet, is he? I've known Donagh to tie a woman's tongue in knots, but never the other way about. But then it's a rare thing for the lad to come face to face with someone prettier than he is."

As compliments went, it wasn't much. Yet she felt herself blushing, as if he'd just told her she was the most beautiful creature in the universe.

A silence settled between them. Out on the diamond, the Mutuals turned a double play and the crowd cheered, but Emma wasn't watching. Thunder rumbled in the distance; the skies had grown darker. She thought he could probably hear her heart beating.

"Were you really going to be a priest yourself?"

"Bria told you that too, did she?" He was sitting with his

elbows resting on his thighs, his hands hanging loose between his knees. He bent over and plucked a blade of grass to twirl between his fingers. "When I was a boy I loved the Mass with all its holy mysteries and ceremonies. For a time, in them, I found a meaning for my life. And then . . ." He shrugged. "I didn't anymore."

Then you found a meaning for your life in Bria, she thought. And now you've lost her, as well. That day on the beach, when he had let her hold him while he wept, she hadn't been able to think of what to say to him, and so she had said nothing, only held him. But now . . .

"Mr. McKenna?" He turned his head to look at her, but his face showed her nothing of what he was thinking. She hoped he could see nothing in hers. "There's a thing I've been meaning to tell you for some time now, and I don't know as how I'll get another chance . . . I wanted to say that whatever happens to me in the rest of my life, I know I will be a different, a *better*, person from having known your wife. She taught me how to be a friend and how to have one. And how to live and love unconditionally."

He wasn't looking at her anymore, but she saw his throat work as he swallowed hard. He was watching Bria's brother leave the refreshment tent with two buckets of beer in one hand and strings of *chourice* in the other. But then the priest stopped to talk to a man in a wrinkled linen suit and a straw boater.

What Emma said next she hadn't planned on saying. It just came out before she could stop it: "Sometimes . . . sometimes I don't think I should marry Mr. Alcott, for I doubt he and I will ever have what you and Bria had."

A moment passed when she didn't think he would answer her at all. "A marriage isn't made with the proposal of it," he finally said. "It's a thing that's done living one day at a time together. Glorious days like the one when you watch your wife put your firstborn babe to her breast. Or those sorrow's own days, when you'd sooner be giving the stupid, stubborn ass of a fellow you've married a great clout on the ear as look at him." He flashed her a sudden, startling smile. "And simple days, like this one, when you're watching a baseball game together, and wondering if you're going to get rained on before your dawdling fool of a brother-in-law makes it back with the beer."

She smiled back at him, but she wanted to tell him that she knew already she would never have a day like this with Geoffrey and any children they might have.

Still, perhaps he read her thoughts on her face, for he said, "Your life will be what you'll make of it, Emma Tremayne . . . And I do believe that it will be a grand one."

He was being kind, and kindness wasn't what she wanted from him. And she thought, but didn't say, that for all he loved his Bria and she loved him, Bria's life was still what *he* had made of it.

She heard the crack of a baseball leaving the bat and then she realized that the people around them were shouting and waving their arms. She looked around and up . . . and saw the ball coming at her on a long, high arc through the air.

She didn't have time to duck. She threw up her hands and the ball smacked right into them, stinging her lace-gloved palms something fierce, but Emma barely felt it. She was that surprised and excited, and overall pleased with herself.

"I caught it!" she exclaimed, laughing, turning to him. "Did you see, Mr. McKenna, I . . ."

He was looking at her, looking at her hard, and she saw something flash in his eyes—a sort of wild and desperate hunger. And she felt the piercing sweetness of suddenly losing her way, of being utterly and magnificently lost in that look in his eyes.

But then it began to rain, big drops that rattled on the bleachers like dried peas, and what she had seen—whatever she'd thought she had seen—was no longer there.

"Merry!" he suddenly shouted, his gaze shifting beyond her. "Bloody hell. What is she doing?"

Emma looked around. Noreen and Father O'Reilly were hurrying toward them, and Noreen was holding her hands over her head, trying to shelter it from the splattering rain. But Merry was running *away*, around back of the bandstand and toward State Street and the harbor.

Then the clouds seemed to collapse, and the rain fell in sheets and torrents, and the little girl was lost from sight.

"Merry!" Shay shouted again, and took off running after her. Emma gathered up her skirts and followed, almost slipping on the wet grass. The rain, driving in from the bay, scourged their faces as they ran. The wind sounded like sails flapping.

Merry was all the way to the Thames Street wharves when they caught up with her. She had climbed onto a pier, and for a moment Emma had the horrible fear she was going to jump into the water. The storm was whipping the bay into white-fringed waves that spewed foam onto the gray, weathered boards.

Merry went all the way to the edge of the pier, and then she stopped and turned around and seemed to be waiting for them. She was humming so hard her whole body shook with it.

Shay got to her first, scooping her up into his arms. But she began to buck and writhe, her humming now so high-pitched it was like the whine of an overturned beehive.

Noreen came running up, with Father O'Reilly on her heels, still carrying the beer and sausages forgotten in his hands. Merry reared so violently in her father's arms, he nearly dropped her. Her humming turned into a screech.

"Nory," Shay said, panting. Rainwater streamed down from his cap and hair into his eyes. His face was white. "God save us. Nory, what's she saying?"

Noreen's eyes seemed to swell and fill her face like two

black wells. She was shuddering so hard her teeth rattled. "She's . . . she's saying the mill's on fire, and Miss Emma has to come for us, to get us out."

They could see the mill clearly from where they were. With its granite stone walls and gray slate roof and tall brick chimney, it looked as hulking and forbidding as a prison in the rain, but there were no flames or smoke.

"It's not on fire," Shay said. He tried to turn the hysterical child so she could see for herself, but she kicked and flailed her arms, and hummed. "Look, m'love, you can see from here how it's not on fire."

"She says Miss Emma's got to come for us," Noreen repeated, her voice breaking over the fear that lived always within her, just beneath the surface.

Emma held out her arms and Merry came into them, wrapping her legs around Emma's hips, gripping her tightly, and the frantic humming slowly subsided. Emma held her close, although she staggered a little under the child's weight. "I'll come," she said into the little girl's wet and shivering neck. "I promise, I will come."

He could hear Emma in the bedroom, saying sweet words of comfort to his daughter. She hadn't wanted anything to do with him, had Merry. And Noreen had gone next door to Mrs. Hale's, to fetch the baby, and there she'd stayed. Apparently, she didn't want to have anything to do with him either. Not that he could blame them. He hadn't been around much to give his girls any comfort lately. Mother of God, he hadn't been able to comfort himself.

Emma came to stand just inside the door, with one hand on the jamb. "She's sleeping," she said. "I put a hot water bottle on her feet so she wouldn't take a chill."

He tried to smile at her, but he couldn't manage it.

"You're a wonder with her. A wonder with both girls, and the baby, too, and I know I haven't thanked you properly. Sweet saints, I haven't thanked you at all."

He'd never known someone like her for being able to make her whole self look pleased whenever she was given the smallest compliment. He could see her pleasure pass over her face, like a flash under the skin, and spill out of her eyes.

It was only when you first saw her, he thought, that she seemed so haughty and unapproachable. Now he knew that was only a way she had of protecting herself from revealing how vulnerable she was. And every time he got another glimpse of the fragility in her, he felt a frightening sensation of discovery. As though he was the first man to have seen this in her.

She was showing that vulnerability now, looking around his kitchen, unable to meet his eyes.

"You've made coffee," she said. "But you haven't poured it."

He sat at the table and watched her go to the stove. He watched her lift the blue-enameled coffeepot off the fire, watched the muscles tighten in her pale, slender arm. Her hair had dried, but strands of it had come loose to feather her neck. Freckles of rain pelted the windowpane, casting speckled shadows on her face.

She brought the pot over to the table, and he watched the way the curve of her breast pressed against her silk shirtwaist as she poured the coffee into a pair of tin mugs. Her head bowed, revealing the small bone at the nape of her neck. He wanted to touch the skin there at the back of her neck. To feel that bone and the softness of her skin beneath his fingers.

His hand clenched into a fist on the oilcloth. He pulled it down off the table and into his lap. He felt his own heart beating in slow, dragging thuds.

He'd never known this about desire. No—he'd known it once, long ago, but he'd forgotten it. That the hunger and the wanting can live in you, hiding, and then come out when you least expect it. When you don't want it.

She set down the coffeepot and picked up the book he'd left lying on the table. The book he'd read throughout the long hours of the past night. He hadn't been sleeping much lately. He'd slept so many years with Bria beside him, and now he couldn't seem to do it without her.

He'd been a steady patron, surely, of the Roger's Free Library these past weeks.

She turned the book over in her hands and read the spine aloud, "*Anna Karenina* . . . That one will make you cry," she said, and then he watched the blush of memory spread like a stain over her cheekbones, saw the pulse beating in her throat and her mouth part open on a shock of breath. He almost smiled.

"Not a big tough boyo like myself, surely. Might be it will make my eyes go just a wee bit soft, though."

She blushed brighter, then she laughed, softly and shyly.

She turned away and sat down in the chair across from him. She picked up her coffee, but then set it down without drinking, and he saw a teasing light come into her eyes.

"Did you ever notice," she said, "how inside the Roger's Free Library, the books by male and female authors are kept segregated on the shelves?"

He watched the dimple deepen at the corner of her mouth, and he waited for what she would say next, knowing it would surprise him.

"It makes you wonder, doesn't it," she went on, "what those books get up to once the lights are put out and the doors are locked, and there's no chaperon to be had for a song."

He surprised himself by laughing. For so long he'd been thinking that he would never laugh again.

Smiling, she drew the mug in front of her and rubbed her finger around the rim. Her gaze flashed up to his, then down again to the table, engrossed in watching her own finger move around and around. "There's another thing I've been meaning to speak with you about, Mr. McKenna."

Don't, he wanted to say to her. *Don't share any more of yourself with me, because it scares me. It pulls me into a place where I don't want to be.*

"I've been thinking," she said, "about the problem of schooling for the mill children here in Bristol. Obviously, they can't be attending any sort of lessons after their shifts, for they would be toppling over asleep at their desks after the long grind of the day. But I was thinking perhaps we could establish a kind of scholarship school that would pay the children to attend. That way their families could continue to have their income, yet the children would get the education they will need to elevate their stations in life."

She looked up at him, and her vulnerability, her need to please him, was almost painful to see.

And it scared him. Mother of Jesus, it scared him. So that he couldn't seem to keep the words from coming out of his mouth. "A scholarship school we could establish . . . And just who is this *we*, Miss Tremayne? Or are you meaning yourself? You with your million-dollar trust fund fairly burnin' a hole in your pocket. Are you thinking maybe you've found a way, then, to buy your way into our lives?"

"What a snobbish thing to say," she exclaimed, her voice breaking. She averted her face, blinking hard, and he knew she was fighting tears.

"Aye," he said. He felt his own face hardening and he wanted to stop, but he couldn't. "I admit it."

She had stood up and turned away from him, and he knew she would leave him now. He had hurt her, and he didn't like knowing he could do that. That he could hurt her, and so easily.

But he wasn't going to stop her from leaving.

He wished Bria hadn't put the thought into his head: that Miss Emma Tremayne, one of the high and mighty Great Folk of Bristol, Rhode Island, fancied herself in love with the likes of him.

Because you can't be told that someone is in love with you without it changing how you look at that person. You can't help wondering what it would be like just the once to . . .

Maybe a man couldn't stop the hunger, he thought. Maybe he couldn't stop the wanting from coming, but he sure as bloody hell didn't need to act upon those feelings. And if that meant not looking at her, if that meant staying away from her, he would do those things. If that meant not thinking about her, then fine, he could do that, too.

But he wasn't going to let it happen . . . whatever it was.

The summer storm that had soaked Bristol's first exhibition baseball game blew away during the night. Now the sky was duck's-egg blue, with white, fleeting clouds, and the breeze wafted light and soft as feathers. But then, it would never dare to rain on an Alcott garden party.

The Alcotts hosted a garden party at their Hope Street mansion twice a year, on the first day of June and the last day of August. The tradition had begun in 1792, and every Alcott thereafter had carried on with it, each in grander style than the last.

It was one Great Folk tradition Emma had always enjoyed, and the Alcott gardeners had outdone themselves this year, creating a kaleidoscope of blossoms that seemed to twirl and change colorful patterns with the breeze. Emma walked the path that circled the marble fountain of cavorting cupids. She breathed deeply of the flowered air, which had just a hint of salt bay water underneath it to give it a tang. She lowered her parasol and let her head fall back, soaking in the sunshine like oil.

The parasol was plucked out of her hands and put back where it belonged, shading her from those disastrously browning rays. "Merciful heavens, child!" Bethel exclaimed. "What are you doing? I declare, you have positively *ruined* your complexion this summer. But there's no need to add insult to injury now. And *here*, of all places."

Emma resumed control of her parasol, resting it lightly on her lilac tulle-and-lace-clad shoulder. "I'm sorry, Mama. I shall endeavor to be more careful."

Her mother gave her a dubious look and sighed. "You are a trial to me, Emma. All my children have always been such trials to me."

The fountain tinkled like silver bells, harmonizing with the strains of "Claire de Lune" coming from the string quartet housed in the gazebo. Later, there would be tennis and archery, but for now the guests were content to stroll the gardens and partake of the delicacies displayed on the damask-clothed tables sheltered by a blue-striped tent.

As they passed within sight and smell of the tent, Bethel gazed at it with a blend of yearning and aversion pulling at her face. As though the pâté de foie gras, the chilled oysters on the half shell, and the meringues with strawberries and whipped cream were all cruel lovers she both longed for and feared.

Emma thought her mother did look exceptionally young and pretty that sun-stippled day, in her pale beige satin summer gown draped with yards of creamy lace. But there was a languid, trembling air about her, as if she were on the verge of fainting.

"Mama," Emma said. "Why don't you allow me to bring you a little plate of something? Some lobster salad, perhaps?"

Her mother rejected the offer with a shudder. "I swear, Emma, sometimes I think you enjoy tormenting me. You know that if I get within so much as ten feet of that dreadful tent, I shan't be able to squeeze into my unmentionables tomorrow without Jewell positively having to use a *crank* on the laces. And now that we know for certain your father is coming to the wedding, I don't want to disappoint him. He should feel proud to display me on his arm."

Emma linked arms with her mother and leaned against her, which was the closest she dared to an embrace. "He will be proud, Mama, I'm sure of it." Yet, she felt a tightness inside her as she said so. She believed her father would come, but she also believed he would go away again. What happens, she wondered, when you live solely for a moment that comes and goes, and you find afterward that nothing has changed?

She gave her mother's arm a gentle squeeze. "But the wedding's so long off yet, and in the meantime you are wasting away to nothing."

"Nonsense. You are being melodramatic, as usual. Look, here is Mr. Alcott coming to fetch you. So that you may pay your respects to his grandmother, I don't doubt—the morbid old wretch. Mrs. Alcott, I mean, not your charming intended. Duty is a hard thing at times, I know, my dear," Bethel said as she began to move away, leaving her daughter to the dutiful ministrations of her fiancé. "Yet it must be borne with grace and a cheerful smile."

But Emma didn't need to pretend a smile as she watched Geoffrey walk toward her along a path lined with terra-cotta pots of ruby-red gardenias. He looked dashingly fashionable in a striped jacket and red bow tie.

"Emma," he said, and he took her hand and brought it up to his lips, and she saw genuine happiness flood his eyes. Although he'd been away in Maine for most of the summer, every morning a perfect white rose had arrived for her at

The Birches, always with the same message penned in his elegant hand: *"I am in despair that I cannot be with you."*

"If you've come to coerce me into engaging in a tennis match with you, Geoffrey, I must warn you I positively will not do it. For the rackets you lend me invariably seem to have holes in the middle of them."

He laughed and held her hand an extra moment, before letting it go. "You must come and admit to Grandmama that you are a failure on the court, for she is always insisting to me that you are perfection itself."

Eunice Alcott, Emma knew, had never insisted any such thing. But she answered her betrothed's perfectly turned compliment with a gracious smile.

Geoffrey led her up to the back veranda, where his grandmother was ensconced in a hooded wicker chair among pots of ferns and palms.

She was wrapped up in cashmere shawls, although the day was warm, and her hand shook a little as she raised her lorgnette to her face, but she gave Emma a sharp once-over and announced without any further ado, "I found Prudence Dupres dead in the paper this morning. At only eighty-seven, poor thing. Nipped in the bud."

Emma and Geoffrey exchanged smiles with their eyes, as they settled into chairs beside the old woman. There had been a dearth of deaths among the Great Folk over the summer. "Grandmama," Geoffrey had warned Emma earlier, "has been in a positive frenzy of boredom. Yesterday, she telephoned the editor of the *Phoenix* to complain about the paucity of obituaries in his newspaper."

"They said she died of water on the brain," Eunice Alcott was saying. "Hunh. First they refuse to print any deaths whatsoever, for days on end, and then when they do manage to scrounge one up, they lie about the cause of it. Water on the brain. How does it get there? I ask you. You can't tell me Prue had taken to standing on her head, for I will not believe it. Not when she could barely stand on her two feet without tipping over, although that had more to do with the glasses of sherry she was always sneaking at all hours . . . but never mind that. No, the truth is, she died of a broken heart."

"I didn't know Mrs. Dupres had suffered a tragedy lately," Emma said.

The old woman leaned over to whisper in Emma's ear, but since she was deaf, everyone on the grounds of the Hope Street mansion heard her. "Mr. Dupres had a torrid fling with a vaudeville floozy but a month before they were married."

"Grandmama . . ." Geoffrey sighed. "That particular scandal occurred over sixty years ago. And the man more than redeemed himself by going on to father six children and twenty-seven grandchildren."

Mrs. Alcott rapped Emma's arm with her ivory fan. "That is what comes when one marries beneath one—heartbreak and an early death."

"But I didn't know Mr. Dupres was—"

"He was *French*, my dear. That tells one quite everything, does it not? We all warned Prudence she would be sorry one day, and now see if she isn't. Dead in the paper of a broken heart." She sighed and narrowed her eyes to stare at the linden trees, which were whispering sweetly in the breeze. "Didn't I say to you, Geoffrey, that the sun would shine today?"

"You told me it would rain."

Mrs. Alcott patted Emma with her fan again and leaned in to her to whisper loudly, "He always sees rain, even when there's not a cloud in the sky. Such a regrettable tendency toward pessimism. I can't imagine how he comes by it—" She cut herself off, her eyes narrowing on the marble-paved lane, her chin jutting. "How dare he! How dare he use that poor child to draw attention to himself?"

Emma and Geoffrey turned to see who was daring what, and Geoffrey sucked in a sharp breath of shock and surprise.

"Maddie!" Emma cried, and she was up and running down the lane shaded by linden trees, running so hard she had to lift her skirts above her ankles, and not caring that the whole of Great Folk society was there to see her bad form. Running toward her sister, who was being pushed in her chair by Stuart Alcott.

Maddie wore a white nainsook dress sprigged with tiny forget-me-nots, and she looked so pretty and happy, her eyes bright, her cheeks flushed, her mouth smiling. "I have come, Emma," she said, her voice curling up on the corners like rose petals.

Emma stumbled to a stop in front of her, and she was laughing and crying, both at once. "So I see. Oh, Maddie, so I see."

Stu leaned, arms braced straight out, on the handgrips of her chair. He was more than flushed; he was sweating. His tie was awry, and the starch in his shirt had wilted. Brandy fumes clung to him like oily smoke.

"Well, Maddie child," he drawled. "You have come, and you are here, and now pray will you excuse me? I believe I hear a champagne cocktail calling my name."

Maddie watched him saunter away, shadows already dulling the excited joy in her eyes. She clenched her hands so tightly in her lap the knuckles turned the color of old wax.

Emma reached down and took one of those hands in hers. "Maddie . . ."

"Do you think Mama will be terribly angry?" Maddie said in a small voice.

"She'll never let on while in company, if she is. And I'll help you to weather the storm later."

Emma let go of her sister's hand and began to push the chair toward the refreshment tent, where most of the party was gathered. She looked for their mother but didn't see her.

She remembered noticing her earlier, with Uncle Stanton and Mrs. Norton, strolling around to the south side of the house, where lay the pride of the Alcott gardens—its rose beds of thirty-seven varieties. Emma supposed she was still there, hoped she was still there. For Maddie was going to find this initial plunge into Great Folk societal waters difficult enough without trying to do it under Mama's deep blue frown.

"Oh!" Maddie exclaimed softly as the wheels of her chair bounced and rattled over a crack in the marble flagstones. "I'm beginning to understand now why you dread these things so. It's as if all my thoughts have suddenly been scattered to the winds like a dandelion puff, and I feel sure that at any moment I'm going to do or say the wrong thing."

"Why don't you leave that to me," Emma said a little too brightly. "I've become quite the expert lately at doing and saying the wrong things."

The conversational chatter and laughter hushed as they drew closer to the tent.

"They are all staring, Emma," Maddie said. Her voice sounded high and tight, like a clock too tightly wound.

"They are doing no such thing."

"No, it's worse than that. They look, then they look away and pretend they haven't just seen what they did see."

"It's only because they've grown unused to seeing you away from The Birches," Emma said. "There's bound to be an initial awkwardness, but things will ease with time."

"If Mama allows me another time."

Emma stopped the chair and leaned over her sister's shoulder to take her hand again, gripping it hard. "Maddie, I am so glad you came. I am so *proud* of you for coming."

Maddie twisted her head around to look up at her, her eyes glittering with tears barely held back. "Are you, Emma? Are you truly?"

"Truly."

Maddie pulled her hand free and clasped the armrest of her chair. Emma could see her sister's pulse beating high and hard in the veins of her neck. Two taut white lines bracketed her mouth.

"Then would you push me over there beneath that willow and go ask Stu to bring me a glass of punch? Go, please," she said as Emma hesitated. "I can be by myself for a few minutes, and besides, I see your dear Geoffrey wending his way here to save me from being an utter wallflower."

Still, Emma waited until Geoffrey had joined them before she slipped away. She could trust Geoffrey to take care of her sister. His loyalty and his sensibilities toward doing the right thing had always been as unassailable as his gentlemanly manners.

The same could hardly be said of Geoffrey's brother, Emma thought. She found him standing before the fountain, scowling at the water-spewing cupids as if they offered him some insult. At the sound of her step on the stones, he turned to face her, swaying a little. He held an empty champagne glass in his hand.

"Ah, Emma. Come to fetch me already, have you? Is she feeling neglected? Scrutinized? Criticized? Demoralized? I did warn her, honest and truly I did. I reminded her of how we Great Folk have developed to a high art the ignoring of the unusual and the unpleasant."

She looked at Stuart Alcott's face. He was still handsome in spite of the puffy flesh around the bloodshot eyes and the slack, drunken mouth. "Stu, if you are going to be like this, then why did you—?"

"Why did I what? Bring her here? Because she begged it of me, and I have somewhat of a penchant for lost causes, being one myself." He shrugged and staggered, nearly landing in the fountain. "On the proverbial other hand, if you are trying to ascertain whether my general intentions toward your sister are honorable ones, I'll tell you straight out: I have no intentions. I'm a gambler, a drunkard, and a womanizer of considerable repute, and those are the vices I'll admit to in mixed company. And my lack of intentions includes inflicting myself on any woman for longer than a night. Our Maddie, being virginal and an old friend, shall be spared even that."

He started to walk away from her, but she grabbed his arm. He pulled free, but she had touched him long enough to feel the hard trembling going on inside him. "You can't come home for a summer, turn her life upside down, and then have nothing more to do with her."

"Can't I?" He threw the champagne glass at a cupid's head. He simply lobbed it as though he were tossing a tennis ball, but it shattered nonetheless, sparkling like dewdrops in the sun. "Indeed, I rather think that having nothing more to do with her is the greatest act of kindness I can show to Miss Madeleine Tremayne."

"Stu, please," Emma said. "Please. Don't hurt her."

He turned and stared at her a moment, then he brushed the back of his hand against her cheek. "I can't help it, child. *Life* hurts."

His gaze lifted and focused on something beyond her, and although Emma didn't turn around she knew he was seeing her sister. And that the sight of Maddie—sitting in her chair beneath the shade of the linden trees—hurt him in some terrible and fundamental way.

He walked past her without another word, and this time Emma let him go.

What happens when you live solely for a moment that comes and goes, and you find afterward that nothing has changed?

Summer oozed, hot and sticky, into September. Emma continued to keep her promise. And every time she opened the door to the Thames Street house, her heart would catch a little in expectation that she would see Bria standing at the stove. But she never did.

She began to sculpt again, a joy and an agony that she had put aside during those final weeks of Bria's life. She spent hours out in the old orangery, searching for the artery that led from her heart to her hands, but she felt as though she was using a dull knife to do it with. She would cut herself, but she wouldn't bleed, and most of what she created out of the cold, wet clay, she threw away.

One day, along with the single white rose that still came every morning, Geoffrey sent her a letter from Maine. He told her in meticulous detail how the work on the foundry was progressing. At the end of it he wrote: "As I sit this evening in this shabby, soulless parlor of my boardinghouse (I shall not give it the dignity of naming it a drawing room) and write to you—now is when my arms ache most to hold you, and I long for the time when I can name *you* most pridefully and earnestly: My Wife."

It was the closest he'd ever come to telling her he loved her. She knew his letter should please her, but instead she felt weighted with guilt. She had promised to marry him, she was letting him fall in love with her, and all the while she loved someone else. Someone she couldn't have.

In that place in the heart where secrets are kept, where you know right from wrong, good from evil, and honor from dishonor, she knew she had to end it. One thing or the other had to end.

And then one Tuesday afternoon, as she turned up the path of the Thames Street house, she saw that the violets she and Bria had planted had died.

She knelt and began to pick them, one by one, as if she could make a bouquet of them, only they were dead. She knew they were dead, yet she went on picking them, frantically, tearing them up by the roots now, throwing them into her lap, and raining dirt all over herself.

Her hands stilled, and she shut her eyes. A single tear fell onto the dry and faded purple petals in her lap, followed by another tear and then another, and then she had to press her hands hard to her face to stifle the noise of her weeping.

When it was over, she threw back her head and stared with aching eyes up into a sky of wind-tossed clouds, and she felt as though she'd torn loose from the earth and was flying around up there, lonely and sad and scared.

Then she realized she must be making a spectacle of herself, sitting there at the bottom of the stoop, covered with dirt and dead violets, within sight and sound of Thames Street. So she got up and went into the house, but no one was there, and it was a while yet before the shift whistle would blow.

She stirred up a pitcher of effervescent lemon to go with the jelly roll she'd brought for the girls. She went to little Jacko's cradle, empty now, for he was over at Mrs. Hale's. She picked up his blanket and rubbed it against her cheek, breathing in his baby smell. But then she put the blanket back in the cradle, for it triggered an aching, hollow yearning in her for things she didn't understand.

She wandered the house. She stood before the washstand that Shay used of a morning and thought: This is where he stood just hours before; he touched this razor and this towel. But the hollow yearning came again, and so she turned away from it.

And saw Bria.

Saw her by the stove again, wearing the night rail she had given her. But instead of reaching for the teakettle, she was facing the window this time, looking out, her eyes wide and dark and filled with utter terror.

"Bria!" Emma cried, and in that instant she was gone.

And the coals in the stove—which had been left to go out that morning—burst into flame.

Emma could see the fire glowing red around the crack of the loading door, she could smell it burning. *But that's impossible*, she thought—and in that instant the fire went out.

She walked to the stove on trembling legs. She touched the top, but it was cool. She opened the loading door. The coals inside were gray, burned to ashes. Cold.

She looked out the window. She saw that the wind had come up, but that was all. It was blowing hard, as hard as it had been blowing that day when Merry had—

"The mill . . . Oh, God, the mill!"

Chapter Twenty-four

Emma flew out the door so fast, she caught her heel on the last step of the stoop and fell, hitting the ground in a skid, ripping her skirts and scraping the skin off her hands and knees. She scrambled back to her feet and, gathering her skirts up as high as her calves, she ran around back, to the harbor beach. The wind was whipping the bay into a chop. Yachts and fishing boats bucked and winged over the water, white and henna sails flashing.

She climbed onto the pier and ran, nearly tripping twice on the warped boards, ran all the way out to the end of the pier so that she could look uptown, around the curve in the harbor, and see the Thames Street cotton mill. The wind pressed against her face and flapped her skirts, making a tumult of noise in her ears. She shaded her eyes with her hand against the glare of sunlight off water.

The mill was there: granite stone walls and gray slate roof. A white cloud of steam spewed from the tall chimney stack, as it always did. But no smoke or flames curled out of the high, grimy windows.

"It's all right," she said to herself. "Everything's all right."

But it didn't *feel* all right.

It was four blocks from the house to the mill, and she ran the whole way. She passed an onion digger walking home from the fields, and he yelled at her, "Hey, lady, where's the fire!" She wanted to scream back at him, to shriek with the fear that was now clawing at her, but she was too out of breath.

She ran through the big brick-arched gates and into the empty courtyard. She still couldn't see any smoke or fire. But she ran straight up the iron stairs that led to the tin-plated, iron-banded door of the spinning room.

She climbed the stairs so fast she slammed into the door with the flat of her hands. She reached down and grabbed the latch and jerked up . . . and nothing happened. She jerked down . . . and nothing happened.

The door was locked.

The iron stairs beneath her feet shook and trembled with the force of the throbbing machines inside. Even with the wind she could hear the noise they made, clanging and rattling and humming like a million angry bees.

The wind lulled for a moment, and she thought she smelled something scorching, as though an iron had been left too long on starched cotton. She looked up, but all she could see was the gray slate peak of the roof. And then she saw, curling up from underneath the cornice . . .

Black smoke.

Shay McKenna couldn't bring his dory back from a day of fishing the bay without sailing past the wharves of the Thames Street cotton mill, where his daughters worked in the spinning room. So it was that every day he would look at those gray stone walls and that smoking chimney stack, and make the same vow: "I'll get you out, darlin's. Soon I'll be getting you out of there, I promise."

If you were born Catholic and Irish in a *clachan* called Gortadoo, you were used to being poor, used to scratching like a chicken on a plot of dirt you could never own. You were used to living in a stone hut with straw sacking for a bed and, maybe, if you had the luck of the Irish, a stool or two to sit on. And you were, God save you, used to sending your children out to the potato fields with hoes in their wee hands as soon as they could walk.

He'd been used to it then, back in Gortadoo, but he wasn't used to it anymore.

Bria, lying on their bed at night after a twelve-hour shift, lying on her stomach while he rubbed her aching, cramping legs, talking to him . . .

"Merry's got to stand on a box while she works her spinner, her being too small to tend to her bobbins without it."

"There're cockroaches scurrying all over the floor at your feet. The bobbin boys douse them with lubricating oil and set them alight."

"The o'erseer, he strides out onto the catwalk and blows his whistle, and everyone pulls the levers on their frames and starts their spinning. And then he locks us in until after the shift is over."

"It's the littlest fingers that manage the best. And you got to be swift and nimble with them, to catch the threads when they get tangled or break."

"The cotton lint gets in your eyes, and up your nose, and down your throat. The air's always so damp and dusty and full of that lint."

"Your ears ache from the din, and your eyes start to burn so, what with staring so hard at the threads ballooning, ballooning, ballooning. . . . God save us, I've been seeing them ballooning threads in my dreams."

Dhia, how it tore at his guts to see his girls drag themselves out of bed in the dark hours of the morning to go off to that place with the shift whistle shrieking in their ears, to be shut up all day away from the sunlight, shut up with the dust and the machines and the ballooning threads that would haunt their dreams—

The mill whistle blew shrilly, startling Shay so that he let go of the tiller for a moment, and the boat turned up into the wind, sail flapping, hull creaking. For it hadn't been the short sharp blast that announced a shift change, but the long warning wail of an impending disaster.

He stood up in the cockpit, narrowing his eyes against the heavy push of the wind . . . and saw oily black smoke pouring into the sky from the mill where his girls were. Where his life was.

Emma was halfway down the stairs when the mill whistle blasted into a long, shrieking wail.

Oh God, oh God, oh God . . . Her feet skidded on the metal treads, and she nearly went tumbling down head over heels. *It's on fire and they're trapped in there, Bria's girls are in there, and I promised I would come for them, only I can't, I can't get them out because it's locked, locked, locked . . . It's on fire and it's locked . . .*

Workers from other parts of the mill were already pouring out into the yard, along with streams of acrid black and gray smoke. Emma hit the bottom of the steps running, for she'd seen Mr. Stipple come staggering out with a handkerchief to his face.

She flung herself at him, grasping the lapels of his coat. "Mr. Stipple, thank God, thank God . . . You need to unlock the spinning room—"

He tried to pull away from her, shaking his head. His small eyes, like two round white buttons, stared wildly in his fleshy face.

She shook him, her fingers digging deeper into the rough, greasy wool. "Give it to me, then. Give me the key."

He jerked against her. "No, no. Can't—"

"The key!" she screamed at him, snarling the words into his face so that he reeled back.

"In . . . my office." He shook his head again, his eyes staring more wildly. "I'm not going back in there. The fire's in the mule room and that's too close, too close . . ."

She let go of him and plunged through the mill's cavelike entrance just as the fire bell from the station up the block began to clang.

Her skirt was in her way, tripping up her legs, so she ripped it off. She was in the hall with the yellow time cards lined up in neat soldierly rows on the wall. She still couldn't see any flames, but squall clouds of smoke floated down the hall from the back of the mill. She had to feel her way to Mr. Stipple's office, following the wainscoting on the wall, and she thanked God it wasn't far, for already her eyes were tearing and her chest burned. The door was closed and for a moment she was seized with a terror that it too would be locked.

But the knob turned easily beneath her hand, and only after she'd flung the door open did she think there could be a wall of flames on the other side.

There wasn't.

She slammed the door shut behind her and plunged into a room that seemed strangely dim and quiet after the tumult outside, and considerably less smoky. She gasped and coughed, and sucked in a deep breath of sweet, sweet air.

But she had to hurry, hurry . . .

She started for the desk, thinking the key would be there, and tripped over the rolled edge of the carpet, banging into a big iron safe, bruising her hipbone. She didn't even feel it, though, for just then she noticed a pair of hooks on a wall with peeling, watermarked paper. A worn black derby hanging on one, and from the other, an iron ring heavy with keys.

She lunged across the space between the desk and the wall and snatched at the keys.

The iron ring was hot and it burned her hand, startling her so that she cried out and dropped it. She ripped off a piece of her petticoat and used it as a pad to pick the keys up again. She could feel the room getting hotter, as though she stood in front of the open door of a coal stove. She straightened just as the old wallpaper burst into flames and instantly melted to ash.

She whirled and flung herself back across the room toward the door, knocking into the desk again, sending it skidding over the thin carpet. She reeled into the tall metal filing cabinet, snagging her hair on one of the brass handles, and she couldn't get it loose, couldn't—

She was loose and plunging across the room, reaching for the door.

It crashed open, banging against the wall. Smoke billowed over her in a cloud, thick as sea fog. An arm covered in a yellow slicker and thick leather gauntlet reached through the sooty haze, and she grabbed it.

A startled face, topped by a black helmet, seemed to be floating disembodied in the smoke. "Lady, what in blazes . . . ?" He ran his hands up and down her arms, as if he had to be sure she was real. "Jesus, I got to get you out of here, but first I need—"

"The key," she gasped, choking, as she held up the ring in her hands. "I have it."

He bent over and took her up into his arms then, as though she were a child. He carried her through the door and into a hallway so thick with smoke it was like trying to peer through a wool blanket. Emma pressed her face into his chest and tried not to breathe.

He took long strides at a half jog as the wainscoting

beside them caught fire and they were enveloped in a *whoosh* of heat. But then they were through it, and water from the fire hoses doused them like a sudden downpour of rain.

"Noreen! Merry!"

Shay pushed his way through the crush of people in the mill yard. He nearly fell over a snaking tangle of fire hoses and he stopped for a moment, swaying on his feet as if the shouts and bellows and screams he heard were physical blows that buffeted him.

He flung his head back, looking up, up at the pall of ocherous smoke floating overhead. At the orange and yellow lights dancing, reflecting in the glass panes of the high, narrow windows of the spinning room.

At the flight of iron-plated stairs and the two men wearing yellow oilskin slickers, who were swinging axes at a tin-plated door. Axes that rang loudly as their blades struck the metal plates and left moon-sized dents, and did nothing more.

And then he locks us in until after the shift is over.

Shay hurled himself toward the stairs, shouting and cursing. Out of the corner of his eye he saw a fireman come stumbling out the wide-mouthed entrance to the mill. The man carried a woman in his arms, but he set her down as soon as he was clear of the smoke, and then he was running and shouting, and waving a black key ring high above his head.

Shay followed the fireman up the stairs, their boots rattling on the iron rungs. It seemed to take forever, for the man to fit the key into the lock, to turn the tumblers, to lift the latch, and then at last, at last, the door swung open. Oily black smoke and women and children spilled out of it, choking and gasping, eyes streaming, and their hands in front of their faces to feel their way. One after the other they came stumbling through the door, pushing and shoving in their desperate fear to get out . . . children, so many children.

And none of them his.

Shay wedged his way through them, onto the catwalk, searching frantically through those still inside, but the smoke was so thick it was hard to see. The catwalk's iron grille floor shook beneath his feet. Little hands reached out to him, grabbing for him, and he guided them toward the open door, and looking, all the while looking, for his girls, and screaming, screaming inside his head.

He peered down into the room below. The spinning frames were still running, clattering and clanging, but no one was tending them now. The far wall was on fire. The old wood crackled and spat hissing, smoky flames that were spreading quickly in streamers along the greasy floorboards, raising blisters that popped and bubbled like boiling soup.

A hand grabbed at his pantleg. "Da!"

Shay spun around, snatching Noreen up into his arms all in one motion, and Merry was there too, and he grabbed her up, and he was through the door with them in his arms just as one of the machines below caught fire, exploding into fiery red pinwheels and shooting blue sparks.

He was down the stairs with his girls safe in his arms.

He carried them out to the far end of the courtyard, well clear of the smoke and flying cinders. He set them down and ran his hands over them, over every inch of them. They were frightened and choking from the smoke, but they weren't hurt anywhere that he could see. Yet, he couldn't stop touching them. He kept having to touch them, to feel the warmth of their living flesh. His girls—he'd nearly lost his girls. If he had lost them . . .

A woman came running at them from out of the crowd of gawkers and mill workers, running and shouting their names. A woman dripping water and wearing only a ragged petticoat for skirts, and with tears leaving white tracks in her sooty face.

The woman that fireman had carried out of the burning mill.

Emma.

"She came for us, Da. Just like Merry said she would."

"I know, m'love." Shay sat down on the bed and brushed the damp hair off Noreen's forehead. He leaned over and kissed the heat-flushed skin. But not burned, thank God, thank God.

"It's getting some sleep the both of you should be doing now," he said when he was able. "You know how your mam always said there's nothing a good sleep won't cure."

Noreen gave him a tremulous smile, but Merry only looked at him with wide, haunted eyes. She hadn't hummed once since he'd carried her out of that burning mill. He'd had a hard time convincing her to let go of Emma's hand, though.

"She came for us, Da," Noreen said. "Just like she promised."

"I know."

He had to make his eyes as wide as possible to hold back the tears. He leaned over and wrapped his arms around both of his girls and held them tight, tight. In spite of long, soaking baths, they still smelled of smoke, and he shook to think of it. He couldn't stop shaking.

"I love you, my darlin's," he said, whispering the words for they were already asleep. And those were hard words for a man to say sometimes, even to his daughters.

He got up from the bed, careful not to wake them, and went to look at his son, who was asleep in the cradle he'd made out of old Arbuckle coffee cases. With his lips he traced the fatness of his baby's cheek, then kissed the soft spot on his head. He went to leave the bedroom then, padding quietly in his stocking feet, but he paused at the door and looked back at his son in his makeshift cradle, at his girls asleep now in the white iron bed. He spent a long, sweet, suspended time just watching them, and shaking inside from the power of what he felt for them.

He was surprised to see when he stepped through the door and into the kitchen that it was now blue with the shadows of the coming night.

Emma sat in the rocker, beneath the window.

Even in the confusion of the mill yard, even looking like a rescued mill rat herself, she had been recognized. Both as Miss Tremayne and as the woman who had run into the burning mill to get the keys that unlocked the door to the spinning room, saving the lives of those women and children trapped inside. But she appeared almost frightened by the attention and she kept insisting she hadn't done anything, that a fireman had come for the key practically on her heels, and she had only wound up needing to be rescued herself.

No one had thought yet to question what she'd been doing there. But he knew from the words she'd sobbed and whispered as she'd knelt on the bricks of the yard and clutched his girls to her chest; he knew that she'd been at the mill trying to open the door well before the alarm sounded. And then there was Merry, knowing about it before it had ever happened.

He wasn't going to dwell on thoughts about the strangeness of it, though. The Irish had a saying about how those questions having no answers were either miracles or mysteries, and both had to be taken on faith.

Shay's one thought, once the girls were out, had been to get them safely home. Emma had come with them, as though she belonged with them. But then, Merry wasn't letting go of her hand.

She had helped him to get the girls settled out of their fear and into bed. She had heated the kettle for their baths and poured hot comfrey down their throats. She had wrapped them up in flannel night rails and put a beer jug full of hot water into the bed with them, for comfort as much as warmth.

Now she sat in the rocker by the stove in his kitchen. As if she belonged there.

Her white lawn shirtwaist was gray with soot and pocked with cinder burns. Her petticoat was in worse shape, ripped ragged in places and water stained. She was still modestly covered from neck almost to ankle, but he doubted that any man had ever before seen Miss Emma Tremayne in her petticoat.

She was holding one hand inside the other in her lap, as if it pained her.

He went to her and knelt, and he picked up her hand, turning it over. A red welt lay like a rope across her palm, but it wasn't blistering. He could see her heart beating in the blue veins of her wrist.

He looked up at her, but he didn't know what to say. He'd said "thank you," but that wasn't enough, and yet there weren't any other words.

"You burned your hand," he said.

"Only a little. I wasn't wearing any gloves," she said, in that way she had that was such a strange mixture of haughtiness and naughtiness. Her eyebrows and the front of her hair were singed some, giving her a wide-eyed, startled look. "See, that is what comes of leaving the house without one's gloves."

He smiled, but the smile cracked midway and became something else. He could feel each separate, slender bone in her hand. "Miss Tremayne . . ."

"I really must insist now that you call me Emma." Her hand trembled just a little. "I cannot be Miss Tremayne when I am sitting in your kitchen in only my petticoat and without my eyebrows. It just won't do."

He didn't know when he had let go of her hand, and he didn't know when she leaned in to him and he reached for her. But somehow his hands were in her hair now, and she was sliding off the chair down onto her knees in front of him, and his mouth was in her hair and her face was in the curve of his throat.

He gripped her shoulders and set her gently away from him. Her head came up, and her eyes were two wide, dark green pools in her face. He could see nothing in them but himself, reflected into eternity.

He got back onto his feet somehow, for he couldn't seem to feel his legs. He backed away from her, first one step and then another and another, until his shoulders were flat against the wall.

She knelt on the floor where he had left her. Her eyes swallowed him, swallowed the world.

"I was sitting here remembering," she said, "that day we paid a call on the widowed vixen and her kits. And I was thinking . . ." She stopped, swallowing as if her throat hurt. He could see the pulse beating in her neck. "I was thinking that what I really wanted was to go back to the meadow and see how they are faring. I'll go this Sunday I think, after church. I haven't any guns made from bits and pieces to shoot at the poor snipes with, so I suppose I'll have to bring a basket of something from The Birches kitchens."

He could imagine her arriving at the meadow with a wicker basket full of orange-glazed chicken and terrined pheasant. He nearly smiled, except that his own heart was beating too fast and his chest was too tight even for breathing.

"And I was wondering if . . ." She rubbed her neck where

the pulse beat, above the high lacy collar of her ruined shirtwaist. "Will you meet me there?"

"No," he said, or thought he said. He didn't know wanting her could feel this way. So deep inside there was nothing to do but give in to it.

"Shay," she said, her voice breaking now. "You know what I—"

"Oh, aye. I know, I know."

"I want you to . . ." Her hands had been lying palms up on her thighs, but now she lifted them, spreading them as if in supplication. "There, you see how ridiculous and narrow and hollow my life is—I don't even know the *words* for what I want. All those books, male and female, segregated on their neat little shelves in the Roger's Free Library, and none of them have the words I need to tell you what I want."

"Don't," he said. "Don't say it."

She bowed her head. She stayed that way a moment, her back curved and taut, the nape of her neck showing white beneath the dark swell of her hair. He clenched his hands into fists, digging his nails into his palms.

She got slowly, gracefully, to her feet and looked at him, and now her eyes were soft and gray and cool as a dawn sky. "Sunday," she said. "I'll be waiting for you at the vixen's meadow."

"I'll never be going to that place again," he said back to her, and wondered to himself where he would find the strength not to make it a lie.

Chapter Twenty-five

He ran flat out until his chest hurt. He ran hard, until his feet stirred up a pall of dust that floated over Ferry Road, and his breathing blew harshly in his ears.

He ran and ran, but the pain kept pace with him, matched him stride for stride and breath for breath. The empty, whistling pain.

He flung back his head and shouted her name into the hard, blue, merciless sky: "Bria!"

The road curved. He was running into the wind now, and it was warm and dry on his face. It was a sou'wester, and it came up every afternoon in the summer here, smelling of the sea. The old-time Yankees claimed it fanned the passions and stirred desire.

Desire. And what a queer thing that was, desire. You could choose what you took and what you bought, and what you kept and what you gave away.

But not what you wanted.

He was deep in the woods now. Three months ago the maples and birches and elms were still greening in the late spring rains. Now their leaves were drooping from the wet summer heat. A month would pass and they would be blazing crimson and gold, and his wife would still be dead. And though his heart might clench in unbearable grief to think of it, that didn't change the truth of it.

He wasn't going to choose to stay away from the meadow today, he saw that now. He'd been running down this road for quite some time, all the while telling himself he was running away. Now there was nothing more left to choose, nothing left to do.

But run to meet her.

The meadow was blazing with goldenrod, like a bowl of sunshine. She sat in the middle of it, a girl in a white pleated lawn dress and a yellow straw hat, whose blue ribbon lifted and floated in the breeze.

The light seemed to spill from her flesh, as if the sun lived inside her. He saw her, and he wondered how he ever thought he could feel this way and yet make himself believe and behave as if he felt nothing at all.

He stood within the shadows of the trees and watched her for one long sweet moment. Then he walked out into the sunshine to join her.

She heard him, and turned her head, and her face lightened even more, became buoyant and expectant.

"You came," she said, the relief in her voice tinged just a little with fear. And she didn't even know yet how much he wanted her.

He was dizzy, desperate with wanting her.

He sat down next to her and rested his wrists on his bent knees. The hot, dry wind fanned the dark wisps of hair on her forehead and neck. He wanted to take off that delicious little hat with its wide blue ribbon and let down her hair. He wanted to fill his hands with her hair and bury his face in it, breathe it in until he was full up inside with the smell of her.

He looked away from her, around the clearing. At the dark

evergreen of feathery hemlock boughs. At the yellow splashes of goldenrod and black-eyed Susans. At the purple elderberries plump on their vines.

At the fox's earth that had a bird sitting in front of it—a huge naked, pink bird.

"And would you be telling me," he said, "what the devil is that?"

"It's a capon."

"Mother of God. Those kits will be hard pressed to make do with a farmer's scrawny chicken after this."

She had the laugh of a naughty child. He wanted to kiss her open mouth when she laughed and swallow the sound of it down deep inside him.

"I hope you looked carefully before you sat down," he said, thinking to tease her with the blarney and make her smile, maybe laugh again. "For don't you know, surely, that on hot days such as this, the snakes like to hide themselves in the goldenrod fields?"

Her lips trembled into the smile he wanted. Her mouth was like a delicate bruised rose in the paleness of her face. He wanted to kiss her mouth.

"Perhaps I came here looking to be bitten," she said.

He laughed at her bravery.

"Shay . . ."

He loved how she said his name. It sounded the way woodsmoke smelled, tangy.

"Emma," he said, giving the gift back to her, and he saw her pleasure in the way the ocean depths of her eyes shifted and stirred.

Her gaze fell to her lap, where her hands were gripped together in a tight little fist. "What do we do now?" she said, her voice small and tremulous.

"We lie with each other, Emma. If you still want that."

"Yes, I do," she said on a little gasp. "But what do we . . . How do we begin?"

"Slowly, I think," he said and smiled, for the way he felt inside, shaking and flapping like a sail loose in the wind, "slowly" seemed an impossible thing. "Aye, we will make it slow and sweet. We'll undress each other slowly, and then I will touch you sweetly in all those places you want to be touched."

She made a breathy sound that was half laugh, half sigh, although she wouldn't look at him. She pulled her hands apart and began to pluck at the little pearl buttons on the wrist of her glove, but she was shaking so, and her breaths were coming in soft little gasps again.

He took her hand. "Here, let me," he said.

He turned her hand over and laid it on his knee, and he undid a single pearl button, and then he brought her wrist up to his mouth and kissed the small patch of white, white skin that showed there, then he undid another button, and kissed her again, and again, and again, until all six buttons were undone and so was he.

She was looking at him now, and all of a young woman's first love shone brilliant and vulnerable in her eyes. "Touch me some more," she said. "Touch my mouth now with yours."

As simply as though he did it every day of his life, he kissed her on the mouth. A long kiss that began soft and gentle, and turned rough and hungry, and went searching for all he wanted, and found it.

He undressed her as he'd promised, slowly, and he touched her sweetly. With his mouth and his hands and his tongue, he touched her breasts. He touched her throat with them, and her belly and between her legs. He couldn't speak words anymore. Only touch her.

When he pulled off his own clothes, he wasn't surprised by the daring way she touched him, for he knew that about her, knew how she could be both daring and shy. She touched his flesh, all over, as if she were molding the shape of him with her hands.

He rose above her so that he could see her face. Her eyes were wide and dark, the color of peat smoke. He wanted her so much, so much, and he wasn't going to stop now.

When he entered her, she uttered a little cry, and he caught it with his mouth. He pushed all of himself inside her, thrust himself deep inside her, and when it was time he pulled out of her, so that he could give of himself without giving her a babe.

He eased down beside her, but he kept his arms around her, and he gathered her close. He felt strands of her hair between her face and his. He felt the softness of her breasts against his chest, and the heat and wet of her naked belly pressing against his.

He had wanted her, but just as much he wanted to be held by her like this. Simply held by her, and comforted.

She lay on her back, naked.

The sun melted and flowed over her like hot butter. The wind touched places on her she hadn't known existed before Shay had found them. She felt ripe and bursting with love.

She opened her eyes onto the great windy blue bowl of the sky. The world seemed caught in a simmering hush. Then a wood thrush began to sing, and a bee buzzed by her cheek. And she heard his ragged breathing.

She turned her head, and her whole view of the world was the round, hard bulge of muscle in his arm.

At first she had felt his body with something very like fear, the weight of it, the strength. But that hadn't been an end, only a beginning. For he had done such things . . . He had put his tongue in her mouth. He had suckled her breasts like a babe. He had touched her between her legs with his fingers and his mouth, and he had put his tongue inside her there, as well.

And then he had put himself inside her there.

It had hurt a little, but she hadn't minded. She thought she had been created for that moment, when she would take his body into hers and feel his weight and his need. And when it ended, when they pulled apart, the moment was still there between them, would always be there. They were two; then they were one.

I will never love anyone but him, she thought. Not like this, not ever again.

She pushed herself up on her elbow and looked down at his face. His eyes were closed, and there was a brooding slant to his mouth. She wondered if he thought of Bria. She didn't mind if he did. Bria was the mirror to both their hearts.

She put her hand on his chest and felt him take a breath. Then he opened his eyes.

"Emma," he said, and what she heard in his voice wrapped around her heart and squeezed mercilessly.

She put her fingers to his mouth. "Don't," she said. "Don't say we shouldn't have done it."

He left her fingers on his mouth. He reached up and pushed his hand through her hair. It had all come undone.

"A man," he said, and she felt his lips move, felt how soft they were beneath the hardness, "can ruin a virgin by seducing her, but if she comes to him of her free will, that is her gift to him. I'll not be saying we shouldn't have done it. I'll not be saying that to you."

"I don't want it to end," she said. "Not yet."

He leaned in to her, and his hair brushed her cheek and his breath scalded her neck. "God save me, neither do I."

Her kissed her mouth and then he pulled back again, and his gaze roamed over her, all over her. She felt it as though he touched her with his eyes, and it made her melt inside. As though she were made of wax and his eyes were fire.

"Don't look at me," she said, suddenly feeling shy again.

He smiled at her, a bandit's smile.

He ran his fingers along the curve of her belly, along the dark line of hair that grew there, and into the dark warmth below it. "*Ah mhuire* . . . How can I not?"

The deep purple of twilight was just falling over The Birches when she drove up the long quahog-shell drive in her little black-lacquered carriage.

She turned the equipage over to a groom and then stood alone in the drive, looking back to the big scrolled gates. The wrought-iron bars cast deep blue and purple shadows over the lawn. This summer, wild rose bushes had suddenly grown up on the bay side of the gates. And now, in that evening's warm wind, their white petals were falling silently to the grass like pearl teardrops.

She thought, *I have been with my lover.* And it made her smile to think this. But when she turned her face toward the bay, and the wind stroked her like her lover's fingers, she found that her cheeks were wet with tears.

She turned and walked up the stairs, across the wide piazza, and through the coffered ebony doors, walked carefully as if treading on ice.

Carrews, their butler, appeared before her in his silent, unobtrusive way as she was about to go up the stairs. "They are awaiting you in the front drawing room, Miss Emma," he said.

She thought she was probably staring at him strangely. She felt strange, dazed and disoriented, as if she'd suddenly been plucked up and then set down again and in a place she'd never been before. "But there were to be no guests at dinner tonight," she finally said.

Carrews tucked in his chin and lowered his eyebrows, a gesture he made when the conventions were not being followed to his satisfaction. "I am under the impression that there is only Mr. Alcott present at the moment, and he is not dressed for dinner."

It was indeed Geoffrey's soft, flat voice that she heard as she approached the damask-swagged doors to the drawing room. They were slightly ajar, and for a moment she stood hidden by the heavy green portieres, looking in on her mother and the man she had promised to marry.

They were sitting in the ribbon-backed Chippendale chairs. The antique Chinese rosewood chest supported an elaborate silver George II coffeepot, freshly brewed, Emma knew, for its spout was steaming. They were drinking out of the Sèvres, which meant that Mama had felt the occasion important enough to warrant the best, even if Geoffrey for once wasn't dressed for it.

Indeed, his white linen suit was, incredibly for him, smudged with soot. He sat with his straw boater balanced on his knee, and its brim was bent up on one side, as if he'd crushed it with his fist.

He had been up in Maine when the fire happened, and it would have taken him this while to get here. He must, she thought, have just come from the mill, which had been badly damaged by the smoke and flames. But she knew, for Mama had told her, that the premises, the machinery, had all been insured. Mama—fearing the social embarrassment of her daughter's fiancé suddenly going bankrupt—had already had their banker-cousin investigate.

Yet it seemed strange to see him, Geoffrey Alcott, her intended, here in the drawing room. To find that life should be going on in its old way when she herself had changed so much. When beneath the white lawn and lace of her dress bodice, beneath her jersey webbed corset and her French chemise with its embroidered tucking . . . beneath all the accoutrements that went with being Miss Emma Tremayne was a red mark on the slope of her right breast put there by Shay McKenna's mouth.

To find life going on in its old way when she was still wet between her legs where he had been. When she could smell him on herself.

She must have made some sound just then, for Geoffrey looked up and saw her. He didn't leap to his feet and rush to meet her, for that would have been inappropriate behavior, even for a man who hadn't seen his intended bride in over two weeks. Rather, he rose in a gentlemanly fashion and came forward to take her hands and lead her into the room.

"Emma, darling," he said. "I hastened here as soon as I heard. You weren't hurt, were you? Tell me you're all right."

She stumbled a little so that he had to support her with a hand beneath her elbow. She looked up at him, feeling dazed and dizzy again, and then she realized he was talking about the fire. "No, I . . . I only burned my hand a little. A fireman came in right after me and he carried me out. Everyone got out."

He led her over to a medallion-backed, brocade sofa. He sat on it with her, keeping her hand. She looked down and saw that one of the pearl buttons on her glove was missing. She could feel her pulse beating hard and fast on the wrist that Shay McKenna had kissed and kissed and kissed.

And she felt her mother's deep blue frown on her. It was the talk about the fire. Her "act of bravery" had been written about in the *Bristol Phoenix*, and that wasn't at all the done thing. A lady's name should appear in the newspapers only twice in her life: upon her marriage and upon her death.

"Apparently some bobbin boys in the mule room were

dousing bugs with oil and setting them alight—that's how the fire got started," Geoffrey was saying. "I just don't understand how you came to be there."

Emma's hand trembled in his. She tried to pull it free, but he tightened his grip, just enough to keep it, and so she surrendered. "I was passing and I saw the smoke, and I remembered having seen the keys in Mr. Stipple's office," she said. It was what she told everyone. She hated to think what they said about her. Her act of bravery. All she'd thought about, all she'd wanted, was to get Bria's daughters out.

"At least no harm was done," Geoffrey said.

"No harm done." Emma began to shake inside herself, deep, deep inside; she shook so hard it made her voice tremble. "Will you tell me just one thing, Geoffrey? That door was the only way out of the spinning room. Why was it kept locked?"

His mouth tightened at the corners, and a muscle twitched beneath his right eye. "The spinners, especially the young girls—they were using that door to sneak out early before the end of their shifts."

Emma laughed. She laughed because if she hadn't laughed she would have screamed. But her laughter was loud and laced with hysteria, even she could hear it.

Her mother set down her coffee cup with a sharp click that seemed to disturb the genteel ambiance in the room more than Emma's laughter had. "I declare the child *would* insist on going out and about in the middle of the day in this dreadful weather. I don't ever remember it being so hot this late in September before. I fear, Mr. Alcott, that your dearest Emma is suffering from a touch of the heat stroke." She turned to Emma, her smile brittling at the edges. The shadows that had haunted her eyes all summer were there again. "Perhaps you ought to go up and lie down for a bit before dinner."

Emma lowered her head, hiding her own eyes. "Yes, Mama," she said. She got to her feet, gathering up her skirts.

"Emma, wait . . ." Geoffrey reached for her hand again and stood up with her. "I fear I must have seemed callous to you just now. Of course I care about those women and children and what could have happened to them. There will be reforms, I promise you. Indeed, the superintendent has already been dismissed because of his unavailability during the crisis."

Geoffrey's face as he looked back at her was tender, solicitous. But his gray eyes were like a flat pond in which she saw only the sky and her own face reflected back at her. She had given up believing she would ever come to understand him, to know him, and she had convinced herself that not only was it unnecessary for a Great Folk wife to know or understand or even love her husband—it just wasn't done.

So she wasn't angry with him so much as disappointed. She now understood fully that from the day of the fox hunt, when he had asked her to be his wife, he had been destined to disappoint her. It was a startling thought. That the things that were wrong between them could be his fault as well as hers.

"I really am feeling unwell, Geoffrey," she said.

"Yes, of course you are." He patted her hand. "The strain, the stress . . . You have such a brave and generous heart, my dear. And there is this dreadful heat."

He walked her to the drawing-room doors, where he kissed her cheek before letting her go. Emma went up and lay down on her bed as if she truly had suffered a heat stroke—and perhaps she had.

She brought her knees up and wrapped her arms around her legs, hugging herself. She closed her eyes and pressed her face hard into the bones of her drawn-up knees, making herself into a tight ball. But inside, Emma's heart was beating wild and fast and scared. Like a racing sloop sailing on a broad reach across an ocean with no shore in sight, or hope or promise of one.

Sailing into a world of infinite possibilities.

Chapter Twenty-six

The stars paled and then vanished, and although the sun had not yet risen, it was a new day.

Shay McKenna was making a sweet time of the early morning, getting the dory ready for a day on the bay. He'd filled the bait buckets, and a pot of freshly brewed coffee was in the little galley below.

He'd just bow-lined the starboard sheet to the jib, and was bent over, reaching for the mooring line to cast off, when he heard the dock creak, felt it rock. And a pair of elegant, high-button tan kid shoes appeared before him on the gray weathered boards.

"Miss Tremayne," he said, and sighed. "Would it be troubling you too much to tell me what in bloody hell you're doing here?"

She took a step forward and looked down on him from under the brim of another adorable little hat. This one was of dark blue straw trimmed with a heron feather that pointed jauntily toward the heavens. "I've come to spend the day with you."

"*Dhia*. The day, she says." He looked up and down the beach, but only the fish hawks and gulls were there to see them. For the moment. "What are you thinking, child?"

Her chin came up a bit and her eyes narrowed. "Don't call me a child."

He gave her the look he gave Noreen when she was being difficult. "And I suppose your little black carriage is parked outside my house this time of the morn' for all the world to see and know that Miss Emma Tremayne has taken herself an Irish lover?"

Her chin went up another notch. "Of course not. I walked."

"Glory. And I suppose you did your walking right down the middle of Hope Street, too."

He held out his hand to her, though, so that she could climb aboard before anyone did see her standing there bold as you please on his dock, and with the sun not yet up. His was a big, shallow draft boat, fitted out with a trawl coiled in two tubs, lobster traps, and some handlines and bait for rock cod and haddock. He swabbed it down at the end of every day, but it still stank of fish, and it was hardly in the same universe as her little racing sloop.

The boat was rocking in the tide, but she stood on the deck with that athletic grace she'd always shown at sea. His hand came to rest on the small of her back and lingered there a moment. He put his lips close to her ear, just so he could have the pleasure of smelling her hair.

"Maybe you should be staying below until we're out of the harbor," he said.

She turned her head so that she could have the pleasure of feeling his lips brush her cheekbone. Then she smiled at him with her eyes and disappeared down the companionway. And well she should be looking pleased with herself, he thought, since she'd just gotten her own bloody dangerous way.

On a September morning, Bristol harbor could be as flat as a pond. Shay hoisted the sails, but they drifted for a while, until the canvas finally caught the wind.

The sun came up fiery, painting red slashes over seas of nickel. Shay was laboring with the jib, which was luffing badly, when she came up from below, wearing his pea coat and slouch hat—Miss Emma Tremayne's version of a disguise, he supposed. Hunh. And maybe on some other planet there might be a pair of eyes mistaking her for a Bristol fisherman. The essence of what it meant to be a lady, born and bred, clung to her like a perfumed cloud.

She looked around, getting her bearings, checking to see what tack they were on, and then she swung around to him, and he saw something much like real despair on her face.

"Don't take me home," she said.

He frowned at her, since that's exactly what he'd been about to do—sail right over to Poppasquash Point and put her ashore, where she belonged.

Except . . . except he kept feeling this sweet, throat-aching joy to be having her with him.

He didn't say anything. But he let out the mainsheet, setting the boat on a broad reach toward the middle of Narragansett Bay.

She took a seat in the cockpit out of the way and turned her face to the wind. He wasn't used to having company on the dory with him, but she didn't seem to mind his silence, and she answered it with a stillness of her own. The world filled with the gentle rush of the morning wind over the sails and the laughing spill of the water over the bow.

The sun was full up in all its glory when she said his name. And the way she said it, as if the edges were broken, made him look around at her. She sat like a child with her feet tucked under her and her arms wrapped around her knees. Her cheeks were flushed, and her mouth had that bruised look.

"Shay? When are we going to lie with each other again?"

He breathed a flat, aching laugh. "It's terribly brave you're getting now with your words, Emma darlin'."

Happiness suffused her face in a flash of light, and he knew it was because he'd called her "Emma darlin'." He hadn't meant to, but he wasn't sorry he had.

He wedged his knee into the wheel spokes to steady it, hooked his thumbs in his pockets, and put on the Irish for her. "There was an Irish hero by the name of Cú Chulainn. The lad suffered a terrrrible defeat at the hands of a tribe of warrior women who rode naked into battle. He took one look at the bare-breasted lot of them, turned on his heels, and ran for the life of him."

Her mouth curved into a slow smile. "Are you telling me you want to run away from me, Mr. McKenna?"

What he wanted . . .

After he and Bria had first made love they had talked about their future, not just their tomorrow or the next day, but their whole lives. They had vowed to spend their lives together as man and wife, even before they had done so in church before God.

But with Emma it could only be the moment. A moment that had no past and would have no future, that could have no ambition or hope beyond itself. Sweet and wild and fleeting—the moment simply was.

What he wanted . . .

He thought of her, of the feel of her breasts in his hands, the curve of her belly rubbing over him, and her thighs soft and round against his face. He thought of the taste of her and the smell of her, and what he wanted was to have her again.

"What I was telling you," he said, "is what I ought to be doing. Not what I am doing, surely, since I've already taken myself down to Pardon Hardy's and purchased some French letters."

The little crease she got between her eyebrows when she was worried or confused appeared. "I don't understand you sometimes. What does France have to do with anything?"

He laughed. "French letters, lass, are a thing that keeps a

man from planting a babe in a woman. They don't always work, though. It's a dangerous business we're about, Emma Tremayne."

Her chin came up again; she was getting good at it. "I'm not afraid," she said, but he heard the tremor in her voice. She was coming to know about costs and consequences, was his Emma.

"I am," he said. "I am very afraid."

She stared at him carefully, trying to see if he meant it. When she understood that he did, her gaze fell away, and he saw her swallow hard.

He leaned over and scooped a big, fat sardine out of the bucket at his feet. "Take this and bait a hook with it," he said. He tossed the slimy thing into her lap and grinned at her when she jumped and uttered a little squeak. "If you're going to spend the day with me, Miss Tremayne, you'll be doing it fishing."

She was game for trying, he had to give her that. But she was more trouble than she was worth, because he kept having to tell her what to do and then show her how to do it, and he kept wanting to touch her.

The bay was a flat, glassy blue now, speckled with distant sails. They fished for cod among the small islands that lay scattered between Poppasquash Point and the larger Prudence Island. When they passed a place where the surf beat wildly and the currents eddied dangerously around a pile of jagged rocks, she told him this was where her brother had drowned in a storm six years ago.

"Our father went out looking for him in his own sloop, when the wind was still blowing fiercely. He was so long in coming back, Papa was, and I thought . . ." She shivered, as if that long time of waiting lived within her still. "All that he brought back with him of Willie was his yacht-club cap. He showed me later where he'd found it, floating among those rocks, along with pieces of kindling, which was all that was left of Willie's boat."

"And didn't that make you afraid of sailing?"

"It made me afraid," she said. "But of other things."

When the sun was high and golden in the sky, and the water took on the polish of steel plate, he put the dory in irons and brought out his dinner of corned beef sandwiches to share with her.

"Most days, this is a sweet little bay, the Narragansett," he said. "Not like the wild surf of Gortadoo."

She was sitting by him, close enough to touch, although they weren't touching. The slouch hat that she'd borrowed concealed a good part of her face from him. But it did something to her neck, making it look impossibly long, and he kept thinking how he wanted to run his lips along the long, white arch of her neck, from her breastbone to that place behind her ear.

"Tell me of your Ireland," she said.

He opened his mouth to answer her, and his voice cracked roughly. "My Ireland? Is there the more than one?"

"Bria told me of hers. Now, I want to know of yours."

He was silent a minute, then said, "My Ireland . . . Well, she's a fairy thorn standing in naked loneliness on a hill of black rocks. She's walking across a boggy field and looking up to see a plume of smoke rising from the yellow thatch of your *shibeen.* She's fuchsia hedges dripping scarlet over a famine wall in summer, and turf piles drying in the sun."

She turned her head to look at him, and he was surprised to see tears welling in her eyes. "You make her sound so very beautiful."

"Is that not how Bria spoke of her?"

"No. Although she loved her still, there was more pain in Bria's memories."

"There was, surely," he said, acknowledging the truth she spoke, and accepting the hurt of it.

It was a bittersweet comfort to him that they could speak so freely of Bria. But then their love for Bria was the one real thing they shared beyond their bodies. In a way that he was coming to see only now, in the last weeks of his wife's life they had formed a triangle—he and Emma and Bria. Bria had been the base of it, holding them together. But now she had gone away and left them leaning against each other.

For the moment.

"When I was a lad in Gortadoo," he said into the soft silence that had come between them, "we'd go diving into the waves as they broke on the sandy beach, and afterward we'd climb onto the rocks and watch the sunset. There's a legend, you see, that out beyond the western sun lays a land called Tír na nÓg, a place of eternal youth. But no Irishman has ever gone to look for it. We Irish, we like to dream about leaving Ireland, but we don't really like to do it. And when we must leave her, we are lost."

She had turned a little so that she was facing him, and she reached up now and touched his face with her fingers. Traced the shape of his nose and cheekbones and the ridge of his brow, and the scar on his cheek made when a shroud had whipped loose from the mast during a squall and cut him.

And then she touched his mouth.

"Lost is what I would feel," she said, and her own mouth trembled, "if I had to leave you."

He wanted to put his mouth against hers and leave it there forever. "You will have to leave me someday, Emma. You do know that?"

She nodded, her eyes wide and wet, acknowledging the truth he spoke and accepting the hurt of it.

Somehow they had drawn so close their lips were almost touching, and so he kissed her.

They kissed in a place of salt-scoured air and high sun and dark blue water. He heard his heart pounding in his ears; it seemed to have run amok, his heart, run aground, gone astray. His heart was lost.

He pulled his mouth from hers. "Let's go below," he said.

He took her hand and led her where he wanted to go, or perhaps she led him. This time the love they made had an edge to it, of desperation and greed. Their naked bodies made soft, wet noises, while the boom creaked and the hull groaned. His thrusts went into a rhythm with the lifting and falling of the bow in the water.

My heart is lost, he thought. I am lost.

And then, like all moments, it came to an end.

He set her ashore on the back side of Poppasquash Point, and she watched him sail away from her. She looked around as if she'd never seen it all before, never seen the white birches flashing silver in the sun, or the bay spilling seafoam and seaweed onto the shingled beach. She had never felt a breeze like this, so soft and hushed, or heard a thrush singing quite so sweetly. Nothing in her world, she thought, would ever be the same.

She went into the house and up to her bedroom, and she took off her clothes. She took them all off until she was as naked as she had been with him, and she thought, He touches me there and there and there, in all my woman's secret places. He touches me.

"Each time," she said. "It happens to me each time."

He was lying on his back, his arms flung above his head, his chest heaving. They were lying naked in the meadow, among the goldenrod. But the flowers shivered, as if chilled by the breeze, and the sun had the brassy glow of autumn to it.

He turned his head to look at her, slowly. His whole body felt leaden, as if he'd been beaten with something thick and heavy. "What happens?" he said.

"You happen."

He rolled up onto his side, and she turned in to him. He cupped her breast with his hand and scraped his thumb over her nipple. He watched the heat from his touch move upward, like a blush, over her collarbone and into her throat, and he thought he could almost see the words come out of her, come flying out of her throat, rising fast, like a flock of gulls taking off from the shore.

"I love you, Shay."

He saw her wait, aching, breathless for him to say the words back to her.

He kissed her on the mouth, and he wanted to say, Being with you was not how I'd imagined it would be. I can't be with you without wanting you, and I can't have you without wanting you again. He kissed her on the throat and he wanted to say, I never had any intention of loving you, yet here I am, loving you.

"Emma," he said instead.

She pulled away from him and sat up, crossing her legs Indian-fashion, like a child. She seemed small and vulnerable, sitting that way. Her skin was dusted golden all over by the sun. She had twigs and leaves and goldenrod petals in her hair.

"When Mr. Alcott comes home," she said, "I must tell him I can't marry him after all."

"Ah, *Dhia*, no. Don't be doing that."

She shook her head back and forth, once. She spoke as if her throat hurt, and her heart was in her eyes. "You can't expect to show me a miracle and then think I'll settle for a life without it."

He took her hand and put it between his legs. "*This* is all I've ever shown you, and there's nothing miraculous about it."

Her fingers closed around him, squeezing a little roughly, and he had to close his eyes to fight off a shudder. "No, you are wrong," she said. "It is the one, true miracle."

He sat up so that they were knee to knee. He gripped her face with his hands. Her mouth was wet and open, her eyes like a wind-scoured sky. How had he gotten to this place? How had she?

"Emma darlin' . . . This thing between us, it's a passion of the moment. It can't last. Especially when the one of us would be having to give up all she has and the life she was meant to live to try and make it last. Don't be doing something you'll be weeping sorry tears for later."

She wrapped her fingers around his wrist. She held his hand in place so that she could turn her head and brush her lips across his knuckles. "You told me once my life would be what I made of it."

"And what of the promise you made to your Mr. Alcott? What of your duty to—"

She shook her head, and her mouth brushed across his hand again, and yet again. "I know what duty is. I've lived with duty all my life." She took his hand and began to lower it down the length of her body, down her throat, and over her breasts and the swell of her belly. "Duty is all those endless things you have to do and keep on doing forever and ever, even when you don't want to do them anymore. Even when you can no longer bear doing them."

She put his hand in the warm, dark place between her thighs. "Set me free of it, Shay. Please set me free."

He wanted to say, I started out not daring to hope for anything, and now here I am hoping for it all.

"I can't be doing that for you, Emma Tremayne," he said

instead, "because I'll always be a poor lad from Gortadoo. And I'll always love Bria."

She leaned in to him and brushed her lips across his cheek in a sigh of a kiss, as tender and ethereal as a rose petal falling to the grass. "I know that. It's what I'm trying to tell you. I'll always love you."

She loved him.

She loved him while she was calling on the Carter sisters, sipping tea and talking of the weather. She loved him while she played chess with Maddie and looked over couture plates with Mama. She went to the Sunday service at Saint Michael's and sat in the turkey-red pew, wearing beige this time, and she loved him. She took a breath, and felt herself loving him.

A fir standing in a splash of sunlight would remind her of his eyes. The grate of a saw pulling through wood would cut through her like his voice. The deep, rich gurgle of seawater spilling over the bow of her boat would become his laugh.

It is a kind of madness, she thought, what I feel for him. A love madness. She would tell herself she wouldn't think of him for a while, she wouldn't remember him for a while.

And then she would do all those things, endlessly.

She wasn't going to let him go, anyway, not until the world came to an end, and then she waited with her heart in her throat, beating like a wild thing in her throat, for the world to do just that. To end.

Every day she would wake to see a perfect white rose sitting on her dressing table. I must tell him, she thought. As soon as he comes home, I must tell him. She tried out words in her head. Geoffrey, you are a dear friend, but I have found that we can't be anything more to each other than friends.

Geoffrey, I can't be the wife you deserve and so I am setting you free. Geoffrey, I love another.

I have taken a lover and, oh, by the by, he is a poor lad from Gortadoo.

So many words she could choose to say to him, but she'd never been good with words, and she couldn't imagine saying those things to him without imagining the hurt in his eyes.

She would walk through The Birches, from room to room, looking at her reflection in gilt-framed mirrors and pier glasses, rubbing her hands over the backs of Chippendale chairs and along ormolu-studded bureaus. She held a sterling silver fork in her hand and rested her cheek on a satin pillowcase, and she thought, I can live without all this.

But then she would look at her mother, sitting at the breakfast table and having only black coffee of a morning anymore. Mama, getting thinner and thinner, her heart anxiously set on the return of the husband who would not be coming if there was no wedding.

And one day she found Maddie in the library with her eyes staring wild and unblinking, lost in that dreamworld that seemed more and more lately to have a claim on her soul. Stuart Alcott had left Bristol again the day after the garden party, and Maddie hadn't ventured out of The Birches since. This is what comes, Emma thought, of loving unwisely. This is what they always say will come. But what if this is still what you want?

She hadn't lain with him since that last time in the fox meadow. She told herself he had his fish to catch, and she knew that to sneak off to be with him on his dory was a foolhardy thing she could never do again. And she had her Great Folk duties to perform, her appearances to keep up at tennis parties and whist games and charity cake sales. Only once, when she visited the girls and little Jacko at the Thames Street house, was he there.

That evening they made a family. They ate *colcannon* and soda bread for supper, sitting at the table with its brown, well-scrubbed oilcloth. She could almost make herself feel that she had walked into that kitchen with its faded bird-of-paradise wallpaper and taken Bria's place, there at the stove, with the teakettle in her hand.

Father O'Reilly dropped by, and the five of them walked a way together down Ferry Road, with Noreen pushing little Jacko in his carriage. She and Shay walked side by side, but not so close that her skirt could so much as brush his leg.

The sugar maples were now aflame against the sky. The ferns had turned a rich bronze, the reeds and sedges a tawny yellow. She showed them the Yankee custom of putting the first horse chestnuts of the season into your pocket to ward off the rheumatism. And she told the girls to save theirs to bury in snowballs come winter.

Once, when Father O'Reilly and the girls pulled a little ahead of them, Shay said to her, his voice barely above a whisper, "I want you."

He was staring at her, his eyes green and sudden, startling her with the hunger she saw in them. She felt her breasts, taut and aching, press against all the layers of her clothes. Her legs, encased in silk stockings and drawers, quivered as if they were naked.

"I want you more," she said.

He jerked his gaze away from her, and she heard him draw in a deep, shuddering breath. "This is like the Púca," he said.

She felt her mouth twist into a funny little smile; her heart was pounding. "The what?"

"The Púca. She's a white fairy horse with horns. You'll only be finding her on a lonely road, or rather she'll find you. She'll stop and ask if you want a ride on her. And when she gets you on her back, away she'll go galloping with you, over a cliff."

"I want to jump over a cliff with you, Shay McKenna. I think it would be like flying."

On the walk back they watched the moon rise over the bay. That night from her bedroom window, she looked out and saw the moon there in the sky, as though it had followed her home.

She waited for him outside the scrolled wrought-iron gates.

When he came it was from around back, by way of the birch woods. He came in a hurry, with his pea coat flaring in the wind and his slouch hat shading his face. She was more than a little afraid he would be angry, because of what she'd done.

"I came from right off the dory," he said, as he drew close to her. "Quick as Noreen gave me your letter. Are you all right, then? What's happened?"

She clasped her hands behind her back and held herself tall. "Nothing's happened. I only want to show you something."

"To show . . ." He swung away from her, wrapping his hands around the gate's iron bars, leaning in to them. He shut his eyes. "God save us. I thought we'd been found out."

"Would that be so terrible?"

He swung around to stare at her. He grew cold when angry, she was discovering. And hard. His eyes were as hard as the granite rocks that littered the harbor beaches. "You know it would be," he said. "Don't play the child, Emma."

And in the way of a child, she suddenly wanted to weep. "I'm sorry. I only . . . I couldn't think of any other way of getting you out here. You'd never have come if I'd asked, even if I'd sent around an engraved invitation."

"Sure and I would not have. One of us has to have some

sense." He started to push himself off the gate, but she laid a hand on his arm.

"Don't go, please. I have something . . . It would mean so very much to me if you'd allow me to give it to you. And there'll be nothing scandalous for anyone to find out. Mama is in Providence today, with her Ladies' Luncheon Club, and Maddie always naps in the afternoon."

He looked around him, raising his eyebrows in mock wonder. "And have you no servants around a place this grand? You do it all yourself, then—scrub all the marble floors, polish all the silver teapots?"

"We have fifteen servants at The Birches," she said, and then flushed a little at how that had sounded coming out. "I'm only taking you out to the old orangery, not into the front drawing room or, God forbid, up to lie on my tester bed. If they see you with me in the orangery, they'll think you're a stonemason come to deliver. And now I'm done with excuses and apologies and explanations, Shay McKenna. You can either come with me, or not."

She walked through the gates without looking to see if he followed. At first she didn't hear his step on the quahog-shell drive behind her, and then she did.

Sea light spilled through the glazed glass walls of the orangery, flickering on the black-and-white-tiled floor like tiny waves. She had known she would love having him in this place that she had made her own, that was uniquely hers.

She left him to look around while she wheeled a stand out from deep in one of the corners. On the stand was a piece she had done, shrouded in canvas.

She stood before him, nervous and yet excited. Until now, the only thing she had given him was her body. This was made of the blood of her heart. "I did this for you," she said. "Well, no, actually I did it for myself. But it is meant for you to have. If you want it, that is. You don't need to accept it just to be polite."

"Very lovely," he said, teasing now. He was looking at a clay-stained, paint-splattered drop cloth as if he beheld a masterpiece.

She gripped the edges of the cloth and lifted it slowly, and she thought she could hear the beat of her heart suddenly filling the room.

His hand came up, hovering before the sculpture, but didn't touch it. "*Mo bhean,*" he whispered, his ruined voice breaking rougher. "Bria, lass . . ."

It was Bria. Bria's face as she'd once imagined doing it, a mask of her face with those extraordinary bones there, strong, so strong, but invisible, existing in the infinity of space and in the mind's eye, invisible behind her face that was a shell of bronze as thin as crepe paper.

It was three times life-size and set on the smallest pedestal she could have and still adhere to the laws of physics, so that it seemed to be floating in the air.

Shay's hand began to shake and he let it fall to his side. Emma looked away, for it hurt to see his face. To see the love and the pain that shone wet in his eyes and pulled at his mouth.

She left him alone with Bria's face for a long time, left him in silence to be with Bria's spirit. She looked through the salt-scummed panes. She watched the tide gobble up the pebbly beach, watched the wind stir the yellow leaves of the birches. They were ripe, those leaves. They would be gone, she thought, with one wild blow from the sea.

She left him alone with Bria until the silence in that vast place of glass became unbearable. "It's a bronze done in the lost-wax technique," she finally said, "which begins with a mold made of clay, and so I can cast others. I can do one for each of the girls to have, and Jacko, and Father O'Reilly, if he wishes."

Not to look at him, she decided, was worse. She turned and found that he was staring at her. The last time she'd seen such a look on his face had been the night his son was born.

He came up to her but he didn't touch her, except with his eyes. Eyes that were brilliant with pain, and life. "It's an extraordinary woman you are, Emma Tremayne. You keep giving me things that are irreplaceable."

Her gaze fell before the rawness of the feelings that lived in his eyes. "I loved her, too, Shay," she said.

He touched her then, gathering her within the circle of his arms. She laid her palms on his chest, feeling him breathe, feeling his heartbeat, feeling him live.

"I know you did," he said. "I know."

Feeling him hold her close.

When they moved apart, Emma felt lighter, as though she were floating up in the coved glass ceiling. She took his hand and pulled him over to another canvas-draped figure.

She said nothing, but she watched his face carefully as she lifted the shroud. It was a pair of hands, hewn out of granite, a man's hands carved to life-size and curled into fists.

"Now you needn't fear that I'll ever exhibit it," she said. "Neither Mama nor Mr. Alcott would ever allow me to exhibit my work. It isn't the done thing. Great Folk don't put their talents on display, only their possessions."

Shay was walking all around the sculpture, staring at it with eyes that were a little wide and wild.

"He's more brawn than brain, this fellow," he finally said.

Emma hid a smile. "He's yourself, Shay McKenna."

"Aye, I can suppose that. God save me."

"They're only your hands, God save you. Someday I might be doing other parts of you."

He peered at her from around the sculpture's thick, rope-veined wrists. "What parts of me?"

"All the marvelous, delectable parts of you. I've been

practicing them since first I saw you—that day of the fox hunt." In truth, she'd only dared to do his hands so far, even in clay, but she enjoyed teasing him. His ears were turning red.

"Are you after telling me you had me stripped naked in your mind's eye when you hardly knew me?"

"Didn't you do the same to me, in your mind's eye?"

"Neverrr," he said, exaggerating his brogue. "Well, might be I lifted up your skirts and took a wee little peek at your ankles. In me mind's eye."

Laughing, she backed up until she bumped into the turntable where she did her clay modeling. She sat down on it, spinning herself around, and lifted her skirts, spreading her legs wide, like a vaudeville chorus girl. "And what do you see in your mind's eye now."

"I see a shameless hussy."

He stopped the whirling turntable by grabbing her waist with his big hands. Her knees fell wider apart and he came between them. He bunched up her skirt and petticoat around her waist, and his hand moved up the long muscle of her thigh to the slit in her drawers.

He lowered his head and pulled at her lower lip lightly with his teeth. "You've a few delectable parts of your own."

"No, they are yours. All yours."

He let go of her waist and pressed his palm to the back of her head to kiss her deeply. His tongue thrust, slowed, then stayed, filling her mouth. He ground his hips against her. He was hard.

She flung her head back, her eyes opening wide onto the glazed panes that spun above, fracturing the light into a kaleidoscope of whirling blue skies and yellow suns. He pressed his lips to the throbbing hollow in her throat and his voice thrummed in her blood. "Emma, Emma, Emma . . ."

Sometimes when her dreams wore off and she awakened to the winter that was her life, Maddie Tremayne would be seized with such a restlessness she couldn't bear it.

She would torment herself by throwing off the bedclothes and lifting her night rail, so that she could see the wasteland of her body and revel in her hatred. Her hatred of life and of God. Her hatred of herself.

But even hatred and self-pity palled after a time. Then, if the weather was fair and Mama was not at home to scold her for making a fuss, she would ring for a footman to carry her and her chair downstairs and for her maid, Tildy, to push her around the garden.

That day she had intended to venture across the lawns to the small promontory that overlooked the bay. But then she saw a shadow of movement behind the glass-paned wall of the old orangery.

"There's Emma," she said, looking back at Tildy over her shoulder, "working on her sculpting."

"Should we go an' see if she's looking for company, miss?"

"Oh, I don't know." Maddie didn't want to intrude if her sister was deep in her work. It wasn't that Emma would be rude; she'd be oblivious, and that was somehow worse.

And yet, and yet . . . Maddie had awakened that afternoon feeling so wretchedly lonely. No, more than lonely—she felt empty. As if a harsh wind had blown through her while she slept and scoured out her soul.

And then it didn't matter anyway, for Tildy was pushing her down the garden path, past the pots of geraniums and onto the terrace that ran alongside the orangery's south wall.

Tildy saw them first and gasped, jerking the chair to such a sudden stop that Maddie tipped forward and had to grab the armrests to keep from falling out. Maddie uttered not a sound, for she'd lost all her breath.

Emma was with a man, a man Maddie had never seen before. A rough, working man by the look of him, him in his shirtsleeves and with his ragged hair, and his worn corduroy britches . . . his britches that were pushed down around his thighs. Her sister's hands were pale against the darker skin of the man's bare buttocks as she squeezed the taut flesh almost savagely.

Emma was leaning back across some sort of table, and the man was standing between her legs. Emma's shirtwaist and camisole gaped open, exposing her breast, and the man was sucking on her nipple, pulling at it with his teeth. And then the man's hips began to pump and thrust, hard, so hard the table rocked across the floor.

Emma's head was thrown back and her mouth was open wide, and Maddie thought she could hear her sister panting, but then she realized it was the wind blowing through the birches she heard. That, and her own ragged breathing.

Tildy tried to turn the chair around, but one of its wheels was stuck in the crumbly mortar between the brick tiles.

"No!" Maddie said harshly. "Leave it stay."

Tildy moaned. "But, Miss Maddie, we shouldn't be watching this, surely. 'Tisn't decent."

"You hush up and do as I say."

She watched, she watched it all. And when it was over, Maddie Tremayne's heart pounded as if she'd been running, and sweat pooled beneath her breasts and trickled in runnels between her corset stays.

But when she spoke her voice was steady, resolved. "I wish to be taken back to the house now."

Moaning again, Tildy wrenched at the chair and finally got it loose. The wind seemed suddenly to have died, and now all Maddie could hear was the clicking of her wheels.

My wheels, she thought. My wheels are the only sound my life makes. Even my heart makes no sound because there's no one to hear it beat.

Chapter Twenty-seven

It was a cloudy afternoon, and the lamp had not been lit in the bedroom where Emma Tremayne lay on the white iron bed with her Irish lover.

Outside a foul sort of wind blew, a storm wind with a yellow edge to it.

"I'm going to be having to leave Bristol," he said.

She could only lie there as if winded, lie there and think, In a moment I will breathe again, in a moment I'll go on living. All I need is a moment, a moment . . .

"Donagh says he has a cousin in New York, and this fellow says he can get me a job working the docks that'll make me far more money than I'm doing here with a fishing dory I don't even rightly own."

She was lying beside him, in his bed, and he was telling her he was leaving her.

She breathed; she breathed again. She was learning, growing up. She didn't ask, she told him. "I'm coming with you."

"Emma." He stroked her hair, following the length of it where it curled down around her breasts and over her hip. She knew now why he'd let her come here this afternoon, with Father O'Reilly having taken the girls to a church party and only little Jacko in his cradle for a chaperon. Somehow, what they had was already over, and she hadn't known it.

"Emma . . . Sweet it is between us, surely, and because it's sweet we can't let it alone, and because we can't let it alone, we're someday going to be found out. It's not a thing to be going on and on without costs and consequences."

She got up and went to the window that overlooked the beach. It had begun to rain, and waves were battering the rocks and piers, even in the harbor. She laid her hand flat on the glass pane, as if she would feel the beating of the surf, the ocean's heart, the beating of her heart. Her dying heart.

"If I come with you, it can go on and on. Forever."

"But I'll not be letting you come."

She wrapped her arms around herself, hugging herself, holding herself together. She felt the fear of losing him begin to build in her chest, in her throat, behind her eyes.

"It's my Yankee money, isn't it?" she said. "You are being such a stuck-up Irish snob."

She turned to look at him. He had sat up and was pulling his britches up over his hips, fastening them. "Partly, aye. It's a thing a wee bit hard to overlook, your money."

Those eyes of his, so green, so hard, his eyes burning so hard, all of him so hard. She wanted to reach out and stroke the broken place in his nose, to kiss it. To hit it hard enough to break it again. It was nearly unbearable to look at him. It was unfair that he was the man he was, and that she loved him so much.

"Are you saying I have to give up my trust fund to be with you? Are you making that a condition? Do you think I couldn't, that I wouldn't? Don't you dare try to tell me that I don't love you enough."

"Ah, *mhuire*." He stood up from the bed in that way he had, a sudden yet graceful uncoiling of long and powerful limbs. "You can't even begin to imagine what 'enough' would be. There's more to loving than fucking, and more to marriage than the both of those things. To be husband and wife—it's a sharing. Of dreams and destinies, of histories and ceremonies, and beliefs and faiths. Of things as small as a liking for corned beef and cabbage, and things so grand as the children you come to be making and raising together."

"But I want to make children with you. I want to be a mother to the children you have."

He pushed the hair out of his face with both his hands. "There, and don't you see how it's happening already—with me talking of one thing and you hearing another. I can say to you that I've always been a 'chickens today and feathers tomorrow' sort of man, and you wouldn't have a notion of what I was talking about. Any more than I would have a notion of what it's like to have a million dollars sitting in a thing called a trust fund, and able to attach the word *only* to it as if it were of no more significance than this." He picked up her black velvet hat from the paint-chipped dresser and held it out to her. Then sent it sailing to the bed and gathered up her ecru kid gloves and pushed them into her face. "Or another pair of these."

She snatched the gloves out of his hand and threw them aside. "You are wrong. You've always been wrong about me in that way. You make me sound spoiled and selfish and vain, and perhaps I am all of those things, but I can change. I have changed."

"Changed enough, you think, to come live with us in a Hell's Kitchen tenement, maybe get a job in a mill and learn what sort of 'plight' it is to work at a spinning frame for twelve hours a day, six days the week?"

"But why should I have to? I'm a rich little heiress, or have you forgotten already?"

"Sure and I haven't. So maybe me and the children could be joining you and your trust fund up in that grand silver house of yours, where even the fifteen servants will be snubbing us from the instant we walk through the back door as we go mistaking it for the front one, and—"

He pushed his breath out in a deep, harsh sigh. "It can't be, Emma. Some things, no matter how badly we might want them, just can't be."

A shock of rain suddenly beat a hard and rapid tattoo on the shack's roof. They both started and looked out the window, but they could see nothing now but water washing down the panes.

"You are a coward, Shay McKenna," she said, her voice nearly drowned out by the noise the rain made. "Afraid to try."

"Aye, I admit it. It's scared I am of hurting you and of being hurt myself. Of having to watch my girls and my baby son, who could all come to love you for a mother, suffer the loss of you when you walk out of our world and go back to your old one."

"We can make our own world, Shay, our own special place. Together."

"Ah, darlin' . . ." He shook his head, his mouth softening into a smile that broke what was left of her heart. "And what sort of place would it be, really? You're too high for me to reach for, and I'd only be dragging you down."

The storm had filled the room with a strange yellow light. The light sought him out, catching the sheen of wetness in his eyes, the tick of a muscle along his jaw.

And she understood how, in the way of men, he had decided to make all the choices his.

She understood, but she wasn't going to accept it. If he went to New York, she would follow. She would crawl to him there on her hands and knees if need be, and then she would make him let her stay.

"You—" His voice broke, and he had to start over. "You should be knowing, Emma . . . There'll never be anyone else for me. I love you with all my heart, and I'll be doing it forever, *mo chridh.*"

She began to gather up her clothes, to dress in silence. She got as far as the door before she looked at him. He stood just inside the kitchen, wearing only his britches, and with the top buttons still undone. His hair was mussed, and his cheeks were flushed, and he had a kiss mark on his throat. He looked like some woman's lover, just come from her bed.

"I love you, and you love me," she said. "So perhaps you can explain to your heart why I am leaving."

He said her name once, but she kept on walking through the door.

The afternoon had darkened to a gray twilight now, and the wind prowled the sky. Spume rose, foamy, off the bay. The rain came down in white flashes, making a beating sound like sheets snapping on a line.

She had started down the beach when she heard him shouting, his feet pounding after her. She wasn't going to turn around, but then she did.

He ran up to her. She was shocked to see how the rain had drenched him, and then she realized that she must look the same.

The wind made a sound like a cow lowing, and then she heard him say, "Emma, you didn't sail here, did you?"

"No," she lied, not sure why she did. She wanted only to get away from him now, away, away. "I drove the carriage and parked it in front of the library."

For so long, for forever, they stared at each other through the driving rain.

"Goodbye, then, and take care," he said.

And then he left her.

He left her and went back into his empty house, back into his empty bedroom, and lay down on his empty bed. He lay on his side and stared at the wall. The rain beat at the window, the wind cried wild.

He put his hand on the place in the bed where she had been. But it was cold.

"Darlin'," he said.

But he wasn't sure which loss, which woman, he was crying for.

The *Icarus* groaned like a thing in agony as she bucked and climbed the waves, her sails curving and gripping the wind. The sky was shrouded and furious. Lightning struck in blistering flashes, flooding every crack and corner of the world.

Emma fought hard with both hands to hold the tiller, as the rain lashed her face, blinding her. The lee rail was two feet under white water; the wind howled and shrieked through the rigging. The storm was terrible and it was beautiful, so terrible and beautiful it made everything else in life seem useless and tawdry. But not love, she thought. Love stood up to it.

She threw back her head and screamed with the wind, "I did this of my own free will! I choose this, Shay McKenna! I choose *this*!"

The whole sky exploded in a dense cobweb of lightning. In that flash of brilliance, before the world was swallowed back by the driving wind and rain, Emma saw a thing that stopped her heart.

A wave. A wave meant for an ocean, not a small Rhode Island bay. Even above the roar of the wind and rain, she heard the hoarse whisper a big sea makes as it prepares to curl and break.

"Oh, please, God, no . . ."

But already the *Icarus* was soaring up its black face. The bow pointed to the seething sky, leaping into the roiling darkness, reaching, reaching. . . . For one suspended moment they hung there, the brave little sloop groaning and shuddering, and Emma with her soul stripped naked . . . hanging there on the edge of eternity.

And then they plunged, plunged into a trough as deep and black as hell. Plunged with such force the sloop's hull thundered as it struck the bottom and the mainmast bent like a bow.

A wall of water crashed over them, pummeling them, beating them down . . . and then it was gone.

Within moments, the gale ended as suddenly as it had started. The rain still poured and the sky was still dark, but the danger had followed after the wind.

Emma sat in the sloop, trembling, gasping, more afraid now that it was over. But she felt triumphant as well. She had not won, she thought; she'd done something better. She had survived.

Only a glimmer of gaslight shone on the upper landing of the dark house. Emma's legs shook with exhaustion as she climbed the stairs. She was soaked and chilled through to the bone, and shuddering with it.

If she'd cared she would have thought to wonder why the house was so dark and silent, so possessed of such a soul-freezing emptiness. But all she could think of was how tired she was, so tired.

She opened the door to her bedroom, then shut it carefully behind her and leaned against it, shaking. She suddenly felt an almost irresistible urge to laugh. She wanted to lift up her skirts and spin around and around, making herself dizzy, laughing, until she collapsed in a heap on the floor the way she used to do when she was a child and she'd been banished up here to her room as a punishment.

Something stirred in one of the rose silk armchairs that sat before the fire. "Mama?" she said.

Her mother stood up, and then a man shuffled ponderously to his feet out of the other chair. It was Uncle Stanton, the doctor, coming to stand beside her mother. It was so quiet Emma could hear the rain and seawater dripping from the hem of her skirts.

Her uncle's face was drawn, worried, and now Emma smelled the sharp, sour odor of chloral hydrate.

"What's wrong?" she said. "Has something happened to Maddie?"

Her mother's eyes were staring at Emma, wide and haunted in her too-thin face. Emma took a step toward her. "Is it you, Mama? Have you taken ill?"

"I will not allow this to happen," her mother said. "I will not let you do this to me."

Chapter Twenty-eight

Shay McKenna stood before the heavy wrought-iron gates and looked through the scrolled bars at the grandeur that was The Birches. The big, sprawling house shimmered under the October sun, with all its gables and bay windows and piazzas. Its weathered shingles were like the taut scales of a snake.

A spider had woven a web over one of the gate's leafy scrolls. Its fine threads had caught only dewdrops so far, although they sparkled like diamonds. Shay started to lift his hand to break the web, to destroy it and restore perfection to the gate's elegant symmetry, but then he let it be.

He wrapped his fists around the bars instead, pushed the gate open, and walked down the long white quahog-shell drive.

He'd always thought of himself as a bold-as-you-please sort of man. Aye, so bold he was, and with his heart hammering so violently in his chest, it was a wonder he didn't crack a few ribs.

For although he didn't expect to see her, his gaze still searched the garden with its urns and nymphs and marble fountain, hungry for the sight of a girl in white lawn and a straw hat with a wide blue ribbon floating in the breeze. And by the time he knocked on the big coffered ebony doors, his mind hadn't had to do much of a running leap before he was drinking in the smell of her and feeling her hair in his hands. . . . And when the doors opened, he thought, In another moment I'll see her, and she will smile and say—

"Sir?" said a sour-mouthed man with haughty eyebrows.

Shay stated his business and, not to his surprise—after the visitor he himself had had last evening—he was led across the black-and-white marble floor and into the interior of the house.

The times he had been here before, Shay had had other things on his mind besides admiring the grandness of it all. But today his gaze took in the festooned domed ceiling and fluted columns embellished with gold leaf, the grand double oak staircase and the massive gold-framed mirror above the massive white marble fireplace. There was even a suit of armor in one corner, polished to a nickel-plated shine. When he was a boy back in Gortadoo, playing "castle and knights" with Donagh, he'd never imagined such a place as this.

The sour-mouthed man led Shay into a room with yellow silk damask walls and white and gilded paneling. A woman with pale hair was dressed to match the sumptuous interior in a yellow gown of such stiff cloth she seemed to rustle even though she was sitting still.

The woman, his Emma's mother, was sitting at a shell-carved secretary, writing on a piece of gold-edged paper with an ivory pen. She waited through ten ticks of the ormolu clock on the mantel before she looked up and turned to face him. She had the bluest eyes he'd ever seen.

"I have been expecting you, sir," she said in a soft, drawling voice that made Shay think of hot nights and sultry winds. "I'm afraid you've arrived just when I was about to compile today's menus. If you would be so kind as to wait for just a moment . . ."

She turned her back to him, and picked up the ivory pen

with a hand that was as white and graceful as a dove's wing. She was sitting in a chair with a small engraved silver clock set into its back. Shay had never known such a marvel in his life. It was a beautiful thing, but what good did it do you to have a clock in a place that was always behind you, where you couldn't see it? It was like so much of Emma's world, he thought—beautiful and glamorous and, in strangely perverted ways, useless.

Emma's mother had at last finished with her menus and now gave him her blue-eyed, silken attention. "So? Apparently our first offer was not enough," she said, "and you've decided that coming directly to the source might be the easier way of getting more?"

Shay stared back at her. It wasn't that he didn't understand the question—he'd even expected it. But the hearing of it rose the temper up in him, so hot and full of bile that for a moment he couldn't speak.

"As my lawyer has explained to you," Emma's mother went on, "I am willing to give you a certain amount to resettle in another place, so that you are forever out of our lives. But I warn you, sir, that you will not be allowed to bleed us."

"Faith and begorra. Will I not?" he said, exaggerating his brogue, and looking around the room as if calculating its worth, with all the wide-eyed wonder of a lad from Gortadoo and the bog still stinking on his shoes.

"A fellow with the word *esquire* tacked onto his name, he comes along yesterday and offers me a thousand dollars if only I'll go away and never admit to a soul I've ever seen or heard of the likes of Miss Emma Tremayne. And so I'm thinking we've been found out—and wasn't I always after telling her that would happen. And I'm thinking, too, I'll not be smashing in the face of the esquire if he'll only be taking his money and himself out of my house."

He went up to her, close enough to intimidate her with the big size of him. "But then this esquire, he tells me she's been packed off for a little visit with some cousins who live in a grand house in a place called Georgia. And so now I'm thinking she's pregnant, and if she is, then I'll be taking the babe and her both, and to bloody hell with the lot of you."

He took another step, and the woman shrank down in her wonder of a chair. "Is that why she's been packed off to this plantation place? She never mentioned having such cousins to me."

A tight, nervous smile pulled at the woman's perfect, rosebud mouth. "Are you implying the two of you actually *talked*? I was under the impression . . ." Her hand, white and fragile, waved through the air. "Well, never mind. There is no child, and for that you both should be grateful to whichever of the gods watches over fools. Nor has she been 'packed off,' as you put it. She has gone of her own free will."

Emma's mother rose gracefully to her feet in a rustle of stiff yellow silk and slipped around him, putting distance between them again. "Perhaps she saw leaving Bristol for a time as the only tolerable way to end what she had come to think was an intolerable mistake."

"Perhaps. More likely, though, you were sitting there on your silk-covered arse and lying through your gold-plated teeth."

She was tougher than he'd given her credit for. She stood before him straight as a mast, her face so calm it seemed empty. But then he saw fear in her eyes, shadows that moved like storm clouds flying before the wind.

And why should she not be afraid? he thought. When to her way of figuring, her daughter had nearly gone and ruined everything.

"It is possible you cared for her," said Emma's mother. "You might even have convinced yourself you loved her. If that is so, then you ought to be thinking of her. Let her go,

Mr. McKenna. For her own sake, let her go. What can you possibly offer her but unhappiness?"

Shay looked around the room with its silk and gold walls and its chair with the pretty, pointless clock. "I'm thinking the words sounded truer," he said, "when I was saying them to her."

He left the gilded woman and the gilded room and the gilded house with his hands and belly clenched tight. But he didn't leave The Birches, not right away.

He followed the path through the trees to the beach where Emma docked her little sloop. The *Icarus* was there, her sails lowered but not furled, the sheets in tangles on her deck, puddles of saltwater slopping in her cockpit . . . and the worry came gnawing back at him.

The Emma he knew was too good a sailor to go gallivanting off to some cotton plantation for the winter and leave her boat to rot away in such a sorry state.

But what of the Miss Emma Tremayne who lived in that gilded house, the daughter of that cold, gilded woman? That Emma could doubtless buy a dozen little racing sloops and not feel the pinch.

He was about to leave when a thing lying on the gray, warped boards of the dock caught his eye. It was one of her gloves. He bent over and picked it up, brought it to his face, rubbed the soft leather of it over his open mouth . . . breathing her in.

He started to take it away with him and then he changed his mind and left it there. But in the days and weeks that followed, he couldn't get the smell of her out of his throat.

They kept giving her chloral hydrate to make her sleep.

Some nights Emma refused to take it, so she was strapped into a chair and her head was yanked back by the hair. One of the attendants leaned on her, his knee pressing hard into her belly, while he pushed a wooden wedge between her lips and teeth, prying her mouth open. The matron forced a black rubber tube down her throat, and then funneled the drug, mixed with warm, stale water, down the tube.

Emma couldn't swallow fast enough, and she began to choke and gag and gasp for air. Her chest burned as the water poured into her lungs, and she cried. She kept promising herself she wouldn't cry, no matter how they hurt her, but she always cried.

For after the chloral hydrate was forced down her throat, she was put into a muff—a pair of leather mittens, buckled to hold the hands together, which in turn was buckled to a stout leather belt they had cinched around her waist. Then they put her into a contraption they called a "crib."

The crib was a square wooden box, like a coffin. "That," the matron would say, bringing her mouth so close her spittle would spray Emma's face, "that ought to teach you to behave." And then she would close the lid, and Emma would lie there with a scream trapped in her raw throat, until the drugged sleep overcame her.

The matron had heavy-lidded eyes like a frog's, and gray hairs sprouted from her ears and nostrils. Emma learned to hate and fear her.

But more than she feared the matron, Emma feared the unimaginable things that hadn't yet been done to her. She heard such screams, especially at night, such maniacal shrieks. Screams that sounded as though they came from the souls of the damned.

After she had been in the asylum a week, she was taken into another part of the big gray stone building. Taken into a wood-paneled, book-lined room that could have been a library in a Hope Street mansion. Her uncle Stanton was there, with another man he said was a doctor whose specialty was diseases of the mind. They told her she'd been put in this place for her own good, to be cured of her "excitable" nature.

Her uncle still bore the scratch marks she'd put on his cheek the night of the storm, when he'd pushed a syringe into her arm. That night before she had woken up in this place.

Emma sat on her hands, so they couldn't see them shaking, with her knees pressed close together. "Would you bring Mama to see me," she said to her uncle, and she saw something shift in his eyes before he looked away. Mama doesn't know the true nature of this place, she thought. Surely, Mama would never have done this to me if she had known.

"It is better for you if your dear mother stays away for a time," said the doctor whose specialty was diseases of the mind. "It is easier to facilitate a cure when the patient has a complete break with the familiar. When she is removed entirely from the environment which has led to her excitability."

"This is a place for mad people," Emma said, struggling hard to keep her voice sounding calm . . . sane. "And I am not mad."

The two doctors exchanged knowing looks, and then something snapped inside Emma. She lunged out of the chair, screaming at them, "I am not mad! I am not, I'm not, I'm not mad!"

The matron barged into the room with two attendants in tow. They put a straitjacket on her and dragged her out, and her all the while screaming how she wasn't mad.

"It's hall number twelve for you, my girl," the matron said.

She was put into a cell that was no bigger than her clothes press back home at The Birches. They ran chains from the buckles on her straitjacket to a ring set into the stone floor, fastening her so that she could neither lie straight down nor stand up.

The matron slammed shut the iron door and turned a key in the lock, and the last thing Emma saw before she was enveloped by the cold and the dark was the matron's eyes peering at her through the grate, and then that, too, was slammed shut.

Emma screamed, then—screamed and rattled the chains and tried to wrench herself out of the straitjacket, straining her muscles and bones unbearably and not even feeling it, screaming, screaming, screaming . . . until the iron door clanged open and a bucket of cold water was dashed in her face.

She sat in the dank blackness, wet and shivering, and whispering over and over to herself, "I am not mad, I am not mad," and then she thought, *They will make me mad.* And so she stopped even whispering.

But the screams were still there, building, building, inside her, and the terror was like a wild thing, a mad thing. Such a mad thing that if she let the screams out now, if she let just one out, then she wouldn't be able to stop screaming. She would scream and scream until the screams swallowed up her mind.

When the matron finally came back an eternity later, she said to Emma, "You are going to behave."

And Emma looked down at the floor, humbled, broken, and said, "Yes, matron," in a small, trembly voice she would never have recognized as her own.

"You'll eat and drink what you are given, without making a fuss, and you'll do as you are told."

"Yes, matron."

"You will be put in the fifth hall, then. For as long as you behave. And if you don't behave, it's back to the close room you'll go."

"I'll behave."

The fifth hall was behind a solid, massive, spring-bolted door that the matron unlocked and then locked again with the set of keys that jangled and dangled from the braided cord she always wore around her thick waist.

The "hall" was indeed just that—a wide hall that had six small dormitories feeding off it, each with six iron cots. Along the walls of the hall were wooden benches, with small, barred windows set in high above them.

The hall was crowded with women. Some merely sat quietly on the benches. Others paced frantically back and forth, waving their arms, pulling at their hair, moaning and screaming aloud, some screaming silently, others talking gibberish and cursing foully. One woman was strapped to a wheelchair. She stared at Emma with vacant eyes, her mouth hanging open, drooling.

The matron gave Emma a shove in the back and pointed to an empty place on one of the benches, next to a filthy, wild-eyed, straggle-haired woman who was sitting in a puddle of urine. "Now you park yourself there and behave."

Emma's legs all but collapsed beneath her as she obeyed the matron's pointing finger. The stench in the hall was as rank as spoiled fruit.

Across the way from her, a woman was chained to the bench with her arms bound in a straitjacket. She was beating her head back against the wall, hard, over and over. Her face was a mess of purpling bruises, and Emma wondered how it had gotten that way, when it was the back of her head that she was beating.

But just then the matron went up to the woman and slammed the ring of iron keys into her mouth. Blood spurted from the woman's pulpy lips.

The woman uttered not a sound, but Emma moaned. She sat on the bench, afraid to move, after that. But after a long while, when she felt certain that she wasn't being watched, she stood up on the bench so she could look out the window. The glass was framed and grated in iron, but she could still see through it. A green lawn sloped down to a grove of birch trees so much like the ones at home. Their yellow leaves and white trunks shimmered silver against the clear blue sky.

Hours passed . . . Emma never knew how many because she had already learned that time had no meaning in this place. A bell rang, summoning them to another, smaller hall, where they were seated on wooden benches at wooden trestle tables and fed cold corned beef and cold boiled potatoes. When the woman next to her began smearing the potatoes in her face and hair, Emma's stomach revolted and she couldn't eat. But when she went back to her bench beneath the window, her stomach cramped with hunger.

"Are you one of the crazy ones, or just Yankee stubborn?"

Emma started at the voice in her ear, although it was a nice voice, sweet and chirping like a chickadee's song. The woman who owned it had a face that was both sad and lovely, with bright violet eyes.

But Emma thought of that wood-paneled room and her uncle and the doctor exchanging those knowing looks while she protested her sanity, and she didn't trust either the woman or her words.

Although it shook a little, Emma still managed a haughty lift of her chin. "I'm sure I don't know what you mean."

"Are you sane, or insane?" The woman brought her face up close to Emma's to peer into her eyes. "You look sane to me. Still, it's hard to tell sometimes. And the things they do to us in here would soon have the Christ Jesus himself shrieking and drooling and talking gibberish."

Emma almost smiled, and then she thought of herself shrieking and pulling at the chains in her cell, and she shuddered instead.

"So, what are you in for?"

"What?" Emma said, starting again.

"What affliction do they say you suffer from—melancholia, dementia, hysteria, nervous prostration?"

"I have an excitable nature."

The woman looked Emma up and down, her eyes dancing with an inner smile. "Yes, I can see that. And what did your excitable nature lead you to do?"

"I took a lover," Emma said, surprising herself with the pride and wonder she still heard in those words, after all that had happened. "But he . . . he was unsuitable, and I was supposed to be marrying someone else."

"You suffer from an excess of passion then, an affliction more peculiar to the female than the male. Thus, being female is obviously the root of your trouble. Indeed, being female is often found to be a cause of great nervous distress in women."

Incredibly, Emma found herself wanting to laugh. The woman had a nice smile, although her teeth had gone rotten.

"I'm being incarcerated for the opposite crime as you," the woman said. "It was my husband who took a lover. He wanted to live with her and I refused to divorce him. At the time, I believed divorce was an unbearable disgrace—I would not even allow it mentioned in my presence."

She became lost for a moment in her thoughts, then she shrugged. "Oh, the errors of judgment one can make when one is young . . . So he had me put away in here. I don't know if he's still with her. She could be dead—they could both be dead—and during my occasional lapses of sanity, I pray that they are. I say *lapses* of sanity because since he had me committed, only he can get me let out. Which he can't very well do if he's dead now, can he?"

She huffed a small sigh and said quite matter-of-factly, "I've been incarcerated in this place for over thirty-five years."

Thirty-five years. God, oh, God . . . Emma sat on her hands again so that no one could see them tremble.

The woman's name was Annabel Kane. During the coming days she would sit with Emma on the bench, or sometimes they would stand to look out the window, when the matron was not about to see them. There was a fence and a locked gate, Emma came to learn, on the other side of the birch grove.

They filled their hours with talk. Or rather, it was mostly Emma who talked, and she mostly about her childhood at The Birches, about sailing and riding and, oddly, about Geoffrey, who dwelled in her thoughts more and more now, although she didn't know why.

"I fear I've grown rather dull in here myself," Annabel said. "Every day is much the same as the last."

One day she joined Emma at their place on the bench, her face vivid with excitement. "I'm going home tomorrow!" she exclaimed.

Emma seized her hands. "That's wonderful," she said, the tears starting bright in her eyes. "Is it your husband—has he asked them to let you out? Or have the doctors decided you are cured?"

But Annabel didn't answer, she was that excited. Instead, they talked all afternoon about the things Annabel would do the first afternoon she was free. "I'm going to go for a long walk," Annabel said. "A long, long walk, and I will look up at the wide, open sky and breathe it in, just breathe it all in."

And when Annabel was leaving her, she leaned over and wiped a tear off Emma's cheek. "You take care of that excitable nature of yours, Miss Emma Tremayne. Preserve it well."

But later the next day, walking past the dormitories on her way to the dining hall, Emma saw Annabel Kane lying down with her feet strapped to her bed, her hands muffed, and a broad leather band stretched tightly across her chest. She'd been drugged, for she was snoring loudly, and she was naked.

"Annabel!" Emma cried, trying to go to her. But the matron came lumbering after her, grabbing her arm, and jerking her to such a hard, wrenching stop that she nearly pulled the bone from its socket.

"Oh, God . . . Please, matron. Can't you at least cover her up?"

"She ripped up her sheets last night," the matron said, "and so she's being punished for it. And you'll find yourself getting the same if you don't shut your mouth."

Two days later, Annabel was waiting for Emma back at their place on the bench. She was standing, looking out the window.

"I'm not well sometimes," she said. "I've been in here so long, Emma, so long. All of my life. I was only twenty when I came here. Twenty! I am now fifty-five, an old woman. I shall die in here." She touched the barred glass with the very tips of her fingers. "Sometimes I despair that I shall die here."

That night, Annabel Kane ripped up her sheets into strips and tied them together in a good, strong rope. And then she tied the rope to the copper light fixture and hanged herself.

After that, Emma stood on the bench alone.

She shut her ears to the shrieks and moans and snarls of the other women, the madwomen. She closed her nose to the raw smells of their sweat and urine. She pressed her face to the cold, barred glass and watched the birches outside the window lose their leaves, one by one. One day, she looked out and saw the lawn was dusted with a sprinkling of snow.

She didn't think of Shay because that was unbearable.

She imagined herself walking with Bria along a gray shingle beach, through air that was as silver as the bay.

Chapter Twenty-nine

It was a cold and damp, sniveling day, on the edge of tears.

Maddie, sitting in her chair on the terrace that overlooked the bay, worried that she was about to get wet. But it had been one gray, sloppy, and lonely day after the other for so long—first snow and now this slushy rain—and she had so needed to get out of the house.

She heard footsteps on the flagstones and twisted around, expecting to see Tildy or one of the footmen. Her heart began to thud fast and unevenly with both fear and relief to see Stuart Alcott coming down the path with his long-legged stride. He was dressed for casual riding, in leather breeches, knee-high boots, and a Norfolk jacket.

"What, here again so soon, Mr. Alcott?" she said as he came up to her. She had written him countless letters during the past two months, begging him to come and getting no reply. "Ought I to be flattered, or have you run out of money again?"

He leaned over to kiss the air next to her cheek. "And a good afternoon to you too, Maddie girl. Actually, I've had a phenomenal run of luck at the tracks lately. No, this time I've come to sniff out scandal."

"Scandal?" She had tried to say it lightly, but it came out

brittle. So he knew, then. Probably not the whole, but he knew something.

"Sniffing out scandal amuses me on occasion," he was saying. "When all my carousing and drinking and gambling begin to pall."

He faced the bay. He put a hand in his jacket pocket and braced a foot on one of the ornamental iron vases that stood at intervals along the front of the terrace. He thrust out one hip and squared his shoulders. It was a masculine pose.

"Do you know, Maddie, it doesn't take a lot of effort to lie to our narrow little world here in Bristol and get away with it. For all our money and our hoity-toity Great Folk ways, we are such provincials. But in the nasty, shark-infested circles I sometimes swim in in New York, there are people whose sole reason for drawing breath is to sniff out the lie and the pretense in others and then bring them down."

He dropped his foot off the urn and turned to face her again. Studying her hard, so that she had to look away. She'd been begging him to come so she could tell him the truth, some of the truth, and ask him to right the terrible wrong she had done. But now he was here, and she was afraid. When he learned of her part in the "scandal," he would see her for what she was, and he would despise her.

"Sometimes," he went on, "it amuses my friends to exercise their man-eating talents in uncharted waters, to discover dirty little secrets about us New England pretenders out here in the hinterlands. Especially if we have a tendency to put on airs. And if they do happen to find out any dirty little secrets . . ." He lifted his hands, spreading them. "Well, my, how they do love to talk."

Her heart was pounding now. He knew, he knew . . . What did he know? "Stu Alcott, are you by any chance trying to work up the nerve to impart to me a particularly juicy bit of gossip?"

"In a way . . . You see, I, in my innocence, just happened

to mention to someone one day how my brother's beautiful fiancée has been spending the last two months visiting with cousins of her mama in their fine and elegant plantation home in Georgia—when lo! I am told there aren't any cousins in Georgia. Or, more to the predatory interests of my shark-toothed friend, there are no cousins with a fine and elegant plantation house."

He stepped up to her, menacingly close, until his thighs brushed her knees. "And if there are no cousins in Georgia," he said, "then where oh where is our dear Emma?"

"I don't know what you're talking about. Of course there's a plantation house. Mama's often spoken of her cousins at High Grove." But Maddie was afraid, so afraid, Emma wasn't there.

He leaned over her chair, bracing his hands on the armrests, leaning so close to her now she could see the flaring of his thin nostrils as he breathed, the creases at the corners of his mouth. The black specks floating like dust motes in his gray eyes. And she could smell him. Stale champagne and a faint odor of something like burnt peanuts, sweet and cloying.

" 'Fess up, Maddie girl. What has Emma done, and what have you and your mama done with her?"

A sob burst out along with her words. "I had to tell. For her own good, I had to tell." But that was a lie. She hadn't been going to tell, until she had watched Emma come running back to the house from the gate after telling her lover goodbye. Her sister had had her skirts lifted high, all the way to her knees, and she was running flat out and laughing . . . She had looked so happy.

Stu's eyes were staring at her, judging her, and Maddie couldn't bear it. She averted her face, pressing hard into the chair's cane back.

"Where is she, Maddie?"

Maddie pressed her fist hard into her mouth to stifle

another cry. She hunched down deep in her chair, as if she could press all the way through its cane seat, all the way through the cold winter's earth to the other side of the world, where he couldn't look at her, and she didn't have to face him.

"Mama . . . She said Emma was an embarrassment to the family, and she ought to go away for a while. To—to the p-plantation house." Except there was no plantation. Mama had lied—Mama had always been so good at lying—and . . . Oh, God, what had she done?

Maddie looked up at him in spite of herself, but he had turned away and was staring out at the bay again. The gray, soggy clouds had sunk lower, their bellies sagging into the water.

"I wrote you," she said. "I wrote and wrote you, begging you to come, but you never did."

His mouth twisted a little. "Your letters were a bit vague as to the why of it. But you're right—I should have come anyway." He swung back around to her. She'd never seen his face the way it was now, so bleached of color, almost fleshless. "That fool woman has sent your sister up to the asylum in Warren, hasn't she?"

"Oh, Stu, I've been so afraid . . ." She choked over the words, over the fear and guilt and horror that was building up a dam in her. "It's what she always threatened me with after I became an embarrassment to the family with my chair. She said she'd sent Emma off to Georgia, but I thought, I thought . . ."

He muttered a foul word beneath his breath, and she flinched. "Does Geoffrey know?"

She shook her head, pressing her lips together, hard. The dam was tall and thick now, strangling her. "He thinks she's in Georgia, too. Mama told him Emma's nerves have been delicate and unsteady lately, and the New England winters made it worse." She gripped her hands together in her lap robe, twisting them, afraid of what would happen now that the secret was out. Of what her mother would do to *her.* "What—what are you going to tell Geoffrey? You can't tell him why . . ."

He half-turned away from her, as if he couldn't bear her presence anymore, and his voice took on a mean edge. "What would I tell him as to the why of it? All I have is only a suspicion, after all . . . And one of us has already said too much."

"What do you care so much for anyway?" she shouted, ashamed, scared, oh-so very afraid of losing him—losing him when she'd never even had him. "You wouldn't come for me, not even when I begged you. But you came quick enough for *her.* I suppose you're in love with her like all the other men in the world."

He was silent for a moment, then he surprised her by coming close to her again. "I care because she's my friend. I've never been in love with her, but I've always liked her."

He started to lift his hand, and she thought he would touch her, but he let his hand fall back down to his side. He was, she understood now, never going to touch her, not in the way she wanted, not in the way that rough man had touched her sister, Emma.

"What happened to your heart, Maddie? Did it get broken along with your spine?"

"Of course it got broken!" She flung her head back, and the tears ran out her eyes and into her hair and down into the corners of her mouth. "And what do you know of my life? You don't have to *live* like this . . . She doesn't have to live like this."

"That chair is not Emma's fault."

"No, it's Willie's fault!" she screamed at him, screamed at herself, at Willie dead now and in heaven. "It's Willie's fault and he killed himself over it, and I want to die." She buried her head in her hands, pressing her fingers hard against the bones of her face, trying to stop the noise of her ragged sobs. "Go away."

"Maddie . . ."

"Please just go away."

He was quiet for so long, she opened her mouth to plead with him again. She wanted him away, away, away . . . He was always going away and leaving her. Then she heard his boot heels clicking on the flagstones, walking away from her, leaving her.

Maddie lifted her head just as a sudden gush of icy rain came blowing up off the water. She wrapped her fingers around the slick wooden rims of her wheels and tried to push, but the rubber tires were stuck. Sobbing, she pushed harder and they began to turn, slowly, then faster . . . were turning too fast now, going too fast down the slope of the terrace, toward the edge that dropped off into the bay, flying now into gray water and gray skies, flying—

Maddie screamed once, loud and sharp, as the chair struck one of the cast-iron vases, skidded sideways, and teetered over, spilling her onto the rough flagstones.

She was weeping so hard, her heart was pounding so hard with fear and hopelessness and the utter desperate loneliness, that she didn't at first feel the strong arms come around her. Not until they lifted her, holding her close against the solid comfort of his chest.

She turned in to him, pressed her wet face against his, pressed her lips to the hard bone of his jaw and tasted salt again, but whether they were her tears or his, she didn't know.

"My darling," Stu said. "My poor, broken darling."

He came for her during that time of day when you can sense darkness falling, even though the sky is still filled with light. His pale face was luminous in the gloom of the hall.

"Emma . . ."

He came closer to her, where she was sitting on her bench beneath her window.

"Emma," he said again.

He knelt before her. Her hands were lying on her lap, palms up, and he lifted them gently, tenderly. "I didn't know about this. I swear to you, Emma, darling, I did not know."

Geoffrey chafed her hands with his own. She thought they must feel cold to him. She'd been cold for so long, she didn't notice anymore.

"Do you believe me?" he said. "Say you believe me."

She looked into his face, fair and long-boned, so familiar to her, a face she had known all her life. Looked into his flat, gray-water eyes that she could never read.

"I believe you," she said, although she wasn't sure if she believed him or not, and it didn't matter. He was here now and he was going to take her out of this place. To take her home.

Chapter Thirty

Emma had thought of only one thing since she'd come home to The Birches the night before. To go for a long, long walk and look up at the wide, open sky, and breathe it in, just breathe it all in.

And stepping through the big coffered ebony doors this morning had surely been a wonder—to be able to go somewhere without the matron and her jangle of keys.

But now that she was out here on the piazza, dressed in her sealskin coat and hat, her hands stuffed deep and warm into her muff, she was afraid to take the first step. She felt so broken inside, as though pieces of herself had broken off. Jagged, jigsaw pieces that had settled wrong and wouldn't quite fit together again.

She could go back into the house and ask Geoffrey to come with her, she thought. But when he was with her, she could feel him staring at her and it made her uncomfortable. She wondered what he looked for in her face—marks of Emma's passions run amok, signs of Emma's excitable nature found and lost.

She knew she wasn't mad, had never been mad, but they had broken her anyway. They had made her afraid again.

She thought just then that she heard the old twig rocker creak, but there was no wind. And when she looked around at it, she saw that it was still. The sound, though, so familiar and evocative, gave her the courage to walk down the steps and strike out across a lawn lumpy with old snow. A mist was gathering like smoke off in the birches.

She stopped once and looked up at the sky, letting her eyes fill up with the blueness. Breathing it in.

And when she began to walk again toward the stand of birches, all white and black and gray in the winter landscape, she felt better. Not her old self, though. More like someone else.

A thicker mist, pearly and opaque, rose off the bay. She couldn't tell where the water ended and the sky began. The beach was gray drifts of sand and snow.

The last time she'd been here was the day she'd sailed herself home in the storm. She'd left the *Icarus* in a terrible state, but someone, she saw now, had been taking care of the sloop for her.

"You went and left your sloop in a fine mess, Emma Tremayne," said a grating voice she had not thought to hear again.

And the jagged, broken pieces shifted inside her, hurting.

He came out from among the bare and withered trees, with his hands in the pockets of his black pea coat and his slouch hat shading his face, came right up to her until he was so close she could have touched him. But she was too afraid now to touch him.

"You've come back, then," he said, his breath trailing across his face in thin clouds. His beautiful, battered face.

"Back?"

"From your cousins' fine plantation house. In Georgia."

Her skin was cold and damp, but her heart beat fast and tremulously. He had the most startling green eyes.

I cannot bear this again, she thought.

"Donagh happened to see you at the train station yesterday," he said, "that's how I came to know that you were back."

"Yes." They could have driven down from the Warren asylum, it was only a few miles. But Geoffrey had said they had to come by train, so that no one who mattered would know the truth. Of where she'd been.

"I thought you'd come to check on your sloop first thing," he said. "That's why I'm here. I want to know how you're faring, Emma."

She felt a flash of anger at him. Anger that he had been so right about costs and consequences.

"I'm going to marry Mr. Alcott," she said. "Mama doesn't want to wait the two full years anymore, and so we'll have the wedding in June. In the garden. Mama says he's as solid as the bricks in the mills he owns."

He was staring at her hard, his eyes going up and down the length of her. She looked away.

"Is there a baby, Emma?"

The broken, jagged pieces slipped again. She wanted suddenly to go back into the house, where it was warm. Safe.

She blinked and looked at him again. "You didn't go to New York?"

"No. Not yet." She heard it now, the grayness of unhealed pain in his hoarse whisper. "I needed to know how you were faring. If there was a baby . . ."

When she looked at him, it was hard to remember that she wasn't supposed to love him anymore. Somehow she found the courage to reach up and touch his face, to trace the thin white scar that slashed across his cheek.

"Shay," she said. "Shay McKenna," as if trying out his name, saying it for the first time. "Did you ever love me, even a little?"

"Love you?" He turned his head and brushed his lips across her fingers. "I'm loving you now, *mo chridh*. After

I'm dead, a thousand years from now, whatever's left of me, be it a soul or just a handful of dust, that will be loving you."

Her hand fell back down to her side. "But I'm marrying Geoffrey. It's for the best."

She saw his throat move as he swallowed, saw his chest move as he breathed. "It's for the best if you are happy. Will you be happy, Emma?"

"I'm cold. I . . . I'd better go in now."

She walked away from him, back down the beach and into the birches. She didn't have to turn around to know he was staring after her as though he would never see her again.

Geoffrey stood within the shadows of the velvet-swagged doorway and looked at her.

She stood at the windows, looking out at the birches, but he didn't think she saw them. Her eyes were focused inward, to a place deep inside her. Shadows lay like old bruises under her cheekbones.

She must have gone for a walk after all, for she wore her sealskin coat, although she'd unbuttoned it partway. He could see a band of lace and tiny seed pearls that was the high collar of her dress. It wrapped around a neck impossibly long and thin.

He told himself he needed to be patient, that she'd only been home a day, but he felt as though he were shouting at her from across an endless distance, and if he reached out and touched her she might vanish.

He was afraid he didn't know her anymore, that perhaps he had never known her. No one would tell him precisely what her "excitable nature" had led her to do that her uncle and mother had felt she needed a rest at the asylum to cure her. He'd tried to find out, but not very hard because he really didn't want to know.

He didn't want to know of something he might not be able to forgive.

He went up to her where she stood at the window, close enough to touch, although he didn't. She smelled of her lilac perfume, and cold fur.

"You went for your walk," he said.

"Yes," she answered. She spoke softly, like someone just waking from a deep sleep.

"You're cold." He brushed droplets of mist from the smooth shell-like roll of her hair. He wanted to ask her what she was thinking.

Instead, he turned away from her, picked up a pair of studded leather bellows, and began to puff air at the fire.

In the days of December that followed, Geoffrey spent as much time as he could with her, even though he could never find the words he needed for the question he thought he should ask. He wanted to believe she needed him, and so he was there.

She wasn't always easy to find, though. She spent so much time walking out-of-doors, even though it was close to Christmas, and the winter was a cold and wet one.

Today he found her in the old orangery. He'd never before been to this place where she did her sculpting; he'd never been invited. Nor had she ever offered to show him her work, but then, he thought perhaps she had feared he would think it amateurish.

The door was partway open and he paused on the threshold before going in. A pale yellow sunlight washed down from the glazed glass roof, splashing watery patterns on the tiled floor. She stood staring at a strange something made of bronze, and although he couldn't see her face, she had an odd, suspended look about her. As though she'd been standing there in just that way for centuries.

He walked in, his cane tapping on the tiles. She turned, and he was shocked to see tears streaming down her face.

"Emma, darling," he said, hastening to her side. "What is it?"

She spun away from him to stare at the strange bronze something again. "I've been afraid to come here, afraid of what I might feel, of how it would hurt so. But then I got to thinking. Mama might have smashed Bria while I was away, and at that moment I became more terrified of *not* coming. I had to see, to know that she was all right, and she is. She is! Isn't she beautiful?"

Geoffrey tried to look admiring as he viewed the strange something. It was a mask of a woman's face, he finally decided, but it was hardly . . . Well, for one thing, it was much too large to be a proper face. And for another, the features were much too harsh and strong to belong to a woman. His poor Emma, she really didn't have any talent at all. No wonder she had been reluctant to show him any of her creations before this.

She didn't seem to care whether she had his approbation anyway. She had gone back into that suspended state, where she didn't even appear to be breathing.

"You're not thinking of taking it up again, are you, your sculpting?" He really rather hoped not; her nerves were still much too delicate for such a stress.

She shuddered, breaking her stillness, and looked out the milky windows toward the bay. The water slept, smooth and gray, under the blue-white winter sky. "No," she said. "That would take much more courage than I could ever find right now."

Her face held such a sweet sadness, it made him ache to comfort her. Without quite realizing he was doing it, he slipped his arm around her waist and drew her to him. He had thought to be careful, to give her more time after her illness. But here he was kissing her, and it was too late.

Her mouth was cool and soft, and he ended the kiss much too quickly to know whether he'd gotten a response. And he didn't dare try again.

"I thought we would go skating today," he said. "They say the ice at Collins Pond is the best it's been all winter."

"That would be nice, Geoffrey," she said. But he saw no feeling on her face now at all.

Sunlight danced on the delicate lacy collars of ice that rimmed the rocks and trees, and the harness bells jangled a roundelay tune. The wind the sleigh made cutting through the snow stirred the gray fur of Emma's collar in a soft caress against her cheek.

But she was sorry now she'd agreed to come, for she could feel the fear stirring inside her. When she was at home, at The Birches, in that calm, familiar place, she felt returned to herself, to the girl she'd been long ago. As though she'd just met herself again, after a long and perilous and frightening journey away.

She slipped her arm through Geoffrey's, leaning in to him, hanging on. He turned to her and smiled. In the subdued winter light, his eyes were the soft burnished color of old silver. She thought she and Geoffrey cared about each other, only they didn't always feel it, and that didn't seem to matter so much anymore. Among the many things she was now afraid of, one was letting go of Geoffrey's arm.

They walked down to the pond with their skates tied together, hanging around their necks. Geoffrey had her sit down on a rock so that he could lace hers up for her.

They skated side by side, she and Geoffrey, arm in arm. The cold bit at her nose and cheeks, and the wind in her face felt wonderful, and to her own surprise, she laughed. Although her laughter sounded fragile in the thin air.

At the wide end of the pond, some Irish kids were playing a game of curling, sweeping the stone disk back and forth over the ice. And shrieking and whooping and trying to slash one another with their curved sticks while they were about it. Although the skaters appeared to be boys, for a moment Emma thought she saw Noreen among them.

She uttered a little cry and started after them, trying to pull away from Geoffrey. But he held on to her arm.

"Whoa there, darling," he said. "Where are you going?"

She let him lead her away. She let his gentle, familiar hands lead her back to the rock, where he took off her skates. She let him bundle her up in the cutter and drive her home, where the holly wreath on the door and the lamplight spilling from the windows onto the snow on the sills made a welcoming sight.

As they crossed the pine-garlanded hall, laughter and a tinkling rendition of "Jingle Bells" floated out from the family parlor, and they followed the sound of it.

The parlor was aglow with the white firefly light of the Christmas-tree candles and smelled of ginger lace cookies and eggnog. Maddie sat in her wheelchair alongside the fire, and she was the one who was laughing.

Stuart Alcott stood before her, holding a music box with a twirling ice skater on the top of it.

"Stu!" Geoffrey exclaimed, a wary surprise in his voice.

Maddie looked around and her mouth widened with a smile so bright it rivaled the candles on the tree. "Look, Emma. Stu's come home for Christmas."

"And bearing gifts, too," Stu said. And as Emma watched, he picked up Maddie's hand and put the music box in it. The tune was winding down but neither of them seemed to notice. Stu looked down into Maddie's eyes and he smiled.

A smile that bridged depths, gulfs, worlds, and unimaginable spaces.

And the look she gave back to him went even further.

How she loves him, Emma thought.

How I loved Shay.

Chapter Thirty-one

In Bristol they called it the "unlocking season." That time when snow fell in soft plops from the trees and the ice broke up in the streams with cracks louder than any Fourth of July rocket. When young ferns and flowers first poked their noses out of the warming earth, and the birch and beech leaves began to unfurl.

Emma Tremayne's unlocking came about as slowly as the spring thaw. In those first weeks of the new year, she had often gone back to Collins Pond—not to skate, but to watch the Irish boys play their games of curling. She never thought she saw Noreen again, but still she went. It was the wildness in the boys' laughter that drew her, and the way they hurled themselves across the ice, heedless of thin spots and cracks and the dead branches hiding there to trip them. Their foolish bravery, she thought, was painful to see.

She never could bear watching them for long, and so she would turn with a soft, aching cowardice toward home and the familiar things. The soothing tone of Geoffrey's voice when he spoke her name, the solid comfort of his arm when she leaned on it. The sight of the birches, black and bare, etched against a white winter sky. The smell of wet clay in the old orangery, the clay that she prepared every morning as if she were a real sculptress, with real work to do.

Although she never dared to make anything with the clay, she would knead it for hours. The feel of it oozing through her fingers—soft and warm and smooth as living flesh—stirred a strange, hot restlessness inside her. Like the wild and reckless freedom she could hear caught up in the ice-skaters' laughter, it made her remember too much. And she felt a disappointment in herself, that she couldn't make herself be less afraid.

One morning in March, when the birches dripped with ice melt and the sun rose pale and shrunken in a bleached-blue sky, Emma awoke determined to pay a call on Bria's girls. She told herself it was a promise she had made, a promise she must keep. But that day she only drove as far as the scrolled iron gates before she turned the carriage around and had the grooms put it away.

That afternoon, it snowed again—winter's final gasp. Emma stood at her bedroom window and watched the flakes drift onto the silent woods, and she wished that she could be like the birches and have slept through these past months, to awaken in the spring with her heart healed and her fears forgotten.

It was some time before she dared to try taking the carriage out again, but on that day she made it through the gates, although her heart pounded and her palms were damp beneath the soft leather of her gloves. She drove as far as the corner of Union and Thames Streets, but there she stopped to look at the house from a safe distance.

She was shocked at how shabby and small the place was—that clapboard shack, perched on stilts. How it could be so small and yet hold so much . . . How it could hold all of a woman's heart. She looked at the house, and the broken pieces inside her shifted and ground together, hurting her so that she gasped aloud. *I belong in there*, she thought. She belonged in that kitchen with its faded wallpaper and worn linoleum; she belonged to the family who ate supper at that table with its brown oilcloth, to the man who slept in that white iron bed. She belonged to the friend whose spirit still tended to the teakettle whistling on the stove.

But there was an ocean to cross between knowing where you belonged and having the fire in your heart to go there. And Emma Tremayne had lost her courage to set sail.

One day, when mist clung to the cold waters of the bay and spring was still pent up in tight red buds on the branches of the birches, Emma went to Saint Mary's cemetery and stood before Bria's grave.

The marker was a simple stone, etched with her name and the years of her life. The last time Emma had been here, the dirt had been mulchy brown and raw, the stone freshly carved, the letters white scars in the smooth gray granite. Now already the grave had sunk a bit at the edges, and winter had pitted and scarred the granite marker with tiny cracks.

Emma knelt and traced the letters in the stone. "Bria," she said, and the pain of saying her name was an unbearable thing.

She shut her eyes for a moment, and then she stared up into the infinity of the sky. But if Bria was there, she couldn't see her. Yet the alternative was too horrible to contemplate—that nothing of Bria existed anymore beyond the bones in this grave.

Emma heard a footfall behind her and turned slowly around to see Bria's daughters coming toward her down the cemetery path.

Noreen's chin was up; a wariness was in her eyes. "We always come visit Mam's grave after school," she said. "Lots of times, anyways. We didn't come because *you* were here."

Merry hummed furiously and shook her head.

Noreen glared at her sister, her cheeks flushing brightly. "All right! So Merry said you would be here today. She said we had to come, because you've been looking for us for a long time now."

Emma opened her mouth, but she was so choked with feelings no words came out.

Merry squatted on the ground beside her and took Emma's hand. With her other hand, the little girl began to smooth down the dirt of her mother's grave, petting it as if it were a living thing, and humming softly under her breath.

Noreen remained where she was, studying Emma with dark eyes. "Da said you had to go away for a while, to visit family. He said that's why you stopped coming to see us."

Emma felt tears burning in her eyes, and she fought them back. "But now I've come home again," she said. She tried for a smile. It came hard and trembled on her mouth, yet it unlocked something deep inside her. "So, you go to school now, do you?"

"Da makes us. Merry doesn't like it—she hardly even hums anymore."

"Tell me about it," Emma said. "Tell me all about school and little Jacko—oh, I imagine he has gotten so big! Is he crawling yet? And tell me . . . tell me about your papa. Tell me everything."

A slow, tentative smile spread over Noreen's face, and then she began to talk, and Merry chimed in with long and trilling hums, and the months of winter began to melt away.

Emma came back to Bria's grave the next day, and the girls were waiting for her. After that she told them when she would be coming, too afraid to leave it to chance or to Merry's fey ways.

One day in April, when all that was left of winter were a few tattered, wrung-out clouds high in the sky, Noreen brought sardines and soda bread and they had a tea party at Bria's grave, even though they had no tea. On another day, in May, when the sunshine flowed warm and smooth as melted butter and the air was soft, they went for a walk down Ferry Road and picked wildflowers, which they put in a tomato can beneath Bria's headstone. That day, Emma thought she saw Father O'Reilly come around from in back of the plain wooden church. He started toward them, but then he turned away.

And once, on a day when the whole earth fairly sang of spring, Emma saw a woman in white batiste, with wild red hair and a laughing mouth, standing beneath one of the cemetery elms. She was so real that Emma lifted her hand and opened her mouth to cry out, but in her next breath the woman was gone.

And then there came a day in early June, when the linden trees were in their full, haunting bloom, that Emma came to the cemetery and the girls weren't there. That day, she had brought violets to plant, and so she began the joyful task herself. She knelt in the greening grass and turned the soft, moist earth over with a trowel. This time when she heard a footfall behind her, she was smiling as she turned.

He was jauntily dressed in a lounge suit accompanied by a striped tie, a bat-wing collar, and a derby hat. He walked alone down the cemetery path, walked in that long-strided, confident way he had, walked right toward her.

Emma stood up slowly and carefully, as if afraid of falling. She didn't really go forward to meet him, she only stood and felt the pull of him, like gravity.

And then he was there, standing before her.

"Shay," she said, the color rising to her cheeks as she said his name.

His eyes, startling and green, fixed on her in that hard, terrifying way he had. He had come up so close to her that she could smell the spicy soap he'd used to shave with, could see the way his hair still curled a little too long over his collar.

"The girls and Father O'Reilly—they all told me that you often come here lately," he said. "Surely, darlin', you knew that they would tell me?"

"Yes," she said, but it was a lie. She'd been too afraid to let herself know.

"And you know, surely, that I'd be coming myself someday, that I couldn't make myself stay away forever?"

"No . . . Yes."

How can this be, she thought, that after all this time, even when he's not touching me, I can still feel him touching me?

"And so?" he said.

She wanted to ask him what he wanted from her.

She was terrified of asking him that.

"And so . . . I don't know." She lifted her shoulders in a small, helpless shrug.

He took a step away from her. He looked down at his wife's grave and the violets she had planted there. He took off his hat, and she saw that his fingers were white on the brim.

She wanted to say to him, That we all found each other, you and Bria and I, even when so much should have kept us forever apart—it ought to count for something, shouldn't it?

He turned around to face her again. "And so," he said, "you are still to be marrying your Mr. Alcott next Saturday?"

She wanted to say to him, I will never love again, not like this, not like I love you.

"Yes," she said. "The ceremony will be held in the gardens at The Birches, unless it rains of course. If it rains, it will have to be postponed indefinitely because Mama will have killed herself."

He actually laughed. It didn't seem fair that he could laugh, when she hadn't laughed for so long, so long . . . Since the last time they had laughed together.

"Ourselves," he said, "it so happens we're leaving for

New York that same day. I've a job working for a ward boss down there, settling new immigrants into the borough, providing them with Christmas turkeys and scuttles of coal and buckets of beer and such. It's a political job, so the money's a fine thing to behold. I won't need to be putting the girls in any mill."

She wanted to say to him: Why are you telling me this, when it still hurts so to hear it said?

" 'Course, while I'm settling those immigrants in, I'll be telling them why they ought to be voting Democratic, and I'll be collecting donations for the clan. *Erin go bragh.* Perhaps there'll be a rising in my lifetime after all."

"If there is, would you go and fight in it?"

"No. I'll be staying here."

"In New York."

"Aye, New York, rather."

She wanted to say, I am coming with you. Incredibly, the words had been there, nearly spilling off the end of her tongue. As if there hadn't been anything between this time and the last, as if she hadn't been broken.

"Emma," he said. "I want . . ."

Her breath caught and held, and held, and held.

"I want to thank you," he said, "for sparing the girls a hard parting. When you could've just disappeared out of their lives and always left them wondering." He flashed a quick, sudden smile. "It's a grand lady you are, Miss Emma Tremayne—and I wanted to say that to you as well."

He held out his hand to her, and for a moment she allowed herself to feel it—her hand in his.

And then she was watching him walk away from her.

"Every time it's the same," she said into the empty world that he had left behind. "You happen to me all over again."

Later that afternoon, she went home and changed out of the plain black skirt and shirtwaist she'd been wearing, and into a spring costume of gray-green silk decorated with black velvet knots and buttons, and a large cravat of white chiffon spilling from the neck.

She rode with her mother in the family brougham to the Hope Street mansion, rode back into the safe, familiar territory of her Great Folk life. She walked up the lane of marble flagstones, arm in arm with Geoffrey. The linden trees were blooming, filling the blue sky with floating blossoms and sweet smells. In the still air she heard laughter coming from the tennis court and the genteel pat of the ball against the strings.

We are walking together, she thought, Geoffrey and I. Walking down a lane of marble flagstones, beneath a canopy of blooming linden trees, walking together, arm in arm, and not touching.

A man's heart was a queer, stubborn thing, thought Seamus McKenna. It just went on loving a woman long after it should have stopped.

He stood on the Hope Street sidewalk, next to a cast-iron hitching post, as if he'd just paused there to catch his breath. He looked through the iron gates at the Great Folk drinking champagne among marble fauns and nymphs, and his gaze searched for a woman with a long, white neck, a shy smile, and seafoam eyes full of wild longings.

"I used to know a Seamus McKenna who would've beaten down this gate with his champion's fists to get at the woman he loved."

Shay shut his eyes a moment, then opened them and turned to his brother-in-law. "Can you not be leaving me in peace for more than a minute, then? What are you doing here anyway?"

"Passing by."

"Do tell? And it's a powerful lot of Catholic souls, there are, at this end of town."

"And the cod are fairly swimming, thick as fleas on a hog, down Hope Street as well, I see."

Shay was feeling a pain in his neck from the effort it was taking not to turn his head, not to be looking through that gate for just a glimpse of her. "I had to see her one more time," he said, and he wasn't surprised to hear Donagh sigh.

"You were seeing her fine this morning. If you had the brains God gave a bladder worm, you would've arranged then to be seeing her every day for the rest of your life."

Shay looked; he couldn't help himself. He heard laughter and the clinking of glasses, but the part of the garden that he could see was empty now. "Sometimes," he said, "life leads you to places where no one can follow. Sometimes those who love you can only wish you Godspeed."

The wind blew, sending a snowfall of linden petals drifting down onto their heads. Donagh caught some with his hand, but then he let them go.

" 'Course, it's wise you are," he said, "not to be tempting her into letting life lead her into running off with you. Think of what she'd be giving up—an empty existence and marriage to a man she can't love, surely. Not when her heart fairly burns in her eyes when she looks at you. Think too of what your girls and your young son would be giving up—all their growing-up years without a mother who loves them."

The wind came up again, and Donagh lifted the derby off his head and settled it down more firmly. "Aye, it's a grand and honorable sacrifice you're making on their behalf, Seamus McKenna. Our Bria would be proud."

Shay stared after the priest's broad, black-cassocked back as it walked away from him, passing beneath the leafy vault of maples and elms. Then he looked around him, with eyes that ached as if he'd just spent the last year of his life weeping, looked at the grand mansions with their columns and tall windows.

Donagh was wrong. Champion or no, he couldn't smash an iron gate with his fists. And if he tried he'd only end up hurting himself.

Bethel Tremayne caught herself reflected over and over in the beautiful room's many pier glasses. Even in the soft yellow haze of gaslight she could see the exposed crests of her breasts lifting and falling, rapidly, like the wings of a trapped bird.

He had come.

It was the evening before her daughter's wedding, and William had come home. Just as she had known he would.

He had come sailing on his yacht into Bristol harbor this morning. As soon as she heard the news, Bethel had sent a servant to the Bristol Yacht Club bearing a perfumed note, inviting him to come for an informal supper, just the two of them. Reminding him, discreetly of course, that he still had a bedroom here at The Birches.

She had dithered over where she would first greet him, finally settling on this small, intimate sitting room next to the library. She had chosen the room mainly because of its two lamps that flanked the sienna marble fireplace. The lamps, with their salmon-pink Burmese glass shades, had always cast a becoming glow on her pale complexion. And she liked as well the effect of the room's many pier glasses, which would reflect her beauty to him again and again.

At five minutes before the hour, she had arranged herself on the midnight-black horsehair sofa. It was uncomfortable, but she knew the opaque material complemented the whiteness of her skin and the bright gold of her hair.

And now at last, at last, the grandfather clock began to

strike, its gong banging ponderously. Seven o'clock, the hour she had told him to come. A brassy queasiness suddenly flooded Bethel's throat. What if . . . But no, she was prepared for everything. She had filled the house with flowers, and Cook had prepared a supper of all his favorite foods. She was dressed in her most becoming gown, a watered silk the color of attar of roses.

And she had starved herself until she was as slender and lithe as she had ever been.

When he came into the room, she would leap up to embrace him. Perhaps that was not quite the thing to do, not a thing a Great Folk lady would do. But the young girl he had met on that ballroom floor in Sparta, Georgia, would probably have done such a thing. The girl who had worn gardenias in her hair.

The clock finished striking and fell back into its tick-marked silence. Bethel waited and waited. . . . She waited through the clock striking eight and then nine o'clock. When the door finally opened, she stumbled to her feet, stiff legged and numb. But it was only Carrews. Carrews bearing a piece of folded notepaper on a silver tray.

Bethel's heart was beating in slow, agonized thuds, and her fingers shook as she unfolded the note. But then her eyes blurred so badly with tears, it was a while before she could read it.

He would, William wrote, be residing on his yacht while in Bristol, and dining at the club.

Once . . . once she had danced with him beneath chandeliers that glowed with the warmth and dazzle of a thousand suns. She could remember that night so vividly. So why then couldn't she remember the moment she had lost him?

She heard a sound and looked up. Her daughter Emma stood in the doorway, watching her with those changeling eyes. Standing there with that face that was so much more beautiful than hers had ever been.

She wished Emma would come into the room and sit down beside her, hold her, maybe . . . comfort her. But she didn't know how to ask, and she didn't think Emma would come. Not after what she had done, even though all that had only been for the girl's own good. And the cure had worked, after all. Emma was marrying Geoffrey Alcott tomorrow. She had come to her senses.

"Mama?" Emma said. "Are you feeling all right?"

"Oh, yes," she said, making her smile and her voice go bright. "I was only sitting here thinking about your wedding tomorrow, going over all those endless lists that have been whirling through my head these past months."

The girl started to turn away, but Bethel stopped her, crying out her name so sharply that she startled them both. And then the strangest words came out of her, coming from a place, from a feeling, she had no idea even existed, although they hurt terribly, the words did, cutting her throat like tiny knives.

"I've lived a silly life," Bethel Tremayne said to her daughter. "I had nothing, and then I had everything, and now I have nothing again."

Chapter Thirty-two

On the day of Emma Tremayne's wedding, the sun rose in a glory of red and gold and orange.

Emma rose with the sun, so restless she left the house and went for a walk through the birches and down to the water. The trees were fully leafed now, shiny green and full of promise. She found the landscape of the beach had been changed by the winter, but that was always the way of it. Storms ravaged and wasted the shingled sands. The frost killed some trees, and the cold froze the rocks and broke them. Each spring was never quite the same as it had been the spring before.

As she walked back across the rolling lawn, she stopped to look at the house, shining silver in the sun. She felt a sad wrenching to think of leaving this place, as if she would be gone forever, even though she would not.

She had started to climb the steps to the piazza when she saw her father standing there among the palms and wicker chairs.

This stranger who was her father.

Tall and slender, with mahogany-tinted skin and the white cap and blue blazer of a yachtsman, he stood with his feet braced apart and his hands clasped at the small of his back, as if he stood on the quarterdeck.

She finished climbing the steps, but stopped when she was still a ways from him. "Hello, Papa," she said, unsure what to make of him. Unsure what he would make of her. "Thank you for coming."

His teeth flashed white in his face as he smiled, and then he startled her by stepping up and embracing her in a crushing hug. "I wouldn't miss my little girl's wedding for the world." He set her at arm's length and looked her over slowly, up and down, still smiling. "Except you aren't so little anymore, are you?"

She had nothing she could say to that. She hadn't grown any inches since he'd last seen her, at sixteen. Where she had grown was inside, where he couldn't see.

"My little girl . . ." He reached up as if he would touch her face, but then he let his hand fall, and she saw that there were tears in his eyes. "I've missed you, Emma."

She had nothing she could say to that either. She had missed him too, but he was the one who had left.

He let her go and turned away, putting distance between them, and she realized that a moment of closeness with her father—the first she'd ever had with him—had come and gone. She had let it go.

He had turned his face back to the sea breeze, and his gray-green eyes had taken on a faraway look. He has grown older, she thought. His hair was all white now, the wrinkles on his face etched deeply into the skin.

"Would you like to go for a sail, Papa?" she asked.

He lifted his head, sniffing out the wind just the way he used to do when she was a little girl. To see it made her feel sad, even as she smiled. "Not much wind to speak of at the moment," he said. "There's promise of a fine blow later, though."

"But later I'll be married to Geoffrey."

He turned, his gaze searching her face. "And will you be putting away all your toys after that, my little Emma? No more dreams, no more adventures?"

She felt a sudden and frightening desire to cry, and she had to swallow hard. "S-shouldn't I?"

"The world says you should, certainly."

She had so many questions she wanted to ask him, but they were of things that were never to be spoken of. But then she realized that in these last moments she had shared more real words with him than she had in the whole of her life before this. And she had a startling thought as she looked at him—that he had changed inside, as well, where she couldn't see.

"Papa?" she said. "Why did you marry Mama?"

His mouth pulled into a wry smile. "Now there's a question I've often asked myself."

He paused a moment, as if he'd become lost in thoughts, or memories. Then he shrugged. "I wish I had an answer for you, Emma. The closest I can come to a reason is that I was struck when I met her with how strong and courageous and *certain* she seemed . . . All the things that I wasn't and thought I should have been. You know the Tremayne family motto: He Conquers Who Endures? Your mother has always been able to live it far better than I do. Perhaps that's why I married her—so that she could be the man I wasn't." He breathed a soft, and somewhat bitter, laugh. "We all must admit she's filled the role admirably."

"So then if you . . . admire her so, why did you leave?"

She thought he would say it was because of Willie's suicide, because of what they had all done to drive his only son off into the storm that night.

"There came a time," he said, "when I realized I didn't have the least understanding or liking of her, and that I didn't really want either to understand or like her, and so I left."

It couldn't be that simple, Emma thought. It should not have to be that simple. Poor Mama, plotting and scheming and starving herself all these months to win him back, when she had lost him irrevocably a long time ago.

When she had never even had him in the way that mattered, because she was never the woman he could have loved. Bethel Lane hadn't changed, but the way he looked at her had.

Her father was gazing out over the water again, and it was as if she knew already in her heart what he would say.

"No, I'm wrong to be blaming it on your mother. It wasn't only her. I left because I was so unhappy in my life, and nothing she could do or not do was ever going to change that. Suddenly, it seemed terrible to me to always be so wretchedly unhappy."

Emma took a step toward him, and then another. She wrapped her arms around his waist and she smelled his warm neck and throat.

"We will have that sail later," he said. "Whether you are Mrs. Geoffrey Alcott or not."

"Yes. Later," she said, pulling away from him.

She stopped in the doorway before going inside and looked back at him. But he was the one who spoke. "Are *you* happy, Emma?"

She replied without thinking. "Of course, I'm happy, Papa," she lied. "After all, today is my wedding day . . . I thought I'd have some coffee. Do you want any?"

"I've had some already," he said, and that smile flashed across his face again. The smile that belonged now to her father, this stranger still. "Thank you, though."

She tried to smile herself, but her eyes blurred instead, so that she nearly stumbled over the threshold on her way into the house.

She went into the breakfast room for the coffee and found her mother there. Bethel sat at the lace-covered table surrounded by bone china and sterling silver. She was dressed as always in a close- buttoned, high-collared shirtwaist, her hair carefully arranged in an elegant pouf.

She looked the epitome of grace and refinement . . . except for the scone dripping with cream that she held in her hand and the dollop of strawberry jam that clung to her lower lip.

"Mama? Are you . . . are you feeling well?"

Bethel set down the scone and fingered the jeweled basket brooch pinned to her neck. "Of course I'm feeling well. It's your wedding day, after all, and getting married is the biggest thing that will ever happen in a girl's life."

"Will it be the biggest thing ever to happen to Geoffrey?" Emma asked.

Her mama's hand went still for a moment, and then she said, "It's different for men."

Emma started to tell her that Papa was out on the piazza, but then she looked at the scone and the crumb-littered plate and the strawberry jam, and she realized her mother already knew.

Emma took the sloop out by herself. Before she left she stole one of the white roses from her bridal bouquet.

A thin mist lay over the water, as though a cloud had fallen from the sky. But there was enough wind now to fill the sails. She went out to the place where Willie's boat had been found, stove against the rocks. Where Willie had chosen to give up not only his wedding day but all of his tomorrows.

For a long while she just watched the seafoam breaking over the rocks, over Willie's grave.

If you were here, Willie, she thought, *I would ask you: Are you sorry you did it this way? In the very last instant,* when the water had closed over your head like a crib lid, and your lungs were bursting with the pain, did you wish you'd chosen another way?

For a long time she had thought his choice had been her fault, hers and Mama's, and because of what had happened that night. But she knew differently now.

It had been her first kiss, that night.

He was a friend of Willie's, from the university, coming for a visit during that last week of May. His name was Michael, a boy so handsome Emma had thought he could pose for the angel in a church painting. She was only sixteen, watching him during dinner that night, staring at the fullness of his lips as he talked, drank, ate, and wondering what it would be like to be kissed by such a boy. To be kissed by any boy.

Had he sensed, somehow, what it was she wanted? Apparently he had, for she had found herself out in the garden with Michael's arms around her waist, and those full and magical lips on hers.

He'd just started to do an extraordinary thing—he'd just started to push his tongue into her mouth—when Willie came upon them.

"You whore!" Willie had shouted. But he hadn't been looking at her when he'd said it. His eyes, full of utter hurt and betrayal, had been on the boy.

And then standing behind him, staring at all three of them as if they were a tableau vivant arranged in the garden for show, Emma saw their mama.

Emma had fled into the house in tears. But much later that night, her aching, bewildered heart had driven her to Willie's room, to apologize for her shameful behavior, certainly. But maybe even then she had wanted him to explain what had been behind that look in his eyes.

But their mama had gotten there ahead of her. The door hadn't shut properly and Emma had heard her saying, in a voice thick with anger and disgust, "How *could* you bring him to this house?"

Willie had murmured back something that Emma couldn't hear.

"It is an affliction that can and must be overcome. You can begin to overcome it by looking at once to the performance of your duty as the Tremayne son and heir. By this summer's end I expect you to have found the woman who will be your wife and bear your children. And you will not go near that boy, or any other of his ilk, ever again."

But he hadn't gone back to Yale or met the girl he would marry that summer. Instead, Willie Tremayne had chosen that night to sail his boat out into a storm and drown.

Perhaps, Emma thought now, he had hoped that if he could destroy his body no one would notice how his soul had come unstrung.

Once, when they were children playing in the woods at Hope Farm, they had come upon a trap that held the jagged, bloody remnants of a red-furred foot. With its own teeth, the fox had severed flesh and sinew to be free.

Willie had cried over the fox and what he had done. But Emma had thought, looking at the severed foot, that she was seeing something beautiful.

"Willie . . ." Emma said now, looking down into the tide-eddied depths of the bay where he rested. And if not in peace, she thought, at least he rested.

The breeze was blowing stronger, eating at the mist. The sun seemed to be floating on the water. She started to toss the rose from her wedding bouquet onto the rocks, but the sight of her hand stopped her.

She wore two things on that hand. The sapphire and diamond ring, given to her by the man she was going to marry. And a tiny scar, given to her by the man she loved.

Sometimes, she thought, the price you had to pay for doing what you wanted, for being what you wanted, for being what you *were* . . . sometimes the price you paid was terrible.

But not paying it was always worse.

The train belched a cloud of wet steam over the Franklin Street Depot. It was the 10:05 for Providence, which connected with the 11:47 for New York.

Shay McKenna was squatting on the station platform, trying to pry his daughter's arms loose from a lamppost. Her strength amazed him—he didn't see how he was going to get her on that train without breaking some bones.

"Merry, darlin', if you don't let go," he said, "I'm going to spank your fanny."

"Faith," Father O'Reilly exclaimed to the heavens. "That threat, surely, is bound to get results—being as how you've never raised a hand to the lass in all her young life."

"There's always a first time." Shay tried to give Merry an intimidating glare. He had known it to work on men in the prizefighting ring. She didn't even blink.

He twisted around on his haunches to look over at his other daughter, who was sitting on a steamer trunk, holding little Jacko on her lap. "Why is she doing this?"

Noreen lifted her shoulders high in a big shrug. The movement jiggled Little Jacko, who gurgled a laugh. "I don't know, Da. She isn't humming."

Shay took off his hat, thrust his fingers through his hair, then slammed the hat back on his head. There was always another train tomorrow. But, bloody hell, he was the father here.

He stood up, then pointed a stiff finger at the red fringed ball that topped his daughter's tam-o'-shanter. "Now you look here—"

"Emmmmmmmma," Merry said.

Shay stared down at her for the length of two heartbeats, then decided he hadn't heard her right.

"Miss Emma," Father O'Reilly said, "is at The Birches, even as we speak, darlin' child, and marrying the wrong fellow."

"Donagh," Shay said.

"Meanwhile, your da is busy crucifying himself on the cross of his own good intentions."

Shay gave the priest a hard, tight smile. "Would you mind terribly removing that cross and collar of yours, boyo, so's I can give you a taste of me fists."

Donagh produced a gritty little smile of his own. "I've always thought I could take you, laddie, champion or no. And I won't be needing to take off a thing to do it."

"Donagh, will you think on it a bloody minute," Shay said, his rough voice breaking rougher. "In the bit of time she's known me, I've been a houndsman and a fisherman and worked the onion fields, and none of them being what you might call positions of social and financial prominence."

"And so? Some men build things, other men build dreams. And then other men lie around on their fat arses, belching and farting and talking Irish politics. There's no accounting for some women's tastes."

"She has this thing called a trust fund. With a million dollars just sitting there in it."

"Isn't it the lucky man you are, then? I always do say if a man is going to marry, he might as well marry money."

"I'm an Irishman."

"Now there you could've fooled me. The Irishmen I know, they've guts in their bellies . . . Ah, Sweet Mary. We've had this talk before, and it's grown tired of it I have. You could've gone to New York any day these last two months."

"Now wait—"

"If you've lingered till now, it's because you've been hoping she'll come to you and say, 'Seamus McKenna, lad, sure and if you're the fine, grand man I've been meanin' to spend the whole of my life with.' Only the way I'm remembering it, she's done that once already and you were the stupid bladder worm who told her you'd be having none of it."

"That's not—"

"Now, no one's asking for my advice, you mind, but if I was to be asked, I'd be saying it's your turn to do the proposing, and that's the last I'm saying on the subject."

"If you'd let me finish a bloody sentence—"

The train's whistle tooted. The two men looked together at the big white face of the clock on the station's tower.

"Rather than be finishing your sentences, Seamus, you'd do better to save your breath for running fast," Donagh said. "If you're going to make it to the wedding on time."

Shay's weight shifted from foot to foot, as if his legs had already set off, before his heart and mind had found the courage for it. "But what if . . ."

"Then all you've done is missed your train." Donagh gave his shoulder a little shove. "Go on, man, go. Meanwhile, the rest of us'll walk on down to Hardy's and get ourselves some ice cream sodas."

Donagh watched the man run. Seamus McKenna ran as if he were going to catch a train to heaven. And perhaps he is, Donagh thought. Perhaps he is.

Shay's daughters, he saw, were exchanging big, fat, self-satisfied smiles.

Donagh's head fell back, and he looked up at the sky, blinking away tears. "Ah, Bria, lass. You always did find a way to get your heart's desire."

Emma looked at herself in the cheval glass. She saw what she'd expected to see: Miss Emma Tremayne in a bridal gown encrusted with lace and seed pearls. The long, sweeping peau de soie train spread around her like a bell. A tulle veil, fastened to her hair with orange blossoms, obscured her face.

But she could sense a strange, faint ripening of happiness deep inside her chest, in the area around her heart. She wasn't sure how she had come to this moment. It had begun on that day Bria McKenna had brought the dead child to the last fox hunt of the season, and it was ending here, on her wedding day. Ending here with the choice she now had to make.

With the choice she had made.

Somehow she had lost her way there for a while, and she'd let it go for far too long. She'd almost let it go too late.

The house was quiet as she went down the great oaken staircase. Mama and Maddie were in their rooms dressing, and Papa was in the library. The rose-covered arbor and the yellow-striped tent and the tubs of champagne were all ready and waiting in the garden, but the guests wouldn't be arriving for another hour yet. She knew that Geoffrey was here, though, for she'd seen his landau arrive.

Fortunately for them both, she found him alone, standing on the promontory that overlooked the bay.

"Geoffrey?" she said as she came up to him, as breathless as if she'd been running.

He turned and smiled, a full, sweet child's grin, and it hurt to see it, for his smile was the thing she'd always liked most about him.

"Emma! What are you doing out here? You're not supposed to let me see you in your gown before the wedding. It's bad luck."

"Geoffrey," she said again. "This is so hard for me to say. I should have said it sooner, done it sooner, and I'm sorry, so sorry . . . but I can't marry you."

His smile started to slip. She saw him struggle to get it back. "Emma, now is no time to be funning with me."

"You were going to make me unhappy, and I don't want to be unhappy. That's a selfish thing to say, I know, and the only thing I can offer in my defense is that I would have made you just as unhappy."

He was looking at her now in silence, as though dazed with an inarticulate pain, and she thought she must have to say more, then; she must have to explain more.

"This life of yours, Geoffrey . . . I don't want to live it."

Something broke over him suddenly, a terrible pain, and in his eyes were a fathomless hurt and an emptiness. And defeat. And she thought, then, that somewhere deep inside him he had been expecting that this was coming.

"I'm sorry," she said again.

"But you can't just—" His voice broke. "What are you going to do?"

She smiled. She couldn't help smiling even though she also wanted to cry. "I don't know. Perhaps I'll sail to Viana do Castelo."

"It's him, isn't it?" he said, his face hardening. "I suspected there was someone else, but a gentleman should always give a lady the benefit of the doubt, and so . . . You're going to him." And then she realized that he wasn't looking at her anymore, he was looking beyond, at the man who stood outside the scrolled gates.

Shay McKenna had his hands wrapped around the iron bars, and then he pushed the gate open and walked through.

She picked up the skirts of her wedding gown and walked down the flagstone path to meet him.

"Emma, don't be like this!" Geoffrey cried after her.

She heard his steps on the path, coming after her, and she was suddenly afraid that somehow he would be able to stop her, and so she picked her skirts up higher and she began to run.

She stopped in front of Shay McKenna, her man, her

heart, her life—breathless, laughing, excited, scared, and in love . . . in love.

"Miss Emma Tremayne," he said. "I've come for you. So are you coming with me now, or no?"

"Yes," she said.

To her surprise, for it wasn't at all like him, he let out a boyish whoop. Then he scooped her up into his arms and began to carry her away with him.

She looked back over his shoulder and saw Geoffrey standing there in the middle of the quahog-shell drive, with his hands hanging empty at his sides.

She turned her head and kissed Shay's neck. "I was going to come after you in New York," she said.

He laughed. "Were you, now?"

"Let's take the sloop," she said. "I want to leave here by sailing away."

They had just cast off when Geoffrey burst out of the trees, running hard after her now that it was too late, and crying her name.

Emma took off her wedding veil and slipped the ring he had given her off her finger. She tied the ring to the veil with a white satin ribbon, then threw the veil into the water, where the tide would carry it back to him.

The mist had burned off and the day was blue, intensely blue, with white gun-puffs of clouds.

Emma stood in the cockpit of the *Icarus*, with one hand bracing on the backstay, and she let the sun and the wind and the sea go through her.

She looked back toward Poppasquash Point, to the pebble and shell beach and the paper birches blazing green with their new leaves.

Her gaze caught a flash of something white on the shore.

A woman in a batiste and lace night rail, standing proud and strong, with her red hair blowing wild in the wind. And then in an instant she was gone, and Emma saw only a stand of birches, their trunks flashing silver in the sun.

But she lifted her hand anyway, and waved. Not goodbye, but a fare-thee-well.

"And is it thinking you are, Miss Emma Tremayne, how you're going to be regretting this foolishness someday?"

She looked at him, into his eyes. She had always so loved his eyes. And the moment was so wonderful, she was afraid that if she so much as breathed it would spill over, and she would lose some of its happiness.

But then she was with her love, and so there would always be more happiness to be found and cherished, even though the future was as unfathomable as the black holes between the stars at night.

"Perhaps I will," she said, smiling, laughing. "But in the meantime it's a grand and glorious time that I'll be having, Seamus McKenna."